Spirit Rock

A Susquehannock Tale

by

Wanda MacAvoy

Spirit Rock

© 2019 Wanda MacAvoy

ISBN: 9781073136001

Dedication

This may seem to general, but I dedicate this book to those
missionaries, past and present, who have left all—some even
giving their lives—to tell others about Jesus.
I'd be remiss if I did not specifically dedicate this to
Joel and Sarah Arnold (our niece).
You have answered the call,
and I am so honored to be your aunt!

CONTENTS

FORWARD

THE TRUTH?

And ye shall know the truth, and the truth shall make you free.
John 8:32

On March 8, 1782, in the Moravian mission settlement in Gnadenhutten, Ohio, approximately ninety-six born-again, God-fearing Indians were brutally massacred by local militia from western Pennsylvania. The Revolutionary War was over, and the western frontier was now the place of dangerous unrest. These were difficult times for Native Americans and colonists alike. Memories of brutal massacres by the Indians were fresh in the minds of many of the Pennsylvania militiamen. They were seeking revenge.

In 1778, the first written treaty was signed by Americans and members of the Delaware tribe. Part of the agreement allowed the Delawares to create a protected country of their own—the Ohio Country. However, like most of the treaties the English made with the Native Americans, it was not honored, and like the main character in this story, the Indians were angry with the white men who continued to expand their grasp of the Indians' homelands—thousands of acres of woodlands where the Indians had roamed freely for centuries.

Settled right on the pathway from the British fort at Detroit to the Americans' Fort Pitt were several Indian settlements made up of born-again Indians living peacefully with their Moravian missionaries. The Gnadenhutten Massacre happened because the angry, grieving hearts of

> True Christianity takes off the blinders of prejudice because the heart has been genuinely reborn with the Spirit of God!

the militia men blinded them to the truth that even an Indian could truly be changed by the power of God. These brave Native Americans sang and prayed as they were mercilessly slaughtered, showing forth true Christianity to men who would have called themselves Christian as well!

What is the truth? Salvation is available to all people, no matter their color or creed. **True Christianity takes off the blinders of prejudice because the heart has been genuinely reborn with the Spirit of God!**

One thing I found while researching for this book is that early Native American history was only recorded by white men. Sometimes that person may have been very biased against the Indians. The other end of the spectrum is the opinion that all European settlers and political leaders were haters and warmongers. I have labored to keep in the middle of that road.

Another very fascinating find was that there were many Indians who became Christians or "Praying Indians" as they were called. David Brainerd's journals give a day by day account of his messages and the natives' varied responses to it. Often, the burden of sin caused them to weep uncontrollably, seeking repentance; however, others scoffed and walked away. And here we are in the twenty-first century witnessing the same responses. One thing is certain:

The rich and poor meet together:
the LORD is the maker of them all. Proverbs 22:2

For there is no difference between the Jew and the Greek:
for the same Lord over all is rich unto all that call upon him.
For whosoever shall call upon the name of the Lord
shall be saved. Romans 10:12, 13

PREFACE

By the time Europeans arrived in "Penn's Woods" in the 1600s, it might more accurately have been called "The Indians Well-Planned and Already Quite Occupied Land." Distinct Indian peoples lived in the major river valleys, from the Delaware to the Ohio. Manipulation of the landscape was evident in their villages, fields, and hunting and fishing camps. The paths they had created to travel and trade among these distant and diverse communities crisscrossed the landscape. Native place names, burial mounds, and mysterious petroglyphs etched into rocks testified to the sacred attachment Indians had developed to this land over thousands of years.

"Penn's Woods" may have appeared a pristine wilderness to European colonizers and explorers, but to the Indians who greeted them, it was most certainly an ancient, sacred, and familiar place.

Quoted from ExplorePAHistory.com

PROLOGUE

March 22, 1737—Sheshequin Trail

Chief Hassun watched the travelers from his perch atop their mountain, which gave him a bird's eye view of the Sheshequin Trail. Thirteen-year-old Ahanu stood silently beside him, trying to see what his grandfather was watching, but the lad was nearly a foot shorter than his grandfather and the trees obstructed his view. He knew Grandfather would tell him all he needed to know when he needed to know it. He stood a bit taller, once again, proud to be the chief's grandson and future chief of his tribe.

The old chief squinted as he watched the mixed band snake its way along the twisted trail. Two pale-faces and three Indians were heading towards the rising sun. He wondered at the sight—the first white men in their valley as far as he knew—and sighed, glancing down at Ahanu. "Our world is changing, Ahanu. In my grandfather's day we were known as the Andaste tribe: a proud, noble people. We ruled all this land," he said as his arms swept wide in every direction. He looked back down the mountainside. "But we were no match for the Iroquois. They nearly wiped us out."

Ahanu could have told their history as well as his grandfather, but he listened intently, relishing this one-on-one time with his elder. The boy's mother had died in childbirth, and his father had remarried a woman who had no time for this chiefly son. For that reason and many others, Ahanu was closer to his grandparents than his parents.

"And now we see the white man coming to our land." He stepped forward and motioned to Ahanu to step up onto the rocks to get a better view. Hassun pointed to the travelers who had stopped by a large elm near the creek. He

11

stared at the tall Indian who was gesturing to the white man and gasped. Ahanu looked up in surprise.

"It is Shikellimy, the great chief of the south land." His eyes clouded in thought as he recalled his encounter with the mighty warrior. Chief Shikellimy was greatly revered for his bravery and his kind heart. Although many warriors in the Five Nations did not agree with his close ties to the white man, Ahanu's grandfather was wise beyond his years. The white man had come to Shikellimy's area long ago, and he was able to accept the fact that they were not leaving anytime soon. Others fought. Shikellimy talked.

"This white man must be a good man if Chief Shikellimy is with him," Hassun said mostly to himself.

"But Grandfather, is there such a thing as a good white man?"

Hassun grunted and walked away from the cliff's edge. "Yes, my son, there is, but we must be careful—you must be careful!" he stated emphatically. "Consider them bad until you know they mean you no harm. They are not going away, Ahanu. We must find a way to live with them, not kill them."

Grandfather's words surprised Ahanu. This was not their way—had never been their way for generations. "But why, Grandfather?" Ahanu asked before he caught himself. It was not the place of a youngster to question his elders, but Hassun seemed to understand.

He placed a hand on Ahanu's shoulder and grew very serious. "When you are chief, you will need to find a way. We cannot kill them all. Many will try. But the white man has seen our bountiful land and will want it. It is too much to walk away from."

Hassun moved to a nearby rock and sat down, motioning for Ahanu to do the same. "When I was your age, my grandfather took me to the land of the rising sun. There I saw water stretching as far as the eye could see. There was no end to it; no land could be seen on the other side!" Hassun grew animated at the memory. "We crept to the cliffs and looked down upon a village like none I have ever seen. So many long houses built of stone, brick, and painted wood. I could not count them, and people were everywhere."

He sat quietly for a moment, and Ahanu knew he was reliving the memory. The old man's eyes darted from place to place as though seeing it all again. "There were canoes the size of twenty canoes, which had no paddles. Instead, many cloths caught the wind and moved them through the water."

"Where was this place?" Ahanu asked in awe.

Hassun shook his head. "I do not know. We walked for days towards the rising sun. The sight made my grandfather angry and sad. He knew as well that our way of life would someday need to change." Hassun turned to Ahanu and laid his hand on the young shoulders that would someday need to carry heavy burdens. "You must know too, Ahanu that your life will be much different than mine, and you must be ready for that change and carry our people through it."

It was a solemn moment for Ahanu, and he promised in his heart that he would care for his people... no matter what it took.

CHAPTER ONE

Seeds of Revenge

For thou desirest not sacrifice; else would I give it:
thou delightest not in burnt offering.
The sacrifices of God are a broken spirit:
a broken and a contrite heart, O God, thou wilt not despise.
Psalm 52:16, 17

1740 — Lycoming Creek, Susquehannock Tribe

Ahanu touched the dried blood upon the rock and swallowed hot tears, anger fighting against resignation. He belonged to the Susquehannock tribe and blood sacrifices were a part of their religion. But Ahanu knew this was more about his submission to tradition than his worship of any god.

He bent down and touched the dark spot wondering how long before the rains would wash it away, and his mind replayed the first time he had seen Sucki, the abandoned bear cub.

He had been gathering wood with his friend, Togquos, when they came across the nearly lifeless form. The cub was emaciated and barely breathing, its thick black fur matted and caked with mud.

*　　　*　　　*

Four months earlier...

As Ahanu approached the cub, Togquos spoke, "No, Ahanu! Leave it." Togquos knew nothing good could come

15

from rescuing a bear cub. It would grow up unafraid of men and become a nuisance. But Ahanu was not listening. His eyes were full of compassion as he approached the cub, and when its head lolled upward to look at Ahanu, the boy's heart filled with empathy. He bent over the bear, looking for any broken bones.

"It doesn't look to be hurt, just weak," he said, mostly to himself.

"Leave it," hissed Togquos fiercely.

Ahanu's head jerked up, and there was fire in his eyes. "No!" He turned back to the cub and gently slid his arms beneath the mottled fur. It made a sound, more like a cat's meow than a bear cub's cry. He took it to a nearby stream and gently began to wash away the mud, cupping some of the cool water in his hand and allowing the cub to drink. After just a few sips, life began to reclaim the little body as Ahanu looked on in wonder, amazed at how little stood between life and death.

He reached into his pouch and pulled out a bit of jerky. The cub hungrily ate the morsel, barely taking time to chew. He looked up into Ahanu's eyes, studying them and trying to understand. It cried softly as though saying, "Thank you." Ahanu laughed. He knew Togquos was watching and that his friend was right—keeping a bear cub would be disastrous. Reluctantly, he stood, took one last look, and began to walk away. "Let's go," he grunted to his friend, but after several long strides, they turned to see the little cub following them down the path.

Togquos gave Ahanu a look which mingled a sneer with alarm. "Now look what you've done!"

Ahanu looked from Togquos to the cub. "Run!" he shouted, and both boys took off through the woods.

Stopping further down the path, they silently stood and listened. Far back the path, they heard the crashing sound of the little creature trying with all its might to catch up with them.

"What are you going to do now?" Togquos asked impatiently.

Ahanu weighed his options. He could circle back and lose the cub, hoping its mother would find it. Or, he could lead it to his hideout and keep it there. Togquos would never have to know. "Go. I'll circle away and lose it."

Togquos nodded, obviously pleased with the decision. He swung himself up into a nearby tree and then leaped several feet off the path, knowing the cub would be unable to follow his scent.

Ahanu lifted his chin in consent and headed in the opposite direction. He slowed his pace, allowing the cub to find him. Once again, the cub cried as though glad to see him. Ahanu bend down and scratched the cub's ears. "I'll call you Sucki, since you are so black." Every instinct in him told him to run away, but his heart had been captured by the lonely survivor, so much like himself.

For several months, Ahanu was able to keep Sucki content. He was amazed at the cub's growth, and soon the two friends were spending most of their time together. Togquos watched him curiously when he made excuses as to why they couldn't do things together, looking hurt and confused.

"I thought we were friends," Togquos grumbled one day, looking sad and dejectedly walking away. Ahanu's heart softened.

"Wait," he called. Togquos looked back questioningly. Ahanu came to him, searching his face. "Come," he said, giving no explanation.

Both remained silent as they made their way through woods. When Ahanu neared the hideout, he whistled. Sucki meandered to the entrance to the cave, but when he saw Ahanu, he cried and came running. Togquos gasped. He watched as the bear came to his friend just like a dog would have done. Ahanu scratched the cub's ears and pulled out a piece of dried fish, feeding it to Sucki.

Togquos shook his head. "Ahanu, what have you done?"

Ahanu looked up, worry etched in his face. "I know this was foolish, but I couldn't just let him die, could I?" he questioned.

"Yes, you could have, but now..." Togquos shook his head and looked at his friend. "What will you do when he follows you home?"

Ahanu looked at the cub and shook his head. "I don't know." He wrestled with the cub, making Togquos laugh and forget their quandary for one brief moment. Ahanu's face brightened as he said, "He's very smart." Ahanu showed Togquos some of the tricks he had taught the little bear and Togquos smiled.

Their questions were answered three weeks later. Ahanu was helping his mother clean fish when a ruckus from the other side of the camp drew everyone's attention. Children ran, baskets and pots were scattered everywhere, and women screamed. When Ahanu saw the black streak heading right for him, his heart sank, but he squared his shoulders and called, "Sucki."

The cub cried out and stopped before him, as Ahanu bent to pat his head and calm the bear's pounding heart. He could feel a crowd gathering and eyes upon him, but he kept his gaze on the cub until an all too familiar spoke in a fiercely quiet voice. It was his grandfather. "Ahanu, explain yourself."

Ahanu slowly lifted his gaze to meet that of his grandfather's, hoping to find understanding. The old, wrinkled face was expressionless.

Ahanu swallowed hard. "I found him in the woods. He would have died," he said quietly.

Chief Hassun sternly looked at his grandson, but his heart was aching. He disliked the woman whom his son took as his wife when Ahanu's mother died. She was not very kind or caring, especially for this only child of Anakausuen's first wife. Still, there was no excuse for this. Ahanu knew the dangers of making pets of wild beasts. Many of the other children looked up to him, and this did not make a good precedence. As much as his grandfather-heart ached, he knew Ahanu needed to learn this lesson well.

"Put him in the pit," he said to no one in particular, but three men came forward and herded Sucki away.

Ahanu looked at his grandfather with pleading eyes, but there was no response.

"He will be sacrificed on the full moon to appease Raweno for your error," he stated loudly for all to hear.

Ahanu wanted to shout, but he stood silently, his head bowed in dejection. He should have known. *Fool!*

*   *   *

There had been no discussion, just a lot of disappointed looks from his father as well as disdain in his step mother's voice. Everyone in the village seemed to avoid Ahanu, giving him a wide berth. The children openly gathered in clusters and whispered loud enough for Ahanu to hear. From their conversations he gathered that their parents had warned them to stay away from the foolish boy, not wanting them to learn of his ways. *Foolish boy*, the tongues of the mothers seemed to click in his direction. The men completely ignored him, which was worse than all the rest combined. He deeply felt the shame.

Usually, the full moon sacrifice was a time of feasting and celebration, thanking Raweno, the creator god, for good crops or success in a hunt. Although food simmered on several fires, the mood was far from festive.

As the sun fell to the horizon, the sky blazed fiery red as though Raweno was displaying his thirst for blood. The people gathered into groups ready to follow their chief and elders to the sacrificial rock. Grandfather came and stood before Ahanu and then nodded to the chief elder who pulled Sucki forward, a rope secured around his neck, and handed the tether to Ahanu. Sucki cried when he saw his friend, for it was their first meeting since the small bear had found his way to their village. Ahanu longed to reach down and pat the soft black head but dared not. He wanted to run and scream and cry, but he was a Susquehannock. He stood straight and tall.

The drums began and the procession moved forward. As they neared the sacred spot, the people began to chant accolades to their god.

Raweno! Great one! Mighty warrior of the sky!
Raweno! Raweno! All we see belongs to you.
We come to worship you.

They chanted back and forth—the people and their leaders. Then Hassun began their plea:

We come to plead with you.
Help us! Make right this wrong.
Mercy on us, Raweno!
Mercy, great one of the sky.
Right this wrong.
Accept our sacrifice of blood.

As they walked, the moon rose above the distant hills, its coloring a strange mixture of red and orange. Spirit Rock, their sacred place of sacrifice, sat on the edge of a deep ravine. It was the highest point of the rock ledge, and the moon's rising was directly to the east of Spirit Rock. Its strange glow seemed to pulse upon the deadly altar.

Suddenly, the drums beat faster and the people began to sway as they picked up the chant, repeating Hassun's words, *Mercy on us, Raweno! Accept our sacrifice of blood.* They danced and cried as they formed a half circle around Ahanu, the bear, and Hassun, who clustered before the sacred rock. Hassan looked into Ahanu's face and the boy knew what he had to do. He hesitated for just a moment before lifting Sucki

20

up and placing him on the rock. He deftly secured his paws, fighting back the tears that threatened to fall. He would not cry! He could not disgrace himself or his family any further.

As the cord wrapped around Sucki's paws, the bear raised a questioning glance at Ahanu and let out a pitiful cry which rose above the chanting and the drums and echoed down into the ravine as well as the heart of his master. Ahanu touched Sucki's head, burying his hands deep into the soft fur.

"Accept our sacrifice of blood!" Hassun cried as he raised his knife. Just as the full moon cleared the tree line, he drove the knife into the heart of the helpless cub. A cry caught in its throat as he raised his head one last time to look at Ahanu while the life blood drained from the gaping hole in his chest. The small furry body quivered once, Ahanu watched as the blood dripped down the side of the rock and puddled at his feet. Something deep inside the young man died that day as well. Hassun watched as Ahanu's face hardened, satisfied that the deed had done its work.

*   *   *

For four winters, Ahanu struggled to regain his reputation in the clan. By the time he was eighteen, he could run the fastest and shoot the straightest. He won every wrestling match, often competing with young men much older and heavier than himself. The spectators watched in wonder, and the women shuddered at his fierceness in the games. But still, the stigma against his name could not seem to be erased. He was the grandson of the chief. As the oldest son of the chief's oldest son, he was in line to be the chief someday, and that fact set him at a higher mark. The fate of the tribe would rest on his shoulders. Could he be trusted to make wise decisions?

He often took long walks into the woods, searching for peace, and his footsteps often took him to Spirit Rock.

The dark stains had washed away long ago, but his heart still twisted at the unfairness of it all.

The time of full moon after the summer solstice—the time of Sucki's demise—was fast approaching. Most had forgotten, but Ahanu knew he never would. He sat near the rock watching the heatwaves shimmer across the valley and stayed until the sun was sending its amber rays through the woods. He was ambling back to the wigwam, deep in thought, when he heard hushed, angry voices at the edge of the clearing—voices he knew well. Ahanu crouched in the shadows of the wooden structure and listened.

"You need to do it. He is not fit to be in line for chief," Taima, his father's wife hissed.

Anakausuen's strong voice rumbled, "He is my son, my first born."

"The blood of our chief runs through Chogan's veins as well."

Silence filled the air, but Ahanu could feel the tension. He leaned forward to hear his father's reply, but Taima was speaking again.

"He is not worthy. What is keeping him from making another foolish decision? You saw his face at the last wrestling match. He could have beat Kitchi in a moment, but he felt sorry for him."

Ahanu's face burned with anger. Kitchi had challenged him even though he was much smaller and younger. Ahanu knew that he could win, but had given the boy the opportunity to feel a sense of hope and accomplishment. Was there no place for compassion among his people?

The silence continued and it made him sick to his stomach. So, his father had nothing to say; he would not come to his own son's defense. As Ahanu rose to his feet, Chogan and his friends entered the village from the other side. He watched as they talked and laughed among themselves, his heart aching for companionship. Togquos had been his only friend, and he was now married and busy with his little family.

As they approached, the others split off in different directions. Chogan did not see Ahanu until he was nearly in his face. He stopped abruptly and the smile that had played across his face quickly disappeared. Both stood motionless, all eyes flashing as though waiting for a challenge. Just then, Anakausuen came out from the wigwam, snapping the flap shut. His face was full of anger, but when he saw the boys, he masked his inner turmoil. He looked at one, and then the other. Ahanu's mind screamed for him to say just one word, but there was nothing. He grunted and strode away.

Ahanu, first born of Anakausuen and the rightful future ruler of their tribe, had made his decision. He pushed past Chogan and entered their wigwam. Taima looked up from her work but said nothing. He went to his belongings and began stuffing them into a sack. He rolled his mat and secured it to the outside of the sack before standing. Turning to face Taima, he took one menacing step towards her—this woman who had hated him from the start. She raised her chin defiantly and spat at his feet. Ahanu's fists clenched, but he would not stoop to striking her. Looking around the room one last time, Ahanu walked out the door.

Chapter Two

Searching

Call unto me, and I will answer thee,
and shew thee great and mighty things,
which thou knowest not.
Jeremiah 33:3

1732—Brainerd home, Haddam CT

Fourteen-year-old David followed his older siblings as the funeral procession made its way from their home and to the cemetery. A cold, damp wind chilled the mourners as they made their way down the road. He glanced over his shoulder and marveled at the size of the crowd that followed them, although he shouldn't have been surprised. Hezekiah Brainerd had been a prominent member of the community. He had died suddenly just five years earlier and now his children were witnessing their mother's burial.

As they climbed the hill to the cemetery, the empty grave gaped before them. The family gathered to one side as the pallbearers placed the coffin beside the hole. David shivered and his sister, Jerusha, pulled him close.

There was a moment of silence until the pallbearers joined their families. Reverend Fiske stepped forward and cleared his throat. He had cared deeply for Hezekiah and his family. Haddam was a close knit community, mostly owing to the fact that many of the faces in the crowd had descended from the same roots. He searched the faces of Dorothy's children. The three youngest ones had lost a great spiritual leader in their home, but even at a young age, the little ones had developed the same godly character as their older siblings.

As he began reading words of comfort, his eyes fell on David, who stared intently at the pastor. There had always been something different about the young man. He had a seriousness about the scriptures that Reverend Hubbard did not find in most adults! The reverend smiled empathetically and continued to read.

David soaked in every word, allowing them to bring peace to his heart. It seemed like just yesterday they had stood here for his father's funeral. Memories of his father had not dimmed for David, and his mind flashed to a vision of their whole family gathering around the table, listening as Father read from the Bible. They were such precious times to them all.

It had been difficult when Father passed away, but the trial had strengthened each of them—their strong faith pulling them through. But Mother had been the shining force through it all, and now she was gone. Mother was gone. He would not cry even though his heart was breaking.

"I will never leave thee," the pastor read. As David rehearsed the words over and over again in his mind, he wished he could be certain. God, the Father—his heavenly Father—would never leave him. His father had left him and now his mother. He longed for the peace he saw on Reverend Fiske's face. *I just need to spend more time in the scriptures and work harder at obeying God's commands*, his young heart determined.

There had been many late night discussions in the Brainerd household during their mother's illness, and it had been decided that the younger three sons would live with Jerusha and her husband. Having acquired a farm of their own, there was much work to be done and the boys would be a great help for the young couple.

David took one last look at the coffin as it was lowered into the ground and followed Jerusha and the rest of his family. Life would go on.

1737

For four years, David, John, and Israel worked side by side farming the land from sunup to sunset. It was hard work, but nothing they hadn't done before. But when the sun set and the evening meal was finished, David found a quiet corner where he studied God's Word, seeking that elusive peace he longed for.

One evening, Jerusha studied the young man from across the room, worry lines etched across her brow. She understood his struggle. Jerusha was only four years his senior and she remembered the years of searching that had kept her awake many nights. However, she had the strong guiding hand of her mother through those difficult teen years. The thought made her feel woefully inadequate. She whispered a prayer before rising from her chair, her tall, graceful figure moving silently across the room. Laying a slender hand upon his shoulder, she sat down beside him.

David looked up with questioning eyes, waiting for her to speak.

Jerusha searched his face and prayed for wisdom. "David, I know your struggle."

He looked up at her but said nothing, desperately wanting her to continue.

Jerusha saw the hunger for truth in his face, and chose her words wisely. "You know the scriptures, David. You know the fear of the Lord. Your life shows a heart for God. Don't forget Jeremiah 13:29. *And ye shall seek me, and find me, when ye shall search for me with all your heart.*"

"But I am doing that, Jerusha," David exclaimed, a bit defiant.

Jerusha put her hand on his shoulder. "Yes, you are, so there's nothing more you can do."

"Why doesn't He hear my prayers?" David's voice choked with emotion.

Tears sprang to Jerusha's eyes as her heart broke for him. "Oh, He does, David. Rest in that fact. The verse is a promise, but it must be in God's time. We cannot know His ways. He is past finding out, but His promises are true and sure. We can rest in them, especially through our struggles."

David smiled weakly. A sense of calm settled over him. "Thanks, Jerusha. I know I don't say it enough, but you are a wonderful sister. I miss our father and mother, but you have truly filled the gap."

The persistent tear, which had threatened to expose itself throughout the conversation, now slipped down her cheek. She reached forward and gathered him into her arms. "Bless you, David. Thank you."

For five years David's life followed the same pattern: work six days, worship and much needed rest on the Lord's Day, and searching the scriptures for the peace his family seemed to possess.

It was now harvest season and the days were long. One evening after the supper hour, as the younger children began to clear the table, Jerusha stopped them. "Please have a seat. There's something we need to discuss." She rose from her seat and walked to the hutch, removing a paper from the one shelf and handing it to her husband.

Samuel took the paper and cleared his throat, looking at all the faces around the table.

"After your mother's death, a property came under dispute which had been in her family. It's taken five years, but according to this document..." He stopped and looked at David. "You have inherited the farm in Durham."

At first, everyone just stared around the table in silence, but soon they were all talking at once. David sat speechless. Why him? It seemed to be the question no one was willing to ask. Instead, it was just accepted from the hand of the Lord.

It was decided that the three young men would work the farm together and try to make it profitable. It had been uninhabited for several years and the fields now lay fallow. The buildings were well structured, just in need of minor repair. The harvest season was upon them, so the young men agreed to stay until after the crops were gathered into the barn.

*   *   *

John excitedly put the last of their meager belongings in the wagon. *Freedom at last!* He was grateful for this sister and brother-in-law's generosity and loving care for the past five years, but he was ready to move on with his life. The idea of the three of them having a place of their own made him wild with excitement.

He stood by the wagon, trying to be patient as Jerusha continued to load it with enough food for the whole year—or so it seemed. They had stayed throughout the harvest as they had agreed, but now he was ready to go!

"Are you sure you have enough..." Jerusha was asking, but Samuel cut in.

"Jerusha."

She looked at him contritely, and he smiled, putting his strong arms around her. "They'll be alright. They are nearly grown men."

"Nearly," she muttered, but remained silent.

The three hopped into the wagon, John and David in the front and Israel snuggled into the back amidst blankets and baskets of food.

John picked up the reins, ready to set them into motion, when David stopped him. He saw his brother's impatience but smiled. "Let's begin this new life in prayer, brother." John sighed but nodded, resting his hands on his lap but still clutching the reins.

David looked down at Samuel, Jerusha and their family—all eyes upon him. "We can't thank you enough for what you have done for us." He held Jerusha's gaze for a moment before looking heavenward. The air was cool as a nip of the coming winter edged the last autumn breeze out of its way. Bowing his head, he prayed, "Our dear heavenly Father, we thank Thee for Thy abundant provision and watch care over us. Surely Thy mercies are new every morning and Thy faithfulness is beyond measure. Bless our dear brother and his family for their kindness, goodness, and guidance. Protect them from the Evil One. And show us Thy way, O Lord. Keep us ever faithful to Thee. In Jesus' name we ask, Amen."

The reins fell sharply and the wagon lurched forward. "Goodbye," John called over his shoulder, and they all waved and laughed as they drove out the lane.

Jerusha wept silently. "God protect them," she whispered. Samuel tightened his arm around her shoulders. "He will, my love, He will."

For two years the three brothers worked hard repairing fences and reestablishing the fields. God truly blessed their efforts: crops yielded bountiful harvests and their herds produced strong stock. But God was also working in each heart, teaching them through their lively, nightly discussions. Yale's move to New Haven and its biblical studies was having a profound effect on their community as well as their own lives. The call to serve was never far from the brother's hearts and minds.

They faithfully attended services. To do otherwise was never even considered—it was law. But it was not the law that bound them to their Sunday morning services, but hearts fully devoted to their God. Late in May, after the fields had been plowed and the gardens were planted as well, Israel came rushing to the house waving a leaflet. He had been sent to town with the shopping list—a task none of them enjoyed.

David and John looked up from the garden plot. "Something has him all riled up," John said, mopping the sweat from his brow. David straightened his back and stretched his neck from side to side.

"Look!" Israel shouted. He handed the flier to David who quickly scanned the content, his face brightening with delight.

"Reverend Edwards will be speaking in a fortnight at Yale," he said excitedly.

"Just enough time to get the crops in," John calculated.

"We'll need to let Samuel and Jerusha know," David said. "There's been so much talk of the recent revival in Northampton under his preaching. Perhaps he will be able to stir the hearts of those students who have grown cold and lazy."

"Aren't you being a bit harsh, brother? Perhaps you are just jealous of their opportunity and wish it was your own," John countered.

David was silent. John was probably right. His soul was restless and he longed for peace. Was he to attend college? It seemed foolish when he had such a good situation right here. He did not need the schooling. He looked at John and shrugged as they all continued their tasks without further discussion, but John's words continued to echo in his mind.

The two weeks seemed to last forever, even though the men kept busy with their work. The Lord had blessed them with perfect weather, and they were ahead of schedule by the time the meetings finally arrived, probably because of their efforts to work harder in hopes of making the time pass more quickly.

It proved to be too much of a journey for Samuel and Jerusha's family, but the young men would be able to make the trip on horseback in a day. Letters were sent and plans were made for lodging. Samuel and his oldest son would look in on the livestock, although none of the cows were calving and the pasture was lush with spring growth. The stream was flowing full, so water was plentiful—there was no need for worry.

Spirits ran high the night before the journey. Their bags were packed and their hearts were brimming with anticipation. It had been a long time since any of them had been to Yale, and they feared they wouldn't sleep that night for excitement.

The morning dawned clear and bright as they checked the livestock one last time before taking off. Israel chattered like a magpie; he was so excited. This would be his first visit to the famed college. Now he would see for himself the place which dominated so many of their conversations.

"You know, if you would be quiet for just a few seconds, we might see some wildlife," John rebuked.

Israel's face flushed, but he rode on in silence. John was right. Just a few yards down the road, a doe and two fawns walked silently across the road. Further down the way, a flock of not-so-silent turkeys squawked noisily as they strutted into the road on their way to Farmer Brown's field for breakfast. They cackled and ran as though a fox was on their trail. When the trio approached, the gaggle was already picking through the fields and had quieted down.

After a short stop by a stream for their lunch, the three were once again on the trail, anxious to reach their destination.

The Brainerd children had been taught to work hard and they had, squirreling quite a bit of money away. Now, they were looking forward not only to the preaching but hot meals and clean beds which they did not have to wash or prepare.

The town of New Haven was still bustling with activity even though the day was waning. Israel had never seen so many people in one place!

"Do you think it's so busy because Jonathan Edwards is here?" asked Israel.

David laughed. "Well, that might be partly true, but most of what you see is the citizens of New Haven." As they rode down Church Street towards the village green, the salty ocean breeze filled their lungs. "Just over there," David said as he pointed to the southeast, "is the port. Now there's where you would see even more people and of every walk of life."

"Best stay away from there, little brother," John said with a wink.

Israel looked confused, which just made his older brothers laugh.

John pulled his mount closer to Israel and leaned towards him, whispering, "There are women there of whom mother or Jerusha would not approve."

Israel blushed beet red, bringing on another round of guffaws.

The village green was like a beehive with scholars clustered in small groups, while others hustled to and fro. The Brainerd brothers took in the sights as they turned off Church Street and on to Chapel Street.

In spite of all the excitement, the three were weary by the time they dismounted and walked their horses to the stables. A young boy was pitching fresh hay into a stall, but when he saw them coming through the barn doors, he put down the pitchfork and greeted them warmly. "I'll take good care of your horses, sirs. How long will you be staying?"

"Three days," John offered. He could see the look of excitement in the boy's eyes as he calculated his income. *Three horses for three days!* "Thank you, sir," the boy said with delight and led John's mare to a stable. The other two horses followed serenely, more than happy to comply.

"Let's get settled in. Then we can have some supper," David said. He led the way out of the barn and down the street to the inn. Westgate Inn was not the most expensive place to stay, but David knew that many of the students gathered there for theological discussions. He hoped to take part in some of them, mostly listening, of course.

Their room, spacious and airy, was in the front of the inn and overlooked the Green. Their clothes were hung, the beds tested, and satchels stowed away under the beds. Israel's face beamed with delight and his mood was infectious. After a splash of water on their faces and clean clothes, the trio headed downstairs for supper. Already, the inn was getting crowded with students as well as travelers. It was a cheery group, and much laughter circled the large room, bouncing off the low ceiling and echoing up the stairs.

Innis and Mildred Sanford were the proprietors, and much of the success of their establishment was due to their jolly personalities. They welcomed the boys as though they were long lost relatives, and Mildred smothered them with motherly love just like she did all 'her boys.' Surprisingly, the young men did not mind her mothering; in fact, many alumni returned to visit their mother-away-from-home, proudly showing her their brides and offspring.

The three brothers settled at a table in the corner and ordered their food. After a scant lunch, the hearty beef and potatoes were greatly enjoyed.

"This is delicious," Israel exclaimed.

John mocked insult. "You mean it's better than my savory squirrel stew?" They all laughed. As they finished the meal, hating to leave the comfortable room, a commotion at the entryway drew their attention as well as everyone else's in the room. Soon questioning whispers turned into excited exclamations in every corner. "It's Jonathan Edwards!" was the unexpected surprise.

As he entered the room, many of the students stood. Soon everyone in the room was standing out of reverence for the great preacher. Reverend Edwards circulated among the students, shaking hands and greeting each of them warmly.

The murmurs died away, and it was as though they were all waiting for him to speak. Not disappointing them, he looked around fondly and began.

"How could I not stop into one of the dearest places on earth and see my good friends!" He looked around at all the faces smiling at him.

Edwards had been a student in the early twenties and then pastored under his grandfather before taking the senior pastorate. Then, just four years into his ministry, revival broke out in Northampton. Manuscripts of his sermon entitled "Justification by Faith" were circulated by every New England newspaper. Fame of the revival had spread throughout the colonies, and its effect could be seen and felt in the moral fiber of many communities.

"I am honored by your courtesy and look forward to tomorrow's services." He looked directly into the faces of the students. "Make your calling sure, men, and then strive to follow our Lord's command and take the Gospel to every creature. Times have changed over the past hundred years since our forefathers came to this land seeking religious freedom. When facing difficult challenges—even death—they stayed the course. But in our day, many have strayed. Our churches are filled with cold, indifferent hearts, and we wonder if many need to answer the call, 'Ye must be born again!'" His voice rose and many "amens" sprang from hearts which thrilled to his message.

Reverend Edwards warmed to his subject as well and preached on for another half hour, but no one minded. His fervent spirit and tender heart beckoned to each listener, and by the time he had finished, tears were flowing down the faces of not a few. He closed in prayer and once again circled the room, especially focusing on those whose hearts had been touched by the Spirit.

There was such an ache and longing in David's heart that he wanted to cry like a baby. *What is wrong with me,* he questioned inwardly. *Am I one of them, Lord—have I not sought to please You?* he chided. Edwards was praying with a woman at the table beside them who wept uncontrollably. His words of comfort brought peace to the poor woman's soul, and by the time they had finished praying together, her face was alight with an unspeakable glow.

"Thank you, sir," she whispered, shaking his hand and staring into his eyes as though she could see right to heaven through them. "The hand of the Lord is upon you."

"His hand longs to guide you and make you strong. We have an enemy but he is no match for our Redeemer," Edwards assured her.

As he turned to depart, his eyes fell on David, and for a brief moment, the young man feared as well as desired that he would speak to him. Edwards searched David's face. He sensed the young man's inner struggle but could also tell that he was not ready for absolute surrender. He moved forward and held out his hand to John. "Are you here for the preaching?" he asked.

John rose to his feet, taking the offered hand and shaking it warmly. "Yes, sir. We are three brothers. This is David," he said nodding to his brother. "And Israel is our youngest." He looked back at Jonathan, "I am John Brainerd. Perhaps you knew our father, Hezekiah? We are from Haddam."

Jonathan thought for a moment. "I believe I've heard of him. Did he not serve in the legislature?

John brightened. "Yes, he did."

"And are any of you considering attending the college?" Jonathan continued. His eyes seemed to wander to David as though the question was meant for him.

David cleared his throat. "I have considered it."

Reverend Edwards nodded slowly and once again his gaze made David uncomfortable. "That would be good, but as I said earlier, make your calling sure." He continued to look directly at David, praying as he did so. He wanted to say more, but did not feel led by the Spirit. He shifted his gaze back to John and continued. "Well then, I will look forward to seeing you tomorrow."

That night, David lay on his bed staring up at the ceiling long after he heard the even breathing of his sleeping brothers. He wrestled in prayer throughout the night, begging God for peace, but finding little.

The hall was already half full when the Brainerds arrived. Hurrying to get a seat as close to the front as possible, they decided to separate to get better seating: John and Israel sat close to the center and David to the far right near an exit. For several years, David had suffered with a nagging cough that would throw him into spasms. He never knew when the fits would strike, making him seem reserved as he drew away from a crowd. It could not be helped, but if he could be near a doorway, he could make a fast retreat if necessary.

The buzz of excitement ebbed and flowed as people continued to pour into the chapel, and shouts of excited hellos from visitors who hadn't seen each other in years filled the room. A spirit of anticipation electrified the crowded hall as everyone anticipated Jonathan Edwards' message. Some were there merely out of curiosity. Did this man have something up his sleeve that could make men quake at their sin? But most came because of concern for their own souls and a yearning for fresh words from a New Light.

At the sound of the tower bells striking the hour, the group quieted to whispers. The organist entered and began the service with the Doxology, a tradition for the college, and then another hymn and prayer warmed the hearts of the congregation. David relished the music nearly as much as the preaching which would follow. It was full of life, and spirit, and hope.

Jonathan Edwards scanned the crowd as he walked to the pulpit but wasted no time in beginning his message. Time was of the essence. "Both riches and honor come of thee, and thou reignest over all; and in thine hand is power and might; and in thine hand it is to make great, and to give strength unto all (1 Chronicles 29:12)." He paused, allowing the Word of God to find its place in the heart of every man. "I present to you the all-powerful God. He owns the cattle on a thousand hills and the hills also, and He bountifully sends forth riches and honor to His faithful servants. In His hand is power and might." He looked up to the vaulted ceiling and continued. "Is there anything too hard for our God?"

For forty-five minutes, Jonathan Edwards presented his powerful God to the congregation who listened intently. Using verses from both Old and New Testament, he left no room for doubts concerning the power of God to create as well as destroy, to save as well as condemn.

David was enthralled. Before he knew it, the closing prayer was given. Oh, how he wanted more! He wanted to know Jonathan Edwards' God! Had he been worshipping a puppet god? And if so, how did you find this powerful God who sounded so different than the God he read about in his Bible? The yearning in his heart became so great he hardly knew whether to sit or stand but numbly followed the movements of those around him.

He was standing rather in a daze when John and Israel found him. "Wasn't he wonderful!" exclaimed John. David looked at him and into the shining eyes of his little brother.

"Yes," he said quietly. They both stared at him, wondering if he was ill. The uncomfortable feeling that his brother may be sick in front of all these people snapped John into action.

"Come on. Let's get some fresh air," he said as he nearly ran down the aisle. Israel followed, somewhat confused, and David brought up the rear. The three walked slowly across the lawn to a bench where the crowd was thinner. John turned to David with concern. "Are you alright?"

David's eyes were haunted, and he stumbled for the right words. "Do you know the God that he is talking about, John?"

John looked confused. "Of course I do and so do you." He looked at Israel and then back at David. "We all do, David. What are you saying?"

David shook his head. "I'm not sure, but as he spoke, I had to wonder if I even knew the God that he described."

John didn't know what to say. Belief came easy to him and he never questioned it, unlike his brother. "You're too hard on yourself, David."

David was silent.

"Look. Let's walk a bit and then get a bite to eat after the crowd has eaten. The exercise will do us good."

Without a word, the three walked away from Yale and onto a residential street. The tree-lined cobble road provided some shade, even though the sun was anything but hot. A cool breeze stirred the daffodils in a flowerbed along the street, making them merrily nod their heads. Dogwood trees had started to drop their downy petals, sending forth a shower of white before them.

"I love spring," Israel offered, trying to lift the mood.

David forced a smile. "Me too, lad." He ruffled Israel's hair, much like he did when Israel was younger.

John sighed, thankful the darkness had passed momentarily; however, as each night's preaching became more fiery, David became more sullen. He was determined to keep his thoughts to himself, closing out the world, not wanting to spoil their time together, but Jonathan Edwards preached with so much Holy Spirit power, it was all he could do not to fall to the ground and weep.

On the final night, he would later wonder if it was Satan that induced his coughing and drove him from the meeting. Near the finish of the message he could feel a cough rising in his throat. He wanted to stay—needed to stay—but he would not disrupt the service. Pulling his handkerchief from his pocket, he rose to his feet and quickly made it to the door just as a cough exploded from his throat. By the time he regained his composure, the service had ended, and a heaviness weighed down upon his soul, nearly toppling him to the ground.

He stood leaning against a pillar, feeling the weight on his soul, when John came out of the building. He took one look at David and pity filled his soul. "A coughing fit?" he questioned.

David looked up at him, his handkerchief still at his mouth and nodded. *Tell him*, a voice within seemed to shout in his ear. But this was his fight—his battle. He would find peace, beg God for peace.

*　　*　　*

Spring turned quickly into summer as temperatures rose unusually high for June in Connecticut. The tiny green blades of new plants burst through the dark garden soil as though on a race to the sun, and the weeds soon followed. The boys were busy once again from morning till night, but as they worked side by side their conversations were filled with thoughts concerning all that they had heard during their short stay at Yale.

Over and over, each message was reviewed, discussed, chewed on, and enjoyed with new relish. John stopped hoeing after one of his rather extended remarks and stared across the rows. "This all seems rather pointless, doesn't it?" he asked no one in particular. Both brothers stopped as well and waited for him to continue but he remained lost in his thoughts.

"If a man shall not work, neither shall he eat," David reminded him.

John turned to face him. "Yes, but can you imagine digging into the Word and preparing spiritual food for others?"

"I cannot deny that the thought has also been on my mind ever since we visited Yale," David admitted. But as soon as the words left his lips the same ones that had haunted him night and day echoed in his heart. *Make your calling sure.* He looked away and began to hoe once more.

John looked across the rows to Israel who shrugged and continued his work also.

The weeks stretched into the summer, but each of the brothers sensed an unrest—a longing for more than farming. What had seemed like the golden opportunity now became an albatross.

One Sunday afternoon, David excused himself after the dinner dishes had been cleared and put away. As was their custom, long engrained into their hearts and minds, the afternoon was given to Bible reading or other religious books, and they would then share each other's thoughts; but David was pressed more than ever to get alone with God.

He walked across the yard and into the woods, thankful for the coolness offered by the shade. Their pastor had challenged them that morning to consider their love for God, explaining that, as a religious people, we often move through our religious motions only because it is the thing to do, not out of a heart for God. The thought had stopped David short, and he knew he needed to give it some private thought.

He prayed as he walked all afternoon, but today, his prayers were halted and disjointed as he sought to pray in earnest, trying to focus on who God was and not on what He did. He had been reading First John that morning, and now one verse kept flashing through his mind: *We love him, because he first loved us* (1 John 4:19).

"We love him, because he first loved us," he mused.

As the sun began to dip closer to the horizon, suddenly it all became clear, and the truth nearly took his breath away.

"Herein is love, not that we loved God, but that he loved us, and sent his Son to be the propitiation for our sins" (1 John 4:10). He fell to his knees trembling and looked up into the treetops. "Oh Father, how could I have ever thought that anything at all was required by my hands?" He raised his hands and looked at them as though they belonged to someone else. "How could these hands do anything?" he clutched his chest. "How could this heart ever love Thee enough?" David buried his head in his hands and wept. "It is all of Thee, O Lord. Thou hast shed abroad in our hearts Thy love by the Holy Ghost which Thou hast given to us" (Romans 5:5).

He raised his tear-washed face and beheld the glory of God as never before, understanding for the first time true salvation. "Not by works of righteous which we have done, but according to Thy mercy Thou hast saved us" (Titus 3:5). O Father, why did I not see this before?"

You were too busy trying to earn my love, my son. David gasped at the clarity of the thought. "He is right," he whispered. "I thought I needed to do something, but there is nothing to be done but receive Thy forgiveness, Lord. And yet now the desire to serve Thee is fourfold as great! Can you use this weak, wretched man, O Lord? Is there a task for me, dear Father?" He smiled weakly. "I believe I have made my calling sure."

He rose to his feet feeling light as a feather. The heavy burden of sin and misunderstanding was gone. All he wanted to do now was to learn of his Lord and Master.

*   *   *

Within a month, David Brainerd was heading to Yale to begin his studies. His heart was full of joy and he was ready to learn. Sadly, the spiritual temperature on campus was cold—lukewarm at best, and the foolishness of hazing was ridiculous to him. As though Satan had plans to stop the young scholar at every turn, David developed measles and had to return home that fall, staying once again with his sister and her family. However, David could not be stopped. He had a mandate from God and he would follow God's direction no matter the difficulties.

Returning in November, David soaked up every lesson, studying into the night as long as he was permitted. The scriptures came alive to him, and he was often sought out for guidance and understanding.

As he began his third year, he came back to Yale full of joy and promise, excited that John was now at his side. That year another event took place which would have its effects on not only David, but on the entire college as well. The students had formed a new group called the New Lights. Many students who had been revived by the preaching of Jonathan Edwards were tired of the status quo attitude of many professors. They were growing restless and frustrated, which often was interpreted as rebellion by the administration. David became a part of the movement, empathizing with the students' hearts who desired change.

*   *   *

As Professor Whittelsey droned on, David looked across the lecture hall at all the disinterested faces, and it frustrated him. *There is so much to learn and these young men are as hungry as I am,* David fumed inwardly as he recounted the lively evening discussions that occurred at the Westgate Inn. *More learning is taking place without these windbags than under their tutelage,* he thought.

As the lecture ended, he gathered his books and headed for the door to meet with some of his classmates. Jason rolled his eyes as did some of the others. Their conversation grew heated as they strolled across the green.

"Whittelsey just drones on and on about church laws of the fifteenth century. He has no more grace than a chair," David spouted and the others laughed.

"Did you hear that Whitcomb was also fined for trying to evangelize at the docks?"

David stopped in his tracks, looking around at all the faces. They all had heard, but he had not. "This is ridiculous! I'm surprised that the good Lord doesn't strike the Rector dead for such foolishness. Isn't that why we are here, to give the Gospel to every creature?"

"I don't think the Rector has much compassion for the dock workers," someone replied quietly.

"Have they no souls just as destined to hell as you or I?"

The discussion grew heated, and no one noticed as some of the other students whispered to each other as they passed by.

The following morning, David Brainerd was called into President Stiles' office. David's words were repeated verbatim, and he was asked if he had said such a thing. He began to argue but knew it was useless.

"Yes, sir."

The president was obviously agitated. "And do you consider this statement to be a show of respect and honor to your elders?"

"No, sir."

The silence in the room was thick and choking, only stirred slightly by the heavy breathing of President Stiles. He did not understand where such insubordinate behavior was coming from and greatly disapproved of it. These New Lights believed they had all the answers, lifting themselves above men who had been in the ministry and taught at the college long before they were out of their nightshirts! He would make an example of this one!

"You are expelled from this school," he said coolly. "Please gather your things and leave at once."

David looked incredulous, which only fueled the older gentleman's fury. "Do not speak to anyone about this and do not spread any more of your malice, in the name of God. If you have any respect or honor for the Almighty, you will obey these orders without fail!"

David stood, nodded curtly, and left the office shocked beyond belief. He headed to his room, hoping to see John before he left the campus. He thought through his schedule and realized that his brother might be in their room. He climbed the stairs two at a time and was thankful to see their door open. John was sitting at his desk, deep in thought. When he heard the fast approaching footsteps, he turned to face the intruder, thankful to see that it was David. His face brightened but only momentarily. "What's wrong?" he asked as soon as he saw David's face.

David quietly closed the door behind him and sighed deeply. "I've been expelled."

John looked at him blankly, not able to comprehend the words. "What?"

David walked across the room and looked out the window. They had been so blessed to have this room together. It was so quiet and peaceful here. He loved to sit there by the open window, looking out at the street, and pore over his books. Now, that was over. "I've been expelled for my words about Professor Whittelsey. Someone must have overheard the conversation and reported it to the President."

"Oh, David. I'm so sorry. You know you didn't say anything that all the others were not thinking, including me."

"I believe they are making an example of me." He sighed deeply and sat on the edge of the bed. "What am I to do?"

"Do you think you could make an appeal?"

David shook his head. "If you could have seen his face. It was set like a flint." A spasm of coughing came on suddenly, leaving David weak and breathless. "Perhaps it's just as well. This coughing is so unpredictable."

John came to sit beside him. "What will you do?"

"Rev. Mills of Ripton once offered for me to stay with him. I would be able to continue my studies there."

"God is in this, David. He has a plan for you, for all of us." He shook his head. "These are dark days at Yale, but change is coming. They cannot hold back the hand of God, no matter how many students they expel!"

David smiled faintly. "I'll miss you, John. I hope this doesn't cause you any difficulties."

"Never fear. I'll be a saint!"

They laughed together, sitting for a moment for one last time. "I am sorry for my words, even though they are true. I will apologize to all involved."

In spite of all David's efforts, the board would not budge, and by week's end, his college career had ended. However, his learning continued and by November he was ordained in New Jersey as a minister of the gospel by the Presbyterian Church. Shortly thereafter, a member of the Society in Scotland for Propagating Christian Knowledge approached David, asking him to pray about pastoring in Long Island. He gladly accepted the post, but God had been burdening his soul for another area, and within the year, all plans seemed to fall into place.

He sat across the desk facing the sweet, wizened face of the Society leader, thinking how different the countenance of this face was from the president of Yale.

"We are so pleased with your work, Brother Brainerd. Your heart is tender to the Lord and His people."

"Thank you, sir. It has been my privilege to serve."

"Yet, Mr. MacFadden said that you wished to make a move?"

David shifted slightly in his seat, leaning forward. "Yes, sir, but it has nothing to do with the dear folks at the Long Island church. The Lord has so burdened my heart with the Indians that any other work seems tedious to me."

Mr. Campbell smiled and nodded. "Well, this is not a surprise to me, David. As you know, we are always seeking missionaries to work among the Natives. There is such a need and too few laborers." He stared at David for a moment, not wanting to offend the young man before him, but knowing it needed to be said. "Do you think you're strong enough for the rigors of missionary life, David? Your cough concerns us all."

"I understand, sir, but I believe the Lord will carry me through, don't you?"

The earnestness on the young man's face brought shame to Mr. Campbell's heart. "Of course He will. Your faith astounds me and, quite frankly, everyone in the society."

They continued to discuss the details of the work and it was decided that David would start his mission in New York.

Chapter Three

A New Beginning

For I know the thoughts that I think toward you,
saith the LORD,
thoughts of peace, and not of evil, to give you an expected end.
Then shall ye call upon me, and ye shall go and pray unto me,
and I will hearken unto you.
And ye shall seek me, and find me,
when ye shall search for me with all your heart.
Jeremiah 29:11-13

1742—Great Island, Pennsylvania

Siskia sat at the water's edge on the outcropping of rocks and dangled her feet in the water. It had been three winters since her family had left their Iroquois tribe in the North and traveled to this island in the Siskëwahane River. There had been bad blood between her father, Shawátis and his brother, Chief Deganawidah. Her father wanted peace. Deganawidah wanted war. *Why must there always be fighting,* Siskia thought. Oh, how she longed for the days of her childhood, when life was so much simpler. They lived, and laughed... and loved. With the thought of love, images of Pontiac sprang to her mind. What was he doing? Did he miss her? Would he come for her? The same questions always tormented her soul.

And did he still follow Jesus? She couldn't understand his desire for another god. They had more gods than they needed already as far as Siskia was concerned! But this god was different. Pontiac's belief in Jesus had changed him in a good way. His strength and determination only seemed to be strengthened by his new belief. He had tried to explain it to her but it made no sense. The missionary was a white man. Why would she believe anything a white man said? True, there were good white men, but most of them only brought grief and pain.

She splashed her feet, kicking the water and sending droplets flying out into the river. The air was hot and humid, but the water was refreshing. She was about to jump in when she heard her mother calling her name. Sighing, she pushed herself up and ran to the village.

Teres shielded her eyes from the beating sun, watching the heatwaves shimmer across the field. It was hot, but there was much work to be done. *Where is that girl?* Teres grumbled inwardly. Siskia was a good girl, but she did like to wander off when there was work to be done. Soon a spot down by the water grew into the figure of a young girl. She was running like a deer, graceful and free.

Teres smiled inwardly. Her daughter could have the pick of any brave, even though she showed no interest in any of them. Her face darkened momentarily as thoughts of their past played in her head. *She still sulks for that Praying Indian.* Teres missed her home and her family, but she didn't miss the conflict the white man's beliefs had brought to the village. So many of her tribe had become Praying Indians. What must the gods think? Was that why they were having so many problems and trials? Were the gods punishing them for their unfaithful hearts?

Siskia was the chief's daughter now that they had come to this new place. The loosely knit village was mostly made up of Iroquois and Munsee people. Some Delawares had come from the way of the rising sun. Others passed through their village on their way to new homes having lost their land to the white men —snatched from their grasp— much as Shawátis had lost respect for Deganawidah. The village did not seem to have any leadership when they had

50

arrived three summers ago, and Shawátis was a natural born leader. Humble, yet direct, he had not pushed his way in, but came as a servant. A smile played on her lips as she thought of her husband. How proud she was of him!

"Sorry mother. I came as soon as you called."

Teres hid her smile and grunted. "Some of the women are heading to Otstuagy to trade with the people there. I need you to take corn and trade it for fresh vegetables. And your father needs tobacco."

Siskia's face brightened. She loved going down river to Otstuagy. It was a larger village than their own and had a marketplace where natives would gather and barter their goods. The place buzzed with excitement, and there always seemed to be something happening. Many of her people passed through Otstuagy when traveling north or south and she often wondered if Pontiac might have been so close to her without knowing. She followed her mother to their long houses and readied for the journey.

Teres handed her the pouch heavy with corn. "Our corn is good. Get a good price. There may even be enough for you to buy something for yourself." Her mother's eyes glowed with excitement which Siskia had rarely seen since their move. She smiled and nodded.

"I will do my best, Mother."

The others had already assembled at the far end of the village. It was mostly women, but some of the older boys were going along to help row and carry back their purchases. Siskia brightened when she saw that Mausi was going along. The young Delaware girl was about Siskia's age, and they had become good friends in the time that Siskia's family had been on the island. Mausi turned back towards the village as though looking for someone, and when her eyes fell on Siskia, she squealed with delight. Leaving her older sister, she ran back to her friend.

Taking Siskia's free hand she squeezed it. "I am so happy that you are going with us. I had hoped you would." Mausi's dark eyes shone with joy.

The two girls walked to the water, chatting like magpies. They dumped their sacks into the canoe, which Mausi's twin brother held secure, and hopped in. Kor rolled his eyes at his sister but favored Siskia with a smile, even though she paid him no notice. He sighed, pushed the canoe into the current, and hopped in, taking the paddle and deftly steering the craft away from the other canoes.

The trip to Otstuagy went quickly since it was located downstream from the Great Island. As they approached, they could already smell fish frying over the fires and a mixture of a hundred different scents. A group of women were tanning hides from a recent hunt while others hoed dirt in gardens planted near the river. Somewhere someone was smoking tobacco reminding Siskia that she needed to get some for Father.

As Kor steered their canoe towards the sandy shore where the Lawisahquick Creek met the mighty Siskëwahane River, the girls' attention was directed to the strong voice of a white man speaking in a strange tongue. They stared in open curiosity, as did all the others from their village. He stood before a crowd of Indians who had gathered and were quietly listening as a young Delaware translated his words.

"You come this day to the market to purchase food for your body, but I tell you of One who purchased my soul," Zinzendorf said in a strong, yet calm voice. His passion could not be missed.

"Jesus, the only Son of the true and living God paid for my sins with His blood. His wounds were meant to purchase me. Those drips of blood were shed to obtain me. I am not my own today. I belong to another. I have been bought with a price. And I will live every moment of this life so that the Great Purchaser of my soul will receive the fullest reward for His suffering."

Siskia did not notice his strange, dark clothing. She did not think about the beads of perspiration that gathered on his forehead. She only heard the name, Jesus, and her mind raced back to Pontiac. *This man believes like Pontiac believes,* her heart sang.

Zinzendorf saw the newcomers and rejoiced that the Lord had brought them. "It does not matter the color of your skin, the Almighty God sent His only begotten Son to die for every man and woman who has every walked the face of the earth. We are born in sin. Surely you know that and can understand our trouble!

"But what will become of you when you die? Must you pay for your sin—be punished for your sin for all eternity? But no! The blood of Jesus Christ cleanses us from all sin. No other god has ever sacrificed His Son for man, only the One, true God sacrificed His Son, and His name was Jesus. Will you believe that Jesus died for your sin? He was nailed to a cross. Nails in his hands and feet, and hung there for you and me."

He gestured with his hands and looked heavenward. "Oh, let us in thy nail prints see, our pardon and election free." Turning his gaze back to the seeking faces before him, his voice rang out with the heart-cry of his soul, "Will you believe?"

Nicolaus Zinzendorf searched the crowd for open hearts and found many that were nodding, seeking the release of their burdens of sin. He took several more minutes to explain salvation and prayer—our way of communicating with God. Several in the crowd bowed their heads as Zinzendorf led in prayer. Others scoffed and strolled away.

Siskia forgot everything and everyone. Her heart had been stirred by this man's words and she finally understood what Pontiac had tried to tell her. His words echoed along with the white man's, and the Spirit found a home in her heart. When the prayer finished, Siskia looked up at the man, her face wet with tears. She did not wipe them away, but listened as Zinzendorf continued to talk to the others.

"Siskia, what is wrong?" Mausi asked urgently.

As though coming out of a dream, Siskia focused on her friend's face. She reached up and wiped the tears from her eyes. Siskia was a proud young woman. She would never show weakness with tears unless she was wailing for a lost loved one. But today she had no pride left, only peace and satisfaction. "Nothing is wrong, Mausi. Everything is right. I have told you of Pontiac and his God. This is the God he knew, and now I know Him too!"

Mausi stared at her friend with a furrowed brow. She could not deny that something was different, but she did not understand. "You are different. What has changed?"

A new wave of tears sprung to Siskia's eyes. "My heart is clean, and I am one with this God as well as with Pontiac. I may never see him again, but I know I will see him in the next life."

Mausi pondered her words and nodded slowly. "Will you explain it to me?"

Siskia smiled. "Yes." The two walked to the river's edge, and Siskia explained all that she knew. It was enough for another to join God's family, and the two girls rejoiced together. As they laughed and talked, Siskia's face grew serious. "Mausi, we cannot tell my father. I know he brought us here to get away from the Praying Indians, as they were called in my village. He would not be happy."

Mausi nodded and the two babes in Christ walked to the market to make their purchases, their minds never far from the words of the white man: *And I will live every moment of this day so that the Great Purchaser of my soul will receive the full reward of His suffering.*

1744— North-central Pennsylvania

For two years, Ahanu roamed the woods north of the Siskëwahane River. He kept to himself, moving with practiced stealth along the ancient trails and staying in the shadows when anyone came near. The hurt and rejection drove bitter roots into his soul, and anyone from his village would have hardly recognized him. His features were as hard as his heart.

He often returned to Spirit Rock. The place gave him a sense of strange comfort, but when the sun began to set and he needed to move on, the spirit within him grew as dark as the midnight sky. He had not been back to his village and decided to take the familiar trail. As he drew closer, the thirst for blood filled his mind, as though the only way to avenge Sucki's innocence was in taking the life of another, and he knew exactly who that person would be!

His steps quickened as darkness filled the woods. Had he not known the way, he might have strayed off the right path, so dark was the night. As he approached, he slowed his steps, cautious to make no sound. When the clearing came into view, he was surprised to see complete darkness—not even one glowing ember from the usual bank of coals in the fire rings.

He stepped cautiously into the clearing, listening for a sound, any sound, but there was complete silence—dead silence! As his eyes adjusted to the semidarkness of the clearing, he noticed that the wigwams were in disrepair... and empty. The village was gone, completely abandoned. He found his family's dwelling and hesitated before the doorway. Images of his last time there flashed in his memory: his father's anger and silence, Chogan's look of disdain. Slowly, he pulled the flap open and gasped. The floor of the wigwam was covered with the remains of skeletons—his family's dead bodies! It was obvious that they had been food for the beasts of the woods.

Ahanu slowly backed out of the structure, away from the horror. *They had not been overtaken by another tribe. Natural disaster had not destroyed the village.* His mind whirled as he realized the truth. *Disease had come and claimed them all!* He had heard of other villages that had been completely wiped out by the white man's diseases. He looked around not wanting to stay a moment longer. All thoughts of revenge against his people were quickly replaced with revenge and hatred for another—the ones responsible for his village's demise!

Blindly, he crashed through the woods, not caring if he made any noise or not. Who would hear him? Everyone was gone! The thought only propelled his legs to move faster. When reason finally slowed him down, he found himself along the ridge of the mountain across from Spirit Rock and stopped to catch his breath. His sides heaved from the exertion, and he bent over to ease the pain. Slowly, he stood erect and walked to the edge of the cliffs, looking across the valley at Spirit Rock. His toes were curled around the lip of the cliff and he leaned forward. Was there reason to live? If he just leaned a little bit further, he could join his ancestors and live in peace. Peace? Would there be peace for him? He didn't think so. No matter how much he had tried to do right, it never seemed to work out for him.

His breathing became erratic, and he stepped back, shaking his fist at the sky. He would not only avenge Sucki, he would avenge his tribe! It was not to appease Raweno, it was not to prove his manhood and loyalty to his father. It wasn't to prove his worth to become chief—he had no tribe! It was for his own satisfaction, because nothing else would satisfy the bitter weed wrapped around his soul.

The next morning, as he crawled out from beneath the pine boughs of a giant pine, he heard voices and silently returned to the cover of the branches. Perhaps his opportunity for revenge was coming his way, but as he listened he realized they were not white men. They were speaking in the tongue of the Six Nations. For years, his people had been threatened by these tribes, but they had managed to hold on to their lands. He listened intently, trying to discern their mission.

He counted three different voices. They sounded young and their talk was just the small talk of travelers.

They passed close by but were unaware of his presence. As they passed he decided to follow them, keeping his distance. When they stopped beside a stream to eat, he once again drew close enough to listen. This time he was rewarded for his patience. They were Seneca braves dissatisfied with the decisions of their elders. More and more white men were taking their land and bringing deadly diseases to their people. Many had died.

Suddenly, a squirrel began to chatter noisily in the tree where he hid. The conversation stopped and he knew his presence would be discovered. He decided to take the first step and came out into the clearing.

The trio tensed but relaxed somewhat when they saw that it was another Indian. Ahanu approached casually, wanting them to know he meant them no harm. He sized them up as he walked, in case they chose to be agressive. He knew he could easily take two of them, but the combination of all three was out of the question, and they knew it.

The tallest of the three stepped forward to greet Ahanu. He nodded once and spoke.

"I am Savanukah son of Ostenace, chief of the Seneca."

Ahanu nodded. "Ahanu, grandson of Hassun, chief of the Susquehannock."

The three young men looked at each other with surprise. "But we just passed by their village."

"I have been away from my village for two winters. I just returned last night."

"Then you know what happened to them?" Savanukah asked.

"The same thing that is happening all across our land." Ahanu spat out the words as though they were poison.

There was a moment of silence as they all exchanged glances, sizing up one another and weighing their next move.

"I've been following you for some time. I heard your conversation. I too am seeking revenge."

Their talk became animated as they shared their experiences and discontent.

"We have heard the Delaware are fighting south of here," Savanukah said.

"We go to fight," Kanatase added. "It does not matter who dies, just so someone dies." He was young and wiry, not much older than fifteen winters, and his face was as hard as Ahanu's.

"We go to the Great Island along the Siskëwahane River to meet with others," Degataga added. This one was a follower. His demeanor was that of a servant looking to a master for direction. Lean yet muscular, Degataga followed Savanukah not for revenge but because he always had.

Ahanu smiled faintly. He knew of the Great Island but had never been that far south. Perhaps he had found the outlet for his thirst for revenge.

Degataga and Kanatase looked to Savanukah, who obviously held the highest rank. Savanukah wondered if this young buck, not much older than himself, would be able to submit to his leadership, and it was obvious that Ahanu was asking himself the same question. Something about the chance meeting caused an ache in Ahanu's heart —a longing for fellowship. He had traveled alone long enough.

He bowed his head and held both hands before him, palms up—a gesture which would convey his message. "If you will have me, I would be honored to join you," he said, his head still bowed. But when he raised his head they saw cold hatred in his eyes. "I seek revenge for my people as well."

Savanukah stepped forward and offered his hand, and Ahanu took it gladly. The others joined in with the acceptance gesture as well.

"Good," Savanukah said. "Four are better than three. We will see how well we fit together as we travel, but I am sure your coming to us is a good thing. Come and eat before we continue."

As the four ate together, a bond was already beginning to forge, which would serve them well in the months to come. Their common desires and backgrounds made conversation easy as they continued down the trail. Ahanu fell in step behind all three, not wanting to cause contention in any way, but he knew his heart was in step with Savanukah. They were both chiefs' sons and it made a difference. They were born leaders, and the others seemed to sense it as well.

Ahanu took in his surroundings as they walked, not wanting to forget the way home. *Home? You have no home,* a taunting voice whispered into his already stony heart, causing his lips to curl into a frown. He found himself salving the wound with the evil thoughts of blood and conquest.

As the small group came close to the creek, he heard the familiar cry of an eagle and looked up just in time to see the majestic bird streak downward into the water. The giant pumped his wings, working hard to lift his body and that of a fish nearly his size from the deep, still waters. He soon disappeared around a sharp bend, and Ahanu realized their path turned more southerly as well.

He was just about to speak, when Savanukah raised his hand to signal for silence. Ahanu followed noiselessly amazed at the change in the men's demeanors. Fear was etched into every feature. What was this place? Inadvertently, they picked up their pace. The trail narrowed and they walked in single file through the thick underbrush. On either side of the creek the hills jutted upward, and a sense of foreboding fell upon them. Ahanu did not know if the feeling came from the place or from the hearts of his comrades.

As the hills fell away, the creek twisted its way through dismal swamps and meadows littered with skeletons of fallen trees baked lifeless in the summer heat.

Tangles of debris clung to anything strong enough to support their arrival by the spring flooding. In places where the waters had scoured the earth bare, the sun baked the soil until it cracked. They picked up their pace even more until they were running through this hell hole.

When they reached the other side, their pace slowed to a walk, and they stopped to rest in the shade of a mighty maple whose branches spread benevolently across the edge of the woods.

"What is that place?" Ahanu asked still looking across the seemingly haunted plain.

Savanukah shrugged. "No one knows, but it is believed that it is the home of many demons. So much destruction in one place certainly makes it seem true."

"I hope to never see this place again," Kanatase hissed, trying to hide the quiver in his voice. He was more superstitious than the others and often suffered from their pranks, but no one was taunting him now. They were all in agreement which made Ahanu wonder. Was he ready to cut all ties to his homeland, even if he had no tribe or village? Could he someday return and start a family of his own?

Ahanu felt a twig on his arm and looked up in surprise to see a big grin on Kanatase's face. "Where were you? You looked like you were thinking about a woman," Kanatase teased and the others guffawed.

Ahanu's face reddened causing more comments and pokes.

"He must be quite the brave to be able to think about a woman after just coming through the swamp," Savanukah teased. "Tell us about your maiden."

Ahanu shook his head and smiled. "There is no one, only dreams."

*　　*　　*

Great Island

Shawátis looked up from the circle of councilors when he heard advancing footsteps. Four young men were approaching from the east. He sized them up quickly: three Seneca and a Susquehannock. That seemed strange, but in these times his people would make alliances that were unheard of in his younger days. He stared at the obvious leader of their small band and nearly smiled at the swagger and assertive steps of one so young. *Obviously, a chief's son,* he thought, and then his breath caught. His eyes widened as he recognized the face of his nephew, Savanukah, his sister's son.

The others in the circle had stopped talking and were watching their leader. Every eye turned to look at the young man who had caused such a reaction, following Shawátis as he walked towards the young men to greet them.

Savanukah stopped suddenly. Could it be? He looked at Shawátis, the uncle who had mysteriously left the tribe nearly three winters past.

"Savanukah," his uncle said.

"Uncle! What a surprise!" Savanukah was shocked into silence. He looked past his uncle to the men who followed him, hoping to see other faces he might recognize, but they were all strangers to him. However, he could see that Shawátis was their leader, and the thought made him proud. *So he had not been shamed as many had rumored,* he thought. He was glad. Shawátis had a daughter that was close to his age, and they had been very close before they had left—before so much had changed. He took another glance back towards the village.

"She is here," Shawátis answered as though reading his mind. He smiled. "We are all here for now." He held Savanukah in a manly embrace and then turned towards the others. "Degataga I know, and Kanatase too, but who is this one?" he asked jutting his chin towards Ahanu with a look of distrust, scrutinizing him from head to toe.

Savanukah had already grown fond of Ahanu. They had shared each other's stories and were surprised at the similarities. Savanukah was the chief's second oldest son which meant that he wasn't in direct line to be chief; however, his older brother, upon whom the honored position would fall, had shown no interest in being chief or developing his needed leadership qualities. He was lazy, which was anathema to the Seneca mindset.

When his father started making an alliance with the French, it turned Savanukah's stomach. They did not need or want the white man's help or cooperation, no matter if they were French or British. The French trappers desecrated their land and the British stole it. By the time his brother started taking leadership, Savanukah could stand it no longer and took off with his friends. They had warrior blood and they would fight!

Shawátis' face relaxed. If this Susquehannock had found grace in his nephew's heart, then he must be good. "Come," Shawátis commanded, and they all headed for the village.

Great Island was a perfect place for an Indian village. Surrounded by two flows of the Siskëwahane River, it was high enough in places to avoid flooding but sloped gently down to the water's edge, making it very accessible by canoe. Easily defensible, large enough for gardens and crops, it was a virtual haven. The island had been occupied by different tribes for generations, but most recently had been taken over by the warring Munsee group of the Delaware tribe.

Many powwows had been performed on the sacred area of the island, and it would continue to serve as a meeting place for Indians and Europeans as they tried to forge a way to live together peacefully. However, trying to meld two societies, which were as different as night and day, into one would prove impossible in the end.

Shawátis had joined the Munsee settlement for personal reasons, although few knew why. To most, he was just another warrior who had tired of the European invasion of their land. From the Five Nations, his home had been far north near Lake Okswego. Trading with the French had brought wealth to the Five Nations, but what need did they have for the white man's gold?

The white man had also brought word of their God, which did not concern Shawátis until their earnest message began to penetrate his daughter's heart.

Many in their tribe had become Praying Indians, and that changed everything for them. They no longer worshipped Ha-Wen-Neyu or did sacrifices. They wanted peace at any cost and embraced the ways of the white man. It would ruin their society—their homes, and Shawátis was determined to not let it invade his domain.

When Pontiac, Siskia's intended husband, became a Praying Indian, it was the last straw. He had admired the young brave's strength and leadership—qualities he wanted for his daughter's husband, but there was something false about Pontiac. Even with this new god he seemed to only play the part to gain favor with his elders. This new belief was just another action to gain more favor with the French, something Pontiac valued greatly. Shawátis made plans, and in the quiet darkness of the night, he stole his family away and never looked back. Siskia mourned the loss for days, but she would not question her father's decisions, even though he often found her looking over her shoulder. This was now their home, far away from any talk of Jesus.

As the men approached the village, the sights and scents nearly overwhelmed Ahanu. It had been so long since he sat at a fire surrounded by family. He choked down any sentiment, biting his cheek and stiffening his back. He walked beside Savanukah, something that had become one of their habits on the last leg of their journey together, and he was glad of it.

The dogs signaled their arrival, and the village came alive, reaching out to welcome them—first, the little children, then the men, and finally the women.

Siskia had been drying fish with the other women, lost in thought. Although the activities were much the same as in her homeland, and the people had welcomed her and her family, her heart continued to bring images of Pontiac to her mind. At first, she knew he would come looking for her. Every visitor made hope spring anew in her heart, but as time passed, so did her expectations.

When today's signal of visitors came, she was tempted to ignore it, but then a visitor meant a break in the monotony. She finished laying out the fish on the rack and washed her hands in the river, absently pushing the stray strands of her thick, black hair back into her long braid.

As she followed the women, she saw her father scanning the faces of the crowd until he found her. He gestured to her to come, and Siskia hurried her pace, her eyes scanning the newcomers. The one she did not recognize, but when her eyes fell on Savanukah, she gave a little squeal and pressed forward.

Savanukah had been talking to her brother, Machk, shaking hands and slapping backs when he saw her coming towards him. He wanted to break into a run, but held himself like a man, his eyes dancing with joy. She had been another reason that he had left.

"Savanukah! What a surprise," she exclaimed softly. "What are you doing here?" Her black eyes sparkled with delight, only adding to her beauty.

"I've come for much the same reason your father is here." Savanukah's face darkened momentarily but brightened once again. "But that is for later. You are here. I never thought I'd see you or your family again."

Ahanu watched the exchange with curiosity. Who was this bewitching woman? He had never seen a woman like her. His people were large and strong, even most of the women. It was a mark of respect and was well admired. However, this maiden, although strong, was tall and slender and moved with the grace of a swan. He had watched her from the moment she came into view, attracted by her blithe gait. Yet, as she grew closer, he noticed that her face looked as though some deep pain had etched it into a permanent frown which never seemed to leave her eyes even though her mouth was smiling.

For the first time in two years, Ahanu looked down at his clothing. They were nearly rags hanging on his over-grown body. His grandmother had sown his clothes for him just weeks before he had left his village, but that was two years ago—two years of living in the wild. He had thought to do something about his needs this summer but the thought of being with people, even his own, kept him from the task. Now he wished he had made it a priority!

The sound of Savanukah's voice speaking his name pulled Ahanu from his reverie.

"This is Ahanu, grandson of Hassun, chief of the Susquehannock." Both young men saw Siskia's face darken at the mention of one of their warring enemies. "But his village was destroyed by the white man's disease." Siskia's face softened and Savanukah continued. "None of his people are left," he added for emphasis.

Siskia had scarcely taken notice of the stranger and now determined not to stare at his rags. She trained her eyes on his, holding his gaze for what seemed like an eternity; but Ahanu just stared back, trying not to give away his discomfort. "Welcome to our village," Siskia spoke like the chief's daughter she had become in this place. As she stared, something within her stirred, but she pushed it down. There was something about his haunting eyes that reminded her of Pontiac and it made her angry.

Ahanu nodded, thankful when her attention moved to Degataga and Kanatase; however, he noticed that they were as bewitched and uncomfortable as he was. What was it about this woman?

As the group processed into the village, an air of festiveness enveloped them. They were taken to Shawátis' long house and treated to a bounty of food and drink while they shared each other's journeys over the past few months.

The boys had left early in the spring, hoping to be settled by the end of summer. They had heard of the gathering at Great Island. Now, seeing the place and finding familiar faces only heightened their excitement.

Siskia came and went, but every time she entered she felt Ahanu's eyes on her, and it made her angry. *Who does he think he is?* she wanted to shout. She finished her serving as quickly as possible and was glad to go back to her dried fish.

"We heard talk of fighting," Kanatase finally interjected when the conversation had a lull.

Shawátis stared hard at him in silence considering how to answer. "A warrior does not seek out a fight Kanatase, but when the fight comes he is prepared."

Kanatase nodded curtly out of respect and looked down at his feet, knowing that he had just been rebuked.

"There is fighting along this river," Shawátis continued as though the conflict had never happened. "Chief Bald Eagle is always ready to fight. As you know, the French are also ready to do battle." He stopped and looked at each of the young men. "But we do not want a fight here," he answered sharply. "We want to live peacefully. Raise our children. We wish to pass on when the Great One takes our breath, not when an arrow pierces our hearts!"

He could read the disappointment on the boys' faces and understood the need to fight. But he also knew that their way of living could not survive in this new world of the white man. Shawátis was a forward thinker and would make choices that brought life, not death, to his family.

That night, as the four young men walked along the river, they weighed their options.

"I love my uncle but he is an old man, He is tired of the fight, but we are young and we must fight," Savanukah hissed. "He believes our way of life is passing, and it will if we do not fight." He nodded at the grunts of agreement that he heard. They walked in silence for a time, their pace quickening as their pulses did the same, until they were far past the edge of the village. "Tomorrow we go to Bald Eagle and offer our help to him."

"Can we stay long enough to..." Ahanu did not know how to ask but looked down at his clothes.

Savanukah smiled with understanding and slapped Ahanu's shoulder. "You are a mess, Ahanu. We will find new clothes for you. Then perhaps Siskia will notice you."

Ahanu's head shot up, and he was thankful for the darkness to hide the color crawling up his neck.

"I saw the way you looked at her," Savanukah teased. "But I don't think she was too impressed with you."

The others laughed good-naturedly and Siskia became the topic of their conversation.

Siskia tossed and turned on her mat, unable to sleep. Visions of Ahanu and his ragged clothes haunted her mind. *His village was wiped out by the white man's disease... all of them.* How horrible! As much as she missed her home and her family, she knew they were safe. But did she? Images of Pontiac replaced the ones of Ahanu, but to her great sadness, she couldn't remember his face. Tears choked her, and she quickly sat up. Silently, she left the long house, not wanting to awaken her family—the steady snores assured her she need not fear. On her way to the doorway, she glanced across the sleeping bodies to where Ahanu slept. He was facing her way, and she stopped momentarily to watch him sleep. He looked so peaceful, so gentle, even kind. She could see the boy as well as the man, and it made her blush. Quickly, she moved on.

Once outside the house, she took a moment to breathe deeply, looking up at the myriad of stars and enjoying the silence. A whippoorwill sang his night tune in the distance and a long way off she heard a wolf's howl.

As her eyes adjusted and she picked her way across the clearing, an idea began to form in her mind. At first she wrestled it down, but the more she thought about it, the more she knew it was the right thing to do.

Ahanu had slept well, although his dreams were filled with visions of the lovely Siskia. As he rolled to his back, he stretched out, thankful that he had awakened before dawn. His mind went back to the previous day and then to the events which had led him here. Again, Siskia's face smiled at him, and he wished that the others had chosen to stay on Great Island. Maybe he would stay. The thought excited him, but then the image of his village came into focus. *Revenge!* He must avenge his people! He quietly sat up and pulled on his clothes, once again chagrined at his appearance. As he quietly pulled back the flap, movement ahead of him caught his attention. It was Siskia!

Siskia was pleased with her work. It had taken her most of the night, but as she looked down at the new clothes, she felt thankful she could do something nice for this young man. A smile played across her face and a giggle nearly escaped her lips when she too caught sight of movement. Her plan had been to place the clothes at Ahanu's feet, hoping that no one would ever know of her deeds. She didn't want him or anyone else to get the wrong idea! And now, there he stood—rags and all!

She froze and so did Ahanu as they stared at each other through the darkness. Once again thankful for the cover of the predawn shadows to hide the flush of her cheeks, Siskia's mind raced. Quickly, she walked to him, shoved the clothes at him, and hissed. "Tell no one!" Pushing past him, she quietly reentered the long house.

Ahanu looked down at the clothes and turned just in time to see the flap snap shut. He looked at the clothes again, bewildered. He had not had many dealings with women but this one had him totally baffled. He would honor her wishes, but the thought that she had made clothes for him warmed his heart and made him smile.

For the next few days, it became a guessing game between the four young men as to who had sewn Ahanu's new clothes. He was determined to not tell them, and when

Siskia was nearby, he enjoyed watching her cheeks flush and the hint of a smile play on her lips. But revenge took the place of curiosity, and soon plans were made for their departure. Ahanu hoped that the thought of him leaving saddened Siskia, but she gave him no indication that it was true or that she had anything but contempt for his hide.

By the time of the full moon, the four young braves were once again on their way. They left with no fanfare, for the intent of their journey was known by all and the Great Island village who sought peace and a future, not war and more bloodshed. Chief Bald Eagle, though revered for his bravery, was looked upon with trepidation edged with fear by some and out and out disdain by others.

Many nodded to the braves as they passed out of the village, but the eyes which Ahanu and Savanukah hoped to see were disappointingly absent. Savanukah shrugged but Ahanu carried pain in his heart, fueled by the previous evening's chance meeting.

He had hoped to talk with Siskia and, once again, thank her for her act of kindness and had purposely kept an eye on her dwelling most of the day. His diligence had been rewarded, and he noiselessly followed her to the river. She bent to the water and deftly washed the post and utensils she had been carrying, humming as she did so.

Ahanu stood and watched her, realizing that he wanted Siskia for more than just a friend. As he left his hiding place behind the thick bushes which grew along the river's edge, Siskia looked up startled.

How had he gotten so close without her hearing him? She prided herself on having keen eyesight and sharp senses. Even her father praised her for it. Siskia finished her task and stood to face Ahanu, her ruffled demeanor obvious in every movement.

Ahanu was taken aback but was undaunted. He determinedly stepped closer, willing himself to be kind and gentle, even though she looked like a mountain lion ready to attack. "I wanted to thank you again before we left."

Silence.

Ahanu breathed out slowly, his nostrils flaring, his mind racing. He chose his words carefully. "I want you to have this." He pulled a necklace from his pouch and fingered it reverently, stealing a glance at Siskia but only receiving a scowl. He wanted to rush on but kept his actions quiet and controlled. "I once had a pet but it was taken from me and sacrificed." He thought he heard a sharp intake of air but chose not to look up. "The next day I returned to the sacrificial rock and took a bone that wasn't completely charred and carved this." He fingered the tiny image of a bear. Until today, the necklace had always hung around his neck, close to his heart.

Slowly, he raised his head. "I have nothing else to offer to you. It is the only thing of worth, the only thing I cherish." Their eyes locked. Ahanu wasn't sure which emotion he saw first. She was certainly surprised, but surprise quickly turned into confusion, and confusion turned to anger.

Siskia didn't know what to say. She knew he was heading into danger, doing battle with their enemies. She did not want any more bloodshed, but she didn't like what the price of peace had cost her father. To refuse his gift would be the worst insult she could give him, but to accept it meant something she was not willing to own—a commitment.

"I cannot accept it," she said flatly.

Ahanu looked down at the tiny bear and fingered it taking a moment to choose his words wisely. "I have no one. I don't mean anything by it but to say thank you." Without looking up, he held out the treasure. He heard a huff and the brief touch of her hand as she snatched it from him. The *clink* told him that she had tossed it into one of the pots. He looked up in time to see her back as she hurried up the path. He watched her go hoping for one backward glance, but it never came. Walking to the water's edge, Ahanu kicked at the stones, choosing a flat one and skipping it across the placid water. He wanted to prove himself to Siskia, but why should she think of him as anything but a vagabond? The thought only fueled his vengeful fire. He would show her! He would show them all!

Chapter Four

The Taste of Revenge

For the love of money is the root of all evil: which while some coveted after, they have erred from the faith, and pierced themselves through with many sorrows.
1Timothy 6:10

Middleburg, Pennsylvania

"Don't be a fool Jamison!" John Andrew urged.

But Ralph Jamison's mind was made up. He was heading west, and he couldn't wait for the others. He knew that his wife, Betsy, disagreed with him. It figured—she always sided with her brother when push came to shove.

Four families were moving into the little known valley west of Shamokin. Ralph had followed the Indian trails through the woods and into the valley next to Spring Creek. It was a perfect place to settle, and Ralph had big ideas for a future millwork there. But he had to get there first! He knew his brother-in-law had ideas as well, and they always left Ralph at the bottom of the barrel.

He decided not to tell even Betsy of his plan until bedtime. That way, she couldn't go running off to tell big brother. They had already sold what they didn't need and purchased every item they would need to start fresh. The children were settled down for the night, and Betsy had readied for bed when he laid out his plan.

"We're leaving as soon as it's light," he said nonchalantly.

Betsy looked up in surprise. "But what about the others? John's still waiting on that wagon wheel. It won't be ready until the end of the week."

Ralph grew impatient. "I know that Betsy, but you know as well as I do that when we get to the land, John is going to take charge as he always does." He was getting angry, and his voice was loud. Betsy hushed him, and he worked to gain control. "I'm sick of him always lording himself over us, Betsy. I have dreams and plans too! I want what is best for us. We can do this! They'll be along in a few days." He looked at her pleadingly. "What's a few days?"

Betsy desperately wanted to follow her husband, but fear of the Indians kept her up at night. Ralph saw the fear in her eyes. "Betsy, there ain't been Indians in that area for years. It will be okay. Can't you trust me?" he pleaded, taking her gentle hands into his work-worn ones.

She smiled weakly and nodded. Ralph pulled her into his arms. "You'll see, Betsy. We're gonna make it big." He definitely had enough enthusiasm for them both, but that was Ralph's way. He was a good worker but was always looking for easy money. He chuckled. "Who knows, maybe someday there will be a town called Jamisonville!"

*   *   *

Chief Bald Eagle watched as the four braves found their way along the creek trail. His lookouts had called for him when they had spied the strangers. Bald Eagle squinted, staring intently.

"Do we know any of them?" he asked.

"No," came the reply nearly in unison.

"They do not look as though they have traveled far. I wonder if they are more braves that are sick of Chief Shawátis' weak ways."

The two lookouts grunted their agreement. Bald Eagle had met with the French and knew of their plan to fight the British. He didn't trust any of them, but he knew the British were pushing in from the East while the French had plenty of room to the North and West. The only place for the British to go was their land. He would join anyone to keep them out and would use anyone who showed himself worthy to join his band.

As they watched the four young men make their way along the creek, he learned more than many would see in a lifetime about their qualities. "Bring them to the village," he said and walked away.

Bald Eagle was the ruler of the expansive Bald Eagle Valley which stretched several miles between two mountain ranges. The land was flat and well-watered and had been the home of his people for centuries. As Bald Eagle made his way back to his village, he thought about the four recruits. He knew why they were here. One was especially tall. If he didn't know better, he would have thought that he was a Susquehannock, but hadn't they been either destroyed by the Iroquois or driven out of the area years ago? And his dress was that of the Iroquois. Perhaps the rumors that a Susquehannock village to the north had survived, hidden back in one of the valleys off the Sheshequin Trail, were true. Perhaps the supposed demons in the flatlands along the Lycoming Creek were really bands from this forgotten tribe. No other tribe knew the trails to the north like them and no native could slip into an area unnoticed like the Susquehannock. It had always amazed him, considering their size, that they could be so silent. The others looked to be either Iroquois or Seneca, but he couldn't be certain.

By the time the chief had returned to the village he had his plan in place for testing the mettle of these young bucks.

*   *   *

Ahanu had just thought to suggest they be on the lookout for any watchmen from the village when two young braves seemed to appear out of nowhere on the path before them. They looked anything but friendly. The slight differences in their hair cut and clothing told the braves that they were Shawnee. Chief Shawátis had also told them that most of the villages towards the setting sun were from that tribe.

"Come," one of them spoke, "Chief Bald Eagle is waiting."

The young men looked at each other. *We should have known we were being watched.* The thought passed through each of their minds, and they conveyed the matter with their eyes. Silently, they fell into step behind one Shawnee while the other brought up the rear.

It was only a mile to the village, but they traveled it in silence. Savanukah could sense Degataga's angst. He was not a fighter by nature, and their future seemed to point to a fight. Savanukah wondered if Degataga would survive.

As they approached the village, it was obvious their arrival was expected. This village was much larger than any Ahanu had ever known. His tribe was small, and they had stayed away from other tribes and villages as much as possible. People seemed to be everywhere. Some were working, while others gathered in small groups openly gawking at the new arrivals.

The village was called Bald Eagle's Nest and was a common stopping place for traveling Indians, so it wasn't unusual for them to see strangers. However, Chief Bald Eagle's entrance into the village told them these four would not be passing through. He had already gathered the Council and told them to be ready for instruction. He had also met with some of their best warriors, carefully selecting four and telling them to be ready.

Ahanu took in his surroundings, not missing the four warriors who stood directly behind the chief. The biggest one kept his eyes on Ahanu, his lips curled into a sneer and his jaw clenched. Ahanu stared back, masking any emotions, a trait he had honed into perfection throughout his childhood. If his intuition was correct, there would be a tournament—a test—and he was staring at his opponent. The brave was several fingers shorter than Ahanu, but his arms and chest bulged with muscle and his thighs were thick and sinewy. Ahanu noticed an ugly scar that ran from his left ear down across his square jaw and to his chin. It would be quite a match, but Ahanu knew that his skills— that of a Susquehannock warrior—would serve him well.

They were brought to stand before Chief Bald Eagle, and Ahanu felt proud to be standing shoulder to shoulder with his friends. They stood tall, not knowing what would come next, but they would face the challenge together.

The chief, seasoned with years of leading his people and fighting for their protection, was pleased with what he saw in the four young men. Already, he could tell that two of them would make good warriors. One of the others was a follower, and the other brave was thirsty for blood. He would fight, but he would need to learn the ways of Bald Eagle before he could be any use to the mighty leader. Silence stretched on as the four young men faced off with the leaders of the village. Bald Eagle was in no hurry and had found much could be learned with silence.

Finally, he spoke. "You have entered Shawnee territory. State your purpose."

Without hesitation, Savanukah stood a bit more rigid and began. "I am Savanukah, son of Ostenace, chief of the Iroquois." He heard murmurs of surprise among the people, but continued. "My uncle, Shawátis, is now chief of the Great Island. We have recently come to the island in hopes of revenge against the white man's deeds, but my uncle chooses not to fight. He sent us to you."

Without any comment, Chief Bald Eagle's eyes shifted to the others, and Savanukah continued. "Degataga and Kanatase have come from my people far to the north." Savanukah stopped, allowing Ahanu to introduce himself.

"I am Ahanu, grandson of Hassun, chief of the Susquehannock." Another murmur rose from the crowd.

"My village has been destroyed by the white man's disease, and I too come seeking revenge."

Bald Eagle furrowed his brow. "Where was your village?"

North of the Sheshequin Path in a small valley among the mountain ridges beyond the Legaui-hanne Creek."

"Then it is true what we have heard, that the Susquehannock survive?" Bald Eagle questioned.

Ahanu's jaw clenched. "Of others, I cannot say, but of my village, my tribe, my people—they are all gone." Much to his dismay, his voice grew husky as he spoke, but he continued. "I have wandered alone for two winters until I found these travelers. We are now a band, and we come to you seeking to fight. We have heard that you are a true Indian chief and warrior and are defending our people and our land."

The people gathered, nodding their heads, but still no one spoke. Their eyes were on their leader.

"You must show your worth. Tomorrow we will see if you are ready or useful to us. Each must prove his skill and find a place among us." He raised his hand, motioning to the four warriors. "You must choose. Enata will race." The tall, lanky native of the four stepped forward. "Cuapea will shoot arrows." Another of the warriors only nodded slightly. "Deuquot will use the sling." Another nod. "And Lakose will wrestle." The bulky warrior, who had eyed Ahanu and their arrival, slowly and purposefully stepped forward once again staring at Ahanu. His mouth was set in a firm line and his arms were crossed on his chest, accentuating his muscles, but Ahanu was not intimidated. Chief Bald Eagle was satisfied.

The young men were treated as welcomed guests, and a feast was set before them. The village was filled with excitement at the thought of a tournament and Ahanu feared he might not sleep that night; however, it seemed as though he had just lain down when the first light of day crept in under the door flap. He shifted to his back and felt eyes upon him. Turning to his right, he found that all three of his companions were awake. Shifting to an upright position, the four formed a circle, ready to discuss the day.

"It's obvious who you will be fighting," said Savanukah with a wry grin. His face grew serious as he faced his friends. "Kanatase, you will run." Kanatase nodded, pleased that he didn't have to shoot or wrestle. He was as fast as the wind and knew he had a chance to win. "Degataga, do you want to shoot arrows or sling?"

Degataga thought for a moment. He was good at both, but he knew that Savanukah was excellent at shooting. "I will use the sling," he said quietly. Savanukah smiled warmly, knowing he made the choice for his sake. "Thank you Degataga." Degataga nodded and a faint smile quickly appeared on his lips, but vanished just as fast.

"Whether we win or lose, if we are not accepted here, we will push westward until we find our place."

A glimpse of Siskia danced before Ahanu's eyes. He wanted to stay here, close to her, but he would keep silent and wrestle to win!

As they left the long house, the sun was just rising, and its rays were just beginning to streak the far end of the valley. The smell of cooking food wafted through the air from cook fires where women bent to stir pots while children sat nearby rubbing the sleep from their eyes. The sky was clear, but it promised to be another hot day. Ahanu was glad the tournament was in the morning. He and his friends walked towards a knot of men that were deep in discussion at the edge of the village. A grassy clearing spread towards the creek, smooth and flat, obviously the place of the challenges. All faces turned towards the approaching four and, for the most part, the faces were friendly. Lakose's surly face towered above the rest, and Ahanu wondered if he ever smiled.

The leader of the games stepped forward with Chief Bald Eagle. "Wematin will oversee the competitions." An older man stepped forward. He was tall and muscular and had the look of a winner. Ahanu wondered how many tournaments he had won.

"Have you chosen your game?" he asked.

The boys nodded, and Savanukah stepped forward. "Kanatase will run. Degataga will sling. I will shoot and Ahanu will wrestle."

Everyone seemed pleased with the choices. The rules were discussed, and the order of the games was decided: Running first, sling second, arrow shooting third, and wrestling—the most exciting challenge—last. Ahanu had thought it would be this way, and he was glad. That way the others would have no pressure of finishing well. That challenge was his own, and he accepted it gladly.

Soon the entire village had gathered around the game area. The route had been decided for the foot race and several younger braves had scrambled out into the woods to stand as sentinels as well as human markers. It would be a close race. The two men were of the same size and stature. Kanatase looked confident as he stood beside Enata, ready to race. They crouched at the signal and took off running when a gunshot sounded. The people cheered wildly, Enata the obvious favorite. Across the grassy field they went in a flash, heading for the creek. There they would follow the trail away from the rising sun to another designated spot. The path then shot nearly straight up the mountain, across a stony flat halfway up, and then back down the mountain where the trail forked. They would follow that trail back into the village, across the creek, around a marshy area, through the village, and to the finish line.

Everyone waited excitedly, keeping an eye on the village and beyond, even though they knew it would be quite some time before they would appear. Some of the children had raced to the other end of the village to keep watch, being able to see the path as it came back out of the woods at the creek.

Soon, the children came running and shouting. "They are coming! Both are still coming!"

"Who is leading?" someone asked.

"We could not tell. They are side by side," one child explained.

All eyes turned toward the path through the village. It would still be several moments before they would appear, but soon they were spotted entering the village. Everyone crowded, near the path, keeping back to give the runners room. Sure enough, they were neck and neck, both straining to gain the lead. Ahanu watched as Savanukah gave Degataga a knowing smile, and then turned his attention back to the race.

As though he had wings on his heels, Kanatase suddenly took off as though he had been standing still. He sprinted past the crowd putting several feet between him and Enata. Enata strained to run faster, but it was no use— Kanatase had crossed first.

The village stood still, stunned by what they had just witnessed. Savanukah, Degataga, and Ahanu rushed to Kanatase who was walking around the field, allowing his muscles to slowly relax. They thumped his back, grinning broadly and rejoicing that they had won the first contest.

Others in the village came to Kanatase and congratulated him, looking at him with a sense of awe. When they were alone, Ahanu quietly asked, "How did he do that?"

Savanukah smiled. "Iroquois value speed a great deal. It is a matter of pacing yourself. Most braves run with all their might from the very start. Did you notice that Enata was ahead by the time they reached the creek?"

Ahanu thought back to the beginning of the race. His eyes opened in wonder. "Now that you mention it, yes."

Kanatase had been leaning forward, hands on his knees, but now stood erect and smiled at Ahanu. "Enata sneered at me as he sped ahead. I let him set the pace and think he was the faster runner... until we neared the village.

By then, it was too late. He was spent, and I had much left to give."

Ahanu shook his head in wonder.

The others were already setting up for the sling shot contest. Several green horse chestnuts were lined up on posts which had been driven into the ground. A brave was pacing off the distance and placing sticks in various places as starting points. The three friends gathered around Degataga who swaggered to the first starting line with pride. Another brave, nearly as cocky, came to stand beside him. The two glowered at each other, and Wematin began the contest.

At that distance, both men easily knocked off the horse chestnuts. Everyone cheered as they stepped back and the nuts were replaced on the posts. The second round was also an easy task for both contestants who had been handling a slingshot almost as long as they had been walking.

From the third distance, which was twice as far from the nuts, both men missed one target, keeping their score tied. They looked to Wematin for direction as the crowd cheered.

Wematin stepped forward. "In the case of a tie, I will toss two nuts into the air. Whoever hits the nut will be the winner."

Again, the two braves sneered at each other, readying themselves for the toss. Wematin took the two nuts and tossed them high into the air. Both young men aimed and both nuts went flying. Everyone was wild with excitement.

The tosses continued until one finally missed a flying nut... it was Degataga. Everyone cheered, running to Deuquot and slapping him on the back. Several went to Degataga as well and congratulated him for a fine competition, but most were already looking to the next match.

To win this match was a great honor, for every Indian took great pride in his ability to hit a target. The posts were used for the arrow shooting as well, and a pretty, young squaw carefully marked each post with a brush of white paint. The mark was barely visible from a distance.

Starting much like the slingshot contest, Savanukah and Cuapea stood erect behind the branch that marked the starting point. Both easily hit each target. Young boys and girls ran to the posts to retrieve the arrows and ran them back to each contestant. The men moved back, and round two was a repeat of the first. Another round also ended in a tie, which was expected, and the villagers anticipated the next phase of the contest.

Wematin motioned to several men and they carried several cages to the playing field. Each held small black birds. Wematin walked over to face the contestants and the crowd. "We will set off two birds at a time. You may not take aim or shoot until I have counted to four."

Both men nodded and readied their bows, holding towards the ground, strings taut and arrows ready to fly. At Wematin's nod, the birds were released. Steadily, he counted with a shout, "One, two, three, four." By then the tiny birds were high in the sky, but each man aimed and the arrows found their targets. Shouts went up, and another cage was opened. After three more rounds, the score was still a tie. Faces shone with excitement, and the final match began.

Two horses were brought to the field and led to the shooters. Cuapea smiled, but Savanukah looked concerned. He had not ridden this horse. It seemed unfair, but he rose to the challenge.

Wematin stepped forward. "You may take a moment to ride your mounts and familiarize yourselves with them. Savanukah, this is not Cuapea's horse. We want this test to be fair."

Savanukah nodded and sighed with relief. Cuapea still had the advantage of knowing the horses and the lay of the land, but he would do his best. They both mounted the backs of the animals and rode them across the field, trotting and jogging the animals at different speeds. Again, Wematin explained the rules.

"You will begin at the creek, ride to the posts and shoot. You may shoot at any time, but the arrow that hits this post first wins." He pointed to the last post in the row. "Everyone move back."

Savanukah and Cuapea brought their mounts to the starting place and waited for the shout. Savanukah leaned towards Cuapea and spoke. "You are a worthy opponent. It has been an honor to compete against you."

Cuapea looked surprised, but schooled his features and nodded. "You as well," was all he said.

The shout went up, and they were off racing toward a brave that stood at the creek with his hands held out as far as he could reach. Both riders had to touch his hand before returning across the field. Neck and neck they rode, one moment Savanukah was in the lead, then next Cuapea pulled ahead.

As though in unison, they reached the creek at the same time, turned the huge animals faster than seemed possible, and were racing back to the post. From the corner of his eye Cuapea was amazed to see that Savanukah was already taking aim. Quickly, he pulled up his bow and readied to shoot, but it was too late. Savanukah's arrow had already hit its mark.

The people looked in amazement. Who were these young men? They cheered and shouted, running to Savanukah and welcoming him as a conquering hero. The four home boys were not so enthusiastic, and Lakose was seething.

After the commotion died down, Lakose purposefully walked out onto the field and Wematin followed him. He turned back to look at Ahanu and was glad to see that he too was heading to the field. The sun was now high in the sky and Ahanu's skin glistened. He wondered if it was from the heat or from nerves—probably both.

As he walked across the field, he noticed for the first time there was a circle cut into the grass and two sandy spots directly across from each other. Lakose was already on the far side bending down to rub sand into his hands. Ahanu did the same, grinding the sand into his palms until they hurt. He mopped his brow with his sleeve before removing his shirt and tossing it outside the circle. The two men stood ready, facing each other and waiting for their instructions.

Wematin walked into the circle and beckoned for the two fighters to come to his side. He looked directly into Lakose's eyes as he spoke.

"These young men have all competed well. We can see their earnestness and character in the way they have conducted themselves. We will show them a clean match." He emphasized each word, but Lakose's expression only grew darker.

"You know the rules, Lakose, but we will review them for our guest." He looked to Ahanu. "You may not step out of the circle or you forfeit the match. There will be no weapons, no biting or scratching. We will have a winner when one man has succeeded in pinning his opponent to the ground for a count of five." Wematin waited for a response from Ahanu, who nodded his consent, and then turned to face Lakose. The grizzly of a man nodded as well and turned on his heels to take his place in the sandy spot. Ahanu walked beside Wematin as he left the circle. "Do well, my friend," Wematin whispered before leaving the ring.

Ahanu was surprised but took courage from the remark; however, it also made him wonder what the reason was for the statement. He soon found out.

At the sound of Wematin's shout, Lakose came barreling towards Ahanu at full speed, growling as he did so. Ahanu was nearly taken by surprise, but just before Lakose reached him, Ahanu deftly leaped out of his way. The surprise move, combined with Lakose's forward momentum, caused him to stumble. He nearly tumbled out of the circle but caught himself in time. Ahanu took advantage of his being off balance and came behind him, pulling him hard to the ground. Again, Lakose was taken by surprise, but the moment only fueled his anger and strength. Just as quickly, he rolled over and pulled Ahanu's feet out from under him, but Ahanu was ready for the move and rolled over, pushing himself back to his feet. Lakose did the same.

The two warriors circled, leaning forward, arms and hands ready for an opportunity. When Lakose lunged for Ahanu's leg, Ahanu sprang out of reach, pushing hard on Lakose's back as he sailed by, again causing Lakose to stumble and fall. But Ahanu stayed back, calculating his next move. Lakose was furious. Like a mad bull, he roared and lunged at Ahanu. This time at the last moment, Ahanu crouched down, coming under Lakose, between his legs. He caught both shins and lifted Lakose over his shoulders, throwing him once again to the ground.

Lakose was so surprised that he lay for a moment before gathering himself to his feet. Once again they circled. Lakose was breathing hard, but Ahanu looked as calm and controlled as though out for an evening stroll, which only fueled Lakose's fire.

Lakose faked an advance, sneering at Ahanu's quick reaction. He did it again and again, but Ahanu waited. For the first time, Ahanu saw the slightest flicker of concern in Lakose's wrathful glare. On the next faked advance, Ahanu sprang at Lakose as he was pulling back and leaped in the air. Both feet landed on Lakose's chest and drove him to the ground, but he was ready. He latched onto Ahanu's legs and dug his nails into his calves. Pain seared through Ahanu's legs but he ignored it, keeping his focus on the fight. As he fell forward, he bent his knees and pushed with his hands, but he couldn't shake Lakose's grip. Blood was running down his legs, which actually served to his advantage. Lakose was losing his grip.

Ahanu swung to the left and toppled to the ground, kicking at Lakose as he fell and freeing himself from his hold. Just as quickly, Lakose rolled over and was on top of him, but not before Ahanu was able to bend his legs under him. He unintentionally caught Lakose in the groin and kicked him off of him. Lakose's groan turned into a roar. He continued to roll away and staggered to his feet. Blood was smeared on Lakose's hands and chest where Ahanu had pushed him off. Ahanu's legs throbbed, and he was ready to end the match.

Again they circled, looking for an opening. Lakose wasted no time in lunging at Ahanu. This time, Ahanu ducked to the right and caught Lakose's arm as he passed and kicked Lakose's leg out from under him. The burly man went down with a crash. He started to roll over, but before he could Ahanu was on him, pinning his legs and arms to the ground. Lakose roared once again, but before the sound died in his throat, Wematin's voice could be heard.

"Three, four, five," the man shouted and Ahanu sprang from his opponent. Lakose lay still for a moment, unable to comprehend that he had lost. Ahanu offered him his hand, but Lakose spit at it and marched out of the circle and away from the village.

Wematin was about to say something, but he knew any words would fall on deaf ears. He shook his head and joined the others in congratulating Ahanu.

With great pomp Chief Bald Eagle walked to the center of the circle and beckoned to all seven of the contestants. Lakose was nowhere to be seen.

"You have proven yourselves to be honest, brave, and able warriors. Most of our men have played well." He frowned in the direction which Lakose had gone. "But you have won the victory. Welcome to our village."

A roar went up from the crowd. The young men all slapped each other on the back, complimenting each other on their skills. The four winners were left in the circle as the others joined the villagers. In the distance, drums and singing could be heard as a procession made its way through the people. Behind the singers and drummers were four beautiful maidens dressed in ceremonial costumes. Each carried a crown made of leafy vines. They came to stand before each winner, smiling up into each face. The men leaned forward and the maidens placed the crowns on their heads. Another cheer went forth.

"Come, let us celebrate," Chief Bald Eagle shouted as he led the four winners in a procession back into the village. The food that had been cooking was now spread out before them. As honored guests, they led the way, taking the food which was offered to them and joining the chief and his council.

They feasted well into the afternoon, sharing stories and tales of their pasts. Though many of the villagers were from different tribes—Shawnee, Delaware, Muncee, Lenape, Iroquois—their stories were much the same. Ahanu's heart ached for their tales of displacement because of the white men. It made his blood boil, pumping more life into his desire for revenge than he had ever known.

Far into the evening they enjoyed dances and stories, but when the children and women started to head for their beds, the men gathered around the fire, waiting for their chief to speak.

His eyes reflected the flames of the fire, and he looked as though he was seeing scenes from his past, recounting all the hurt and pain that had brought him to this place. Slowly, he stood. Ahanu thought he looked to be the bravest man he had ever known.

"Our stories are all the same. We retreat and the white man takes our land." Murmurs of agreement came from every throat. "This valley has become our home, but soon they will come here too. But we will be ready," he said ominously. He turned his gaze upon the four newcomers.

"This was only the first part of your test. You have proven to be strong, talented, and fast. But can you truly kill as you say you desire?"

They all looked at him but kept silent. It seemed like a rhetorical question. Degataga looked at the others and jumped to his feet. "We are more than ready to fight, to kill, to do what it takes to keep our homes."

The chief eyed the young man. He had watched him after his loss and admired his self-control. Perhaps he had misjudged him. Bald Eagle nodded slowly. "Yes, I believe you are, and you will have your chance to quench your thirst for blood tomorrow night. Several settlers have just arrived over South Mountain near Spring Creek. There have been others riding and looking, but these mean to stay. You will kill them all and bring back their scalps. Enata, Cuapea and Deuquot will show you the way, but the task is yours to finish."

Degataga looked at the others nervously. "Do you mean the children as well?" he asked.

Chief Bald Eagle's eyes narrowed and his breathing became erratic. "White children grow up to be white men. They are the ones who will take the land and live here instead of our children."

Degataga looked down, shame flaming his cheeks.

When they were back in their long house for the night, they lay in silence, all pondering the morrow's task. Barely above a whisper, Savanukah's voice broke the silence. "What will you do, Degataga?"

"I don't know," came his answer after a long silence.

Ahanu heard Degataga roll to his side. "You must go with us. We will fight together, but you can stand guard for us. We will need extra eyes, and yours are the best."

It was true that Degataga could not only run the fastest but he could also see the farthest as well.

"And you, Ahanu? Will you be able to kill even small children?" Savanukah asked. He needed to know.

Images of skeletons of every size strewn across the village in every wigwam danced across Ahanu's mind, taunting him. "Yes," came the one word answer, and he rolled over away from the faces of his friends. He would avenge his people!

The entire village seemed to be in a solemn mood contrasting greatly with yesterday's festivities. There was much discussion about the activity of the night. All knew what was about to take place, and they also knew that it put their whole village in danger of returned vengeance.

A middle-aged warrior named Askook seemed to be in charge of the raid and prepped the young men on what to expect. He drew a map and outlined the details of the raid. "You will need to be certain that all are asleep. They will have a dog, I am certain, and it will signal your arrival. The man will awaken and have his gun. They have not yet built a cabin and are living in their wagon, so your task will be made easier."

He looked into the faces of each young man and was pleased with their understanding. "Divide up. One of you take the man, and the others finish the work." He didn't need to clarify.

At dusk, the men painted their faces, mostly dark with a streak of red across their foreheads. They checked their blades and arrows and reported to Chief Bald Eagle when they were ready. He looked them over, once again pleased with his good fortune to have them do his work. If there was any retaliation, he would hand them over. They meant nothing to him.

As the sun crawled to the horizon, the sky became ablaze with color. Streaks of gold turned to rose and then blood red as though announcing their evil deeds. They mounted their horses and headed for the mountain in the distance. They would ride as far as they could up the side of the mountain. The settlement was on the other side in the next valley.

Enata lead the way, then Cuapea and Deuquot. Savanukah followed, then Ahanu, Degataga and Kanatase brought up the rear. Degataga wanted to run, ride off and never come back, but his loyalty to Savanukah kept him in place. Just as they reached the peak of the mountain, the sun dipped below the trees as though hiding from the horror to follow.

They stopped and looked across the shadowed valley. Enata pointed to a sliver of smoke floating up from the trees. "They are camped along Spring Creek. They use our paths, so they are easy to find," Enata explained as though they were looking for deer.

"We will ride to the valley edge and then approach by foot." All nodded and they proceeded.

The path crisscrossed down the mountain, making the descent possible. When halfway down the mountain, Enata stopped and dismounted. "I will run ahead and make sure there are no lookouts," he explained. Ahanu realized that this was not the first raid these men had made and he wondered how many had died by the edge of Enata's knife.

When they reached the bottom of the summit, Enata was waiting for them. His eyes glistened with excitement. "All is in place," he whispered excitedly. "I was able to take care the dog, so they will have no warning. It's only one family which makes it easier."

Ahanu's stomach lurched momentarily, but he pushed down his angst with memories of his people. It had been decided that he would go in first and take out the man. Silently, they approached. It was so quiet, they could hear the man snoring in the wagon. They listened. A child whimpered in its sleep and a baby cried. The wagon creaked as someone shifted to quiet the baby. Degataga's eyes were as wide as moons, and for a moment Savanukah thought he was going to run. Their eyes met, and Savanukah pleaded with him to stay. He took a silent breath and nodded.

As Ahanu washed the blood from his knife, the events of the last hour played over and over in his mind: the man's look of horror, the woman's scream as she ran to her children, the little boy and baby's whimpers... the silence. All his life, Ahanu had been trained for war, but this was not war—this was a bloody act of cowardice. Then he once again thought about his village. He rehearsed all the stories his grandfather had told him about the great Susque-hannock tribe—his tribe... his people. Gone! They were all gone because of this tribe of white men and their stealing ways and deadly diseases. He breathed hard and forced his heart to be cold.

They had covered their tracks and rode away from the wagon towards the setting sun, following the creek to Lake Nitanee, a common watering hole for many tribes. There would be no chance of anyone tracking back to Bald Eagle's Nest.

The others were in a festive mood, cheering each other on and proudly displaying their scalps. They rode through the night, entering the village just as the sun peaked over the horizon. Once again, they were hailed as conquering heroes, and a feast was held in their honor. The whole mood of the village had changed in just two days. Every face glowed with admiration... except one: Lakose.

That evening a council fire was planned. It brought a flood of memories back to Ahanu and for the first time in four long years, he felt like he belonged. The fire was blazing by the time the procession of elders gathered to make the inner circle. Ahanu did not remember seeing many of the wrinkled faces, but then, he had been quite busy over the past two days. Behind these ancient men sat the middle-aged men of the village, and the young warriors made up the outer circle. The four newcomers had the honored place of sitting directly to the chief's right, even though they were part of the outer circle. As they sat around the council fire listening to their elders recount tales of their history, Deuquot leaned close to Ahanu who was sitting next to him and whispered in his ear. "Beware of Lakose. He seeks revenge."

Ahanu looked across the circle and found Lakose's dark stare on him. Deuquot noticed as well and hid his face behind his father, who sat directly before him. "He has no honor, only strength," Deuquot added. Ahanu continued to stare back in defiance, but broke his gaze, lifting his chin and concentrating on the men who were speaking. He could do nothing about Lakose, but he could learn these people's story.

For two years, Ahanu and his band made frequent raids on any white settler who ventured too far west. Degataga had stopped coming with them. Their bravery seemed to be enough to secure his place in the village, and, surprisingly, Bald Eagle seemed to understand the young man's dislike for human blood. He became a runner for the chief, often delivering messages many miles to the west.

With each raid Ahanu's heart hardened more and more until even his facial features reflected his sin-cursed soul. Truly, he had earned the label of a savage. Chief Bald Eagle fanned his vengeance by praising him for his passion and favoring him above all the rest. He had even begun to give him copper coins for every scalp he brought to the village and using him more than the rest. Many times, he was sent out alone, accomplishing his gruesome tasks faster and more completely than ten men. He was the conqueror, but Savanukah wondered if he was going too far.

As they entered their wigwam after the latest raid to the south, Savanukah waited until all was quiet, knowing that Ahanu was still awake. He crept to his side and motioned for him to follow. They walked in silence away from the village and into the field. It seemed like ages since they had competed for acceptance. In some ways, Savanukah wished they had never come.

Ahanu grew impatient but waited for Savanukah to begin.

"You've changed," he simply stated.

"We've all changed," Ahanu countered.

Savanukah turned to look directly at Ahanu who kept his gaze on the distant mountains. He could feel Savanukah's cold stare upon him, and he turned to face his dearest friend on earth.

"You like it," hissed Savanukah. "You like all the killing."

Ahanu formed his thoughts carefully before speaking. "I want our land back," he retorted. "I want this to bear our name, not theirs. I want my children to hunt and live here!"

Savanukah sighed heavily. "So do I," he said dejectedly. "But I cannot keep doing this—killing innocent people unsuspectedly in their beds. I came to kill, yes, but I came to fight men, not scalp children!" Just speaking the words left a bitter taste in his mouth. They stood there, both deep in thought, staring across the field to the mountains they crossed to do their deadly deeds. The sky was brilliant with stars seemingly close enough to reach, and for just a moment, Ahanu forgot about all the bloody massacres and gazed upward into the evening blanket of lights. Living in the mountains had never afforded him such a clear view of the stars, and he had been overwhelmed by their splendor when he first came to Great Island. He stared at their beautiful canopy and let their beauty wash away all the ugly images in his mind. He wondered if Siskia was looking up into the stars as well. She was never far from his thoughts, and he hoped that his victories would show her that he was a man.

Savanukah's words cut into his thoughts bringing him back to reality. "I've heard some of the older warriors say that they are heading west to fight with the French."

Ahanu continued to stare at the beauty before him while he pondered the thought. West was not the direction he wished to go. "I want to see Siskia."

Savanukah was not surprised. Ahanu often called out her name in his sleep. "I think you will make a better impression than the last time you met." Ahanu could hear the teasing in his voice. His words were like rain on crumbled, drought-worn earth. How long had it been since any humor had tried to reach his heart?

Ahanu turned to face his friend. His eyes glistened with tears he would not shed. "My friend, you are more than a brother to me." He laid his strong hand on Savanukah's shoulder who was surprised by its strength. "You speak the truth. I am weary of this life too, but I had to give it my best. You understand that, don't you?"

Savanukah was touched and relieved. He drew in a long, jagged breath. "Yes. You are a true warrior. I should have known that you were not just blood thirsty."

"Revenge thirsty, yes, and that requires blood—it will always require blood, but blood thirsty... never!"

The two talked well into the night and decided to leave as soon as possible. First, they would visit Great Island and stay there for a while. Then, they would head west.

Chapter Five

The Passing

*May the Lord of the harvest send forth other laborers
into this part of his harvest,
that those who sit in darkness may see great light;
and that the whole earth
may be filled with the knowledge of himself. Amen*
David Brainerd

Great Island

Chief Shawátis was breathing hard by the time he reached his destination—Turtle Rock, which jutted out from the side of the mountain offering a splendid view of the entire river bed as well as the rolling hills to the north. The cliff's peak was shaped like the head of a turtle which then rounded out before disappearing into the mountainside as though the turtle was crawling out from some primeval mud and was eternally frozen in time in its quest to climb free.

Shawátis pulled himself up to the rock and bent forward to ease the pain in his side. After a moment, he straightened and walked to the edge, making himself comfortable. The cliff was cut so that one could rest his back against the cool rock while sitting on the ledge.

Chief Shawátis took in the view before him: the gently rolling river, Great Island, and the vast expanse of mighty forest beyond the river. An eagle came soaring downstream, its majestic wings spread wide as he rode the air current. His eyes were on the water, and as quick as a flash, he plunged downward, coming out of the water with his catch. Shawátis watched as he flew down river to his nest and shared his meal with his family.

The scene brought his thoughts back to his family and himself. He had hoped that Siskia would have shown some interest in one of the young braves, but as yet, she remained as aloof as a yearling doe. It certainly wasn't because of a lack of attention on the boys, part. He smiled as he recalled some of their clumsy attempts to win her.

Something had changed about her, and he thought he knew what had caused it. Some of the others had also returned from the trading journey to Otstuagy exclaiming about the Jesus man. When he heard them, his eyes immediately flashed to Siskia. Their eyes connected for only a brief moment before she looked away, but he knew... she was now a Praying Indian. Despite all his efforts to protect her, he had failed.

And then the blood started flowing whenever he relieved himself. At first, it was just once in awhile, but lately, it was every time. And he was weak. He knew his time was short and that he would need to tell Terés. She watched him like a hawk, but he knew that she would not ask. And what was he going to do about Siskia? He leaned back against the cool rock and closed his eyes. Was he afraid to die? He wanted to shout, "No!" But when he was alone—away from his family and people—a cold chill ran down his back at the thought of dying. He had overheard some of the women talking about this Jesus—that He died for his tribe and for all men of every tribe. Who had ever heard of a god dying? But not only that, He had risen from the dead! Had any of their gods ever conquered death? Not that he knew of. What king of a god could become a man and yet remain god—enough to battle against death and win? If he was honest, he knew it was a god to be feared!

He is God of all gods, one of the women had said and the others all agreed. He knew that some of the women, including Siskia and his wife were meeting to talk and pray to this god. At first, he was going to put a stop to it, but all over the village, a change was taking place. There had been less squabbling and fewer conflicts to resolve. He knew some of the men were wary as well, but they also liked the affect this Jesus seemed to have on their women. Had some of the men chosen to follow Jesus as well? He did not know.

As his mind played through every scenario, it was as though all the pieces of a broken rock were now fitting together. Even Machk had succumbed when Siskia talked to him. Machk had always had a temper, and his sister bore the brunt of it. He heard them out behind their long house one day, whispering fiercely back and forth. Siskia told him it was a sin for him to be so mean. Machk shot back that he didn't even know what sin was. Quietly but with great urgency, Siskia calmly explained that sin was breaking God's laws. There had been a long silence before Machk told her he was sorry, in a husky voice. Shawátis was shocked, but was even more so when Siskia continued to talk to him and tell him that Jesus alone could forgive his sins. Shawátis wanted to run out of the room and shake them both, but when he heard Machk talking to Jesus as though he was right there with them, he froze. An overwhelming ache consumed him.

Could he believe? He thought back over a lifetime of god worship, fetishes, and chants. It was all part of their heritage, but none of those things drew him like thoughts of Jesus now tugged at his heart. The Holy Spirit drew near, beckoned by his silent cry, and Chief Shawátis made a choice. He cried out to the living God, begging for forgiveness. He felt God's peace rush in. All the anxiety of pending death was gone, and in its place was a yearning to know more.

He continued to "talk" to God, praising Him and thanking Him for the great sacrifice. He couldn't understand it, but then, who can understand a God who sacrifices his own Son for His tribe?

*   *   *

Just three weeks later, Chief Shawátis lay deathly ill. Word was sent to Savanukah and the others. They had already been planning to visit and now raced back to Great Island, hoping to outrun the angel of death.

The dying man had shared his faith with his family, and they all rejoiced that their circle was now complete. Since then, they took turns to be at his side every moment of the day, and now Siskia sat there, praying silently and watching with eyes full of sorrow. *Must you take him now, Father God? I still need him!*

Shawátis' eyes fluttered open. The pain was nearly unbearable but he would bear it like the warrior chief he had proven himself to be.

Siskia's eyes were not closed, but her lips continued to move in prayer. He watched her. A tear rolled down his cheek. "You question God?"

She looked at him, astonished that he knew her thoughts. Siskia reached for his hand. "How will we go on without you?" she whispered.

Shawátis wanted to hold her but any movement caused more pain than he could bear. He squeezed her hand. "I go to join your Father in heaven. We are not gone, just in another village."

A commotion outside the dwelling drew their attention to the flap just as Savanukah cautiously rushed through followed by his three friends who entered more subtly. Siskia started to leave but her father motioned for her to stay.

"Uncle, we came as soon as we head," Savanukah said. His features were brave but his eyes were filled with grief. Chief Shawátis reached up to touch his nephew's face and Savanukah caught his hand, shocked by its weakened condition. Chief Shawátis was also shocked by the strength he felt and the broadness he saw in Savanukah's shoulders. The chief looked past Savanukah to the others standing behind him and realized that two winters had grown them into men. He looked intensely into each face, looking past the eyes and into the heart. Kanatase had lost his impatience and replaced it with determination. Degataga maintained his tender heart but was now surer of himself, not just Savanukah's shadow. The Chief's eyes remained on Ahanu for what seemed like an eternity. The young man was even taller and stronger than the Susquehannock that had come to their village. Bravery and determination oozed out of every pore, but deep inside, the struggle to satisfy his vengeance had scratched and scarred his soul with so much pain, that Chief Shawátis wondered how he had survived. The more he stared at Ahanu, the more his admiration grew.

There was no time for small talk. Shawátis knew he was already on borrowed time. "All leave except Ahanu," he barked hoarsely. Siskia and Savanukah exchanged glances but did as they were told. The others followed as well. Silently, they filed out of the long house, each lost in his thoughts.

Ahanu's heart raced, but he kept his composure and waited for the dying man to speak.

"My only concern is Siskia," Shawátis stated quietly. He was glad to see a spark of interest in the stalwart young man's face. "She loved another but I took her away for reasons that do not matter now. She is beautiful and smart. She is also headstrong and needs a firm hand to guide her."

Ahanu could barely breathe. Was he about to hear what he had longed for all along?

"I give her to you, but you must win her heart."
The young warrior was speechless. He nodded once but remained silent.

Chief Shawátis studied him once more. "I see much pain in your heart. You have been wounded by the past as well as by your own actions. This is my only hesitation. You are strong enough and brave enough, but can you love?"

For the first time in a long time, Ahanu showed signs of emotion. He blinked several times and his mouth fell open. The sight forced a chuckle up his throat and a faint glimmer of humor pushed the pain from his eyes. "So you can feel more than vengeance."

Ahanu smiled faintly. "Yes and gladly."

Siskia paced back and forth in front of their dwelling wondering--agonizing over what was being said between her father and Ahanu. She couldn't help but notice his muscular build, and when she brushed against him as she passed by, her heart raced and her breath caught in her throat. She fumed at her reaction.

Savanukah had learned all the details of his uncle's illness and now turned his attention on his irritated cousin. Slowly, he put two and two together and understood her agitation and smiled wryly as he watched Siskia's furrowed brow, arms crossed--the picture of a storm rising.

"Siskia," Savanukah said.

She stopped pacing and turned her storm upon him.

"Your father knows what is best for you."

She scowled and continued to pace.

"Besides, Ahanu dreams of you every night." He got the reaction he wanted. Siskia turned on him like a mother bear robbed of her cubs.

Just then the flap opened and Ahanu's tall, muscular frame filled the entry. His gaze fell on Siskia, but she could not read his thoughts. "Your father wants you." Ahanu stood like a statue, holding the flap open. He flashed a glance her way but quickly diverted his eyes to the ground.

Siskia looked at Savanukah with wide, horror-stricken eyes, and her cousin's heart ached for her. She was young, and strong... and very independent. His eyes softened and he squeezed the hand that was clenched around his forearm. "He's a good man," Savanukah whispered, but Siskia didn't know whether he spoke of her father or his friend. The fact that Savanukah had accepted Ahanu spoke volumes to her heart.

She slowly let go of Savanukah, squared her shoulders and walked past Ahanu and into the domed hut. She stepped to her father's side and knelt there, taking his hand and trying to communicate all the words she could not speak through that tiny gesture.

Shawátis opened his eyes and tried desperately to ignore the pain. He squeezed her hand and looked into her eyes. "I will soon be gone, Ayashe."

Siskia gasped at his use of her pet name, Little One, and tears sprang to her eyes.

"You must trust me on this. I have prayed much for you and your future."

Ahanu tried not to listen, feeling as though he were intruding on a very private moment, but when he heard Shawátis speak of prayer, his head snapped up. What did the chief mean? Deep in thought, Ahanu missed the rest of their conversation until he heard his name.

"Ahanu, come kneel by my side," Shawátis commanded in a strained voice.

He wanted to bolt, but he stood erect and did as he was told. He kept his eyes diverted from the pathetic figure just on the other side of the old warrior's emaciated body.

Shawátis lifted his hand, and Ahanu took it. Slowly, he pulled their hands together, putting Siskia's small one into Ahanu's firm grip and cupping them both in his shaking hands. He could feel Siskia's tension, knowing both young people would have gladly run away if they could.

"Our people are in a great struggle. The tribe of the white man grows in number every day. These woods are no longer just our home. It will be taken from us." At his words, Ahanu tensed, and he stared at Siskia. She could feel his gaze and lifted her eyes to defiantly meet his stare. Would he question her father's words of wisdom?

"It is not what we want, but it is their destiny." Shawátis' arms ached but he kept on going, determined to finish the task. "The destiny of our people is to be strong in body and in soul." He looked at Siskia. "You are the chief's daughter. You are an Iroquois. We are a strong people."

He turned his head to look at Ahanu. "You are a chief's grandson. You are a Susquehannock. Our people fought in the past, but now we unite to become stronger."

He pulled both hands to his chest and pressed them close. "You are young and you are both strong leaders. Learn to lead together... Learn to love together."

Shawátis' eyes were misty as continued to hold tightly to both hands. He took one last look at Ahanu and then at Siskia before looking upward. "Father, keep them in your care. Lead Ahanu to You and make him complete." As he prayed his eyes widened. Slowly, he let go of their hands and tried to reach upward, but the effort was too great. As his arms fell to his sides, a smile formed on his lips. He sighed deeply and closed his eyes in eternal sleep.

Ahanu just stared, but Siskia took his hand, calling to him and falling upon his chest weeping. She put her arms around him—something she hadn't been able to do in fear of causing him more pain.

"Oh Father!" she wept.

If Ahanu thought that he had loved her before, he now knew it was true. He wanted to protect her and care for her—comfort her with a love he had never received. Gently, he reached out and laid his hand on her prostrate back. At first, he could feel her stiffen, but slowly the muscles began to relax.

"Siskia, I want to talk to you, but that can wait. I will go and get your family."

She knew she should say something, but all she could do was nod. She felt his hand leave her back, and when she heard the flap swing open, she raised up to catch a glimpse of his vanishing figure. She looked back at her father. He looked so peaceful with just a hint of the smile still on his lips. *What must he see? What does he know?* Her mind raced with questions. Was her father in the presence of Jesus? The thought brought fresh tears to her eyes and gave her more peace than she had ever known. Tenderly, she lay down beside her father for one last time.

*   *   *

Throughout the burial and ceremony, Ahanu came to realize that much had changed in the village at Great Island since he had left. Shawátis was buried in a simple grave and many prayers were offered—prayers to an unknown god named Jesus. There had been tears but no wailing for the dead. Everyone seemed calm, even happy for the man's death. Savanukah and he talked late into the night, but his friend was a perplexed as he was.

Ahanu took long walks in the woods trying to sort out his thoughts as well as come to an understanding of his obligation to Siskia. He hadn't told anyone about Shawátis' demands. As much as they pleased him, he wasn't certain what Siskia's family would think. He could tell by their demeanor towards him that she had told them, but without Shawátis there to take command, nothing had been said.

The opportunity to speak alone with Siskia came one evening. All the family had gathered around their fire. The night air was cool, and the leaves would soon be turning color. Brilliant reds of the oak tree mixed with the bright yellow maples, flashing their colors across a backdrop of stately pines. Siskia rose to tend to the fire just as Ahanu came near the circle. Their eyes met, and he only nodded and walked away, hoping that she would follow. She did.

They walked in silence to the edge of the water. Ahanu had been pleased to see that a little bear carving now hung from her neck and gained hope that his quest may not be as difficult as he had thought.

"Your father was a great man. I admired him greatly even in the short time I knew him. Savanukah has become my best friend and talks often of your father and family." He shifted from foot to foot as they stood side by side facing the river. Ahanu crossed his arms over his chest and turned to face Siskia. "I agree with your father that our future is uncertain, but this much I know..."

He stopped and slowly uncrossed his arms and took her hands. The fire they ignited within him clouded his thoughts, and he needed to work hard to concentrate on what he was saying.

Siskia had done a lot of thinking in the past few days. She wanted to fight all this, but soon realized the only reason for the fight within her was that she was being told what to do. She liked Ahanu. Savanukah had sung his praises often to her since they returned. She could see bravery, courage, and a fearlessness in Ahanu that almost frightened her. But as she watched him, she realized that there was a hidden part that almost seemed like an child uncertain about which path to take. That was the part of him she realized that she loved the most. There was hope that he would believe in Jesus and allow him to fill the hole of uncertainty in his life. She looked up into his searching, almost vulnerable eyes and smiled sweetly.

"I want you by my side no matter what comes our way." His heart was pounding in his chest. He had faced many foes fearlessly, but this woman in front of him had the power to make him grovel at her feet!

Siskia's smile lightened her eyes, and she tucked her chin coyly. "Are you sure? I can be headstrong. I might make your life miserable."

His eyebrows shot up, and Siskia laughed. She broke from his grasp and took off running. Ahanu stood shocked for a moment but was soon in hot pursuit. She knew the lay of the land like the back of her hand and was able to keep out of his reach at first, but soon he was right behind her. She glanced over her shoulder just as he lunged for her and caught her in his arms. She laughed and tilted her head back, catching her breath, enjoying his closeness.

Ahanu loosened his hold and reached up to touch her hair, something he had wanted to do as long as he knew her.

"When I first saw you walking up to your father that first day, I knew then that I wanted you." He looked into her eyes, still sparkling with mischief.

She grew serious. "When I heard you were a Susquehannock, I despised you, but when I heard your story, it made my heart sad. I am far from my tribe but I have always had my family." A shadow crossed over her face. "I miss my father so much."

Ahanu drew her close. "I want to help you and care for you… and love you." He was so hungry for love that he felt as though he would die if she did not love him.

Siskia sensed his uncertainty and longed to put his heart at rest. She reached up and touched his smooth face and reached behind his neck, pulling him closer, inviting him into her heart.

*   *   *

The village was alive with activity for the next few days. There would be a wedding as well as officially making Machk as the new chief. It was decided that both ceremonies would happen the same day with one grand feast. Machk would become chief first so that he could perform the ceremony.

Siskia was busy sewing and beading moccasins for Ahanu while her mother sewed her wedding dress of white deerskin and blue beads. The arms, bodice, and skirt were all edged with white rawhide fringe, and a belt decorated with intricate designs of mostly blue pulled in the waistline.

Machk was also busy preparing himself for the task ahead of him. Many council fires were held, and all questions were answered satisfactorily.

Ahanu was busy as well, making something for Siskia, but he kept to himself and kept his project a secret even to Savanukah.

One evening when all the family had gathered into the hut for the night, Machk asked Siskia the question she had been dreading. "Have you told Ahanu about our beliefs?"

Siskia bowed her head, not needing to answer.

"You must talk to him before the wedding."

Siskia's head snapped up, her eyes flashed. "You did not see his face when Father prayed." Her features softened. "I don't know how to tell him."

Machk was silent. He too could have talked to Ahanu but felt the same hesitation, and it shamed him. "We will talk to him tomorrow night." He looked around the room. "We will all talk to him."

Ahanu listened and wondered. He had been coming back to mention something to Machk when he heard Siskia's desperate voice talking about him. He remembered the situation, but he had not been angry but surprised. He had never heard anyone talk to a god the way her father had. He sounded as though he was talking to a friend, and Ahanu was shocked. Now, he wished he had not heard. They had a secret. What could it be?

Several from the village decided to go downstream to French Margaret's Town. It was a smaller village than Otstuagy, but they knew they would be able to get all they needed there. Visiting another village was always exciting, but visiting and boasting of a wedding and a new chief had everyone animated. They would leave tomorrow mid-morning.

Chapter Six

The Truth

*How then shall they call on him in whom
they have not believed?
and how shall they believe in him
of whom they have not heard?
and how shall they hear without a preacher?*

*And how shall they preach, except they be sent?
as it is written, How beautiful are the feet of them that preach
the gospel of peace, and bring glad tidings of good things!*
Romans 10:14, 15

September, 1746—Susquehanna River, West Branch

David Brainerd marveled at the pristine waters and massive forests along the Susquehanna River. Yes, it reminded him of the beauty of the Delaware River where most of his work had been done thus far, but here there were few settlers—just remote towns scattered along the banks of the river, like Shaumoking where he had gathered his supplies for this trip. But Shaumoking had been the last white man's town that he would see. From here on, it would only be Indian villages.

The Susquehanna Indians he had met so far had been a mix of attitudes: some seemed receptive, others aloof, while still others openly showed their disdain. He was certain it had as something to do with their interaction with the white man, but David prayed the Holy Spirit would bless this journey and that he would be able to break Satan's centuries of bondage.

His body was weak from the ravages of tuberculosis, but that didn't weigh him down like the heavy burden of his great work—impossible work if it were attempted without the strong arm of the Almighty. *How many times must I sink down and forget Thy blessed fountain full of grace?*

It was a fifty mile journey up the Susquehanna towards the Great Island. He had hoped to get further the first day, but by mid-afternoon, he knew he needed to stop. Their guide, Logan, found a suitable place for camp, and David gladly rested while the others constructed a lean-to for the night. He was glad to have the son of Chief Shikellimy with them. The chief was a believer and a great help with negotiations between the Indians of the area and the colonists. The young man had learned much from his father and his travels between the Five Nations to the north and Shaumoking.

But sleep eluded the young missionary. Fever had set in, and he sweated throughout the night and into the morning light. His interpreter looked in on him and shook his head. How this man kept going was beyond him. But since his own conversion, he started to understand the man's passion. Moses Tunda Tatamy had been lost, and he knew how that felt.

"Sir, it is time for us to move on," Moses said quietly.

David rolled over to face his faithful companion. His whole body ached, and he prayed silently for strength. "Thank you, Moses. Our Lord knew how much I would need someone of perseverance as well as compassion, so He called you to my cause." David smiled faintly. "Just give me a minute to gather my thoughts and talk to our Father."

Moses nodded and backed out of the lean-to. He would brew some tea for his friend and warm the bread.

That evening, David was worse. Their company had split—several of the travelers were heading east. While

Moses started the fire, David climbed a young pine tree and cut off several branches with his knife. There had been a bit of an argument when the others left taking their only axe, but in the end, the axe headed east as well.

As the clouds rolled in from the west, it looked like it would rain. David feared if he were chilled on top of the fever that still raged, he would wake in glory. As he lay beneath the pine boughs listening to the rain, he slipped into such a deep melancholy that he thought he would die.

"Oh Father, help me," he prayed. Psalm 61 came to mind, and he prayed the verses to his Lord. "Hear my cry, O God; attend unto my prayer. From the end of the earth will I cry unto Thee." *I'm certainly at the end of the earth,* he thought.

"When my heart is overwhelmed: lead me to the rock that is higher than I." His mind went back to the rock ledges along the river at Shuamoking. His Indian guides had told him several Indian stories about those cliffs. "O Father, again I thank you for this opportunity to tell these poor creatures of Your great love! 'For thou hast been a shelter for me, and a strong tower from the enemy.' How thankful I am that I am among friends tonight and not enemies."

He continued to pray the rest of the prayer, allowing all the melancholy and worry to fall away. Before he knew it, the sun was rising. He had sweated a lot again that night, but he rose strengthened. The fever was gone. "Thank you, Father," he prayed.

They arrived at Otstuagy by mid-morning and were disappointed to find some of the men already drunk. David was tempted to be discouraged, but they found a few Indians that listened to their message with great earnestness. As the Word went forth, many souls were touched by their message. As was their custom, David and Moses mingled with the crowd, answering questions and sharing scripture. The Indians seemed to gravitate to Moses, amazed that one of their own kind knew this foreign god so well and accepted his teachings. David went to him and together they shared the Gospel.

After the noon meal, they prepared to travel eight miles upriver to French Margaret's Town. As their Indian guides pushed the canoes out into the river, David once again thanked God for His calling on his life. He watched as an eagle flew high above, and a trout jumped in the water. Once they navigated away from the mouth of the Lawisahquick Creek as it joined the Siskëwahane, the river was wide, deep, and peaceful. Logan's strong arms dipped the paddle into the water, pushing the canoe upriver with ease. The sun was high and the warmth of its rays seemed to bake life back into David's weary body.

As Logan pushed the canoe past the mouth of the Legaui-hanne, David could see the village on the western shore. Many of the villagers had already spotted them as he drove the canoe to the shore. David's feet had just stepped onto the sandy shore when he noticed other canoes coming down stream. *O Lord, may they be coming here and may they want to listen to Your message.*

Reverend Brainerd had no trouble knowing which Indian was French Margaret. As they walked into the village, a woman came out of the long house much more elaborately dressed than the others, and she walked like a queen.

When Moses explained who they were and the purpose of their visit, Margaret grew very animated. "Welcome, and thank you for coming," she said to Moses. She turned her attention to David as Moses made the introductions. "Welcome. Come and tell us your message."

As conversations hummed around the village, people came close, cautious yet curious. Just as David was getting ready to preach, the other canoes reached the shore and the passengers were making their way into the village. Their conversation revealed that they had come to barter for goods, but when they saw the white man they too seemed curious and came closer. One young man, who appeared to be in charge, stepped closer and spoke to Moses. Something in the way he looked at David made him hopeful.

"They want you to preach, and they will listen," Moses said excitedly.

David nodded, praying silently and thanking the Lord for His speedy answer to his prayer. As he spoke, his eyes scanned the faces, looking for any signs of interest. He was surprised to see that several seemed hungry for the Word, taking it in and longing for more. He worked his way through the Gospel, passionately expressing God's love but also emphasizing the price of sin.

One face near the back seemed nearly unreadable. The Indian had come on the canoes and was much taller than the rest. There was something almost stately about him. *He carries himself like a prince,* David thought. For a moment, he stumbled over his words. It seemed as though the Lord was directing him to Romans 12:19. Inwardly, he resisted the Spirit's wooing, but he couldn't resist God's call. With the skill of an orator commissioned by God to preach His message, he wove the text of revenge into the Gospel.

"Jesus is calling to you. Do not resist. Your soul is in His hands and the Almighty says, 'Vengeance is mine; I will repay.'"

Ahanu had hung back, not wanting to get too close to the white man. The faces of the terrified victims who died to satisfy his bloody-thirsty vengeance danced before him. He tried not to listen, but when the man held up a book—the same book which the settler had held—Ahanu's face blanched. In his mind, he heard the voice of the young man as he read from a book—that book. He remembered in stark reality the man's face and heard his cry before Ahanu's knife did its deadly deed. "Lord Jesus, help us!"

"...vengeance is mine; I will repay." The words came crashing into his mind. He wanted to run, but he had to hear the rest.

"Jesus did not seek revenge on His enemies, He died for them! Only His blood can wash away your sins. Can you believe this?"

It seemed as though the voices of a thousand demons were screaming in his ear. Ahanu looked around wildly. He had to run—get away! As quick as a flash, he slipped out behind the long house and into the woods. He ran and kept on running away. He never stopped until he was at the edge of the dreaded valley where Savanukah and the others had rushed through, driven by fear.

He continued to run, around the swamp, through the thick brush, to the place where he had joined Savanukah. He sat for only a moment, fearing his friend would come after him. If he stopped here, they would find him, but if he kept going until he reached the rock, he would be safe.

The ascent to the top of the mountain would have slowed down an ordinary man, even an Indian, but Ahanu was home and he was a Susquehannock. These were his mountains, his lands. His people had roamed here for more winters than he could count.

When he came to Spirit Rock, he felt as though he was home. He stood on the rock and looked out onto the expanse that he had just traversed. No people. No structures. No... god? Standing there, panting from his run, he filled his lungs with air and gave a great battle cry. As the sound echoed down the valley, He stood tall, and purposefully calmed his breathing—slowly breathing in and blowing the air out through his mouth.

He looked over the edge, thinking about the time he nearly threw himself off of it. He was in such despair then. Was he in despair now? No.

He sat on the rock, looking out towards the setting sun. It blazed its hot rays upon him, his chest and forehead glistening in the light. He needed to think through all he had just heard—all that he had done... all that he had become.

Vengeance is mine; I will repay. Ahanu began to recount all the injustices that had been done to him and his people. He tried to work up the anger that had fueled too many of his actions, but he couldn't.

Vengeance is mine... Had he done anything to anger this God? The voices and faces of the man with the book and his family came into view—their looks of terror, their cries for mercy. They were this God's people, and he had killed them mercilessly.

I will repay. Ahanu shook with fear. How could he hide from a god, the Almighty God, for that's what the man had called Him! His heart cried out for mercy, and tears wet his cheeks.

"I did not know!" he cried. "What can I do to stop your vengeance?"

He tried desperately to recall the other words of the white man. Hadn't he also called this God a God of love? Didn't he say that He had a Son and that He sacrificed Him for men... all men?

Ahanu crawled off the rock and knelt before it. He touched the place where Sucki had lain, seeing once again his trusting eyes, feeling the pain of watching him die.

And he was only a bear cub. How would it feel to watch your son die? His mind whirled back to Siskia. He imagined her presenting him with a son, and then taking the beloved child—a symbol of their love—and driving his knife into its heart. The image was so real that he cried out in fear. "No!"

He thought back to the conversation the night before in Machk's long house. Were they talking about this God? Did they all believe? Had they found a way to appease this dreadful God? For if a God would slay His own Son, what might He do to someone like Ahanu? He remembered Chief Shawátis' peaceful face as he passed into another world—God's world. If he knew and Machk knew—if Siskia knew then he could know too! The thought gave him hope.

Ahanu stood once again staring across the deep valley he once called home. He had a new home—a new life. He would go to Siskia.

*   *   *

The moment the man had started preaching, Siskia was in another world. Time stood still, and she listened with near rapture as the man once again spoke of Jesus. Her mind went back to Pontiac, and her face burned with shame. She glanced over her shoulder to find Ahanu, but he was at the far end of the circle. She quickly looked away, not wanting him to read her thoughts.

Silently, she thanked God for Pontiac. He had brought the truth to light, but she now belonged to Ahanu and she was glad. She prayed his heart would be tender to the message.

Too soon, the white man's words ended. She could have stood there for another hour listening to this man. Oh, he had explained it all so clearly! She would go to Ahanu, hoping that his face would reveal a heart change; but first, she needed to talk with the preacher.

Waiting her turn, she listened as others questioned him, learning much for the exchange. The conversation grew animated as Siskia and the others joined in.

"Siskia. Siskia!" Machk needed to call twice to get her attention, but when she looked at his face, she knew something was wrong.

"What happened?" she asked, looking past Machk in search of Ahanu.

"He's gone," he replied, answering her searching eye more than her question.

"Gone? Where? Did he take a canoe?"
Machk shook his head urgently. "No, and no one seems to have seen him leave."

Siskia's brow furrowed. What did this mean? "Did you ask the villagers?"

"Yes. We have asked everyone, but he was standing in the back and no one noticed when he slipped away. We don't even know which way he went."

Siskia's heart was full of dread. What did this mean? Was he that angry with them for their beliefs? She searched the crowd for Savanukah and saw him bartering with a man near the edge of the village. Without a word to Machk, she hurried to her cousin.

Touching his arm, she asked, "Do you know where Ahanu went?"

Savanukah looked past Siskia to Machk, questioning him with his eyes.

"No one seems to have seen him leave. He did not take a canoe. Where would he have gone?" Machk asked.

Savanukah looked around the village, half expecting to see Ahanu strolling back into the crowd. "Perhaps he needed to ..."

Siskia rolled her eyes. "That wouldn't take this long." Her eyes were ready to fill with tears.

Savanukah's face lit. "We came through here when we came from our village. We ran into Ahanu on the way. It wasn't too far from here."

Siskia looked from her cousin to her brother and back to Savanukah again. "Do you think could find him?" she pleaded with her eyes.

"Do you want these beads or not?" the impatient seller barked, waiting for his payment.

Savanukah quickly traded his arrowheads and snares for the brightly colored beads and shoved them into his pouch. "Go! Tell the others to leave us a canoe."

In a flash, Machk was off. On his return, the three headed out of the village following the path to the north. It was a well-worn trail—the north-south connecting route for tribes traveling down to the Great Shaumoking Path—and they ran with urgency. Savanukah and his friends had followed this same path when they found Ahanu, or more correctly—Ahanu found them. He didn't want to get Siskia's hopes aroused, neither did he wish to discourage her, but if Ahanu had veered off the trail, he knew they would never find him.

Ahanu's mind was full of doubt and dread. Though his steps would lead him to the truth, Satan did not wish to lose this choice warrior to his enemy. He pummeled his mind with all the host of hell as Ahanu made his way down the Sheshequin Path.

When he stood at the edge of the supposed demon-filled valley, his eyes could see the demonic tribe taunting him, jeering and dancing across the desolate, storm-ravaged creek bed. Falling to his knees, he held his head, crying out for mercy.

"Look!" Siskia cried. "There he is!"

Savanukah looked as she pointed to the other end of the haunted trail. Ahanu was writhing as though in pain. Siskia started to cross the deserted stretch when Savanukah caught her arm. "Wait!"

She looked at him impatiently. With terror in his eyes, he explained. "This place is home to demons, many demons." He pointed to Ahanu. "If you do not believe me, just look at him!"

Siskia stared at Savanukah in disbelief and realized her cousin did not know the true God either. She grabbed his arm. "Savanukah, were you not listening? My family—father, mother, and even Machk—we all serve the great and powerful God." She shook her head, her eyes brilliant with a Spirit that Savanukah feared nearly as much as the demons. "I do not fear these puny demons!" Instantly, she tore across the dismal wilderness to the man she loved.

Ahanu looked up, trying to focus on who or what was running towards him. At first, his eyes glazed in terror, thinking that it was Raweno, coming at him in anger. But as the figure drew close, he realized it was Siskia. Before he could rise to his feet she was with him, wrapping him in her arms as though shielding him from the angry mob.

"Ahanu," she panted.

He pulled her close, weeping into her hair. "He wants to kill me for my wicked actions."

"No, Ahanu," she whispered. "He wants to save you."

Ahanu pulled away and focused on her eyes. "The demons," he cried fearfully. "They are all around us, Siskia. Raweno is angry."

Siskia's eyes filled with defiance, not towards Ahanu, but towards the one who sought to keep her man enslaved. She rose to her feet and turned to face the howling wilderness. "I do not fear you, Raweno. You are no god. Jesus is my Savior. He is the Son of the true and living God." She stood there for a moment like a mighty warrior defending her ground against the enemy.

Ahanu looked on in wonder as they all fled. There were no more voices, only a silence that left his soul empty, begging to be filled.

Siskia turned to Ahanu and knelt before him. Her eyes were shining with joy. "I should have told you, Ahanu. We believe in the one true God that the white man spoke of today."

Ahanu shook his head, bewildered and overwhelmed. He could say nothing.

Siskia took his hand. "Why did you leave? Were you angry?"

Shocked by her words, he slowly shook his head. "No, I was terrified." As he heard the words that he never would have uttered to anyone, he realized that a greater power than his own was at work. He looked up to see Machk approaching. Standing to his feet and pulling Siskia to him, he called to his soon-to-be-brother.

"We are fine, Machk, but we need to talk. Can you let us find our way home?"

Machk smiled at the irony. Did Ahanu know the double meaning of his words? "Good! I will go," he said and turned to run the other way.

Together, Ahanu and Siskia crossed the desolation and rested beneath the shade of a tree—the same tree where Ahanu had longed for a wife. Siskia waited, sensing that Ahanu needed to talk.

He took her hand, holding tightly as though he feared his words would drive her away. Perhaps they would, but she needed to know. "We left the Great Island and found Bald Eagle's Nest. Chief Bald Eagle welcomed us, but put us to a test to know our strengths and talents." He went on to describe each tournament and the victors.

"We thought that was all, but it was only the first part of the test." He bowed his head, continuing in a small voice. "Our next test... was ... to kill settlers who were moving into the valley south of us."

Siskia barely breathed. She longed to end his torment.

"For two years," Ahanu's face crumpled. He swallowed hard. "For two years we have raided every settler who dared to enter our land." He took in a jagged breath before continuing. "One settler had the book that the white man held."

Siskia gasped, but Ahanu went on.

"He cried out to Jesus, just before..." But he could not say the words.

He pulled her hand to his lips. She felt the tears wet on his face. "You see, I killed His children. He will now kill me!"

"No, Ahanu," Siskia pleaded.

Ahanu turned to look at her. "But He killed his own Son. What will He do to me?"

Siskia's eyes were tender with love—love for this man and love for the truth. "Ahanu, you know that we would sacrifice animals to appease the gods, right?"

Ahanu nodded, thinking once again of Sucki. As though reading his mind, Siskia reached for the tiny bear and held it out for him to see. "The white man's God required animal sacrifices too, but they were not enough to take away our sin." She took both of his strong hands into hers. "He did not sacrifice His Son out of anger; He did it out of love."

Ahanu stared at her. It made no sense, but she continued. "Today, someone asked the same question that I see in your eyes. Why would He do that? I did not understand this until today. Jesus is God's Son, but that makes Jesus, God!"

Ahanu stared at her for a moment and then shifted his gaze across the creek bed, trying to understand. Siskia sat quietly, watching as the truth began to take shape in his mind and desperately praying for his soul. He nodded slowly. "So, this Father God killed His God Son because only His blood was strong enough to erase our sin."

Siskia nodded as the tears flowed down her face. "But Jesus did not stay dead. He arose from the dead!"

Ahanu's eyes went wide. He looked at her questioningly, and she slowly nodded as the wonder of this incomprehensible truth washed over her afresh.

"Do you know of any god that strong?" she asked.

He shook his head, once again staring out into nothingness.

Siskia took a deep breath and prayed. "Can you believe He did all that for you, Ahanu?"

Ahanu's mind rehearsed the last several hours: his fear, his panic, his attempt to escape from the eyes of this God. He thought back to the other side of this wild stretch of wilderness—to his demon-tortured soul. He thought about Sucki's sacrifice and the emptiness and the yearning and the despair. Then he looked into the peace-filled eyes of the woman he loved and nodded.

"Then talk to him. Tell Him your sins and ask for His forgiveness. Ask Him to save you, Ahanu," Siskia explained with quiet earnestness.

She bowed her head, and Ahanu did the same. There in the shadows of the woods, Ahanu found release from all his pain, from all his vengeance, from all his grief; and in its place rushed in the peace of God on the wings of His Holy Spirit.

*   *   *

Siskia walked across the field dressed in her wedding white. The autumn colors made a majestic backdrop, enhancing her beauty and intensifying the whiteness of her dress. Both were carrying the traditional wedding baskets. Ahanu proudly walked beside her in his wedding white as well, thankful for all that God had done in his life. He felt as though his heart would burst. It was clean for the first time and it was overflowing with love for the woman he was about to unite with.

They were from different pasts—different traditions, but none of that mattered. Today, they united as believers in the One True God. He looked at Machk—Chief Machk— who stood in front of the long bench where Teres sat. For one brief moment, his heart sank as he looked at the empty spot where his mother would have sat if she were alive. But he pushed the thought away. This was a day for celebrating life with the living.

Siskia and Ahanu walked past Machk and took their places in the center of the bench, facing the people. Chief Machk greeted the people with a short speech concerning marriage and all it meant to everyone involved. It was his first official leadership role, and both bride and groom watched proudly.

Though young, Machk had proven himself to be a good leader. Ahanu smiled inwardly, realizing he was now the most sought after male in the village. Already, mothers were falling all over him, but Ahanu felt certain that Machk had already made his choice. Chenoa, a shy little maiden from the Delaware tribe lived up to her name: beautiful. Like the others, she nearly worshipped the ground he walked on, but her heart demeanor reflected a strength in character as well as the God she served.

He turned to face the couple, and Ahanu saw the relief in his eyes and nodded his approval. Machk's eyes shown with thankfulness, though he kept a solemn face.

Looking at his mother he asked the five questions that all people from the Iroquois tribe could have recited— the same questions that had been asked for generations.

"What is your daughter's name?"

"Siskia," Teres answered loud and strong.

"To what clan does your daughter belong?"

"She belongs to the Iroquois tribe."

Do you think that your daughter is capable of fulfilling the responsibilities of marriage?"

"Yes," came the resounding reply and many grunts of agreement could be heard throughout the assembly, bringing tears to Siskia's eyes.

"Are you satisfied with your daughter's choice?"

Without a moment of hesitation, Teres replied. "Yes!" In her heart, she felt that she was answering for her husband as well.

"If hard times come, and your daughter and her husband become homeless, would you open your home to them and their children?"

Another resounding "yes" brought more sounds of approval.

Machk then turned to Siskia. He could not hide the pride in his eyes.

"Are you prepared to be the wife of the man that you have chosen for the rest of your life?"

"Yes," Siskia answered, quiet but firm.

"Will you prepare food for your husband and children?"

"Yes."

"Will you care for your husband if he becomes ill?"

"Yes," she said with shining eyes.

"When it is dinnertime and your children are out playing with others, you are to call ALL of the children in to eat. If they have dirty faces, you will wash all their faces, just as if they all were all your own children. Do you accept this responsibility?" he replied, a smile playing on his lips.

It had always seemed like an odd question, but she had seen the command in action many times.

"Yes."

"As a wife and mother, it is your responsibility to prepare and bring your children to all group ceremonies. Marriage is a partnership and no one has the authority over the other; you do not dominate your husband nor does he dominate you."

Siskia nodded, thankful for her people's ways.
Machk paused for a moment as though memorizing the scene before him, anxious for his turn at the bench.

Chief Machk turned to Ahanu and paused for a moment. When the young Susquehannock had first come to the village, Machk had hatred in his heart for him. The old feelings against an enemy were not easily erased. He was thankful when he had gone, noticing the way he looked at his sister. But much had changed since then, and now he gladly welcomed him into the family.

Ahanu wondered if they would just skip the questions to his mother since she was not there, but to his surprise Savanukah stepped forward and stood in the empty place. A lump came to Ahanu's throat which he found difficult to swallow.

"What is this man's name?"

In a voice loud and strong, Savanukah thundered. "Ahanu, son of Anakausuen, grandson of Chief Hassun."

"To what clan does this man belong?"

"This man is from the great and glorious Susquehannock tribe!" Savanukah's voice rang across the field and echoed off the mountains. To Ahanu's amazement, many grunted their approval. He had truly been accepted into this community, and the thought nearly overwhelmed him.

"Do you think that this man is capable of fulfilling the responsibilities of marriage?"

"Yes," he answered in a way that brought chuckles from the group. If anyone knew how much—how long Ahanu had waited for Siskia, it was his friend.

"Are you satisfied with this man's choice?"

"Yes!" Savanukah laid a hand on Ahanu's shoulder, signifying just how much he was satisfied.

"If hard times come, and this man and his wife become homeless, would you open your home to them and their children?"

"Yes," Savanukah said warmly.

Machk asked the same questions to the groom, changing them somewhat to fit the position of husband.

One of the council elders stepped forward and gave the traditional Thanksgiving Address. In his hands he held a beaded wampum—a symbol of the village's wealth. He had been chosen because he too was a believer, and the couple would long remember his prayer. He thanked all the guests for coming and urged them to support the couple with both hands and heart.

Chief Machk then turned to face the people to give the Speech of Marriage. He had thought long and prayed hard over what he was about to say. Unlike the opening speech, these words came from his heart. His village was divided. Some believed but most still held to the traditions of the past. He knew if he had not been the son of the chief, he would not have been chosen because of his beliefs. Since his father had become a believer after he was chief, it had been tolerated. Machk desperately wanted to be what his father and his God wanted him to be.

He began by explaining the responsibilities and duties of both wife and husband, reminding all who listened that accomplishing them would continue to strengthen the marriage for a lifetime.

He paused, praying for wisdom and then continued. "Our times are changing. Many of you never saw a white man in your childhood. Now, they are here. Some bring trouble. Some bring Good News of Jesus. Chief Shawátis chose to believe in Jesus... and so do his wife, his daughter and her husband... and his son."

"This does not change our traditions as you saw here today. We proudly keep them and will pass them to our children. Jesus does not change that, but He changes the heart—the spirit within us."

Machk was encouraged to find that many were truly listening, and it gave him courage. "As a tribe, we will always keep our spirits free. Others may take our land. They may take our wampum. They may even take our bodies, but they cannot take our souls out of the hands of Jesus!"

He knew he had said enough. He turned back to Siskia and Ahanu, ready to finish the ceremony. He motioned for them to stand and face each other, nodding to Siskia to speak.

She looked into Ahanu's eyes. "In my basket is material. I will care for you and our future children. I will sew, and mend, and clean for our family." Her eyes sparkled with the secret that only they knew concerning her sewing. Ahanu marveled at the symbol so unfamiliar to him and realized afresh just what it had meant to Siskia to sew for him.

He cleared his throat and held up his basket. "In my basket is a cake of cornmeal, sweetened with honey. I will care for you and provide for you and our children as well as all the children of our community."

Machk turned to the elder and took the wampum belt. He gave one end to Siskia and the other to Ahanu. All the family formed a circle with the council leaders and passed the wampum from person to person. As they held the belt, they offered words of praise and advice to the couple.

It was done. All gathered around Siskia, who had always been a favorite, and Ahanu, shaking their hands and congratulating. Because this was also a feast for the new chief, the tables were heaped with foods of every kind.

The celebration lasted into the night with dances and laughter and feasting. One by one, the families slipped away to their clan's long house. Siskia eyed Ahanu wondering if he had any qualms about staying with her family. From what he had said, his people had separate wigwams. It would be very different for him.

As though reading her thoughts, Ahanu took her hand and silently led her away from the others. No one seemed to notice as the feasting and dances continued. They had done their part as a couple. Now it was time for themselves.

He enjoyed the feel of her small hand in his and smiled to himself, knowing that she wondered where he was taking her. "I have a surprise for you," he said, wanting to calm any anxiety she may be feeling. "We will join your family later. They will understand." He had already talked to Machk to make sure that he was not offending the family.

The great bonfire grew smaller and smaller as they neared the woods. As they followed a trail into the darkness, Ahanu was thankful for the full moon. Its rays cast dancing shadows throughout the forest's thick canopy. As they drew near their destination, Ahanu gripped her hand tightly. He stopped before a lean-to and waited for her reaction. She looked first at the lean-to and then up into his searching eyes, which so desperately looked for approval.

Words could not express her gratitude. She reached up to touch his cheek. "Thank you," she whispered. His act of kindness erased any doubts she may have still had about this man. He would take care of her and meet her needs, no matter how small or seemingly foolish. Could she ask for more? Gently, he swept her off her feet and carried her inside.

It was nearly dawn when they made their way back to the long house. Before they slipped in, Ahanu took Siskia in his arms once again wondering how he had ever lived without her.

"I would like to show you my home," he whispered.

Siskia rested her head on his chest, so happy she could not answer but only nodded. As they entered the long house, Siskia led the way to the place she had prepared for them. The fires were just embers and cast as warm glow to the interior of the large building. As their eyes adjusted, Ahanu counted seven fire rings which meant that seven families from Siskia's clan shared the shelter. It was neatly divided into sections by the placement of their pallets. He wondered if he would be able to get used to living with so many and was thankful when Siskia led them to a semi-secluded corner.

*   *   *

Everything was better for Ahanu. As they packed some things for their trip, and stashed it in a canoe, it felt so good to be heading out with his wife. They stored the canoe at French Margaret's Town and headed north up the Sheshequin Path.

When they came to the place where Ahanu understood and believed for the first time, they stopped and prayed, thanking Him for His goodness and wisdom, and prayed for guidance for their future.

Ahanu first took her to his village or what was left of it. Some of the wigwams still stood, but most were in ruins. Any sign of human life was nearly erased from the clearing. Saplings had sprouted throughout the village, and in a matter of years it would all be taken back by the forest.

As they walked away, Ahanu knew in his heart it was probably the last time he would be there. Every day rumors of white men coming reached Great Island.

They stopped at a waterfall for their lunch before heading to Spirit Rock. Ahanu had told Siskia about the sacred place, and they had both rejoiced that their new God required no more sacrifices, sobering by the reality that

Jesus' sacrifice was the reason. The fact always left Ahanu feeling overwhelmed and unworthy, and he determined that nothing would come before his love for God.

It would have been shorter to come straight from his village, but they were not in a hurry, and he wanted to show Siskia the waterfalls as well. It would also bring them in from the other side affording them a view of the cliffs from below.

The climb was steep but Siskia's graceful moves once again amazed Ahanu. He watched for a moment, mesmerized by her blithe stride. Her long, thick braid swung in rhythm to her steps as she ascended the mountain as though she were walking across a flat field. Stopping when she did not hear his steps, she turned to look his way and tilted her head in question; but when she saw the admiration in his eyes, her face lit as though sunbeams had just broken through leaves of the majestic trees around her and kissed her cheeks.

She ran to him and jumped into his arms. He swung her high, his strong arms encircling her slim waist and lifting her as though she were weightless. He kissed her neck and cheeks until his lips found hers. Siskia breathed hard, knowing it was not from the exertion of the hike.

"I never knew it would be like this," Ahanu breathed into her ear.

Siskia laughed. "Me neither. It always looks different when it is your parents." She laughed until she saw his face, and then she grew somber. "I'm sorry. I didn't think." She felt pain in her chest, knowing that her words brought painful memories of his loveless life.

Ahanu shook his head. "You do not need to apologize. It does make me sad, but more than that, it makes me feel empty." Slowly, the hurt faded and into its place grew an expression of tender love. "You have already filled it more than I ever thought possible."

Together, they continued up the mountain hand in hand. By the time they reached the top, they were now breathless for other reasons. Slowly, Ahanu led her to the rock. He showed her the markings that had been etched there to appease Rawano and tell of their beliefs. He traced them with his finger, deep in thought. He knew what he needed to do.

Taking his knife, Ahanu began to chisel a cross into the top of the rock. Siskia sat beside him, rubbing his back and watching with admiration. She glanced across the valley admiring its beauty. In spots, the Legaui-hanne Creek shimmered against a backdrop of green. In a meadow far below them, a mother bear ambled out of the woods with two cubs following her lumbering stride.

Ahanu finished, running his fingers across the deep cuts. He looked up at Siskia and smiled. He took the pouch that was tied to his waist and opened it, pouring the coins out onto the rock.

Siskia looked at them in amazement. She had never seen so much wampum although she had heard that white men called it money. "Where did you get this?" she asked wanting to touch them but fearing to do so.

Ahanu's lips were drawn into a frown. "This is blood money, Siskia. We could use it in many ways, especially in the future, but I do not want it." One by one, he dropped the coins into a crack in the rock. They listened as the coins jingled and clinked against the rock, finally landing far below.

Siskia nodded with understanding. "You are a noble man, Ahanu, and I am proud to be your wife!"

They sat in silence for a long time, each lost in thought, listening to the sounds of the woods around them. A welcome breeze cooled their faces. Ahanu took Siskia's hand and together, they walked away, never looking back.

Chapter Seven

Change

Trust in the LORD with all thine heart;
and lean not unto thine own understanding.
In all thy ways acknowledge him,
and he shall direct thy paths.
Proverbs 3:5,6

1747

Ahanu stood in the shadows alongside Machk and watched as the white men's canoes came up the river and stopped just short of Great Island. For two years the village had lived in peace while rumors of Indian attacks to the southwest accompanied the many Indians who traversed the Great Shaumoking Path from the west. News of the French near the Ohio River was not much better.

Some of the young braves from Great Island joined the passing bands of warriors and headed west to help the French fight the British. Ahanu and Siskia stayed at Great Island, building a home there. Within the year, the Lord blessed them with a little baby boy and Siskia gladly named him Sucki.

From the lookout high above the river, the two men watched as six men pulled their canoes to the south side of the river. They sat and listened. Soon, strange noises could be heard.

"What do you think they are doing?" Machk asked, never taking his eyes off the place where they had landed.

Ahanu shook his head. "I don't know."

As they watched one of the white pines—the biggest in the area—began to quiver and shake. With a loud cracking noise, the mighty giant crashed through the surrounding trees and landed on the earth with a thud that was felt even by Machk and Ahanu. They looked at each other, stunned and confused.

More sounds of axes resonated up and down the valley. In amazement they looked on as the naked tree trunk was pushed into the water. In no time, the men were back in their canoes, guiding the huge log down the river.

Without a word, the two friends and leaders of their community, raced down the mountainside to the place where the tree had just been taken. They had never seen such destruction. Broken tree limbs hung loosely from the trees where the giant had crashed to the ground, looking like broken arms trying to wave in surrender. The ferns and undergrowth were trampled and mangled and the sawed off limbs were strewn everywhere. The earth had been torn and dug up where the log had been drug to the river, and the lush green water plants were broken and pressed into the mud.

Machk shook his head. "I don't understand," he said looking mournfully at the devastation.

Ahanu's brow furrowed. "I think I do." He stared at the retreating canoes, now only the size of needles. "My grandfather told me once of the white man's villages. He said that they had canoes which were as big as twenty of our canoes, and many, many long houses, all made out of wood. Their canoes had many large pieces of cloth attached to a long pole." He was silent for a moment. "The white men will come for our forest."

There was much discussion in the village for the next few days and weeks. Summer would soon be upon them and no rain had come for several moons. The crops were failing, and Machk worried about his village.

By the end of summer, it was obvious something had to be done. They could not stay on Great Island. That evening at the council fire, it was decided that they would move west, but the group was divided.

"We do not know that they will come," some argued.

"Did you not see the white travelers the last time we were in Otstuagy? Did you hear their questions? They see the tall trees and rich ground. They want it!" Machk argued.

"But we will fight them," another younger brave shouted, and many sounded their agreement.

There was a moment of silence as Chief Machk looked around group. Many of the men were much older than he, and at times like these, he wondered why he was the chief. He shook his head sadly. "I talked with Logan, the preacher's guide. He comes from Shaumoking where the white man has been for many winters. They are not leaving, and there are too many of them."

"Then we stay and make them choose their lands while we keep ours. There is plenty of room for all."

"Logan also told me when that happens—our people and the white man live together—we lose our children to their ways."

Another long silence—the only sound was the crackling fire and the hoot of a distant owl on the mountain. Discouragement and sadness etched lines into each face.

"Then we will go," spoke Abukcheech, one of the oldest members of their tribe. He was a Muncee and had come from the land of the rising sun as a youth. He never said much about his childhood, but they all knew he was forced from his lands several times before coming to the Great Island. His look of resignation angered some and saddened others.

"Where will we go?" asked Degataga. The beautiful dark eyes of a certain maiden at Bald Eagle's Nest often visited his dreams.

Savanukah spoke. "We will go to Bald Eagle's Nest, but I would like to go further. It is only a matter of time until they too will face what we are facing."

"How do you know?" asked one of the older men.

Savanukah looked at Ahanu. They had not talked much with the villagers about their time with Chief Bald Eagle, but by the look in Savanukah's eyes, he knew he did not wish to continue the deadly raids on innocent people, no matter the color of their skin.

"We made many raids on settlers to the south of Bald Eagle's Nest," Ahanu said quietly. He looked intently into the eyes of the people he now counted as his family. "I will not live that life again."

"Are you afraid to kill a white man?" Keme thundered. He had secretly hoped to have Siskia for his wife and still held a grudge against Ahanu. He was not a believer and felt the white man's religion only made men weak.

Ahanu knew all this and fought to control his anger. Since his conversion and marriage, the Lord had been pressing him about this, but he had seen victory in his life, and it encouraged him. "I have already killed more white men than I hope to ever see in my lifetime." His statement brought murmurs of astonishment around the fire.

"We plan to go farther west, perhaps into Ohio. We know many of our people have joined the French there and are fighting a war against the British," Savanukah explained. Ahanu's look flashed his thanks to his friend for taking the light off of him. "We will fight for our people, but in a war, not in senseless raids."

The discussion continued well into the night, but it was decided each clan could make their choice. By morning, the majority of the villagers had decided to follow their chief and his clan wherever he went. Their words of confidence to Chief Machk humbled him, and the weight of the responsibility pressed down upon his heart.

That evening, he made a choice as well. Walking to Chenoa's long house, he asked her to walk with him.

Chenoa's eyes were red and he knew she had been crying. He wasn't sure, but he was afraid that her father would choose to stay on Great Island.

They walked in silence part way down the path along the river. He had grown to love this place—the wide, peaceful river, the tall grasses that grew along the water's edge, the sloping mountainside to the south and rolling hills to the north. His heart ached at making yet another move and thought once again about Abukcheech, wondering what the circumstances were that he received his name: mouse, but mostly wondering if his life would follow the same pattern as the old man.

When they reached their favorite spot where the shore had lost its greenery because of the all the canoes which launched forth from the place, Machk stopped and faced Chenoa. He looked into her eyes. She knew what was coming—the day she had longed for as long as she had known Machk.

"Will you be my wife, Chenoa?" He searched her eyes, seeing the turmoil. "I need you by my side. I cannot lead these people alone," he said in a husky voice. "You know my feelings for you, don't you?"

Chenoa's eyes shone with affection mingled with unshed tears. She could only nod.

He pulled her into her arms, rubbing his smooth cheek against her hair. "Please say yes," he begged.

As he held her, and his breath, waiting for an answer, he sent a prayer heavenward. In a voice as quiet as the turtledove's coo, he heard her answer. Joy flooded his soul and he held her tightly, listening as the evening cricket sang his song. A bobwhite chose that moment to begin his evening melody, and they stood in silence, enjoying the sweetness of the moment and the night sounds. He could feel her heart pounding, but as he held her, little by little, its rhythm slowed.

*   *   *

Most of the villagers chose to follow Machk's leading and walked away from the comfort of the Great Island and into the unknown. Although many natives had come to their village as they journeyed, none in their tribe had ever been further west than Eagle's Nest. They came to that village by midafternoon and Machk realized that he would need patience for this trip. He was no longer traveling with young warriors but also children and the elderly. Their pace would be slow, but they were in no hurry.

Ahanu walked proudly beside Siskia. He still wondered at the realization that she belonged to him. Her beauty surpassed any maiden he had ever known; her kind heart showed forth in her gentle, yet strong spirit. Most of all, she knew the true God and sought to please Him. They didn't know much, but the young couple's hearts showed them the way led by the Holy Spirit. Ahanu often awoke to find her kneeling in prayer—her hands clasped and her lips moving in silent praises to God. He did not deserve her, and now, as they walked into Eagle's Nest, he was nearly overcome with dread and worry.

Siskia noticed the dark cloud that moved into Ahanu's heart and cloaked his eyes. She reached for his hand and gave it a firm squeeze. His eyes met hers and, without a word, he knew that she understood.

Their group numbered fifty-eight, and Machk knew from experience that the lookouts had already sent word of their coming. Chief Bald Eagle and his elders met them warmly at the creek-side path which led to their village. His eyes sought Ahanu and the others who had been with his warriors. Ahanu stood straight, making him nearly a head taller than the others. Chief Bald Eagle's eyes were steely. The young bucks had left abruptly with good reason—Savanukah's uncle was dying—but Ahanu was certain Chief Bald Eagle had expected them to return. Of all the raiding parties that the chief sent out, Ahanu's was always the most successful... and brutal. Now, the memories made his face burn with shame, but he would not show it.

"Welcome," Chief Bald Eagle called to them. Machk stepped forward, throwing the older man off guard. Certainly this one was not their leader; however, Machk's strong, assertive voice left no doubt as to who was in charge.

"Thank you, Chief Bald Eagle. We seek shelter just for the night."

The chief looked surprised. "Where are you going with so many?"

"We are uncertain of our destiny, but have come to the realization that our time at Great Island has ended. We will journey towards the setting sun, possibly settling in Ohio.

Chief Bald Eagle's countenance changed quickly as though thunderclouds had suddenly rolled across the sky to cover the sun. "You are cowards? We must stop the white man!" His eyes fell on Ahanu and the others. "You have brave warriors who can do the task—have already done so!"

He darted his fiery gaze from one to the next until they landed once again on Ahanu. He had had high hopes for this one—he had fire in his blood. The old chief's eyes were riveted to Ahanu only making the young warrior stand straighter.

Chief Bald Eagle studied him as though he could see into his soul. His lips curled with disdain. "You have become a woman," he jeered, spitting in Ahanu's direction. "You could have been great. Now you are less than a dog."

Ahanu felt more than he saw Savanukah, Kanatase and Degataga ready themselves to come to his defense. The chief had hurled the greatest insults any Indian could have said, using them to draw Ahanu into a fight. "You are right, Chief Bald Eagle," Ahanu answered calmly. He heard the gasps around him. "I have become weak; in fact, I am dead—dead to your ways but alive to the one true God. He gives me more strength than any of your bravest warriors could have in their little fingers."

"Then fight!" shouted Bald Eagle.

"No!" came the strong, still voice of their Chief Machk. "We do not come to fight our people." He scanned the faces of his men—brave men who would have fought to the death for their friend—and then turned to Chief Bald Eagle. "We will fight our enemies but not innocent settlers." He turned and walked back down the path, away from the village, but Chief Bald Eagle shouted to him.

"Stop!"

Out of respect, Machk turned to face him once again, but Bald Eagle kept silent. The two leaders stood facing each other as all the onlookers seemed to hold their breath. Without another word, Chief Machk walked away and his people followed.

Ahanu, Savanukah, **Degataga** and Kanatase stood still, letting the others pass by. As Chief Machk walked on, he prayed that his men would make the right choice. It would take humility not to defend their honor.

Ahanu's friends stood next to him as though waiting for his next move. The old, familiar taste of revenge burned hot in Ahanu's heart, and Satan's host fanned the fire. At that moment Sucki gurgled and cooed, breaking the silence. The sound was a message straight from His Master, and the demons fled, the fire fizzled out, and Ahanu walked away.

No one spoke as the group headed west, through the great valley which seemed to stretch forever into the horizon. As the sun began to set, the travelers were weary of their journey. The trail which followed the **Siskëwahane** River offered several places to camp for the night, places which had been used for centuries by other travelers. Their group was large, so several of the young warriors forged ahead with Ahanu leading the way.

Sucki was fast asleep in his carrier on Siskia's back by the time they made camp, but as soon as Ahanu started to loosen the straps he was awake. He rubbed his eyes and began to cry as Ahanu handed him to his mother.

Every time Ahanu watched Siskia with Sucki his heart swelled with pride and his eyes were full of wonder. She was so patient and loving with their child, and she seemed to know what the little papoose needed before he did. He took a moment to watch as she deftly changed his swaddle and then brought him to her breast. The sight nearly brought tears to his eyes. He would never tire of watching Sucki's eyes roll shut in deep satisfaction. Siskia looked up, surprised to find Ahanu still watching. Most men did not pay much attention to mothering, but Ahanu seemed to hunger for it.

"Will we sleep under the stars tonight, my husband?" Siskia asked coyly. It was her way of saying, *get busy!*

Ahanu smiled sheepishly and knelt down before her. He touched the downy head that was nearly asleep and then drew his gaze to Siskia. "You are a wonderful mother and wife. I am blessed."

A knot formed in Siskia's throat, and she blinked back tears. They were all tired and a little bit frightened of the unknown, but their men were strong and brave, and she knew that God would lead them. As Ahanu rose to go, she smiled up into his gentle eyes. "You are a wonderful father and husband." She reached out her hand, and Ahanu drew it to his lips before turning away.

After the lean-to shelters were finished and the women and children were asleep, the men gathered around the fire. Ahanu and his men had circled back to meet with Machk, feeling that was safer than the others joining their fire. At this point of their journey, they feared what they had left at Eagle's Nest more than what lay before them. Ahanu did not miss the look of fiery revenge in **Lakose**'s eyes nor the way he eyed Siskia. It made his face burn with anger as he clenched his jaw.

Machk had not missed Ahanu's dark eyes as he stared into the fire and wondered if it had to do with the bulky man who shot him through with looks of daggers. He chose his words carefully, wanting to get his message across but not wanting to create any more tension than that which already circled the fire.

"Our God will lead us and protect us from evil," he said quietly, but he emphasized every word. His eyes moved from face to face, trying to calm the hearts of the young warriors who had been so badly shamed at Eagle's Nest.

"Ahanu said it best when we were among the others. He showed the true and living Spirit to those who still live in darkness."

"But you saw their faces. Don't you think they will seek revenge?" one of the older men spoke. Although many admired the beliefs of their chief and the others, they did not understand the change in their ways.

"We will be ready." Ahanu spoke in such a low, commanding voice, no one dared to question him except his chief.

Machk stared into the fire for a long time before he shifted his gaze to Ahanu. "I know you were cut deeply with their words, Ahanu, and I trust you to do what you believe is best."

Ahanu would have felt better if Machk had reprimanded him. His eyes softened and his shoulders drooped slightly. He could not look into Machk's eyes, but only nodded.

They sat in silence, listening to the night sounds and any other noises which did not belong, when the sound of a twig breaking sharpened every nerve. Someone was coming, and they all had heard it. Degataga silently left his spot and melted into the woods behind him. He circled around the area where the noise had been heard, pulling his tomahawk in readiness. His eyes were as sharp as an eagle, and as he silently made his way through the woods, he soon spotted the silhouette of one person. He searched to the left and right, looking for others, but saw no one.

Without so much as the sound of his breath, he crept forward. As he drew near, he was certain that it was not

Lakose. The shape was too small. He was nearly behind the person when the silhouette turned to face him.

Degataga pulled back in surprise! "Hurit," he whispered. "What are you doing here? I could have killed you!"

Those big, beautiful eyes that had haunted his dreams now filled with tears. "Degataga, I had to come and warn you. Lakose and some of the others are coming!"

Degataga took her hand, and rushed through the woods to the fire. The others were on their feet by the time he came crashing into the clearing. "Lakose is coming!" he whispered fiercely.

Machk took charge, although the others knew what to do. They had expected trouble and had made a plan as they set up their camp. The clearing was easily patrolled from the ridge that nearly encircled the bend in the river. With men stationed at the top of the ridge, their families would be safe.

"How many are there?" asked Machk.

Hurit thought for a moment. "No more than five. Lakose does not have many friends. Most of the talk after you left was that we must stop fighting each other." She swiped the tears away, trying to look brave. In reality, if her heart had not belonged to Degataga, she wondered how she would have made it. When he first saw her, his look of surprise had made her wonder if she had come in vain, but when he took her hand and held it so firmly, hope revived in her heart. Now, she realized he was still holding her hand, and it made her heart soar.

As the men dispersed, Degataga took her with him in the other direction. He was on a later watch. He walked in silence until they were away from the others, feeling questioning eyes upon them but not stopping to explain what he was not certain of himself.

They were nearly to the other camp when he suddenly stopped and led her to a fallen log. Without a word, they sat near the water's edge waiting for the other to speak.

"Thank you, Hurit. You may have saved our lives and the lives of our loved ones," Degataga said in a low voice. He hesitated, not certain he should speak his heart, wondering if he had only seen what he wanted to see when he had been at Bald Eagle's Nest.. "I am glad you came," he said as he squeezed her tiny hand.

Hurit's eyes shone, and a shy smile came to her lips. "When you left the village, I feared I would never see you again," she said shyly. She dropped her gaze momentarily, remembering Lakose's advances. He had made it very clear what he wanted.

Degataga watched as her eyes grew so sad it nearly broke his heart. "What is wrong?"

She looked up into his strong, honest face. How could he have gotten any stronger? Was he a follower of this God that Ahanu had spoken about? "Lakose..." She didn't know what to say but she didn't need to say any more.

"No!" Degataga nearly shouted. He took her hands, working hard to compose himself. "Hurit, ever since we left, I have thought of only you. Will you go with us?"

Hurit had no family to speak of. Her mother and father had died when she was still a child, and her uncle had taken her in. Although she thought of him as a father, she also knew he would be happy for her to join Lakose, and she knew she couldn't do it. She looked up into his handsome face as a smile spread across hers. "Yes, if you will have me," she whispered.

Dagataga, still holding her hand, bent close and kissed her cheek. Hurit's heart raced as he pulled her close. "Surely our God is powerful. He has done the impossible."

Hurit pulled back and turned searching eyes on him. "When I saw Ahanu's bravery and heard his strong words, I knew what I had to do. Can you tell me about your God?"

Dagataga nodded slowly, smiling.

Lakose raised a hand and blew softly into his cupped hand, creating a nearly inaudible sound of a breeze. The other warriors froze in their tracks, all listening for any sound. Lakose sniffed the air, trying to find any trace of his enemies' camp. They couldn't have gone much further with the women and children in tow.

Ahanu had seen them pass and held his breath. They were heading right into camp, but had not heard or seen him or Savanukah who was on the other side of the trail. This would be easy.

When Lakose motioned his band forward, Ahanu lifted his hand to his mouth and made the hooting sound of an owl. When Savanukah and the others heard it, they prepared for the attack.

Almost simultaneously, Ahanu and the others let out a war cry. Lakose whirled around to face his oncoming enemy, but he never had a chance to even focus his eyes before Ahanu was on him. Kanatase and Machk came up the trail to join their fellow warriors, and the deed was swiftly done. Savanukah looked down into the blank stares of their native enemies, his heart sad. "These were good men who chose to follow a bad leader."

The others nodded in agreement. Ahanu stared at Lakose who lay silent in his tracks. "Lakose hated us from the start. We are not guilty of these men's blood," he said quietly. "They brought this upon themselves."

"We are indebted to Hurit," Machk said, and all heads nodded in agreement.

Degataga had heard the war cry in the distance and quickly rose to his feet. He was fairly certain that the cry was from Ahanu, which meant that they had the element of surprise, but he wanted to be on guard just in case. The other men came from their shelters as well and quietly took their places along the trail. It seemed like an eternity to

Degataga as he waited, but soon he heard the careless footfall of the men and knew they had won the battle.

The men huddled around the dying embers where a fire had been built earlier and listened to the young warriors' account of the attack. Machk watched the faces of his people as Ahanu told the tale. This was his first battle as chief and, although he was pleased to see the loyalty and admiration in the faces of all the men, he wondered how many more battles he would need to face before they could live in peace.

Siskia's eyes were wide open when Ahanu entered the shelter. With movements faster than a cat, she sprang to him and buried her face in his chest. Ahanu held her close, thinking how nice it was to have a wife.

"Be strong, Siskia," he whispered. His words brought shame to Siskia's heart, and she blinked back the tears. "I'm sorry, Ahanu. You are right. But I saw the hatred in Lakose's eyes, and I knew his knife was meant for your heart."

Ahanu brushed her face with his finger and looked into her eyes. "His blade is no match for our God."

Siskia saw the earnestness in his eyes in spite of the darkness, her face full of wonder. She nodded slowly, once again amazed at the spiritual strength of her husband. "Your physical strength is only second to your spiritual strength."

Ahanu's eyes widened. It was the greatest compliment she could have given him.

Together, they snuggled down between the blankets—Ahanu's arm cradling Siskia. They lay in silence listening to Sucki's even breathing and the sounds of the evening woods. "This was the right move," Ahanu spoke. "God is with us."

Siskia snuggled closer, feeling more peace in her heart than she had ever felt before.

*   *   *

Some of the older men in their group were familiar with the **Great Shaumoking Path** that they were following. The trail was clearly visible, made by the steps of a thousand feet throughout centuries of travel. Both red and white men used the trail, for the white traders were welcomed by the Indians.

The way along Marsh Creek was lush, and the air was filled with the sweet perfume of the last of the summer lilies. The creek offered a cool drink and mosses which grew along the path soothed weary feet. With each step forward, the little band felt less alarm and more hope of a promised land. They were survivors, and the Praying Indians among them knew God was leading them in the way they should go.

By midafternoon the travelers had reached Chingleclamouche, the first Indian village of any size, situated on the banks of the **Siskëwahane River**. Seeing the river felt as though they had reunited with an old friend.

The children quickly sought out the village children and were soon playing games along the water's edge, sharing stories and telling of their adventures. The men gathered with the elders of the village, explaining their mission.

"You and your people are welcome here," said the old chief. He had liked what he saw in the young chief and knew that he and his warriors would be great addition to their small clan.

Machk shook his head. "We are not certain of our destination, but we plan to go further."

The chief's face clouded with sadness. "There is only fighting in the land of the setting sun. The white men come through here, but they do not stop. They are friendly to us and have promised to leave us alone."

Machk looked skeptical but did not want to offend his elder. He nodded. "Then it is a good place for you, but we must move on."

Knowing the young man's mind was set, the conversation turned to small talk. One of the elders eyed

Ahanu curiously. "You look like my ancestors, the Susquehannocks," the old leader said.

Ahanu's face showed his surprise. "Yes. I am a Susquehannock. You are of my people?" Ahanu asked excitedly.

The old man's face brightened. "Yes, my great grandfather was a Susquehannock. He came here and settled with the others." He shook his head sadly. "We were a strong people, but now we are scattered." He shook off his reverie and looked up at Ahanu. Slowly, he rose to his feet and Ahanu was surprised to find that he was looking straight into the eyes of another. "Come. Let us walk and you can tell me your story."

Savanukah smiled as he watched his friend leave. *This will be good for Ahanu,* he thought. *It is always good to find a link to your people.* His mind went to his own family and he wondered if he would ever see them again.

In the morning, after a hearty breakfast, the travelers were on their way, but this time by canoe. The men were thankful to be riding instead of carrying the canoes, and the air was festive. The river twisted and curved its way through dense forest and open meadows taking them on a zigzag path to their destiny.

Siskia watched as Ahanu's strong arms dipped the paddle into the water and pushed them forward. Sucki had fallen asleep, and the gentle rocking of the canoe had made naptime easy. In fact, she found herself dozing as well.

When Sucki stirred, Siskia was surprised to see that the canoes ahead of them were pulling off to the side of the river. She looked at the sky in alarm. How long had she slept?

Ahanu's quiet chuckles drew her attention. "You will be twice as beautiful now with all that extra rest." His smile was cocked to one side, and she knew he was teasing her. Her eyes narrowed and before Ahanu knew what was happening, she had dipped her hand into the water and splashed him. His eyes flew open in surprise, and Siskia laughed. Sucki looked from one parent to the other and clapped his little hands with glee.

"Perhaps, since you are so rested and I have battled the river all day, you should make the lean -to for tonight," Ahanu quipped.

Siskia's chin shot out. "Fine, and you take care of Sucki's needs," she shot back. As the canoe reached land, Siskia scooped up the sodden Sucki, deposited him into his father's lap and ran up the river bank laughing. She looked back over her shoulder, her dark eyes dancing with delight as she disappeared into the woods.

The next leg of their trip was the most difficult thus far. Carrying the canoes and following the path which made a gradual ascent was difficult. Thankfully, the path then descended into Punxsutawney. By the time they reached the settlement, everyone was ready for a rest. Machk was surprised at the size of the village. Dozens of long houses, or stockades as they were called here, were scattered over the land. Fields of corn and wheat formed a patchwork design among the cleared areas and stockades. He had never seen so many people, not even around Lake Okswego. His heart ached, and he wondered it this would be their new home. Somehow, he doubted it.

The group had not been in the village long before they understood why the settlement was called Punxsutawney. Sand flies swarmed everywhere, and soon the cries of frustrated children and infants could be heard all around their group.

When the people of the village came to greet them, Machk and the others noticed that their faces and arms were smeared with a foul smelling greasy substance. Soon the women were offering it to them, encouraging them to do the same. "It will keep the flies away," explained one woman with a toothless grin.

Machk looked at his men and shrugged as he dipped his finger into the grease and applied it. The others were doing the same and were amazed at how quickly the flies fled.

"Welcome," boomed their leader as the women departed. His face was also smeared with the stuff, but his had a darker, nearly black color, which Ahanu found out later was something of a distinction. As they mingled with the people, it seemed as though different groups claimed different colors. It was quite a sight to behold.

That evening after a time of sharing food and information, Machk and the others gathered in a guest shelter. They had been traveling for several days and some of the children and older people were weary. Machk looked around the group before speaking. "I believe we should stay here for a while and strengthen our people, but I do not believe this is to be our permanent dwelling." Heads nodded in agreement and Machk smiled. A chuckle grew into a full grown laugh as he took in the sight before him. "Although, I think the grease suits you, Ahanu." Machk's eyes sparkled with mischief. He had overheard Ahanu grumbling to Siskia about the grease, refusing to apply it to his skin, that is until every sandfly for miles seemed to descend upon him. Siskia giggled but hid her face, and Ahanu only grunted.

"You couldn't get me to stay here for all the treasures of every land!" Ahanu hissed under his breath, not wanting to be overheard.

"I agree," added Savanukah. "How can they live here?" he questioned.

"You heard the contentment in their voices as they spoke of good land and good crops. They also seem to have a good trade agreement with the white men in this area," Machk said. He shook his head slowly. "They are all things to consider. Perhaps it is just for a short season that the sandflies come."

Chenoa shook her head. "I asked one of the women. She said they fly until the first frost and come with the spring rains."

Others murmured their disapproval, and it was decided that they would only stay until the weary were rested and strengthened.

Three days later, they were traveling again. The people of Punxsatawney sent them on their way with fresh supplies and words of wisdom concerning the Mahoning Creek. It would be a long trek as the creek wound its way through the woods, but at the end of the tributary was the Allegheny River and a land of hope and promise. Plus, they would be flowing with the water's current and not against it.

As they pushed away from the shores of Punxsatawney, their excitement ran high. If all went well, the villagers told them that they could make the trip in one day—one long day.

Sucki sat transfixed by the fast moving water as Ahanu plied their way through its murky depths. Siskia loved to travel by canoe. The smooth ride and fresh, clean air on her face filled her heart with joy. She looked around at the other canoes and smiled. They were making a new start, and this time she hoped it would be their last move, although she never tired of seeing new places.

As they swiftly sped along, the men were soon vying for the front of the pack. Like young boys, they laughed and paddled with all their might until Sucki's eyes danced with delight and squeals of joy could be heard from the children. Women laughed, men shouted barbs to each other, and life was a holiday. It nearly brought tears to Siskia's eyes; she was so happy.

Soon, the race was on between Savanukah, Ahanu, and Machk, the three canoes all aligned with each other. Siskia smiled at Chenoa and became a bit alarmed. The young bride was pale, and Siskia wondered if there would be a little one joining their family by this time next year. Her smile became filled with empathy, and Chenoa blushed, making Siskia nearly certain of her conclusion.

"Savanukah needs more riders in his canoe," Ahanu called. "And you only have little Chenoa."

"Are you saying that my sister is fat?" Machk laughed.

Siskia tried to look insulted but only laughed. "Ahanu, show them what you can do," she cried.

As though he had only been plodding along to this point, Ahanu dug deeper into the water with such force that Siskia fell backwards. Their canoe shot forward and outdistanced the others at such an amazing rate that the others soon called him the victor. Ahanu panted as he pulled his paddle into the canoe, his face split with a winning smile.

Siskia reached forward, having righted herself and laid her hand upon his bare back. Her eyes sparkled with adoration, and Ahanu had never felt so full of joy. The others soon joined them as they drifted with the current, allowing the others to catch up.

"Way to go, big brother," Machk said reaching out to grasp Ahanu's hand. But Ahanu saw the mischief in his eyes and quickly grabbed his arm, pulling him out of the canoe and into the water. Savanukah laughed, and Chenoa showed her surprise, working hard to keep the canoe afloat, but all the confusion had frightened Sucki who started to cry.

Siskia picked him up and soothed him as Machk hoisted himself back into his canoe. "Poor baby," he said with exaggerated tones. "What a nasty father you have."

"What a pouty uncle you have," Ahanu countered, and Machk drew an enormous pout, making them all laugh.

The rest of the trip was uneventful except for the sight of several elk and bear along the water's edge. They glided past noiselessly enjoying the sight. By the time they reached the banks of the Allegheny River, the sun was nearing the horizon. With practiced ease they navigated the strong current of the river, paddling a short distance before gathering together in the middle of the river where the water ran deep and calm.

Machk looked around, assessing the mood and strength of each paddler. "I say we paddle to Kittanning. It's just down river a ways, and I believe we can make it before dusk."

All nodded in agreement, and soon they were once again moving swiftly down river. The river was much wider than Mahoning Creek, and the canoes aligned themselves into three rows, making an impressive sight.

When the lookouts saw them coming, word was immediately sent to the chief. By the time the canoes reached the shores of Kittanning, a welcome party had been formed, and a grand procession was taking place. They pulled onto the shore, and Chief Machk, summoning all the courage and age that was within him, walked proudly before his people. The children were tired and the women weary, but they held their heads high, making an impressive entry.

Kittanning was a young town by any Indian calculation, established only twenty-three years earlier. But it had become an important stopping place and center of Indian activity. As the tension increased between the French to the north and west and the English to the east and south, Kittanning marked the spot of nebulous demarcation.

Delawares from both the Turtle and Turkey clans had moved west as the white man continued to gobble up the land. Disgruntled by the unjust dealings of the Walking Purchase in 1737, many of the Delawares still carried anger in their hearts. Kittanning was a smoldering pot, filled with hatred towards the settlers, as Machk and the others would soon find out.

The chief was followed by many warriors, and Machk felt a bit intimidated. The Spirit within him also seemed to be sending signals that this was not the place for his people. He could tell by the men's demeanor that they were fighters. Sadly, the whole scene reminded him of their first encounter with Chief Bald Eagle, but he wanted to keep an open mind.

"Welcome to Kittanning. I am Captain Hill." As he said his title, he could tell from the strangers' reaction that they were not used to hearing a red man referred to as "captain."

"I have received this title from my enemies because I am a leader and a warrior." Captain Hill's mouth twisted in a cruel smile.

Machk sensed movement behind him and knew that the others were drawing closer to him to show their support. He raised his chin slightly, not wanting to offend this man but also not apologizing for who they were. "We have fought for Bald Eagle." He let the statement stand and saw admiration in the captain's eyes. "We are not afraid to fight, but we wish to know who our enemies are."

Captain Hill's face was expressionless. He liked the looks of these men and did not wish to offend them. He could use them and their strength, but first he must win the battle of words.

"We too seek to destroy our enemies," he said in a strong voice, but his tone grew quieter as he added, "And we know who they are." It wasn't a threat and Machk knew it. This man was a leader not by birth but by proving himself worthy.

Machk stared at the man with no expression on his face. He wanted to be strong, prove his leadership and pride for his people. The first encounter with another leader sets the stage for what will follow, and Machk wasn't quite sure just what would follow. He wanted to keep his options open.

After what seemed like an eternity to most of his people, Machk spoke once again. "We will stay and listen to your story."

Captain Hill nodded. "We will gladly tell it." His hand slowly raised into the air, and the people behind him whooped and shouted, moving forward and welcoming the new arrivals.

The people of Kittanning proved to be wonderful hosts. Fires were soon blazing, and meat and vegetables were roasting. They were ushered to a long house at the end of the settlement where they could put their belongings and little ones. Some of the older children begged to be allowed to join in the festivities, but mothers firmly settled the matter. It had been a long day and little bodies needed their rest.

Once all the women and children were fed and settled, the leaders gathered around the fire, even though the long journey had all of them longing for their beds.

The pipe was passed and questions began. Machk told of their village on Great Island and the visit from the white men who took down one of the giant trees and floated the trunk down the river. He stared into the flames before he continued. "There are several Indian villages in the area, but we do not want to mix with the white men. We would rather find our own place than live among them," he said quietly. "As you can see, our clan is small. Most of the villagers came with us."

He looked up into the eyes of their leader. "Do you know Shikellimy? Have you traveled far to the rising sun?" Machk asked with pleading eyes. "The white man comes in droves. They have taken much of the land."

"That is why we must stop them," Captain Hill argued. Machk heard the grunts of agreement circle the group.

"I agree but would it not be better to strike at the underbelly than at the tail?"

Captain Hill cocked his head, "Yes, but I do not understand what you mean."

Machk became animated. He had been thinking about this idea throughout their whole trip and even longer. He had shared some of his thoughts with Ahanu and the others, and they agreed. "The white men are divided. They come from different tribes, these French and British. I am not certain which are stronger, but both sides want our help."

Another of the warriors chimed in, "But why would we fight with the white man. We need to kill them all!" he shouted.

Machk leaned forward. "Find the stronger and help him to strike the belly."

There was silence as the idea was tossed about in their minds. Finally, Captain Hill spoke. "The French have lived alongside the Indian for over a hundred years. They have traded with us and treated us fairly, but the English make bad treaties, like the Walking Purchase."

Some hissed their disapproval and stomped their feet, sounding like snakes and tom toms.

Machk hesitated before he went on. "This is true, but these two tribes are very different. Both clans have good and bad men within them. Some good men come and tell us of their God, the Almighty God." He stopped momentarily, letting the words sink in, but he could already sense the resistance. He sat tall and looked around the fire and into the eyes of his men. He saw their affirming looks and continued. "We are followers of the One true God, and we pray to Him for wisdom."

Captain Hill's lips curled in disdain. "It is the white man's god," he spat.

But Machk did not back down. "You are wrong Captain Hill. This God is for all men. He has helped us and made us stronger than we have ever been before."

Captain Hill sat back, eyeing Machk and the others. "Are you willing to put those words to the test?"

Ever so slowly, a smile spread across his face. "We are, but if our God leads us to victory, will you consider Him to be the God of all men?"

A look of astonishment passed quickly over the leader's face and then vanished. Astonishment was a sign of weakness. He stared at Machk, then at his men, and then back into the faces of the strangers around his fire. Who were these men? He had heard of Indians who followed another god but had never met any. Did they possess a power beyond human strength? The thought both scared him and intrigued him.

"Agreed," he affirmed and murmurs of excitement circled the group.

The meeting was over. It was late and soon pockets of men were going in every direction. As Ahanu and the others fell into step with Machk they were all silent until they stood before the long house. Ahanu looked around, but no one was in sight. "Do you think that was a good idea?" he asked. "What if we lose?"

Machk smiled. "Do you think our God will let us lose?"

"But," began Degataga, "did you see the size of some of his men?"

Machk chuckled. "We'll leave the big ones for the winner of the canoe race."

Ahanu rolled his eyes and went inside. He could feel Siskia's eyes upon him as he readied for rest. She waited patiently until he was nestled beside her. He looked at her briefly before reaching to her other side where Sucki lay sleeping peacefully. He stared at the sweet calm that rested upon his son's face, wondering, not for the first time, what he would face in his lifetime. He brushed his finger over the smooth warm cheek and then fixed his gaze on Siskia. How beautiful she was!

"We will have a tournament tomorrow," he said in a low voice.

Siskia wanted to question him but waited.

There was really nothing to say and Ahanu rolled to his back.

Siskia reached for his arm and squeezed the rock-solid muscle. "You will win," she whispered excitedly.

He turned to look at her. "Pray that we all win. Machk has made this a tournament of honor to our God. If we win, the chief has agreed to listen to our words but if not..." He left the sentence hang, not wanting to state the obvious.

Siskia snuggled down into his embrace. "Then we will pray," she stated simply, and he knew she was doing just that.

The sun rose bright and hot into a cloudless canopy of vibrant blue. It would be a hot day for the tournament. Machk had called the men to follow him into the woods before sunrise, and, after finding a secluded dell near a cheery brook, they all knelt in the cool shade of giant fir trees and sought the aid of their Heavenly Father. Their prayers were simple but heartfelt, filled with more faith and trust than many prayers which ascended arch-ceilinged structures of stone and stained-glass windows.

When Machk closed their prayer meeting, they all sat back on their haunches for a moment, taking in the peaceful surroundings that seemed to match the peace that rested upon their hearts.

Finally, Machk stood and faced the others. "We will be true, whether we win or lose. If we win, then we will know that God is in this place, and we have a purpose, but if we lose, then we will know that their hearts choose to remain in darkness."

The others nodded.

Akopee and Blue Feather watched from their hiding place as the strangers walked back towards the village. They looked at one another not certain of what they just witnessed.

"Who do you think they were talking to?" Akopee finally asked.

Blue Feather shook his head. "It sounded as though they were talking to a friend not a god."

Akopee grunted. "How could a god be a friend?"

Blue Feather shrugged his shoulders and silence pervaded the woods. Only the sound of the first bird songs of the morning could be heard in the distance. Akopee would compete with the sling and Blue Feather with arrows in the day's competition, and Captain Hill had told them to keep an eye on the strangers. The two warriors had camped outside the visitors' long house that night.

"Strange," Akopee continued. He rose to his feet and led the way back to the village, both men deep in thought. Just who or what would they be facing today?

After a small morning meal, the two groups gathered near the open field where the games would take place. Targets had been set up for the bow and arrow competition and Ahanu looked at the tamped down circle of dried grass in the center—the wrestling circle. He eyed the crowd, looking for the biggest man. He wasn't hard to find. Beedeedee stood with his arms crossed over his massive chest smirking at Ahanu. Ahanu's heart sank. The man was a giant!

Siskia felt more than saw Ahanu's reaction and pulled on his arm. She jerked her head away from the crowd, summoning Ahanu to a quiet spot, turning him to face her. Her eyes danced with excitement. "Ahanu, I just remembered a story that the missionary once told us as children back in my home village. It was about a boy, or very young man, who fought a giant. He used a sling, but that's not what killed the giant."

Ahanu watched as her eyes flashed with more than just excitement. He saw her faith in her God and in him as well.

"All the other warriors were too frightened to fight. But the young man who was not even a warrior volunteered to fight the giant... because he knew the battle was God's, not his." She searched Ahanu's face for understanding. "Don't you see, Ahanu? You are that boy! Yes, you are a warrior, and you are brave, but you are so much more! You are God's child! He will strengthen you and help you in ways that even you do not understand!"

Ahanu bent low and kissed her, their faces close enough that he could feel her breath. "Will you still trust me and God if I do not win?" he asked quietly.

He saw the shocked look on her face. "Of course I will. Our God knows everything. He will do what is best." She squeezed his hand. "And I will follow you to the ends of the earth," she added fiercely, her eyes blazing with loyalty.

Ahanu squared his shoulders and walked proudly beside his wife.

Captain Hill and several other leaders ceremoniously made their way into the wrestling circle and turned to face the crowd.

As Ahanu listened, his mind went back to Bald Eagle's Nest and another fight. That contest led to a part of his past he wished to forget, and he wondered what this contest would accomplish. He tuned back into the chief's words when Machk stepped forward. Savanukah, Degataga, and Kanatase were not far behind and he joined their rank. As he did so, he saw the giant step forward with three others.

Captain Hill looked pleased as he surveyed his warriors. They were all strong, talented men. "Akopee," he called out and one of the warriors stepped forward. Captain Hill faced Machk. "He will compete with the sling."

Degataga stepped up, but his eyes then darted to Hurit who stood with his people. He would win not only for his God but for Hurit too.

"Running Fox," Captain Hill called. Another man stepped forward and stood beside Akopee. "Running Fox runs like the wind," Captain Hill nearly shouted and the people cheered.

Without a word, Kanatase stepped forward. He eyed his opponent with no expression showing on his face.

He nodded to Running Fox and stood erect.

"Blue Feather will fight with his bow," Captain Hill shouted, and a young man blithely stepped out of the crowd and took his place. Savanukah did the same.

"Beedeedee," Captain Hill began but was interrupted by the hoots and stomping of his people. The giant swaggered through the crowd and towards Ahanu. He did not stop to stand beside the others but walked up to Ahanu and towered over him, sneering with delight, but Ahanu stood his ground.

Seeing no response, Beedeedee harrumphed, and joined his ranks. Ahanu moved forward and stood beside Savanukah ready to fight. He felt a strange calmness come over him and looked up into the sky. Never before had he felt such a presence of the Lord. He gasped slightly and noticed that some of the others looked in the direction he was staring, expecting to see something or someone approaching.

An uneasy murmur passed through the people of Kittanning, and Captain Hill knew he must put an end to it.

"We will begin!" he shouted. "We battle in the traditions of our people," he stated, emphasizing the word "our." "You know the rules. We compete with fairness." He looked around to see if anyone questioned his meaning and then nodded to Beedeedee who took his place in the ring.

They were all surprised that the wrestling was first, but Captain Hill knew that Beedeedee would win and he needed to shake whatever spell these strangers had put on his people.

Ahanu would always remember that day. He knew he would win before he even fought. Beedeedee's confidence was in his strength, but Beedeedee was awkward and clumsy, even more so than Lakose.

Beedeedee wasted no time and came lunging at Ahanu, but Ahanu simply dodged him. The crowd laughed at Ahanu, taking him to be a coward, but when Beedeedee crashed to the ground, they were silenced.

Machk watched on, wishing that he could have competed as well, but now he realized that his battle was with the unseen hosts of heaven and hell, and he began to pray.

Beedeedee picked himself up and roared like the mad bull that he was! He charged Ahanu again, but once again Ahanu simply stepped out of the way. This time, however, Ahanu balled up both his fists and smashed them into the giant's side. Beedeedee cried out in pain. He did not fall but turned quicker than anyone would have thought possible. Any other fighter may have been taken by surprise, but Ahanu's skills were as much mental as they were physical.

He knew he would need to engage in physical battle soon enough, but Ahanu also knew that if he got within the grasp of this man, he would not survive. Beedeedee's hands were huge, and his legs were like tree trunks.

Ahanu danced in front of Beedeedee, taunting him. He wished that he had a sling like the boy in Siskia's story. That would have been easier!

Beedeedee ran for Ahanu, who continued to skirt the edge of the circle. He zigzagged back and forth, and at just the right moment, he came at Beedeedee with his shoulders down and aimed for the giant's right knee. As Beedeedee reached for Ahanu, everyone could hear a sickening crunch, and Beedeedee's leg buckled and he lay on the ground, writhing in pain. He struggled to get up, but his right leg would not hold his weight.

Ahanu waited. Was this it? Would they call the match? As the crowd watched, the giant tried again and again to rise to his feet without success.

The leaders looked back and forth and then to Captain Hill. What could they do? Reluctantly, one stepped forward and raised Ahanu's arm in victory.

Machk and his people cheered wildly. Their God had done this! Ahanu walked out of the circle, never looking back. He found Siskia and held her close. Tears were coursing down her cheeks, and Ahanu was surprised. She was always so strong, one of the characteristics that had drawn him to her. But as he looked, he saw that they were tears of joy.

The other contests all ended the same: Chief Machk and his people were the victors. Some of the villagers seemed shocked while others looked angry, and Machk wondered if their victories would be enough to prove to these people that their God was the one true God.

That evening, after the festivities and feasting had ended, Captain Hill stood before his people, bringing silence to the group. The night was still, and the fire crackled sending sparks into the air as a log fell among the coals. He surveyed his people and then turned to the others. "You are a strong nation. You have proven that today." He stood in silence as though weighing his next words carefully. "We will listen to you. Tell us about your God." Without ceremony, he sat down and waited.

All of the people looked to Chief Machk, and he wished that his father were still alive. He would know what to say to these people! What did he know? *Tell them what you know, and it will be enough,* a still small voice said to him inside his heart. He had prayed for his warriors; now they were doing the same for him.

He stood to his feet and looked into the fire. "After a great day of tournament and feasting, our people would then make sacrifices to our god, thanking him for our victories. It is customary for the winner to honor his god— to offer an animal to show our worship." He paused to gather his thoughts, and when he continued, his voice was strong, filled with power from the Almighty God.

"But we offer an even greater sacrifice. We offer ourselves." Murmurs rumbled as the unbelievers tried to comprehend. Would these strangers kill themselves?

"What if we could die but stay alive?" He looked into the questioning faces around him and grew animated.

"What if we offer our lives, our hands?" he said as he raised his hands to the starry sky. "What if we give Him our feet to go where He wants us to go? We become a living sacrifice, and we live for Him."

He could see their confusion and looked to the others, urging them to pray more. "We give him our hearts because He sacrificed His own Son on a cross many winters ago. I see the confusion on your faces. That makes no sense to us. We are strong people, but we are slaves to our gods. They are false gods who try to destroy our souls. But the one true God knew we needed a warrior to fight for us against the enemies of our hearts." He pounded his chest. "There is no greater warrior than the son of a chief." His eyes found Chenoa's, trying to imagine sacrificing the child they had not yet seen.

He looked back across the crowd, his voice barely above a whisper. "How much love would it take for a chief to sacrifice his son for his people?" Another murmur of surprise could be heard.

"This is what the one true God did for us—for all His people everywhere—here in Kittanning and even across the great waters. Why would He do such a thing? He knew it was the only way to rescue our souls from the fire." He stared into the golden flames before him. "The eternal fire that eats at our souls but never consumes them. Only the blood of His Son could take away our sins, because only His Son had the power to die and come alive again." He continued to stare into the flames, lost in his thoughts until he realized that they were silently waiting for him to continue.

"This is the God we serve. He helped us win today. He gave us strength to walk away from our homes, and He will give us the strength to continue on to where He wants us to go.

"We can stay here if we are welcome, or we can go to the Ohio Country to start our new life."

Machk sat in the circle of men, not certain what would happen next. The air was tense with warring spirits. He had felt certain that if they won, the people would receive them and their God, but now he wasn't certain.

Finally, Captain Hill rose to his feet. He too had sensed the rivalry between the spirits and didn't like it. What would their gods do if they forsook them, especially now as they prepared to fight the white man like never before? And how would this white man's God feel about them warring against the white man?

"You have won this fight, and you have told us of your God. Now, as chief of Kittanning, I will say that you must go." Like a silent rush of wind, the sense of satanic victory swept the air. "You may stay as long as you need before you move on, but you must go."

Machk rose and nodded his understanding. His heart was sad, but his soul was relieved. He could feel the opposition not only in the people but in the gods they served.

*   *   *

Kittanning was abuzz with activity for the next few days. Although the visitors were treated kindly, there was a sense of unrest. No one had shown any signs of desire for their God, and the longer they stayed, the bolder they became in their resistance. Some even called them names and whispered loudly as they passed by. It was time to move on.

They had decided to leave in three days in order to gather food and supplies. The women were busy drying fish which the boys had caught, when a large party of canoes could be seen coming from the north. Siskia looked on with the others who worked just a stone's throw from where they had entered the village just a short time earlier, watching with general unconcern as the canoes approached.

The villagers grew more and more animated as the troupe came near, obviously recognizing some of the approaching Indians.

The women chattered in delight, and the men pushed forward to meet the welcome guests.

Siskia could see some of the faces and realized that some of them were French traders. Memories of her childhood home came flooding into her mind as the scene unfolded. How many times had she done the same thing, excitedly welcome anyone who would break the chain of daily drudgery? She smiled as the canoes made land, busily placing the meat on the racks to dry.

"Welcome Chief Pontiac," Captain Hill shouted, and Siskia's head snapped up as her heart dropped to the bottom of her stomach. He was there, Pontiac.

Chapter Eight

A Different Kind of Enemy

Yea, mine own familiar friend, in whom I trusted,
which did eat of my bread, hath lifted up his heel against me
Psalm 41:9

Siskia stared at the seemingly familiar Indian as he got out of the canoe. His tall, slender figure and the way he tipped his head as he greeted the chief all solidified the truth: Pontiac was here and now a chief, but of what tribe? Where did he now live? What was he doing here? Her heart raced with questions to which she wasn't certain that she wanted to hear the answers. Before Siskia could look away, Pontiac's eyes found hers.

For as long as Pontiac could remember, it had become his habit to survey the women's faces in search of the one he feared he had lost forever. Long ago, hope had died in his heart.

When Tsiokwaris had left their village, Pontiac knew the Praying Indians were part of the reason. He also knew that Tsiokwaris was not happy with Chief Deganawidah's plans to fight. *That hadn't gone the way they had planned!* Pontiac thought to himself. The chief and his sons had all been killed along with many of their warriors.

Pontiac had had no designs of becoming chief, but the mantle had fallen upon him, and he took it. But many were not happy with the idea of having a Praying Indian as their chief, and soon other rivals began to rise to the top, demanding a match to prove true leadership. He had declined and became known as the wandering chief— searching for his lost love. A small band of discontented men and women chose to follow him, choosing the life of nomads, much like their forefathers had done on coming to their home by the lakes of the north. It was a good life, but Pontiac was lonely and longed for Siskia. Where had they gone? Logic told him to head west, which he had.

Now he was making his way back to the land of the rising sun, determined to find her or someone else to take her place. And now, there she was!

Their eyes locked, and Pontiac saw no one, heard no one. Captain Hill watched curiously as his friend seemingly ignored him. Pontiac had stopped in the village on his way west, and the two had shared the same heart-desire to have their lands returned to their people. He watched with intrigue as the young man bee-lined to a group of the visiting women.

Siskia wanted to run. She wanted to cry. Oh, where was Ahanu? All the women stopped their work as Pontiac approached. Wearing several eagle feathers in his hair to signify his leadership, he presented a striking appearance as he strode forward with purpose. But as he approached his pace slowed slightly. He studied Siskia's face looking for the joy that he had in his heart, but it was not there.

The children who had been playing at the water's edge came near as well, and Sucki ran to his mother, clinging to her leg. Pontiac stopped mid-stride and took in the scene. What did this mean? Was the child hers? Perhaps he was only a nephew or stranger's child under her care. But as he studied the face of the child, there was no doubt in his mind who had given him birth!

His eyes shot up to Siskia who stood transfixed. Her eyes were pleading and sad. She reached down and scooped up Sucki and headed for the long house, never looking back.

Pontiac watched her go, his jaw twitching as he realized a truth he had never considered. Siskia belonged to someone else.

The other women watched curiously but soon returned to their task, leaving the stranger to himself. Trying fiercely to gain his composure, Chief Pontiac, squared his shoulders and returned to the greeting party.

"Forgive me," he said to the captain. "I seem to have made a mistake."

Captain Hill looked at him questioningly, but Pontiac did not reply. "Come, my friend," Hill replied. "We will talk." The two leaders left the others and went to the chief's longhouse where they could talk in peace.

Siskia felt the hot tears running down her cheeks as she nearly ran to the long house. Thankfully, no one was inside—there was too much to do. She sat down on their mat and hugged the little boy fiercely. He enjoyed the attention but looked at her questioningly. "Mommy sad?" he asked.

She did not answer but rocked him back and forth. Just then the opening of the hut darkened as the form of a man filled it. Ahanu came to her with concern written on his face. "Siskia, what is wrong?" he asked, sitting down beside her.

She leaned close and wept but did not answer. Sucki looked at his father in fear, and Ahanu lifted him to his lap. He stroked Siskia's long hair and waited for an answer, praying for his wife. He knew he did not have to ask again. She would tell him when she could.

Slowly, the tears subsided and Siskia lifted her tear-stained face. "I love you, Ahanu," she whispered.

Ahanu cocked his head to one side and looked confused.

Siskia swallowed hard. "Pontiac is here," she said.

Ahanu's brows raised, but he still looked confused. "He is no threat to us."

"He is a chief," she explained. "What if he chooses to take me away?"

Ahanu thought for a moment. It was true that a chief had great power. He had seen wicked men trade women like cattle. He looked at Siskia. "But you said he is a Praying Indian. Surely he would not do this if he follows the true God."

"You did not see him, Ahanu. His eyes were so full of hurt when he looked at Sucki. He knows I belong to someone else. And by the way Captain Hill greeted him, they are good friends. Perhaps he has forgotten God."

"But he has no claim on you..." Ahanu stopped and looked at Siskia. "Does he?"

Siskia's eyes grew wide. "Only a childhood promise," she whispered. Tears filled her eyes. "When we knew we would be parted, we promised that we would be true to each other no matter how long we were apart. I looked for him for three winters when you came to the Great Island." She looked as though her heart was breaking. "My heart belonged to him until you stole it."

It sounded so serious, and yet in Ahanu's mind it seemed trivial. He shook his head. "We have a child and a future together, Siskia." His face grew serious. "I will not let him take you away. God will not allow it." He purposed to calm himself and reached for her hand. "We will pray," he said quietly and bowed his head.

Together they committed their lives to their almighty Father. "Give us your wisdom, dear God. May Pontiac remember You and choose to do right."

Chenoa flew to find Machk. She did not like the look that the new chief had given Siskia. And then she had run off. Surely something was not right.

She found him with the men and stood before him. He didn't miss the urgency in her face and rose to his feet, leading her to beyond the thicket which bordered the woods. "Chenoa, what's wrong?" he asked, searching her troubled face.

"People have come to the village. The chief came to Siskia and looked at her as though he knew her. She ran to the long house. I heard her crying."

Machk searched his mind for answers. "Did you hear the chief's name?"

"Chief Pontiac," she panted, still trying to catch her breath, knowing that her breathing was affected as much from the excitement as the run.

Machk's face showed recognition.

"You know who he is?" she asked.

Machk nodded. "He was in love with Siskia. He is from our home village. He was part of the reason that we left."

Chenoa looked at him questioningly.

"He was a Praying Indian, and my father didn't want that for his daughter."

Chenoa shook her head. "So much has changed."

Machk reached for his wife and held her close for a moment. "I will go and see him," he said with authority. "You do not need to worry. We were friends."

Chenoa shook her head against his chest. "You did not see his face, Machk. Please be careful."

Machk hugged her once more, squeezing her shoulders to encourage her to be strong, and walked towards the long house. He had not worn his feathers since they had first arrived, but knew he needed to show his authority. He didn't want any trouble, but he did not trust Captain Hill.

Savanukah, Degataga and Kanatase followed their chief to Captain Hill's house. Two warriors stood as sentinels signaling that the chiefs were not to be disturbed. They stood even more erect when they saw the group of four striding toward them.

Chief Machk stood before them speaking loudly in hopes that the two men inside would hear them and intervene. "I have come to see Captain Hill and my friend Chief Pontiac."

"They are not to be disturbed," said the one, but had hardly finished when Pontiac came out, followed by Captain Hill. His eyes shone with delight, and he went to Machk, embracing him.

"My brother," Pontiac said, his face lit with joy. Before Machk could answer, Pontiac looked past him to the other three, naming each of them.

"Savanukah, Degataga, Kanatase!" He pulled each into an embrace while his new friend looked on with a hint of disdain on his face.

Chief Pontiac turned to face Captain Hill. "These are my friends. They are from my home village," he explained. Captain Hill only nodded understanding. "You must excuse us, Captain. We have much to discuss."

Without another glance, Pontiac strode off to the other end of the village, the five young men walking side by side.

They chattered about their lives and the joy of seeing one another, and Pontiac led them to a clearing in the woods where logs formed a circle around a fire pit. After they had settled in, Pontiac turned to Savanukah first. With sadness in his voice, he told them of their demise, his call to leadership and his mission.

"I am seeking to help the French in their battle against the English. I have traveled far to the west and am once again heading towards the rising sun to rally our people to join us." He paused for a moment before continuing in a low voice. "And I have been searching for Siskia as well for nearly five winters," he added. No one missed the anger in his voice.

He looked up at his friends, especially Machk. "And now I find her with a child—her child," he nearly shouted. "Please tell me that the father is dead!"

"I am not dead," came the menacing voice from the edge of the woods. Machk turned to see Ahanu striding into the circle. His eyes were full of fire.

Pontiac looked at the giant of a man and his lips curled in disgust. He looked back at Machk. "A Susquehannock! How can this be?"

Machk felt the tension as it circled the group. As though on cue, Savanukah, Degataga, and Kanatase rose to their feet and went to stand by Ahanu.

Machk and Pontiac both rose to their feet at the same time. "Pontiac, you know we left partly because you were a Praying Indian. My father became a follower of the true God as well. And so have we." He looked at Ahanu with love and compassion. "Ahanu is a Susquehannock. He is my brother in body and spirit. Siskia chose him for her husband, and I am proud to say so."

Pontiac looked from face to face, his own hot with emotion. His lips curled once more. "But we promised, and Iroquois keep their promises. You are calling Siskia a liar. I will not believe this until I speak to her face to face... alone!" Pontiac turned and marched away.

Machk started to follow but Savanukah caught his arm. "Let him go."

The five friends came together in a tight circle. Savanukah was first to speak. "I do not trust him, Machk. He is like a raging mother bear who has lost her whelps. He grieves but anger is clouding his senses."

"But what can he do?" asked Ahanu.

Machk looked into the hurting face of his friend. "I fear that he will try to steal her away. Their lives were entwined together for as long as I can remember."

Ahanu's eyes flashed.

"This does not mean that she does not love you, Ahanu. You must know that, but Pontiac has searched for her for five winters, all the time thinking she was waiting for him. His pride is smashed, and the thing he has hoped for is now gone. But he will convince himself that she will love him if he can get her away from you." He paused for emphasis and added emphatically. "He is wrong, Ahanu! He is deadly wrong."

Pontiac seethed as he headed back to camp. His mind raced for a plan. He was certain that Siskia still loved him. Could he force her to go? What would his people do? Blinded by rage, Pontiac could only think of one thing—getting Siskia, and the sooner the better. They would not think that he would just steal her away, but they were wrong!

He knew they would be making a plan, but by the time they hatched their scheme, he would be gone! He ran to the long house where she had gone. Sure enough, she was still there—alone!

Siskia looked up in surprise as Pontiac came crashing into the house. She gasped. "Pontiac," she cried and he took that as a good sign, hearing joy instead of surprise in her voice.

He came to her and grabbed her arm, pulling her to her feet.

"What are you doing?" she cried.

"You are coming with me," he spat. "You will one day thank me, Siskia." He looked at the sleeping Sucki in disgust and pulled her to the doorway, but Siskia fought hard.

Afraid that she might cry out, he gagged her and tied her hands together. He then threw her over his shoulder and ran away from the village and prying eyes. He knew Captain Hill stashed several canoes down river in case of enemy attack and headed that way. He smiled, realizing that his plan was working. He would be long gone before anyone was the wiser. She would thank him. She would.

The men went back to their work, and Ahanu would join them, but first he would check on Siskia. She had been pretty upset when he left, and he wanted to assure her that he would not do anything drastic.

He entered the long house and waited a moment for his eyes to adjust to the darkness. The stillness set him on edge but he pushed aside the thoughts of any harm coming to his dear ones. Quickening his steps, he found Sucki snuggled down on the soft animal skins, puffing gently. Ahanu scanned the room. Perhaps she went back to the river to help the women, and yet, he didn't think she'd leave Sucki unattended. Maybe she needed to relieve herself. He swiftly crossed the room and checked the nearby woods. Nothing. His strong strides took him to the water's edge where the women worked, chatting and laughing together. No Siskia!

"Did Siskia come back to work here?"

They all looked at one another, alarm growing on their faces as each one shook her head, "no!"

Ahanu looked about wildly trying to think of what Pontiac would have done. He raced to Captain Hill's house and barged in, in spite of the sentinels.

"Where is Chief Pontiac?" he cried.

Captain Hill looked up in surprise. "He's with his friends," he sneered.

"You haven't seen him since then?" Ahanu demanded.

Captain Hill did not hide his annoyance. "No," was all he said.

Ahanu rushed from the house. Who could help him? Time was of the essence. Where would he go if he was going to get away quickly? He looked at the woods and then the river and took off running towards their canoes. Without a word to anyone, he quickly jumped into the canoe and headed downstream, paddling with all his might. If he were wrong... he wouldn't think about that! *Oh, Father! Please help me to find Siskia!* he prayed with each stroke.

Siskia kicked and rocked the canoe until Pontiac bound her feet and legs. She looked at him with pleading eyes, but he ignored her, needing to put as much distance as he could between them and that Susquehannock!

She continued to rock the canoe as much as she could, knowing that it would slow them down. She was right. Pontiac's goal was to get to the fork in the river before the Susquehannock caught them, but it was half as far as they had already come.

Ahanu's powerful arms pushed his canoe through the water at break-neck speed. He purposely chose the fastest flowing parts of the river, and hope sprang in his heart when the river straightened, and he could see another canoe in the distance. It was only a dot on the water, but he knew it had to be Pontiac!

As he drew nearer he could see the canoe rocking wildly and praised God for Siskia! The sight served to drive him forward.

Pontiac was nearly to the fork when he glanced behind him and saw a canoe approaching speedily. Like a wild animal, he dug his oar into the water and raced forward, but it was no use. Ahanu was nearly upon him.

As Ahanu drew near, Pontiac lunged for Siskia and pulled her to him, also pulling his knife from its sheath. "Stay back if you want her to live," he shouted.

Ahanu sat motionless, not certain what to do. He eyed Pontiac and saw sheer panic on his face.

"Pontiac, she is my wife," he said pleadingly. "Please do not hurt her."

"She is mine," Pontiac shouted like a madman, and his lip began to quiver.

Tears ran down Siskia's face and fell on Pontiac's hand. He looked at the wetness and then into Siskia's eyes. They pleaded with him.

Slowly, he loosed the gag from her mouth and brushed her disheveled hair from her face. "Oh, Siskia, why did you not wait for me?"

Siskia sobbed. "I did wait, Pontiac. I waited three winters but you did not come."

"I didn't know where you were," Pontiac cried. He saw the surprise in her eyes.

"I thought you knew."

As they both considered each other's thoughts, Pontiac's face softened. "You waited three winters, thinking I knew where you were but didn't come?" He shook his head. "How could you think that I would not come?" But even as he asked the question, he knew he was not being fair to her. She honestly thought that he knew.

He held her close to his chest as she cried. Methodically, he cut the straps from her arms and legs but continued to hold her close. The sight nearly drove Ahanu crazy, especially as the sun glinted off the blade he still held in his hand.

"Do you love him?" he whispered.

Siskia pushed herself away and looked into his face. It was contorted with pain, and it broke her heart.

"Oh, Pontiac, you know that I do. We had a taste of sweet love, the wonder of first love. It will always be in my heart, but, before our heavenly Father, I vowed to love this man and be his wife. Can I break that vow, Pontiac?"

He looked into her eyes in wonder. "Are you a believer, Siskia?"

She smiled and nodded. "Ahanu is too. We all are. The white man came near our village, and he told us the way of truth." Tears came fresh to her eyes. "I thought of you, Pontiac, when I heard his words."

She laid her hand on his cheek. "You began my journey to God, but Ahanu must finish it, not you." Her words were strong and forceful, and he understood. He held her once again and then released her, putting his knife back in its place. His eyes found Ahanu, and the two men stared at each other.

Ahanu was the first to speak. "I do not deserve her, Pontiac."

The words startled Pontiac. He looked in wonder at the love that he saw in the big man's face. Ahanu's words had softened Pontiac's face and heart. "If you truly believe that, then, in the name of our God and His Son Jesus, I release her from her promise."

Ahanu drew to the side of the canoe and held it while Siskia gingerly stepped across. He wanted to hold her, to hug her and kiss her, but he did not want to offend Pontiac or make him any sadder at his loss.

Siskia, however, had other plans. She threw herself into Ahanu's strong arms and wept. Ahanu looked over her shoulder and made a helpless gesture, and Pontiac offered him a weak smile.

As they rode back to Kittanning, Siskia and Pontiac caught up on each other's lives while Ahanu listened. He thought about his own childhood. Had he ever had such a friendship as these two shared? The thought made him sad.

"Why do you frown?" Pontiac asked abruptly, thinking that their talk made the man jealous.

Ahanu looked into Pontiac's eyes, reading his thoughts. "I never had a friendship like you and Siskia share when I was a child. I can hear the friendship roots go very deep."

Siskia sat silently, pondering his words and feeling a bit awkward. It was Pontiac who broke the discomfort. "We have been friends for a long time." He looked at Siskia, amazed at the change in his heart. It was as though God had momentarily removed the painful desire to have her as his own, and now he was able to just enjoy her company while her husband watched. "But I can also see the love you have for each other. It runs deep and is good—better than a childhood love."

Siskia blushed. It was time to change the subject. "Why are you friends with Captain Hill? He has no time for the true God."

Pontiac smiled at her frankness—the thing he missed the most. "He is not a believer, but we share the same thoughts about the white man. We must not allow the English to take more land. I believe the French will deal fairly with us when the English are driven away."

"I wish they would all just go away," Siskia murmured, making Ahanu remember his grandfather's words: *They will never leave. The white man has seen our bountiful land and will want it. It is too much to walk away from.*

"The white man has seen our bountiful land and will want it. It is too much to walk away from," Ahanu said. "My grandfather told me these words when I was just a boy. He had seen many white men with his grandfather many, many winters ago. We have given away too much already. They will just keep coming and coming across the great waters." His voice dropped. "We cannot stop them."

"But we must try!" Pontiac said fiercely. "If we do not try, our people will all be dead."

Ahanu's battles had been with the Iroquois not the white man, but Siskia and Pontiac had seen first-hand what the white man could do.

"We are heading west in three days. You can go fight your wars. We want peace for our son," Ahanu said. He heard the sting of his words and knew that Pontiac had felt the barb. They rode in silence the rest of the way.

The village was in turmoil when they arrived. Machk and his people were preparing their canoes for flight and the Kittanning villagers were in heated discussions with Pontiac's people. When their canoes reached the shore, all gathered round to get the story correct—so many tales had been circulated among them in a short time.

Ahanu and Siskia walked to Machk. Relief spread across his face but soon grew stern. "We need to leave now," he said emphatically.

Although they had many questions, Ahanu just nodded and walked with Siskia to find their son. When Sucki saw his parents, he cried out and reached for them. Chenoa smiled and handed him to Siskia. "All is well?" she asked timidly.

Siskia smiled weakly and nodded.

When the final items had been placed into the last canoe, Machk and his people gathered on the shore. Captain Hill stood beside Chief Pontiac in solidarity and silence. Machk walked to Pontiac and reached to embrace him. "Be careful, friend," Machk said quietly into Pontiac's ear.

"You too, brother," Pontiac replied. "I hope we will meet again."

Machk nodded. "We will find a home in Ohio Country. Perhaps when this war is over, we will find friendship once again."

"God goes with you," said Pontiac, sensing the daggers from his comrade.

"And with you," Machk offered. He turned to his people, and they readied to depart. But no one saw the curl of Pontiac's lip as he watched his one and only love glide noiselessly away in the canoe of another man. His thoughts turned cold, slicing into his heart like a knife, dissolving all thoughts of God.

The village of Kiskiminetas was not far down river and they arrived there in the early evening. The children were tired, and the travelers were thankful for the warm welcome they received. A much smaller village than Kittanning, Kiskiminetas was like stepping back in time. Nestled in the woods beside the Allegheny River, the place was peaceful and not interested in fighting. Siskia wondered if it might be a good place to settle down, but after listening to the men talk, she agreed they were still too close to the rising sun.

They retired early, planning on rising at dawn and continuing down the Allegheny, hoping to reach the village of Toquhese before too late in the day.

As they laid down in another guest long house, Ahanu held Siskia close in the darkness, longing for time alone with her.

"Are you settled with today's affairs?" Ahanu whispered into her hair.

She nuzzled closer, resting her face against his chest. He felt the wetness of her tears. "I was so afraid you would not find us."

He squeezed her hand and brought it to his lips for a kiss. "I would hunt until the day I died to find you," he said huskily. "You are my greatest treasure."

She was once again amazed at his tender words, which brought a fresh flow of tears to her eyes. "I know," she whispered.

They lay in silence for a moment, listening to the evening sounds of love and sleep which could be heard around them. "And I will love you forever because of it," she added.

Ahanu's chest heaved as he drew in a long breath to quiet his heart before it burst from his chest.

The morning dawned with dark, foreboding clouds overhead and the men wondered if they should wait until the weather cleared before proceeding. The elderly chief assured them that the village of Toquhese was only a short distance down river. "You are more than welcome to stay, but the good people of Toquhese will also make you feel welcome if the rain comes hard."

It was decided that they would push on, but were only a few rods down river when the thunder cracked and the clouds burst forth with their bounty. For all the rumbling that followed, the rain was gentle and finished in a short time.

Soon the sun was peeking out from behind the clouds and feathery, higher white streaks could be seen above the dark puffy ones. Ahanu looked on in wonder. The clouds had always fascinated him, and he wished he knew more about them.

In spots where the shoreline was sandy, steam threaded its way skyward. Siskia breathed in deeply, enjoying the fresh, clean smell. The river continued to deepen and widen into a gently rolling liquid highway as they neared its convergence with the Monongahela.

Machk and Savanukah steered their canoes to Ahanu's, both wanting to hear the details of his chase. Pontiac and Ahanu had walked into camp in silence, Siskia walking proudly beside her husband but between the two men.

As others quietly gathered around them, the two warriors exchanged nods before Siskia and Ahanu went to their people. Siskia had stopped and faced Pontiac, her eyes full of meaning. She had forgiven him, and their friendship had been restored, but there was a look of loyalty in her eyes as she turned to her husband and gratefully took his hand.

As they left the circle, Ahanu and Siskia had heard questioning murmurs, the volume rising and falling as Pontiac answered their questions.

Ahanu had said very little, but his look was enough for his trusted friend and leader to give the order to get ready as soon as possible and leave this place.

Savanukah paddled to the left side and Machk to the right, but Ahanu ignored them—the three canoes continuing to cut through the water in silence.

Finally, Siskia could stand it no longer and reached out of the canoe. Her hand dipped into the water and quickly slapped the surface, sending droplets across Ahanu's back.

He stiffened but remained silent, plunging the oar into the water.

"Ahanu, shall I tell them about my conquering hero?" Siskia asked.

Ahanu grunted and she turned to face her brother. "He had the power of a mighty bear, the cunning of a fox, and the swiftness of the eagle," she began to sing, adapting her words to a common tune among their people.

"He is brave and strong. His honor rises above the clouds, and his courage runs deeper than any water." She continued to sing his praises until Ahanu motioned for her to stop. She wondered if he doubted her sincerity. Surely not!

"Pontiac made a mistake," he said quietly. His paddle resumed a normal speed. "If I had been him, I'm not sure what I would have done, but his love for Siskia was genuine. Sadly, his aching heart clouded his vision, and I am afraid for him."

"What do you mean?" Machk asked.

"He has searched for Siskia ever since she left with her family. Now that he has lost her, his heart is like a mother bear robbed of her cubs." He shook his head sadly. "How will he cope except to pour himself into his mission?"

"Do you mean fighting the English?" Savanukah asked.

Ahanu nodded. "But without Siskia in his future, he will fight like a dog or die to restore the past when she was in his life." They were all silent as they pondered his words. "He will stop at nothing."

"But isn't that why we are here as well?" All faces turned to see Kanatase beside Machk. He had been listening and wondered at Ahanu's words.

"I too have left everything to fight the white man."

"Yes, many of us are here for the same reason, but we must decide who we are fighting, and that is why we left Kittanning so quickly." Machk explained.

"Pontiac has clearly joined Captain Hill to fight against the English, but we trust the English," Ahanu said.

"I trust no one," grumbled Kanatase.

His words shocked the others. Kanatase had been wrestling with these thoughts for a long time. Perhaps these thought had kept him from finding a mate. A single man fought with unreserved fury, and he had always been a fighter.

"Kanatase, the English brought us the truth," said Ahanu.

"So did the French," countered Kanatase. "And the French did not drive us from our homes. I hate them all. It does not matter to me who we fight—just so we fight." Kanatase's face was as dark and foreboding as the clouds that seemed to follow them.

"It becomes a question of who we can trust more," Siskia said. Her voice was full of emotion. Could it be that they would find themselves on the opposite side of Pontiac? As much as she had hated what he had done, he was still a longtime, childhood friend, and the thought of watching these men whom she loved fight against him made her heart ache.

"We will stop at Logstown and pray for answers," Machk said sternly. "Captain Hill told me both the French and the English are vying for the support of the Indians there. We will watch, and listen, and then we will decide."

It was nearly dark when they weary group traveled the last leg of the day's long journey. The sun had set and sleepy children had been bedded down among their things. A nighthawk flew overheard, swooping down.

Fires dotted the village indicating just how large it was. As they glided closer to the clearing, dogs began to bark, signaling their arrival.

The usual greetings were much shorter, and everyone was thankful for a place to rest for the night. Siskia was amazed at the amount of Englishmen who freely mingled with the Indians, and it reminded her once again of her childhood home, except the white men had been French. Part of her sided with Kanatase, remembering the French missionaries who first taught them about Jesus, and again her mind went to Pontiac. He had changed, and she wasn't sure that his words were true.

When Ahanu came from the meeting Machk had called and slipped in beside her, she rolled into his arms and snuggled close, hugging him fiercely.

Ahanu was surprised. "What is all this?" He felt wetness on his chest and knew she was crying.

"Thank you for wanting peace for our family."

Ahanu was silent for a moment, considering her words. Machk and the others wanted to stay and support the English. He knew that would mean more fighting and not peace.

Siskia sensed his hesitation and pushed up on her elbow even though it was too dark to read his face. "What has my brother said?"

Ahanu smiled in spite of the seriousness of the subject. Siskia always referred to Machk as her brother if she sensed he had made a decision that she did not like. "He has decided we will most likely stay here and support the English."

Siskia huffed as she dropped down beside him. "Will he feel the same when the baby arrives?"

"What baby?" he asked in surprise.

Siskia shook her head. *Men!* "Chenoa is expecting a baby. He will most likely come in the spring."

Ahanu let the thought roll around in his mind. Was he different in his thinking because he was now a father? Without a doubt—yes! He thought back to Machk's words, wondering if they were prompted because of Pontiac's actions. "Were Pontiac and Machk friends in your village?"

Siskia thought for a moment. She had always thought that they were, but as she thought about it, several images of Machk's disapproving looks towards Pontiac came to mind. She always thought they were just brotherly concern. "I don't know." She rolled back into his arms. "I must tell you, Ahanu, I hate the thought that you may one day find yourself fighting against Pontiac. He will continue to support the French."

Ahanu shook his head. "Who would have thought our people would one day take sides against each other but with the white men?"

"Oh, Ahanu, I just want to run away! Could we?"

"I've run before. I will not run again." His words were clipped and forced, and she knew better than to say any more.

Machk and his clan would soon find out that Logstown was not just another Indian village. It stood on the banks of three important waterways—important to the French, the English, and many Indian tribes. Many council fires had been held in this spot, and now both white men tribes wanted to control it as well.

The Indian village had been established in 1725 by Shawnees, Delawares, Mingoes, Senecas and others which made the village appealing to Machk. His group was from several of these tribes, and the mix made for friendly relationships. The English presence also made the place attractive.

Machk walked along the shoreline in solitude looking for answers. Should they stay, or should they push on? He wanted to do what was best for his people. Many of the young men wanted to fight, and this seemed like the best place to make a stand. To the west was the Ohio country—a land promised to the Indians by both sides. Perhaps if they stayed and helped the English, they would be satisfied with all the land they had already taken.

He thought about the vast forests they had just passed through and the streams and rivers. The land stretched far to the north and also to the south, he had been told. *Isn't it enough, Father? Can't they be satisfied with what they already have taken? Could we make these mountains the dividing line like so many of our people have suggested?*

He struggled to keep the anger out of his heart. How much had he already lost! Now, he just wanted a place to raise his family. The thought brought a smile to his face.

Watching Ahanu and Siskia and realizing that they too would have a little papoose in the late spring did something to his heart that he had never felt before.

He looked out across the water towards the setting sun. A few lingering clouds slowly slipped across the darkening sky. Patches of yellow, red and orange dotted the forest and he stood still for a moment taking in the surrounding beauty. A fish jumped in the river, and he caught a quick glimpse of a turtle's head before it bobbed beneath the water. A pair of otters played on the opposite side of the river, splashing and chattering as they dipped and slid on the moss covered rocks. It was a good place. They would stay unless the Lord led them otherwise.

Chapter Nine

War!

"The French claim all on one side of the river [the Ohio], and the English all on the other side. Where does the Indian land lie?" – Old Indian Chief

Shawande Village (southeast of Logstown)

Pontiac watched the group of young braves as they wrestled and bantered back and forth. This trip had been very successful. He had recruited quite a few young bucks to his cause, once again thankful for the education the French missionary had given him. His knowledge of the English and French cause and his ability to express himself with confidence had earned the respect he needed among his people and the French, and already he had made a name for himself among the English as well.

However, with those thoughts of his childhood came visions of a young Siskia learning alongside of him, smiling at him admiringly. Lately, those visions had been replaced with a more mature, more beautiful, more alluring vision of the woman he loved—full of life, grace, charm... *Stop!* He chided inwardly. *She is another man's wife!*

"Yes, a man who sides with the English," said the taunting voice, which also tormented his thoughts. *Perhaps she can be yours once again.*

It was not a new thought. Since leaving her at Kittanning his heart had turned to stone, and thoughts of revenge against the white man bled over onto Ahanu. He would not force the hand of God, but if he had the chance in battle, he would do his best to make Siskia a widow!

August, 1748—Logstown

Chenoa watched with pride as Machk sat with other chiefs. They were all much older than her husband, especially Tanacharison, a chief of the Six Nations. He looked older than time and had been one of the founders of the village over twenty winters ago.

Tanacharison, called Half-King, and Scarouady were both respected leaders among the Indians and the English. They were strong men, learned men. Both had spent much time negotiating with the English on behalf of their people and the French, although their last several meetings with the French had not gone well. The French Commandant had treated them more like bad children and had even threatened them.

The conversation around the fire was alive with excitement. George Croghan had visited Logstown with news of another man—an important white man named Conrad Weiser. They had been told this man had lived among the Mohawks and knew their ways. He was a great man to the chiefs, and their excitement was contagious.

As Chenoa listened to the plans that were being discussed, Siskia joined her at the edge of the women's circle.

"It is exciting, isn't it?" Chenoa said to her, but when she looked up into Siskia's eyes, she saw they were filled with worry. "What's wrong Siskia?" she asked, kindness filling every word.

"Could we talk?" Siskia asked. Chenoa nodded. As they rose to their feet and slipped from the group, no one seemed to notice.

The sound of voices and the crackling fire soon faded away as the two women made their way to the long house.

Siskia waited until they were out of the circle of light and away from any curious eyes before she spoke.

"I am afraid, Chenoa."

The statement surprised Chenoa. Siskia was her idol. She was strong and brave. To hear her say that she was afraid—Chenoa couldn't imagine what could have sparked such a confession. "What is wrong, my sister?" she asked anxiously.

The title of endearment warmed Siskia's heart and gave her courage to share her burden. "I am afraid of war and what might happen."

Chenoa smiled slightly. "Oh, Siskia. Your man is strong and brave. And he is very wise. His faith is strong and he trusts the true God."

"But he has a strong enemy," Siskia insisted.

Chenoa looked confused. "Who?"

"Pontiac," Siskia whispered fiercely. "He serves the French. We trust the English. I am afraid he will use this war to kill Ahanu!"

Chenoa was silent, and the words brought new understanding to her heart. "But Pontiac seemed to be friendly to you and Ahanu when you returned to Kittanning."

"I know." Siskia felt foolish. "I don't know what I would do if something happened to Ahanu. So many of our warriors have died fighting the white man."

"But we have a heavenly Father who watches over us," Chenoa said quietly. She felt unworthy to be instructing the one who had taught her so much—had befriended her when no one else even noticed her existence.

Siskia was silent, and Chenoa feared she may have offended her. She began to offer an apology when Siskia spoke.

"You are right, my sister. Thank you for reminding me." She reached for Chenoa's hand and pulled her close. "We will pray that no harm comes to any of our men," Siskia added.

They turned their attention back to the council fire when Half King's voice grew animated. "I told the French father that he and the English are white, and our people live in a country between them; therefore the land belongs to neither one nor the other." Heads were nodding and some even shouted their approval. "But the Great Being above allowed it to be a place of residence for us. Then I told him he must withdraw, but they have not! Instead, they send their puppet Celoron with more of the same words and threats!"

Scarouady picked up the dialogue. "We are done with the French. We will see what the English will do and say." All were in agreement. Time would tell the true hearts of all men.

Three days later, Conrad Weiser came to the village of Logstown, and the Indians were ready. Logstown was teeming with activity. Excitement ran high as word came back from their scouts that Weiser and his men were a short distance away. They had learned from the English the honor of a gun salute and were determined to make Weiser feel welcome. One hundred warriors—each with his gun ready—stood in position wearing native costumes, some more elaborately dressed than others.

Machk, Ahanu, and some of their men had been asked to take part in the salute, which was a great honor to the newcomers. They had not been in Logstown for long, but already they had earned the favor of the leaders who appreciated their character. However, as of yet, none had embraced their beliefs, even though Machk had shared his faith with the chiefs. They had listened with stone faces, which was the norm when a new idea or thought was being heard, but Machk was encouraged by the sincerity he saw behind their silent masks.

All eyes were on the young boy who was perched in the top of a tall maple. He was a chief's son and took this task seriously, knowing the honor that had been bestowed on him.

His eyes were sharp and glued to the river by which they would approach the village. His neck strained and every muscle was taut, like an arrow in the bow ready to be released. Suddenly, his hand shot up into the air. He held it high for the designated moment before dropping it and signaling all the men to fire their guns. The air exploded with the blast of one hundred guns, followed by the whoop of an exultant cry bursting forth from every man, igniting cries of delight from the onlookers.

Conrad looked with alarm at his companions, as the sound of gunfire shattered the stillness. Croghan had assured him that these Indians were friendly to the English, but the shocking boom would have been alarming in any situation. However, when the sound of joyful shouts soon followed, the whole traveling party gave a united sigh of relief.

"Was certainly more than twenty-one guns, I'll wager," Smith said with a glint of admiration in his eyes. He had been traveling with Conrad for nearly twenty years now and worshipped the legendary statesman. Conrad had accomplished much in the colonies, especially for Pennsylvania. His understanding and sympathetic ear to the Indians' ways and needs gave him an air of authority which commanded respect by both the white man and the red.

The day was warm for September; however, there had been an early frost and some of the trees were already showing splashes of color among the greens of the thick forest. Conrad noted the brilliant Virginia creeper climbing a tree along the shore. The contrasts of red, green and gold were breathtaking and, not the first time, he admired the Indians' respect for nature.

His crew deftly steered the canoe to the landing as the chiefs moved forward to greet them. A young boy hopped into the water, oblivious to its cool temperature, and pulled the canoe forward.

Chief Tanacharison the oldest, and most honored chief, stepped forward to make the welcome address. His full headdress trailed after him as he moved forward. Weiser had heard about his chief and his diplomatic endeavors for his people.

"Welcome, Great Tanacharison," Tanacharison proclaimed in a strong voice which all could hear. The name meaning *holder of heaven* had been given to Weiser by the Iroquois, and it went before him wherever he went, opening many doors of negotiation. He only hoped it would do the same here. The governor had sent him here to make a treaty with ten nations including the Shawnee, Delawares and Iroquois. As he glanced across the many faces, he knew that some of these present in this far off place had once peopled the land he now owned. The thought always drove him to do his best to herald their interests.

"You do us great honor by coming to our village. We welcome you and your people."

Conrad bowed low. "Thank you, great chief of Six Nations. I see many different faces and know our time here will be spent wisely."

He bowed once again and then scanned the faces of the other chiefs. Some he knew but others were unfamiliar. It was a large gathering, and he was looking forward to the council fire. However, he also knew there would be feasting and games before any serious business could be negotiated. This had been a long journey, and already he missed his wife and children, but he knew he needed to do this.

*   *   *

1753—Logstown

Tensions continued to rise between the French to the north and west and the English in the south and east. Although the French had better relations with the Indians, their colonies were spread thin throughout New France which stretched from New Orleans up the Mississippi and across the Great Lakes into Canada. The Indians had become dependent on their goods which they traded for the much sought after furs.

In the east, the English colonies were burgeoning with nearly two million Englishmen, and more were arriving every day—outnumbering French settlers twenty to one. The eastern coastline had long been free from any Indian rivals, but as the settlers moved westward, the natives' land was being taken at an alarming rate, and the French were glad to use the situation to influence the tribes to join them in their fight against England.

Settled in the midst of it all, in a little town called Logstown, Indians who were friends to the English continued to make the village their home. Although the village had first been established as a trading post for the Indians by the French, the English traders soon came there as well with more and better items for trade. It was a peaceful time, and for this reason, Machk and those that followed him there enjoyed the peace they had sought.

For six years, Machk and his people chose to stay in this little village. As their children grew and others found mates, they were thankful for the life God had given them. For the first time in a long time they enjoyed normal living: children playing, men hunting, and women keeping the home fires burning. However, the winds of war were blowing, and signs of the tensions were soon felt.

Siskia listened to the sounds of hammers and saws as she tilled the earth. It was planting time and she needed to finish before the rains began. With little Togquos strapped to her back and Sucki watching his sister, Waneek, at the edge of the plot, she kept a steady rhythm with her hoe. Ahanu was scouting with the men and would be back before long to find out what all the noise was about. Someone was certainly making a racket.

That evening the families gathered with their clan. They had moved to the eastern edge of the village and built their own long houses to keep their families together, and they weren't the only ones to do so. Even though they worked together as a whole, their village had several divisions of Delawares, Shawnee, and other tribes which had migrated there. Siskia smiled a bit sadly as she looked across their clan. They were a mixed bunch: some Delaware, some were Munsee. She smiled when she thought of her, an Iroquois married to a Susquehannock! But the Lord bound them all together.

"The French are building a fort just north of us," Machk explained. His brow was furrowed as details were given and questions circled the group.

"But Conrad Weiser assured us that the English would promise us this country—the Ohio Country," one of the older men said. Heads nodded around the group.

"This is true, but the French do not want to lose their control of the waterways. Without the Ohio River, their transportation is severed. If the English control this spot, then the French have no way of transporting goods and people from Canada down the Mississippi," Machk explained. He had listened to the white men and other chiefs as they discussed the white man's politics. *It was not much different than the red man's,* he often thought. How many Indians had died over hunting ground disputes between tribes?

"Will the English protect us from the French?" Savanukah asked. He had found his sweet wife here among the people and had two boys of his own now.

"For now, most of the battles are on the white man's paper," Machk explained. "But if war comes, we will fight," he said.

Heads nodded and murmurs circled the clan. Ahanu spoke for the first time. "We have enjoyed peace and God's blessing here, but if the time comes to defend our families and home, we will do it—we must do it. The English have traded with us and treated us fairly. The French claim hold of this land, but their treaties are meaningless to the English. They are too small."

Machk continued the conversation, for the two men had discussed their situation on their way back from the French construction. "We began this journey seeking God's wisdom on who we should follow. He has made it clear that the English are stronger. They have promised us this land."

"But can we trust them?" Kanatase asked. He also had a family now and had grown in his faith, but Machk doubted that he would ever trust any white man.

"Our trust is not in the English, my friends. Our trust is in God. He sent us the good news of His Son. We need to pray He will send us someone to teach us more. That should be our worry, not the French." Machk longed to know more about his Savior. They had hoped for another missionary to come but so far only traders and government leaders had arrived in Logstown.

"Let us pray now," offered Ahanu, and as a people they bowed their heads and asked the Lord for a messenger. Once the fort was finished, the French were certain to make their presence known at the Forks of the Ohio. Troops were sent to occupy the fort, but it did not have much effect on the Indians. They had kept their loyalties to themselves and continued to hope for peace.

October, 1753—Williamsburg, Virginia

George Washington's long stride moved him quickly down the cobbled street. The air was brisk and fall colors dotted the scenery on each side of the wide road. Brilliant mums of bright yellow, vibrant orange, and contrasting maroon filled the ornate pottery before several homes, and gourds of every shape and color could be seen in baskets. He loved this time of year and he loved Virginia; however, he longed for the wide open meadows and rolling hills of the north.

He slowed his pace a bit as he drew near the Governor's Mansion, wondering again if the urgent sounding message from the governor had anything to do with his volunteered service. He hoped so. With gaining his recent commission into the British army, he was ready to make a name for himself.

Before he could even knock, the massive front door swung open. A stately servant dressed in elegant livery bowed graciously and led him to the governor's office. As he approached, he could hear Governor Dinwiddie's voice and he was not in a good humor. He pitied the secretary who was taking notes.

"In His Majesty's service, etcetera, etcetera. Now go and get that letter ready post haste."

"Yes, sir," the secretary replied and hurried from the room, nearly running into Washington. He looked up with apologetic eyes. "Sorry, sir," he said and hurried by.

"Washington, is that you?" called Dinwiddie.

Washington walked into the spacious room and bowed courteously. "I came as soon as I could. Your message sounded urgent."

"Yes, yes, it was. These French are pressing the limits. We have reason to believe they have encroached even further into the Alleghenies and continue to urge the Indians there to support their demands." Dinwiddie stood and moved to the map hanging on the wall. "We must hold this area, and we have rightful claim to it. Croghan rightfully made the purchase from the two chiefs up there, but, of course, the French do not see it that way."

Washington waited. He already knew of the situation and wondered what his part was in all this. He didn't need to wait long.

Dinwiddie eyed the tall, young man. "You have proven yourself skillful as a surveyor, and you are well acquainted with the area. As soon as Mr. Smith finishes the letter, which demands they end their occupation of the region, I want you to take it to the commanding officer at Fort Le Boeuf."

Washington bowed once again. At only twenty-one years of age, he had already made a name for himself and was well respected.

Dinwiddie returned to his desk and motioned Washington to have a seat while waiting for the letter. "I was sorry to hear about your brother. Real shame. He served his king and country well."

"Thank you, sir. We feel his loss greatly."

"Indeed we do. Without his skill, we may never have been able to establish our presence in Ohio Country."

Just as the governor finished his sentence, the secretary rushed in with the letter. Dinwiddie perused it and melted his sealing wax onto the folded paper, pressing the official stamp of his office into the glistening dark red daub. He blew on it to hasten the set and handed it to Washington. "If this matter were not so urgent I'd demand that you attend this evening's ball. It will be a memorable occasion!" His eyes gleamed with delight. Robert Dinwiddie was known for his extravagant affairs. Washington was glad for an excuse to miss it.

George nodded. "Perhaps next time," he said with a quick smile. They said their farewells, and Washington was on his way, planning the trip and what he would need as he strode across the Palace Green.

Washington left that day and rode to Fredericksburg, where he gathered several men before heading to Alexandria to gather supplies. In Winchester, he got fresh horses and then moved on to find fellow surveyor, Christopher Gist. Washington feared the expedition would fail without the man's help.

Knowing the way would be easy until he crossed over into Pennsylvania, Washington planned to be to Turtle Creek in a few days; however, as soon as they crossed over the South Mountains, the rain, which had been falling nearly nonstop, turned into snow.

"Mighty purdy country," offered John McGuire as they followed the winding path through thick forests and wide meadows.

Washington smiled at the young man's country speech and was again thankful for the education he had received. "Yes, it is John. I suppose even Virginia looked like this at one time."

"Still is the purdiest colony I reckon," John countered.

"Now you don't want to start that already. Do you, John?" challenged Christopher Gist. "It's going to be a long journey." Born in Maryland, his loyalty lay with his homeland, and the two often sparred each colony's virtue. Gist was the expert in the group and highly valued by Washington. He was also knowledgeable about the customs and language of the tribal people.

"I think we'd better dismount and walk the horses for a while. The trail runs steep just ahead," Washington said, hoping to defuse the two.

John harrumphed but scrambled off his horse, giving Gist a look which said, *This ain't over.* Gist just smiled his most gentlemanly smile, which only served to aggravate the servant. He didn't want to ruffle the man's feathers too much, or he might find himself setting up his own tent.

When they reached the Monongahela, the water was swollen from all the rain. A frustrated Gist pulled up beside Washington. "There'll be no swimming the horses across that," he grumbled. The trail across the swollen river seemed to taunt them into trying, but both men knew the danger.

"We'll need to borrow a canoe from Trader Frazier and have some of the men float our stuff down to the Forks," Washington said. He turned to the men. "Barnaby and Henry, you will float the stuff down river to the Forks and we'll go around through the woods." It would add miles to their journey, but there was no choice in the matter.

A quick fire was built and shelters erected. The temperature continued to drop and the wind picked up as the darkness crept in. Thankfully, the snow had stopped momentarily even though leaden clouds made dusk come quicker. All were thankful for the smell of strong tea as they gathered close to the fire.

"Mmm. Nothing will ever taste as good as a hot cup of tea," Gist said, sipping the hot brew slowly.

"I'll agree there," said John. "Chases the cold out of your bones, don't it?"

Washington smiled, too tired to answer. The adrenaline which had pushed him this far seemed to have left him exhausted, and no one argued about an early night. "We'll leave at dawn," Washington said and crawled into his tent. It was small and he was sharing it with Gist, but they would both be glad for the extra warmth of another body.

Washington was surprised by the amount of Indians he found in the village of Logstown. Reports had led him to expect much less. The canoe and their stuff had arrived before them, and the men had their camp ready. Children of every size ran to greet the newcomers, and they looked at the tall, young man with awe. Washington wondered what Currin had told them about him. The man nearly worshipped the ground Washington walked on. The sun had already set, but fires blazed, igniting the village as the firelight danced off the snow. They were ready for them, welcoming them with open arms. Washington heaved a sigh of relief. He had been assured that it would be so by news from Croghan and Weiser and their recent visit, but the area was so volatile—it could all change in just a few short weeks. How well he knew it!

Sucki's eyes gleamed with excitement. He didn't remember any other life than that of his days in Logstown. At times, Ahanu was saddened that his son would not grow up as a Susquehannock, but those days were past.

One day when Siskia was sharing about her past with her children while preparing the evening meal, she caught the sad look in Ahanu's eyes. It didn't take her long to realize his thoughts. That evening she brought it up after they had retired. "You need to share your people with our children," she simply said, and that had started wonderful times of sharing as a family.

Sometimes the others would gather too and add their stories. They all had a story to tell, and they would need to keep telling them or they would be lost.

The children stepped back to let the horses pass but then skipped after them joyfully calling to one another. "Nkiikàmùkehëna! We have visitors," they cried.

Washington and the others were greeted warmly. He smiled down from his steed and reached down to touch the heads of the children. *Perhaps someday I will have children of my own.* The thought surprised him. Children always looked up to him, even during his early schoolboy days. He loved children, and these dark smiling faces had stolen his heart. They were just another reason to succeed in his mission.

It had taken him twenty-five days to make the trip, and his lateness made his heart pound with anxiety. This was only the first leg of the journey.

Scarouady and the others came to greet the Virginians. Last night's council fire had been filled with mixed hopes. It was tempting to have the heart of a woman and hope all the white men would just go away, or to have the foolish heart of the young braves who would like nothing better than to kill them all. Scarouady knew that neither thoughts were possible. They must find a way to work with the English, for the French had shown their true colors.

Washington and Gist looked around for Half-King. Although his name may have sounded weak to the English he was one of the most powerful leaders of the Six Nations—and he was conspicuously absent. The two men exchanged glances which conveyed the thought. What did it mean?

As though Scarouady read their minds he offered an explanation. "Our great leader Half-King is on a hunting trip in Beaver. He will be very thankful that you have come. Your men have already told us of your mission, and we are glad you have come." Without any further conversation, Scarouady turned to the people and raised his hands. "Let the feast begin," he shouted, and the quiet, still group became a beehive of activity. Pots containing delicious smelling foods were uncovered and stirred, sending their inviting odors across the village beckoning all to come.

As they moved towards the prepared feast, Machk stepped forward at Scarouday's signal and held up his hands. "Brothers and sisters, let us thank our God for this bounty."

A surprised Washington looked to Gist who was just as surprised and barely had their heads bowed before the prayer began, not certain what to expect.

"Our gracious and loving heavenly Father, we are grateful for Your watch care over us. Thank you for this land you have given us to raise our children and call home. Thank you for bringing our honored guests to us safely, and may our time be profitable to all and honoring to You. Thank you for this bountiful table, but most of all, thank you for sending Your Son, Jesus to die in our place. In His Name we pray, Amen."

As Gist interpreted the last phrase, he turned his eyes to Washington, but the tall, young man was just staring at Machk with admiration. He would find this young chief later and hear his story. Machk caught the look, and it clogged his throat with emotion. Their hope was in God, but if what the other men said was true, this man was a great leader and would do right by his people.

There would be no council fire that night due to the lateness of the hour, but Washington invited Scarouady and some of the other chiefs to his tent. He was thankful to see that the Praying Indian was among the leaders.

"I have been sent as a messenger to the French general and was ordered to gather all the Sachems of the Six Nations to tell them of my orders." He waited for John Davison, his interpreter to explain, amazed at his fluid tongue. "This is for Half-King," he said and handed him a twist of tobacco and string of wampum.

Scarouady took the prized possessions, which spoke louder than words, with great solemnity. "I will send a runner at first light to tell him and the other sachems of your words. Your men tell of your great name and honored you with their words. The light in the short one's eyes speaks of great trust."

Washington could feel his cheeks blushing and was glad for the semi-darkness. His honest face won the hearts of the leaders. They conversed for about an hour and then excused themselves, knowing that the Virginians must be tired from their arduous journey. As they turned to leave, Washington reached out and touched Machk's arm. Machk turned in surprise. "Can you stay for a moment?" Washington asked. The other native leaders were surprised as well, but schooled their emotions and left the tent.

"Your prayer—it touched my heart greatly." Davison interpreted in a quiet voice. "Are you a believer in the one true God?" Washington searched the young chief's face as he listened to Davison.

Machk's face broke into a joyful smile, and he nodded, his eyes lit with the Spirit, but he said nothing.

Washington's eyes misted, and his voice was husky. "That brings me great joy. My heart breaks knowing that so many of your people live in darkness."

Machk nodded. "We heard the good news at our village on the Siskëwahane River. I believe his name was Brainerd?"

Washington shook his head in amazement. "Yes, he tells of his travels in his journals. He was a great man."

Machk cocked his head. "Was?"

"He died shortly after that visit." He could see the surprise on Machk's face. "He was a very sick young man, but he did not let that stop him. And here you are, fruit of his labors."

The two men stood in silence before Machk spoke. "We wish for the Word of God. We know so little about Him and have no one to teach us."

Washington's face brightened. "Tomorrow is the Lord's day. If you would like, I can read to you from my Bible—God's Word in the morning."

There were no words to describe the look on Machk's face. His eyes glistened, and he could only nod.

"I think he would like that," said Davison smiling.

"Good. Ask him where we can meet." Once again Washington listened to the string of fluid syllables.

"He says that all are not believers, but there are too many for your tent, sir. He suggests meeting in their long house." Davison listened and talked with Machk while he gave directions and then turned to Washington. "He has told me where and asks if full daylight is good, that would be about 8:00?"

"Yes, that would be fine." Washington held out his hand to Machk and they shook. Washington laid a hand on his shoulder. "Go with God."

Machk could hardly wait to tell the others. The women had long ago finished cleaning up and the children were asleep, but some of the men were just settling in. "Washington, the leader is a believer," he said excitedly, "and he will read to us from God's Word tomorrow at full light here in our house."

The news traveled fast and happy hearts slept well, anticipating the morning.

Washington spent some time in prayer that evening, praising God and asking for His leading. He was not a preacher, but he could speak. The weight of the responsibility weighed upon his heart, but he gave it over to His God and slept soundly.

Up before dawn, he was more than ready when the little group gathered. He had told Davison to tell the others of his plans, not wanting to cause any difficulties for the believers. Many came, and the house was packed with others standing at the doorways.

Washington and his interpreter stood in the middle where all could easily see them. He asked Machk to pray, and when he finished he asked them if they knew any hymns. They all looked from one to the other. Finally, Machk spoke up. "We know only that Jesus is God's Son," he said sadly.

"Let us begin then with a new hymn that I will teach you." Washington began to sing Old One Hundred, and Davison aptly translated. The repetition of the words and the simplicity of the text made it easy for the Indians to learn, and after several repetitions, their voices rang out over the crisp morning air, floating down the river on a calm breeze, thrilling all who heard it.

Washington waited for a moment, as the beauty of the music faded away, before he began. He looked intently from face to face. All eyes were riveted to his. Even the young children sat like stone, waiting for the great man to speak.

"By the time of the new moon, my people will celebrate the birth of Jesus. You may wonder, how is it that the God's Son was born?" He looked at the passage he had read that morning and then continued. *"But when the fullness of the time was come, God sent forth his Son, made of a woman, made under the law, To redeem them that were under the law, that we might receive the adoption of sons* (Galatians 4:4,5). When it was the right time, God the Father sent His Son into this world. He was born of a woman but not a man." Murmurs could be heard but all were soon silent once again. "For the one true God to have a Son, He placed

His seed into Mary's womb. Jesus is God, but Jesus is man also, so that He could die for us."

He read the verse again. "God gave us His laws here." He flipped through the pages of the Old Testament. "The law tells us what is right and wrong. Even though you do not have the Bible, God has written His words in your hearts, telling you what is good and what is evil." Heads nodded in agreement as the truth of the Word took root in their hearts. Washington marveled at their openness. They simply believed what he was telling them.

"God's law tells us that we are sinners. He has written many words in His Book to tell us that. But then He made a way for us to come to Him."

Washington deftly read verses concerning sin and God's judgment. They sat in dreadful silence. Then he turned to Isaiah 9:2. "But this verse is for you and for all who sit in darkness. Many of my people sit in darkness too, but listen to this great promise from the one true God: *The people that walked in darkness have seen a great light: they that dwell in the land of the shadow of death, upon them hath the light shined.*"

Once again murmurs could be heard around the house. Some groaned at the thought of their sin, while others wept for the liberty that was already theirs.

Washington began to pray, not certain what else to say. He had been praying this prayer since he was a child and it held a special place in his heart. "O most Glorious God, in Jesus Christ my merciful and loving father, I acknowledge and confess my guilt, in the weak and imperfect performance of the duties of this day. I have called on Thee for pardon and forgiveness of sins, but so coldly and carelessly, that my prayers confess my sin and I stand in need of pardon. I have heard Thy Holy Word, but with such deadness of spirit that I have been an unprofitable and forgetful hearer, so that, O Lord, though I have done Thy work, yet it hath been so negligently that I may rather expect a curse than a blessing from Thee.

But, O God, who art rich in mercy and plenteous in redemption, mark not I beseech Thee what I have done amiss, remember that I am but dust, and remit my transgressions, negligence, and ignorance, and cover them all with the absolute obedience of thy dear Son, that those sacrifices which I have offered may be accepted by Thee, in and for the sacrifice of Jesus Christ offered upon the cross for me..." His mind raced on as Davison continued to interpret, not certain what to say next. *Help me, Father,* he prayed silently. "Help these poor lost souls and give those wisdom who have already found your grace and mercy. In Jesus' Name, Amen."

They all stood staring at him, but he wasn't certain what they wanted him to do. Finally, Machk stepped forward and solemnly asked, "Would you read more to us?"

Washington looked at Davison. "It would be much simpler if you just read and interpreted it to them. Would you do that for them?"

Davison looked a bit embarrassed. "But I don't read the Bible much," he said. "Where would I start?"

Washington flipped to Luke 2. "Why don't you read them the Christmas story?"

Davison nodded and began to read it to himself. Soon the words were rolling off his tongue, and Washington stood back listening and watching their faces. He could tell that Davison was explaining some of the story to them. Washington smiled. He knew that Davison was not a religious man, but he seemed lost in the moment. When he finished, several started to ask him questions, and he turned to Washington. "They want me to read about Jesus' death," he said sheepishly.

Washington took the Bible and turned to Matthew's account and handed it back to him, wishing he could speak the language.

As Davison read, there was a silent dread in the house. When he finished, he seemed sober with the reality of what he had just read.

"Did he do it?" came a quiet voice from the far end of the long house.

Slowly, Ahanu stood to his feet. His eyes were troubled.

"Did he do what?" asked Washington, urging the young man to go on.

"Did God require that Jesus' blood be on these people's children?"

Washington was taken aback by the question. The same question had bothered him as a child. Did God keep the Jewish nation to this statement?

"*Then answered all the people and said, His blood be on us and on our children,*" Davison read quietly, looking to Washington for the answer.

"Yes, I believe God did. They are God's chosen race. He told them of Jesus' coming, but when He came, most of the Jews rejected Him."

Ahanu looked at all the faces—his people. His heart swelled with conviction. "We cannot do the same. We must make certain our children know the truth and do not pay for our cold hearts."

Conversations circled the room and the two Virginians watched in awe as many heads bowed in prayer, begging for forgiveness. Years later after his own conversion, Davison would tell of that day.

It would be several days before the group of white men would actually be on their way to meet the French at Fort Le Boeuf. Half-King returned the next day but needed the "talking wampum" that he had left at his hunting cabin. "I must offer it back to the French to break our alliance." Although Washington was anxious to be on his way for several reasons, the weather being one, he would wait—it was worth the time to wait.

There had been much debate about who would go with them, but in the end, it was only Half-King, an older chief named Jeskakake, White Thunder—another chief, and Hunter, a young man who had grown up in the village. Washington would never forget the trip. The conditions in which he suffered traveling nearly 1,000 miles over treacherous trails in the middle of winter, would help to season him for a future that only God could know. He also learned much about the French and their strengths and weaknesses which would help the English win the French and Indian War. Facing hostile Indians, deceptive French, and swollen rivers—one of which Washington fell into and nearly froze to death—meant a slow return to Logstown.

Washington looked down at his buckskins and moccasins and shook his head. *If my family could see me now!* He huddled in his tent and took out his Bible once again, thinking of the last time he had read or heard the Christmas story. He was ready to be out of this God-forsaken land.

Did he do it? The question came back to him in a flash. Had God also forsaken these people? Some place, long ago, their ancestors had left the ark with just as much truth about God as Shem had been given! When had they forsaken the way of truth?

He read the Christmas story once again, thinking about past Christmas celebrations with friends and family and hoping that he would never spend another one like this!

By the time the whole party returned to Logstown, the New Year had begun. Haggard and disappointed by the French's refusal of the wampum belt or Dinwiddie's orders to leave the Ohio valley, Washington only stayed long enough to refresh his men and horses before heading back to Williamsburg. The supplies were once again being packed when Ahanu approached the great white leader. "May we speak?" Ahanu asked. Washington and Davison looked at each other, but agreed to follow the lone Indian to a small copse of trees near the edge of the village. Both men wondered what the meeting was about, but they didn't have to wait long.

Ahanu wasted no time. From the first time he heard the man's name a dreadful memory had come to his mind. "I have heard the name Washington before," he said quietly. "John Washington."

Washington's face brightened. "That would be my grandfather. Did your people know him?"

Ahanu was quiet for a moment before speaking. "My people are the Susquehannock." He watched for Washington's reaction and knew he understood.

Washington's face grew serious. "Your people called my father Caunotaucarius... Town Destroyer," he said quietly.

Ahanu's face was serious. He only nodded.

Washington sighed. "I am sorry. What is your name?"

"Ahanu. My grandfather was Hassun. Our village was destroyed by the white man's diseases. I am the only one left, but I remember the story."

Washington did as well. His father had supposedly murdered several Susquehannock chiefs when they had come in peace. George struggled with some of the same sentiment concerning the Indians. They roamed the land but did not settle it. There was so much land and opportunities to be had by the civilized man and such extraordinary beauty, but he wasn't certain how the two cultures would ever merge. "I am sorry for the actions of my grandfather against your people."

Ahanu watched the great leader and saw genuine concern in his eyes. He nodded. "Our grandfathers were enemies, but we are brothers in Jesus."

The words shocked Washington. Here stood a savage carrying himself with more grace and dignity than many of the "Christian" white men! He longed to show his love and sincerity with a gift, but what? It had to be something special. His eyes lit and he dug into his satchel. Reverently, he pulled out his Bible. "I want you to have this as a symbol of our brotherhood. It was given to me by my grandmother and I carry it with me wherever I go. Please take it as a symbol of my apology."

Ahanu looked at the precious book. He could not read it but oh how he longed for the Word. Could he take it? To refuse it would be a great insult. Hesitantly, he reached for the sacred book. "I have no words to say what is in my heart. I will learn your tongue and read it to my people."

Washington smiled and placed his hand on the strong, broad shoulders. "Do that and the Lord will bless you always. We part in peace?"

Ahanu nodded, a smile spreading wide across his face.

*   *   *

May, 1754

As the days lengthened and the air warmed, the citizens at Logstown looked forward to planting gardens and the taste of fresh vegetables. As soon as the ground was dry, women dotted the verdant landscape, digging the dirt and pulling out last year's dead stalks. Children ran and played, and newborn papooses cooed from their mothers' backs, nodding to the rhythm of the hoe.

Chenoa had had her baby and was working beside Siskia and Hurit when Sucki came running ahead of a band of children. His face was frantic, and all stopped to hear.

"Smoke, Mother!" he shouted pointing to the column of angry dark clouds rising from the other end of the village.

They all jumped into action, Siskia barking orders. "Chenoa, Hurit, you stay here with the children. I'll run and see what is happening!"

The others watched as Siskia's graceful form seemed to glide over the land. In just a few seconds she was out of sight.

The men had already gathered and were bringing containers of water from the river. George Croghan's trading post was on fire. The hungry flames lapped at the logs and seemed to laugh mockingly at the men's efforts. They soon realized it was useless and worked to contain the roaring inferno.

Ahanu was standing close to Machk and the other chiefs when one asked if Croghan knew who had done it.

"Sure I know," he spat angrily. "Just last week a bunch of Frenchies were here complaining that the Indians were not buying their goods." He scoffed. "I wouldn't buy them either!" His eyes danced with anger. "They threatened me, but I thought that was all there was to it."

He threw the half burned handle he had tried to save into the fire. "Guess I was wrong," he muttered.

It was a somber group that met at the council fire that evening. Was this an act of war? Would the English protect them or counteract the attack? Where did that leave them?

"I don't like that we live so close to the French fort. We are not safe here," exclaimed Scarouady.

A heated discussion broke out, and in the end, there was division concerning their future. Did they wait until the French burned all their houses, or did they find a new home now?

The small band, which had already been through so much, met on their own in one of their log houses. What were they to do? Machk stood when everyone was settled.

"We have asked God to keep us safe and direct our paths. He has made it clear which side of this conflict we are on. Croghan has taught Ahanu his letters and soon we will be able to hear God's Word read to us."

Murmurs of approval threaded their way through the group, and eyes turned on Ahanu making him squirm. He had actually read some of the words just this week and read the name of Jesus! It had brought tears to his eyes which he could not hide, no matter how much he tried.

"But what good is it to us if we are homeless and dead?" cried Sitting Bear, an Iroquois who had married one of their maidens. He was not a believer, and Machk wondered at the young girl's choice, although he had often wondered if she was a believer in name only.

"We will pray about this. Our friend and great leader Washington spoke highly of Allaquippa's Town. He took the time to visit the Iroquois queen when he was here. It is not far." Machk knew that some of the other original residents of Logstown, including Scarouady and Half-King were thinking of going there. They were good men, and Machk leaned heavily on their advice.

No decision was made that night, but the following month's battle of Jumonville Glen decided it for them. Half-King and some of their men had fought beside Washington in the unexpected encounter with the French.

Washington was extending the Wilderness Road when they came upon a French troop. During the skirmish, Half-King killed French ensign Joseph Coulon de Jumonville. Surely, the French would retaliate. It didn't take long for the Indians to pack their belongings and head to Allaquippa's Town.

Siskia felt discouraged. Would they ever settle somewhere for good? Ahanu walked beside her in silence. He watched the excited children who ran and skipped around the band which made its way through the woods along the Monongahela. "We need to be like them, Siskia," he said.

She looked up at him questioningly and then followed his gaze to the children.

"I believe that God calls us His children for a reason. We need to have faith in our heavenly Father." Siskia was silent so he continued. "They are carefree and happy because they trust us to make right decisions. Shouldn't we do the same?"

Siskia shook her head in wonder. "Every day I thank God that He allowed me to be your wife." She linked his arm momentarily, once again amazed at its strength—a strength that she could depend upon. "I trust you too, Ahanu." They walked on in silence, but smiles had touched their lips. "Have you been able to read any more of the Bible?"

Ahanu's face brightened. "Yes. Little words are making sense to me." He looked at her, his eyes soft and full of joy. "I read these words today: God is love."

Siskia cocked her head, mulling over the tiny sentence in her head. At last she nodded, "Yes, He is, isn't He?"

Ahanu chuckled. "You have the faith of a child and the wisdom of a sachem."

Her eyes sparkled at his words. "We are so blessed to know Jesus!"

"Perhaps someone in this new place will be able to teach me more. Maybe there will be a holy man there like the one we heard in Otstuagy." His voice was full of hope. Suddenly, their way seemed much brighter, their future more hopeful. They were standing on the promises of their God.

"I am thankful we are further away from the French, but are you sad we are not moving west?" she asked. She knew Ahanu had always wished to be away from any white men.

George Croghan had gone ahead of the Indians to tell the Queen of the coming group. He had met with the woman before and felt they would be welcome, and he was right. The next day, Machk and his people as well as most of the others from Logstown were welcomed into the village. Soon, new wigwams were springing up like mushrooms. They had wanted to move west, but perhaps here, deep in British territory, they would find peace far away from the French.

However, the British were not happy with the new fort and British Major General Braddock was the man of the hour.

*   *   *

Baltimore, Maryland

Benjamin Franklin sat before the general and took in the tidiness of the place. He had learned long ago that one could gather much about a person's character by his surroundings. The furnishings were expensive and lavish.

Braddock sat behind his desk, erect and commanding. "Mr. Franklin, they told me you would be coming by this afternoon," Braddock said as he rose to his feet and extended his hand. Franklin heard the condescension in the general's voice but chose to ignore it. He did not want to jump to conclusions. He had a job to do.

He shook the hand firmly. "Yes, I've been asked to help you to gather wagons and supplies for your expedition into Pennsylvania. It will be an arduous journey, not only because of the tangled wilderness you will face but because of the Indians who have sided with the French."

Braddock harrumphed. "These savages may, indeed, be a formidable enemy to your raw American militia, but upon the King's regular and disciplined troops, sir, it is impossible they should make any impression."

Another pompous windbag who doesn't know the first thing about savages or forestry, thought Franklin, but he kept his thoughts to himself. His country was counting on him and he would rise above this fool.

"Be that as it may, you will need provisions and it is my responsibility to supply them." He allowed no further discussion and gave the man the needed information, curtly rose to his feet and made a speedy departure.

Braddock looked after the little spectacled man and shook his head. "These colonists think they know everything," he mused. "I'll have Duquesne and the French in hand shortly. Then they will understand who I am!"

May 29th, 1755

Having gathered his 2,200 troops and his supplies, Braddock moved his force out of Fort Cumberland, Maryland and toward his destination. His marching column stretched out for four miles due to the narrowness of the road, which Braddock growled was nothing more than a trail. George Washington and his troops had blazed the wilderness route the previous year, but it was not what Braddock was expecting. He believed that the route was a mere 70 miles when, in fact, it was over 120.

Frustrated beyond measure, Braddock ordered 600 of his men to precede them and widen the road. *Surely this will speed things up,* Braddock thought, but he was badly mistaken. Even with 200 men swinging axes and 100 others standing guard, they only covered 30 miles the first week.

"I've never seen anything like it," Braddock said in disgust to Lieutenant Colonel Thomas Gage as they shared a hot cup of tea around the fire. Gage sensed the commander's frustration.

"Me neither. This wilderness is like nothing we have in Britain, sir."

Braddock's eyes shot up. "That's because Britain is a civilized land of civilized people." His voice had risen throughout his little tirade but he managed to calm himself. He shook his head. "And these colonial colonels we must work beside, and after his botched attempt at Fort Necessity." He left the statement unfinished. He knew that Gage held the same views. It goaded both men that Washington, at the childish age of 23, held the same ranking as Gage. Yes, Gage was only 36, but the difference was more like twenty years in the British commander's mind.

"If it wasn't for his brother, he would never hold such a post," Braddock offered. Laurence Washington, George's older brother, had already been a commissioned captain in the British Navy for nearly ten years and made quite a name for himself before tuberculosis had taken his life. And his brother's sacrificial care of the ailing elder Washington somewhat softened the two men's thoughts towards the young colonial officer.

June 10th

As the march continued over the rolling hills of Maryland, Braddock halted the troops at a rise in the land and raised his hand for silence. Everyone listened as the sound of axes could be heard just beyond the next ridge. Braddock slapped his leg in disgust. They had caught up with the forward attachment.

When the two parties met, the leadership drew aside and laid out yet another plan.

"We will never get though with all this heavy artillery," Washington reminded his superior once again. At the outset, Washington had cautioned the sixty-year-old commander that so much artillery would never make it through the forest. For several years, Washington had been surveying for Virginia. He knew the terrain like the back of his hand, but Braddock brushed him off. Now, it was time to eat crow.

Braddock looked over the column that snaked through the woods behind and before them. How he hated this! He had served his country for nearly fifty years; however, the majority of his posts had been in London and he had never commanded troops in combat. His present rank had been purchased, a practice common in the British army. "Six guns," was all he said. They knew what to do. Six of the original 19 guns would return to Fort Cumberland.

Fires burned around the camp near the Maryland-Pennsylvania line. The troops were discouraged and their respect for their commander had dropped dramatically, especially among the colonial militia. They were a fine, well-seasoned group of men who were ready to fight and had already done so. Daniel Morgan and the young Daniel Boone were proud of this new land. As pioneers from several colonies, these men were rough and ready and bore the spirit of discipline and courage necessary to survive in the wild, and they weren't afraid to speak their mind.

"He's going to get us killed before we even get there," complained Boone.

Murmurs of agreement circled the group. Washington poked the fire and embers flew skyward. "We are bound to the king," he said quietly. "And General Braddock is the king's appointed officer."

Boone spat into the fire, enjoying the sizzling sound that followed. "King or no king, I'm not ready to die protecting a fool."

The men kept their voices low, for all knew their words were treasonous.

"We will all die for God, king and country," Boone added and heads nodded agreement.

Washington stared at the twenty-one year old adventurer. He admired his skill and agility. Boone's eyes lifted to meet Washington's. Although Captain Dobbs of the North Carolina Company was Boone's commanding officer, he was drawn to the young colonel before him. He knew he was a born leader and respected his opinions highly. Washington would always do what was right. Boone, on the other hand, would take risks; however, a pretty young face had caught his attention, and he intended to stay alive long enough to marry her!

"I say we stay alive, keep Braddock alive and concentrate on getting to Fort Duquesne," Washington said. He smiled and the others laughed in agreement.

July 6

Throughout the following days, flashes of movement could be seen just beyond their column and the experienced militia knew Indians were watching their every move. The flying column, the smaller unit which had gone ahead of the main body of troops, was now eleven days ahead of the others. Orders were to proceed to Fort Duquesne and not wait for the others. Two days later they were at the banks of the Monongahela River, just ten miles from the fort. Camp was quickly made and orders were given—Captain Gates would lead a small force across the river first and secure a second crossing site for the wagons and supplies, all under the cover of night. 2 a.m. they would begin.

Braddock looked at his watch. The others had been gone for two hours. He gave the order, and 250 soldiers began cutting a road to the first crossing for the wagons. He smiled inwardly thinking of how sweet victory would soon taste. It had been much more difficult than he had expected. They had crossed five mountain ranges and who knew how many streams and creeks, but now they were ready. His sources had assured him that the fort was a small garrison, easily breached. Yes, he knew the Indians had probably warned the French, but what of it? *We will show them the strength and dignity of the British army,* he had boasted.

Within the hour they were making their final leg of the march. Gates was leading the first attachment followed by the road builders. Then Braddock led the flying column's main section.

Fort Duquesne

Pontiac stood before Captain Beaujeu. His eyes danced with excitement. His scouts had spotted the British troops and had even attacked several stragglers, proudly wearing fresh, bloody scalps on their belts.

Beaujeu smiled. "Well done, Pontiac. You will not be forgotten for your efforts. Now, here is the plan. We will wait until they are crossing the river, and then we will attack."

However, their calculations were inaccurate. By the time they reached the river's crossing points, Braddock was already across! Beaujeu listened for a moment. *They're playing music?* His lips compressed in disgust at their arrogance while his mind raced for an alternate plan.

He turned to Pontiac and the other French officers and chiefs. "Quickly, take your men and fan out along both sides of the trail. We must not let them get to the fort! Wait for Pontiac's war cry, and then you know what to do!" All nodded and moved silently through the woods—their woods!

Pontiac waited for a break in the music and then let out his cry. Immediately, bullets began to fly. To the Indians' surprise, the Redcoats lined up, knelt down and began to shoot. For the Canadian militiamen and many French soldiers who were in their line of fire, it was a deadly blow, but all the while, the Indians continued to fire upon the red targets. Slowly, the British retreated back down the road from whence they had just come.

Pontiac watched as the British regrouped and aimed at Beaueau's battalion. He wanted to shout but it was too late. Beaueau dropped from his horse. Pontiac had always liked the captain, and the sight raised his fury. With another cry he charged into the fray.

When Braddock heard the first shots, he was enjoying the band and admiring the flags furling in the breeze. He would go home a victor! But the blood-curdling cry followed by a massive amount of firepower spurred him into action. He rode ahead, only to find the British troops in disarray. Most of his officers' horses were devoid of their riders, and the soldiers were in a panic. He watched as the American militiamen blended into the woods, fighting just like the savages. It disgusted him, but he must lead.

Ahanu looked at Savanukah at the sound of music— the likes of which they had never heard. What could it be? Curious, they left their hunt and moved towards the sound. As they came near the road, the first shots were fired. They looked on in amazement as the British, clad in jackets, the color of cardinals, lined up and knelt before lifting their guns. By then, their concealed enemy was taking advantage of the situation and picking them off one by one.

Without a word, the two hunters divided and cautiously slipped closer to the enemy, knowing it had to be the French and their loyal Indian warriors. Ahanu took aim just as a French soldier raised his reloaded weapon, his arrow hitting its mark. Sooner or later, Ahanu knew he would need to use a gun, but until then he preferred his arrows. They were silent and deadly.

When Pontiac saw the French soldier fall with an arrow in his chest, he knew they were fighting more than just British soldiers, but whom? He searched the woods, but the smoke from hundreds of muskets clouded his vision. He turned to take down another Brit, but then scanned the opposite woods, looking for the one who had made such an expert shot. Then he saw him. His blood pulsed through his veins until his ears rang with excitement. Ahanu! With a wicked grin he lifted his gun and took aim.

Ahanu would later wonder just how he saw Pontiac in time and would give his God all the credit. He had just placed an arrow in his bow and was ready to take aim when he felt more than saw the barrel of a gun aimed right at him. His eyes shifted in a flash, and with the swiftness of a seasoned warrior, he leaped to safety, hearing the bullet whiz past him and plow into the tree where he had just stood.

He shouldn't have been surprised, but somehow he had hoped that Pontiac would have been true to his word. He continued to slip away until he was certain his location was lost. All the while, he had glanced Pontiac's way, seeing his anger and frustration as he wildly searched the area, but the battle kept him too busy engaged in the battle at hand.

Ahanu's thoughts were jumbled. Why? Why would Pontiac want to kill him? Then the truth dawned like the first brilliant morning rays of sunlight across dawn's horizon—if he were dead, Pontiac would have Siskia. A rush of feelings overcame him. Pontiac with Siskia—Pontiac raising his children—Pontiac stealing his life! His chest rose and fell as anger flooded every nerve. He took his bow and another arrow and aimed.

"Ahanu! Don't!" hissed Savanukah above the roar of battle.

Ahanu turned to see Savanukah a few feet away, dodging from tree to tree. His lip curled in hatred. "He nearly killed me!" Ahanu shouted, and he pulled the string taut.

Just as he was ready to let the arrow fly, a familiar voice rose above the rest. Washington was riding into the fray shouting orders and taking command. Ahanu watched as another Indian took aim at the great leader, and he redirected his arrow.

Braddock watched in horror as the two 6-pounders were abandoned. He headed for Gates but before he was halfway to the man, he was down with a bullet in his chest.

Suddenly, his horse lurched and fell. The animal had been shot. The officer quickly scrambled to another horse, knowing the mount was needed as much as his medals to signify his leadership, but just as he settled himself in the saddle a bullet caught him in the arm and lung, and he fell to the ground.

Washington, having seen the whole ordeal, sprinted to Braddock's side. He lifted the wounded commander to his shoulder, once again thankful for his strength and broad frame, and carried him to the rear of the battle. Gently lowering him to the ground, he looked into the general's eyes.

Braddock focused his vision on the young man, trying to gather his thoughts, but before his mind cleared, his eyes closed in unconsciousness.

Washington looked back into the battle. British soldiers were running for their lives, many throwing down their muskets in order to run faster. For many, the sight of a tomahawk wielding Indian was something they had only heard of from others. Seeing the ghoulish fiends in action, smeared with war paint and bathed in blood, drove the courage from the stoutest heart.

The sight of the scalping of British troops and the wild drinking of rum which the Indians had captured from the British spurred Washington into action. He rode back to the main body of soldiers bringing medical supplies and wagons for the wounded. Dazed soldiers, bereft of their leaders, gladly obeyed his orders, admiring his cool and calm leadership, and soon order returned to what was left of Braddock's army. In the distance, the whoops of victory exploded from the marauding Indians.

Washington thought of his last visit to the area and wondered if the French victory would cause any difficulty for the friendly Indians he had met at Logstown.

Ahanu wanted to go to his friend, but he knew he would be a dead man if he showed himself.

As the two friends left the gruesome scene with great stealth, their thoughts raced before them. They were glad to be heading east and away from the French... and Pontiac.

"I will not tell Siskia of Pontiac's attack," Ahanu said when they knew it was safe to talk.

Savanukah looked at him in surprise.

"She doesn't need to know this about her childhood friend," Ahanu said quietly.

"Your character always amazes me," Savanukah said.

"Even when I tried to kill him?" Ahanu challenged with raised brows.

"I did not know the circumstances. I thought you were only seeking revenge. You had every right to kill him for stealing your wife!" Savanukah understood better now that he had a wife. "Perhaps you should have killed him."

"Saving Washington was the better choice."

Savanukah nodded in agreement. "He is a brave warrior," he said, recalling the image of the young soldier rallying the bewildered British troops. "I'd like to know who their commander was. What a fool!"

As the two men traveled back to Alaquippa's Town, Ahanu was glad to be going deeper into British territory. Surely Pontiac's travels would keep him on the dividing line of the Allegheny Mountains until the French or British were defeated. After the day's obvious French victory, Ahanu questioned their decision to support the British. What kind of a leader would act so arrogantly and march into the enemy's territory playing music? "Do you think the British can push out the French?"

Savanukah's eyes showed his concern as well. "I don't know, brother. Certainly that British officer does not understand our people or our land. But did you see the colonists shooting from the woods?"

Ahanu nodded.

"I believe men like that, led by a man like Washington can win the battle. And they understand our ways."

Another winter was upon them. Life seemed to be on hold, and Ahanu was restless. Would his life ever settle into a normal place?

As the months rolled by, conflicting reports reached the group now living in Aughwick where George Croghan had set up a new trading post. The Indians' confidence in the British was crumbling, and when Queen Aliquippa died, their support fell even further. She had rallied her people to stay by the British, but now she was gone. Her son, Kanuksusy, or Captain Fairfax as he was called by the British, led in her place and had spent much time with the British leaders.

A council fire was called and Captain Fairfax led the discussion. Tension was to the breaking point. Old arguments, like old wounds, were cut open and all the bitterness and anger caused by loss of home and land sizzled out of control.

"We do not trust the British," shouted Blue Feather. "And look at you! You have lost your way. You even take their name."

Kanuksusy stood to his feet, silencing the cacophony of angry words. His reputation demanded respect while his character kept his reactions under control.

"It is true I have been honored by the British. I have met with important men—leaders among their people." He paused for emphasis. "We have powwowed, and the British will win this fight against the French. And they will give us land."

Doubts and misgivings parleyed with confidence. The group was divided, and in the midst of it all was the small group from Great Island. Machk watched and listened as the others argued. He had shared his faith with the great queen before she died, but Aliquippa was too proud to leave the beliefs of her ancestors. Kanuksusy had listened patiently, but his mind was too filled with war and politics to be concerned with his soul.

At times, Machk felt as though his heart could endure no more. These people were more concerned with this life than the next.

He had discussed all this with the others in their group and they were praying for God's leading once again.

Slowly, he rose to his feet. As he waited for the arguments to quiet down, he prayed for wisdom and then began.

"We wish to thank you for taking us in when we had no place to go, but it is time for us to move on."

"Will you run from the battle?" accused Captain Fairfax.

"We have fought this battle long enough—longer than you, my friend. There is no end in sight. You do not embrace our ways. We long for peace. Our children grow before us with no place of their own."

"You think you will find peace in Ohio Country?" scoffed one of the others.

"We seek God's leading," Machk said quietly. He heard the tongues clicking in disgust, but he had heard it before. God had a place for them. They would follow when and where He led.

The direct answer to their prayers came one week later when David Zeisberger and John Heckewelder walked into Aughwick. They were on their way to Ohio to reach the Indians there with the gospel. When Ahanu and Machk overheard the strangers talking to Croghan at the trading post, it seemed too good to be true.

Shyly, they approached the men dressed in black. David's tall, lanky form stood erect as he purchased his items and conversed with Croghan. "You have quite a trading post here, Mr. Croghan."

"Please, call me George," said the jovial trader. Business had been good in Aughwick—even better than at Logstown. Situated on the main road connecting Philadelphia and Forks of the Ohio, travelers knew Croghan as an honest trader who ran a well-stocked post.

"Where you heading?" George asked as he added up the man's bill.

"Ohio Country. My friend John and the others hope to start a mission work there among the Indians."

George's eyes met those of Machk and Ahanu. "Well then you need to meet these two young men here," George said motioning the pair to the counter.

Machk led the way, trying to contain his excitement. He nodded, and David held out his hand. "My name is Machk and this is Ahanu," he said as he shook the stranger's hand. "We believe in the one true God," he added.

David's eyes brightened. "Jehovah be praised. And how is it that you came to know the Lord, my brother?"

Machk's eyes warmed. No white man had ever called him "brother." "My family came from the north where French missionaries told us of Jesus."

David's brow furrowed. "Then you are sympathetic to the French?" he asked.

Machk shook his head. "No. That was a long time ago. Since then, we moved to the Great Island and then to Logstown and now here."

David's face clouded. "We passed through Great Island."

Machk looked at Ahanu. "What do you know of those who stayed behind?"

David shook his head. "Famine and small pox has hit the area. When we arrived, those who were left were sick and starving. We helped them as much as we could."

"Did you tell them about Jesus?" Machk asked anxiously.

"We did, but their hearts were hardened. Yet we never know what our gracious heavenly Father will use to get their attention. Perhaps He sent the drought and difficulties to soften their hearts."

Ahanu stepped forward. "We have been praying about heading to Ohio Country. Could we join you?"

David looked at John. "Jehovah-jerah," he exclaimed. "We have been praying for someone to help in our work. We hoped for an Indian believer, but I'm afraid we had little faith." He shook his head in wonder.

"Will you feast with us tonight? Our people will be so happy to hear the good news," Machk said.

"I would be delighted. But we do hope to leave as soon as our supplies can be gathered and our horses rested."

"We will be ready," Machk said excitedly.

Chapter Ten

Ohio Country

Teach me to do thy will; for thou art my God:
thy spirit is good; lead me into the land of uprightness.
Psalm 143:10

1756—Aliquippa's Town

Spring once again filled the air with fresh scents as tiny young plants pushed their way through the warm sod. The rivers and streams were full and running swiftly—perfect for canoes; however, when Savanukah secretly told Machk about Ahanu and his encounter with Pontiac, they went to the missionaries and shared their concerns. It was decided that they would take a southerly route into Ohio.

"We value your opinions greatly, my friends. Our earnest desire is to tell your people about Jesus Christ, and we prefer to do that while staying out of the fray between the French and British. We are pacifists."

Ahanu looked at Machk and the others to see if they understood the term. They did not and questioned the men of God further. Was this something God required?

John Heckewelder smiled. "This means that we will not lift our hand against another. God alone is the giver and taker of life."

The Indian men looked at each other. They had never heard of such a thing. Machk spoke for all of them. "This is a new idea to us—one that we will need to consider. But it does not change our minds about this journey. We long to

227

learn more about Jesus, and we believe God brought you to us."

David Zeisberger was once again awed by their simple faith. Oh, how he prayed that soon others would turn to Christ! "We will work hard to teach you and to be worthy of your loyalty. I believe you will be a great asset in leading others to our Savior."

Sadly, not all were as excited as Machk, Savanukah, and Ahanu. Kanatase had asked for a meeting with Machk. The young chief looked at the two men before him. Kanatase and Black Hawk stood with arms akimbo as they faced Machk and the others. Throughout the evening's feast with their new friends, Machk had covertly watched the two and noticed their looks of distrust towards the missionaries. Now, while the rest of their group busied themselves for their journey, the two warriors had stated their plans—they would not be going with them. It saddened Machk's heart for he feared that neither of them had truly trusted Christ.

"Why leave us now, my friends? We've been through so much together." Machk pleaded.

But their stance told of their defiant hearts. "We will not run. We will stay and fight," Kanatase offered.

Machk's heart shone in his pleading eyes. "But you have not found peace with God," he said quietly.

Black Hawk scoffed. "We do not need your God."

Machk locked his gaze momentarily on Black Hawk before turning to his childhood friend. "You too, Kanatase?"

He saw just a slight waver in Kanatase's determination, but it was quickly replaced with defiance. He nodded slightly, and held out his hand to his friend. "You have been a good friend and leader, but we do not want to run from this fight."

Machk shook his head. Kanatase had always wanted to do battle and he did so with a relish. He thought back to their time with Chief Bald Eagle. Yes, Kanatase had matured, but the blood in his veins was as cold as his heart. Machk took his hand and pulled him into an embrace. "I will pray for you," he whispered into Kanatase's ear.

It was nearly Kanatase's undoing, but he held his ground. He had left his home and his family to fight for the preservation of their ways. Going with these black-cloaked missionaries just did not sit well with him.

There was no looking back when the small band left the village. Ahanu had mixed feelings. Now that he had children, there was a part of him that wanted to return to his homeland and raise his family there. But live all alone away from these friends and Siskia's family? He couldn't do it. *Someday I will show Sucki his ancestral home,* he thought. His mind traveled back to Sprit Rock. He hadn't thought about it for years, and he wondered about the coins he had dropped into the crevice. Were they still there? What would happen to them? Would anyone ever find them? Had he been foolish to part with so much of the white man's wampum? He shook the thoughts from his mind and looked to the future. He could never have kept it! It was blood money!

The ancient trail wound its way through the dense forest. Their venture had started before dawn, and the air was moist with the morning dew. The evening's fires sent lazy tendrils of smoke into the air as though tired from their evening's trysts. Hasty goodbyes had been given for they had made friends in this little village even though their stay had been brief.

Their travels were slow-going because of all the children who were with them. As Machk looked back over the trail of people, it surprised him to see how far the line stretched! They had grown in numbers since they had left the Great Island, and he suddenly felt the weight of his responsibility. Oh, how thankful he was that God had brought His men to them! They would know more about God's Book and what it said. He could hardly wait to get to Ohio.

However, he didn't have to wait that long before hearing the Word of God read and explained to them. Every night around the crackling fire, either Reverend Zeisberger or Reverend Heckewelder would read from the Bible and then explain the passage to the Indians who sat in rapt attention. They would have spoken for hours, the Indians were so attentive, but morning always came early and travel was best in the coolest part of the day.

By the fourth day they were passing near the Forks of the Ohio and were extra cautious, sending scouts further ahead of the bulk of travelers. They had seen French soldiers and Indians milling about the new fort, but were able to pass by unnoticed.

They had journeyed for two more days when the scouting party returned excitedly describing the crossing at Yellow Creek.

"It is a perfect place for a village," said Degataga, his eyes shining with excitement. "It looks a lot like the Great Island."

Zeisberger looked at Heckewelder. "But we're only two miles into Ohio Country and about fifteen miles from the Fort Duquesne?" Heckewelder explained.

"We had hoped to go further," said Zeisberger.

"But this is a good place. There are several trails that pass through there. You will be able to talk to many people here," urged Degataga.

The two missionaries looked at each other. Perhaps this was the place for them to settle. David Zeisberger looked into the eager faces and smiled. "We will pray about this. If it is of God's choosing, then who are we to argue."

It was a happy group that traveled the last few miles of their journey. All were hopeful that they would finally find peace in a quiet place far from any war.

*   *   *

1756-1774—Yellow Creek, Ohio

For eighteen years the little band of believers' dream had come true. They were now living together in relative peace, even though war raged around them. Yellow Creek was just far enough west that Machk and his people were able to live peaceably; however, one name continued to surface as bands of Indians traveled the Ohio River: Pontiac.

He had made quite a name for himself and was rallying the Indians who were French sympathizers to band together and fight for their land. Many were joining him and council fires were held all over the area. As of yet, Yellow Creek was too far south to be caught in those cross-hairs, but every time his name was mentioned with glowing accolades, Ahanu saw the fear in Siskia's eyes, and it made his blood boil!

However, the Lord spared them from any further encounters with Pontiac, although his successes against the British were frightening. Fort after fort was surrendered to Pontiac and his warriors until it seemed as though the French would win the war, but providence was with the British and slowly turned the tide. Pontiac was finished and his life was snuffed out—not by a white man but by one of his own people.

The news came through a band of Delawares heading back to their homeland after fighting alongside the great leader. Their hopes were dashed, and with slumped shoulders they relayed the story. Zeisberger thought they might be ready to hear the gospel, but their hearts were hardened toward any white man, no matter how eloquent his words.

"It's sad," whispered Siskia that night as they lay awake, listening to the rhythmic breathing of the others.

"What?" asked Ahanu.

"Pontiac," Siskia answered. She felt Ahanu stiffen and then relax.

"His eye was set on a future that could not be, and his heart grew cold."

They both lay in silence, pondering his words. Ahanu turned to face Siskia and put his arm around her. "God spared you, Siskia. Your life would have been one of torment with that man."

"It could have been you," she whispered. "When I think back to your battle with Satan near the Legaui-hanne Creek and your thirst for revenge..." She let the sentence hang.

Ahanu pulled her close. "I will forever be grateful for God's sacrifice for my soul." He kissed her forehead, "and for you."

By 1763, the British had defeated the French, and the conquerors offered the Indians many concessions while the French slowly retreated northward and southward to their claims at the mouth of the Mississippi River.

One land grant to the Indians was the territory of the Ohio Country. Because of the Indians' support in the war, the king granted them the vast forests covering the rolling hills which lay west of the Allegheny Mountains. The Indians were elated; however, the colonists were not. Some marauding bands of Indians, still vengeful for being pushed off their ancestral hunting grounds, earned the reputation of savages by burning, scalping, and kidnapping the settlers of western Pennsylvania.

1774

It was early spring once again, and the women were busy preparing their gardens for seeds. David Zeisberger and John Heckewelder had just returned from a mission trip further west. The two men traveled the area often, but returned to their homes between trips, and their people were always glad to see them. The previous night had been a time of feasting and praising God as the two men told of their success among neighboring villages. The Delawares were especially open to the Gospel, especially when they heard the missionaries had worked with their people back east years before.

David looked around the circle of faces and continued his tale. "Perhaps the most exciting news is of New Comer." He smiled as he saw recognition of the name on many faces.

"He was with us at Logstown," Machk offered.

"Yes, I mentioned your names, and he was excited to hear that you were also believers. He is a wise chief and shows great understanding of God's Word." His face clouded momentarily, and he shook his head. "He even questioned our people and why there are so many divisions of Christianity. I could not answer him." David smiled. "He plans to visit the King of England and ask him personally."

Everyone was astonished at the thought. "But he would have to travel across the great water!" Ahanu exclaimed, voicing what the others were thinking.

"You're right, Ahanu." David chuckled and shook his head. "It would be an eye-opening experience for him. Our homeland across the sea is so different from here." He sat in silence, momentarily lost in his thoughts until he looked up and saw they were waiting for him to continue. "Time will tell if it happens."

The next morning everyone had gathered before the noon meal for prayer and a Bible study. The day was warm for April, and the sky was clear. They chose to gather along the river and enjoy the sunshine as they listened to David Zeisberger share from the Bible.

They had worked all morning and were glad for the break. All sat intently listening to their beloved teacher, soaking in all the promises from their God. David had been pleased at their willingness to forsake traditions which were contrary to Bible doctrine. Many other villages listened to the Gospel but balked at the thought of adopting the "white man's ways." David tried to explain the difference between white men's traditions and Bible commands that transcended all nations and cultures, but many would not budge.

He couldn't blame them, really. Certainly the white man had not treated the Indians fairly in so many ways. It saddened him to think that his people and their ways might hinder many souls from finding true peace in Jesus Christ.

The study was so intense that the group failed to hear the approach of several canoes until they were nearly upon them. Startled by the unnoticed advancement of strangers and chagrined by their carelessness, the men jumped to their feet and hurried to the banks just as the canoes came to shore.

The group included women and children, and the men were relaxed and friendly. They had not traveled far, but the group soon noticed that the canoes were loaded with personal belongings and soon realized that another group of displaced Indians had reached their shores.

David Zeisberger stepped forward and exclaimed. "Logan, my friend! Welcome to Yellow Creek." The tall, muscular Indian gracefully stepped from the canoe and walked confidently toward David. All eyes were upon him, and anyone watching knew by his commanding presence that he was a leader; however, Logan saw no one but David.

Machk looked at his friends to see if they recognized the native and saw that they did, but he couldn't remember where they had met. He didn't remember ever talking to him, but the name sounded familiar.

David turned to his people, his smile broad across his face. "My friends, this is the great Chief Logan, son of Shikellimy."

Many heads nodded for the name was well known. Logan had done much for his tribe, the Mingos, as well as other Indian nations. He had negotiated with the British and the colonists on several occasions and was a great orator among his people as well.

Their Bible study was put on hold while introductions were made. When Logan approached Ahanu, he stopped momentarily and searched his face.

"I remember you," he said with a questioning look upon his face as though trying to bring the memory into focus. "You were at Margret's Town when David Brainerd preached. I saw you—watched your face."

Ahanu looked at him in surprise. "Yes, I was there." He studied the man's face. "But I don't remember you there. I remember you at the great council fire of Fort Pitt."

Logan nodded. "Yes, I was there too, but why is the look in your eyes on that long ago day etched in my mind? I was Brother Brainerd's guide, so you would not have noticed me."

Ahanu's eyes grew tender. "You saw fear in my eyes that day—something rarely seen in a Susquehannock."

Logan's face brightened. "You are a Susquehannock?" He shook his head. "I should have known. You are from a great people. My father spoke very highly of them and traveled far north with Conrad Weiser many years ago."

Ahanu looked at the man in amazement and slowly nodded. "I saw him," he said quietly.

Logan looked astonished. "But how?"

"I stood with my grandfather and watched as your father led a white man's group up the Sheshequin Path. My grandfather told me your father was a good man, so the white man was a good man also. His words surprised me."

Logan nodded. He felt a bond with this warrior and laid a hand upon Ahanu's shoulder. "We are brothers. Our roots travel the same waters and have crossed many winters ago."

Ahanu felt honored. He placed his hand on Logan's shoulder as well. All were silent, savoring the moment of comradeship which passed between the two men.

"This day is a day of rejoicing," David said. "Let us prepare to feast and make our friends feel welcome." He looked at Logan. "It looks as though you seek shelter. Please make our village your home."

Logan's eyes brightened and he nodded. "Thank you. We do seek a new home." A shadow, which every Indian recognized, passed over his face, but in a moment it was gone. They understood the pain and frustration of moving on and leaving your native home behind.

The evening was filled with feasting and laughter. Young bucks sported as their families watched. The village of Yellow Creek had been an Indian settlement for years and was made up of many different tribesmen. When David Zeisberger came to the village, some eventually embraced his beliefs and some didn't. Those who didn't gave him a wide berth. They admired his determination and kind ways, but one thing stood directly in the way of their path to redemption—liquor, and this night of celebration once again made it evident whose side of that conflict everyone was on.

The born-again believers kept an eye out for the poison that turned civil men into savages and were thankful none had been brought forth. The evening looked as though it would end as well as it had begun. Machk and the others were getting ready to call it a night when some of the men who had just arrived with Logan proudly brought out their bottles of rum. The others gave a shout, and the drinking began.

David rushed to Logan and watched with surprise as the man lifted the bottle to his lips and drank deeply.

"Logan!" he shouted. "What are you doing?"

Logan looked at David with a mixture of shame and resentment on his face but said nothing.

"Your father took such a hard stand against liquor, I thought you would do the same," David urged.

Logan's lips curled. "I am not my father," he spat and lifted the bottle to his mouth once again, drinking hastily and rolling his eyes in delight. He handed the bottle to his friend and faced David nearly nose to nose, his hands akimbo.

David stood tall and firm. His eyes were full of compassion but serious. "Wine is a mocker, strong drink is raging: and whosoever is deceived thereby is a fool."

Logan was already feeling the effects of the drink he had guzzled, and his face was red with rage. "No one calls me a fool."

"I am not calling you a fool, God is—the God of your father," David said quietly and walked away. How many times had he done this, wondering if he would feel the point of an arrow enter his back? Once again, God protected him.

Logan watched the preacher purposefully walk away. He was his father's friend. He had performed his father's funeral! Shame burned in his hear,t but the effects of the liquor changed any conviction into pain. He looked at his friends as they passed the nearly empty bottle back and forth and grabbed it away from them, emptying its contents in one swallow. He hurled it in the direction which David had left and heard it smash into a thousand pieces. *Shattered, just like my life*, he thought. In that moment, the party had lost its fun. He looked around and noticed that all of Zeisberger's followers were gone. All that was left was a wild group... of savages.

Back in their longhouses, David Zeisberger and John Heckewelder gathered their group together and began to pray. They prayed well into the night, even after the revelers had quieted down.

The air was still and everyone was thankful for the peace that reigned, at least in their homes and hearts.

David looked at John. "I think it's time to share our plans," he said and John agreed with a nod.

David looked around at each face. He loved this group and would die for them if necessary. The bond that had been forged because of their love for God had been like nothing he had ever experienced. He took a deep breath and began, knowing that John was continuing to pray as he spoke.

"For some time now, we have felt that it may be time for another move." He waited for the news to sink in, but he saw no surprise or resistance and again praised God for this group.

"The conflict between the British and the colonists is only growing more hostile. Virginia land grabbers have their eye set on this area."

"But this is our land," Savanukah protested. "The British promised it to us."

"Haven't they pushed us far enough?" another voice called out angrily and many murmurs of agreement could be heard.

"Yes, they have, but if there is a war and the colonists win, I'm not certain they will honor Britain's treaties."

"But don't they have the same father king?"

David smiled wanly. "Yes they do, but I'm afraid the colonists have reached adulthood and want to be set free." He knew the word picture would help them to understand.

"Where will we go?" asked Ahanu.

David and John spent the next few moments explaining their idea of starting a new village of their own— one that would be inhabited by believers. Others could come, but their ruling laws would be based on biblical principles. David told of a place further west which had already been established.

"The village is called Gnadenhutten, which means huts of grace. It is mostly made up of Indians and any white men and women that are there are missionaries."

"Are there believing white women?" Siskia asked quietly.

David looked at John and smiled. It was a personal joke between the two bachelors who would marry first, although David was nearly twenty years John's senior and quite past the marrying age. "Yes, Siskia, there are white women and children in the village who are very dedicated to the Lord and to teaching as well." He was pleased to see the excitement in the women's faces. This would be a good move. Only one thing held him back. "I would like to stay a bit and try to influence Logan for the Lord. His father meant a great deal to me, and I would be remiss if I did not try to reach his son for the Lord's sake."

Heads nodded, some in agreement and some because of the late hour. David rose to his feet and led the group in a closing prayer, committing their future and Logan to the Lord.

As Ahanu and Siskia settled into their place, Siskia could sense that something was on Ahanu's mind. They had been married for over twenty-five winters and Ahanu sometimes wondered if she could read his mind.

"What is it?" she asked in a whisper.

Ahanu pulled her into his arms and drew her face close to his. He didn't want anyone to hear this conversation, especially not Sucki or the other children. Sucki was nearly a grown man now, and it bothered Ahanu that he knew nothing of his Susquehannock roots. Machk and Siskia often told stories of their family and tribe, and Ahanu did as well, but he wanted him to see, not just hear about his homeland. Ahanu had also seen how Sucki's eyes followed the graceful moves of one of the girls and knew it wouldn't be long before he would want to ask for her hand.

"I want to take Sucki back to my mountains and show him where my village once stood," he whispered.

Siskia tried to keep her voice quiet and calm. "Isn't it too dangerous?"

"I don't think so. If I stay away from the white man's villages, I think we will be fine. He needs to know where his roots began, and I'm afraid if we move any further west it will never happen."

Siskia lay still, pondering his words. She knew he was right, but the thought of not having him and Sucki with them made the move seem impossible.

Ahanu knew her concerns and wondered if the idea was foolish. "I could wait until after we move if it would put your heart to rest."

Siskia's eyes glistened with unshed tears. Her heart was torn. She too saw Sucki's looks towards Bly and knew the girl's heart was taken with Sucki as well. The trip had to happen before a wedding might take place. It only seemed fitting. "No. I think you should go soon."

Ahanu was surprised but pleased. He held her close and kissed her gently.

"The sooner you go, the sooner you will return."

But unbeknownst to either father or mother, Sucki had different plans. When his father told of his plan, Sucki frowned.

"What's wrong, Sucki?" Ahanu asked.

"Bly and I have decided to marry before our move to Gnadenhutten," Sucki said quietly.

Ahanu wanted to argue but he was happy for his son and pleased with his choice. Bly, as her name indicated, was tall and slender. She did not know all of her ancestry and wondered if there was a bit of Susquehannock blood in her veins. Sucki had inherited his father's build and height and the two looked good together, but more importantly, Bly was a solid believer. Siskia had shared her observations of the girl in the women's Bible study time that Bly was devoted to God and His Word. She asked good questions and had a sharp mind.

Ahanu looked up from his reverie to see Sucki's anxious face. Was the boy holding his breath? Ahanu smiled. "It sounds like a good idea to me," he said quietly.

Sucki let out his breath and grinned widely. "Then we have your blessing Father?"

Ahanu felt the lump rise in his throat. He never tired of hearing the children call him father, and in that moment his mind rushed back to his own father and the urge to return to his homeland nearly overwhelmed him. But the thoughts were soon replaced with a Bible verse he had read just that morning. *He is not the God of the dead, but the God of the living* (Mark 12:27). *Thank you, Father,* he prayed silently and shared the verse with his son.

"Someday we will go. Perhaps once we are settled and you have secured your place as a husband we will go."

Sucki's eyes grew moist. "Thank you, Father. I also long to see the place of my fathers."

Sucki had no idea how much it meant to Ahanu that he had referred to his ancestors as his own and not just his father's. Ahanu only nodded and pulled Sucki into a quick embrace.

Chapter Eleven

Winds of Adversity

Good understanding giveth favour:
but the way of transgressors is hard.
Proverbs 13:15

April, 1774—Yellow Creek

The wedding had done more than just unite two young people; it had tied the old with the new: Machk and his people to the villagers of Yellow Creek. It had been a wonderful day of celebrating and rejoicing. Even Logan had honored the wishes of both parents and had left his bottle at home.

Machk had watched the great leader as Brother David performed the wedding which was a wonderful mixture of Indian tradition and Christian beliefs. He determined to talk with the man sometime during the celebration, but Logan had been determined to leave for a hunting trip that day and was gone before Machk had a chance to say a word. He watched as Logan embraced his mother and sister and said a few words to his brother before leaving with some of his men.

Several days later, word reached the village that several of Logan's men had been shot while trying to round up their horses. It wasn't long before the rest of Logan's band, including the women, went to seek revenge.

David watched as they rode away from Yellow Creek. He shook his head, concern written on his face. "We need to pray. This is not good."

That evening as the Yellow Creek believers gathered to pray, Daniel Greathouse, commander of the white men who had killed Logan's men, met the vengeful band as they drew near the camp.

He sat tall and brave on his steed as the Indians approached, holding up his empty hand as a sign of peace. "I have heard what has happened. The man who did this is in prison. We will deal with him justly," he said in their native tongue.

Logan's brother looked around the group, seeking advice as to what they should do, but before anyone spoke, Daniel continued.

"Come, let us make amends at Baker's tavern."

The men knew of the place, and the enticement of rum softened their intent to kill.

"All will be ready tomorrow," Daniel stated. He nodded to them and rode away.

That night, by the light of a full moon along the Ohio River, Logan's men argued. Some wanted to sneak into the village and avenge their comrades. Others argued to wait and enjoy the white man's liquor. "We will satisfy our thirst for rum and then our thirst for revenge."

The others laughed at Bodaway's play on words. There would be no changing their minds. Their craving for rum would cloud any reasoning or thoughts of distrust.

The next day, the band crossed the river and entered the tavern, leaving their guns behind. It would be a friendly visit, they were told. The rum ran freely, and three of the Indians were soon drunk while the others refused to drink—a custom among the Indians. Some would drink while others remained sober to care for their intoxicated brothers.

David Greathouse watched with delight as the Indians laughed and swayed unsteadily, but his eyes darkened as he watched John Petty, Logan's brother. He knew the man was an excellent shot and was concerned that he was one of the sober ones. His plan would not go well unless... His face brightened with a smile. He had a new plan.

"John," he called. "I hear you're a pretty good shot."

Bodaway overheard his words and roared with laughter, nearly toppling to the floor. "He is the best," he slurred.

John looked with consternation at his drunken friend. He didn't like what was happening.

"Well, Petty, what do you say? Are you any good with a gun?" Greathouse goaded.

John had been leaning against the log wall near the door. He stood straight and went to get his gun, and the two other sober warriors followed him out the door. Had the others not been so drunk, they would have seen the look that passed between Greathouse and his men.

Soon the tavern was empty, and all stood and watched as a mark was set, and the two men stood side by side and took aim, the drunkards making fools of themselves while the white men's fingers gently caressed their triggers.

"Perhaps we should see if you really are the best Indian shot here," Daniel suggested. "You three shoot first," he suggested and waited as each eyed the target.

Without a word, each of the Indians took careful aim, glad to prove their skills. The gunfire exploded and three bullets lay within the bullseye, but before they could enjoy their success Greathouse and his men started to shoot, taking deadly aim at the three warriors whose guns were now empty.

Logan's mother and sister screamed and started to run but were immediately shot down. The drunken Indians, seven in all, tried to gather their wits but before they could, the white men were upon them with tomahawks, landing blow after blow.

"How does it feel?" cried one man whose family had been brutally murdered when he had first moved west. There was no answer from the already lifeless body as the man continued to strike until his strength was gone.

Sakari, Logan's sister lay on the ground, clinging to her little girl. She was the wife of Colonel John Gibson, a man Logan had negotiated with in Virginia. The patriot had married Sakari and built a home in Logstown, but military duties had forced him to ask Logan to care for his sister and infant until matters were settled.

As Daniel came near to scalp the child, she cried out. "No! Please. His father is a great man, Colonel John Gibson." Daniel stopped and stared at the child who was crying.

"You Indians would say anything to save your hides." He raised the tomahawk to strike.

"It is true," she wept. "Look at her eyes. Our people do not have blue eyes."

Daniel came nearer. It was true, but the thought only infuriated him. With a loud cry of hatred, he raised the tomahawk and killed the woman, snatching the young child from her lifeless arms.

*   *   *

Yellow Creek was a hive of activity. Like bees whose home has been destroyed by the curious hurd of a boy's rock, the villagers prepared to leave with great urgency. News of the massacre had reached them just about the same time Logan had returned from his hunting trip.

Logan's face of triumph soon turned to anger etched in stone. His family was gone. His people were gone. There was no one left. Without a word, he threw down the bounty of his hunt and rode south.

"Revenge is hot in his heart," Machk said.

"We don't want to be caught in the crossfire," Savanukah added.

The leaders of their village looked from one to the other.

David spoke. "We have our answer, men. We need to leave this place before more blood is senselessly shed." His voice was laced with disgust. "Will they never learn? Red or white, revenge and greed will corrupt the heart, and rum only lights the fire!"

Some chose to stay and defend their village, but most chose to leave. All of Machk's clan followed the man of God, hoping that this place, which sounded like heaven, would be their final home.

A gentle rain began to fall on the newly spaded fields but the Indians continued to choose what they could take and what would be left behind. The sun had passed its zenith when the group walked away from Yellow Creek.

Siskia looked sadly at the rows of vegetables she had just planted that morning. Ahanu put his arm around her shoulders.

"We will plant again. God has been good to us and gave us great bounty last harvest." He shook his head in amazement. "He knew this was coming."

Siskia looked up into his strong features. "I am so thankful you hadn't gone east."

Ahanu nodded. "Siskia, we will never be led astray if we follow close to Jesus."

"Yes, but that doesn't mean the way will be easy," Savanukah said as he drew near his friends. He had struggled more than he wanted to admit with this move. He was tired of uprooting everything and starting over. The more they mingled with the white man, the more of their ways they wove into the fabric of their lives and moving became more difficult. Plus, the added responsibilities of a family added more stress. He smiled wanly as he thought of the few items he had tossed into his pack when he had left home for the first time.

They made camp a few hours later. Silently, they moved to prepare make-shift shelters. The sight of their downcast faces broke David and John's hearts.

"We must cheer them up, John," David offered.

John nodded, and the two men gathered sticks, usually a child's task, and began to build a fire near a fallen tree and pulled another log from the woods and then another until the fire was encircled with places to sit. The Indians looked on curiously. Certainly, a fire was not necessary. They would leave early in the morning and had enough dried meats to satisfy their stomachs. The evening springtime air was a bit cool, but that didn't bother them.

John began to sing one of the hymns they had translated into the Indians' native tongue. David joined in, his face a wreath of peace and joy. It was contagious. Soon, from every direction, the men and women—their people— came and sat down and joined in the singing.

The feelings of doubt and sadness were replaced by God's peace and joy, and the missionaries rejoiced at the sight.

"Friends, brothers and sisters, do not lose sight of our great God in this trial. He made His way clear, just as He promised He would. Isaiah writes, 'Every valley shall be exalted, and every mountain and hill shall be made low: and the crooked shall be made straight, and the rough places plain (40:4).' He is leading us to a place that He has prepared. And though our hearts mourn for Logan and his family, and though we weep at the senseless bloodshed, we go in the strength of our God."

He could see God's hand at work in their hearts and continued. "And what is our part? What did we memorize just last week?" He looked around as their minds worked to remember and the light dawned on their faces, and then began to quote. "Micah 6:8 'He hath shewed thee, O man, what is good; and what doth the LORD require of thee, but to do justly, and to love mercy, and to walk humbly with thy God?'"

By the time they finished, nearly every voice had joined. Their voices became stronger as the Holy Spirit encouraged their hearts.

David waited a moment, allowing their thoughts to continue upon God's Word before interjecting his own. "We walk on, and we do it with great humility, thanking our Father that He has allowed His light to shine in our hearts." Grunts of agreement sounded around the circle.

We will do what is right and just, even when facing injustice and wrong. We will love as our Savior loved, with mercy for our enemies, and God will bless us."

David looked to John, and he began another hymn. They sang every song they had translated and then started over again with the first one, which was everyone's favorite, *Come Here My Creator,* sung to the old familiar tune, *Come Thou Fount.* The two white men drank in the sweet countenance of every face, inwardly praising God for the privilege He had given them to reach many of them with the Gospel. All the trials had been worth it all.

That night, alone in their lean-to, David and John once again prayed that Gnadenhutten would be a refuge to these poor displaced people and that God would be glorified in all that they did.

*   *   *

The next day's journey was much more pleasant, and spirits continued to rise as they drew near their new home. The way had been clear and the rain had stopped during the night. Halfway on the journey, they had approached the Tuscarawas River, and the missionaries led them to a place where they would be able to launch their canoes into the water.

Families gathered to share a quick meal, and David was thrilled to hear laughter bubble up from different places. *Oh, how good Thou art, my Lord!*

It was a quick and happy ride as they wound their way through the forest. The water was high from the spring rains, and the trees were clean from the evening's shower. Hope flickered to life once again.

Siskia watched as Ahanu pushed the oar into the water. Even though he was well past fifty winters his body was strong and lean, and she never tired of watching him. He wore buckskin that chilly morning, but the sun was hot and he had stripped to the waist. She was thankful he maintained their native ways as much as he could without compromising their faith. The muscles across his back rippled with every move, and she couldn't help reaching out and touching him.

Ahanu's startled look made Joseph giggle and Siskia blush. Their youngest had been a pleasant surprise for Siskia and Ahanu. She had thought that her time for childbearing had passed, but then came Joseph. Ahanu's face broke into a wide grin at the boy—the child of his old age. Waneek, now twenty-four, was the spitting image of her mother, and Ahanu adored her, hating to face the day when a young buck would steal her heart. Togquos, named after Ahanu's childhood friend, was only three winters younger than Sucki. He too was spreading his wings and ready to fly.

"Is your mother silly?" Ahanu asked.

Joseph grinned and nodded.

Ahanu's eyes met Siskia's, and she blushed even more. He looked back to Joseph and changed the subject, sparing Siskia any more embarrassment. "Are you ready for a new home?" he asked the boy.

Joseph's eyes danced. "Oh yes!" he exclaimed. "Thomas and I are hoping for more playmates."

Ahanu shook his head. Joseph could never have enough playmates.

The Tuscarawas River reminded Ahanu of Legaui-hanne Creek as it wound its way through the thick forest.

Once again a twinge of longing pricked his heart. He would return... someday.

David and John slowed their canoe as they came around the last bend and motioned to the others. Gnadenhutten was just ahead. John navigated the canoe to the eastern shoreline and anxiously eyed the clearing. In these uncertain times, they were never sure what they would find when returning after an extended time away.

He smiled when he saw the usual activities taking place and waved to Newcomer who seemed to be the first one to see their approach. Soon others were waving and calling to them and to the others. The excitement only grew as more canoes continued to pull to shore. Their spiritual leaders had returned and had even brought more of their people with them!

The new arrivals couldn't help but be pleased at the reception they were given. Only one thing dampened their joy. Machk had seen it and looked to Savanukah and Ahanu who had seen it as well. Their people were dressed in the white man's clothing. They looked like white men in every way except their faces. Even some of the men and women wore their hair as white men. However, there was one who stood out against the rest, and he now greeted them warmly.

"Welcome to Gnadenhutten," called Newcomer in a loud voice. Although the wrinkles on his face told of his age, he was lithe and energetic, and he was clothed in buckskin. He even sported feathers in his hair. A woman came to stand beside him dressed in buckskin as well. Although Newcomer was thankful for the missionaries' efforts among his people, Newcomer was not a believer and did not live at Gnadenhutten; however, he frequented the little town and other villages as well. As a longtime chief of the Delawares, he made his home further west but often checked in on his scattered people.

As the introductions were made, Machk made a mental note to talk to Chief Newcomer later. There was no doubt of the sincerity and heart of the people. He thought back to other times of greeting and feasting that would follow. This was different, he could tell already, but would they need to give up all their traditions to feel as though they belonged?

*   *   *

Machk and the others would soon have their answers. Although it was not required, it was strongly suggested the Indians try to blend into the new fabric which was being woven across the land—a tapestry that would include red and white threads.

As time went on, more and more of their Indian ways melted away, not by choice but by necessity. Skins of animals became less available, and woven material was more practical. More and more foods were grown and not scavenged from the woods around them. Staying in one place and working the land, raising cattle and chickens instead of hunting for their meat was simpler and more practical as well. Their ways were changing, but their hearts would not forget their people or their ancestors.

Other winds of change were whipping up into the storms of war; this time the British father was fighting against his own children. As David had suggested, the colonists wanted freedom from the motherland, but the father-king was not so willing to let them go.

As the new group settled into Gnadenhutten, reports of bloodshed all along the coastline reached the village through the words of traders who were the settlers of the Ohio country lifeline. Time marched on, but Gnadenhutten was spared because of their pacifist beliefs. Most were thankful, but some who were still warriors at heart chafed at this new doctrine. One was Killbuck, Newcomer's grandson. Ahanu had watched the young man, whose heart had been smitten when his eyes first saw Waneek. He had made his advances, but she knew he was not a believer and graciously turned him down. Her parents were so proud of her. There were plenty more in line for her hand, and Ahanu and Siskia rejoiced when she accepted Thomas's affections.

Togquos also found a wife, and soon Ahanu and Siskia were surrounded by grandchildren. Their lives were full and safe, and Ahanu's Susquehannock blood would continue to flow in the veins of his grandchildren and their descendants. The thought brought him great joy, but as the war finally blew itself out, the old thoughts of ancestry niggled at his heart. He would soon be too old to make the journey. Should he just forget it and be satisfied with the future?

By 1781, Ahanu had made a decision. Sucki, now thirty-four with a family of his own would need to make his own choice, but Ahanu would take sixteen-year-old Joseph back to his homeland. The war was over. What did they have to fear?

Chapter Twelve

A Journey Back in Time

Lo, children are an heritage of the LORD:
and the fruit of the womb is his reward.
As arrows are in the hand of a mighty man;
so are children of the youth. Psalm 127:3,4

April, 1781

Siskia tried not to show her worry. After all, they had been followers of Jesus now for nearly thirty-five winters! She shook her head in amazement. Most of her life had been lived as a believer. She took a minute to bow her head and thank God. The sun had not yet risen on this day—the day she had been dreading for weeks. In the stillness of their cabin she listened to the quiet even breathing of both Ahanu and Joseph. Now sixteen, Joseph worked hard, played hard, and slept hard. He had been so excited about the trip that he had tossed and turned far into the night. Now he slept like a baby.

As she prayed, once again giving her family over to God, peace settled into its proper place, and she was ready to face the day's most difficult challenge—saying good-bye to Ahanu for who knew how long. In all their moves and travels, she had not been away from him for more than a few days ever in their lives. With that thought, anxiety tried to creep back into her heart, but she quickly brushed it away with the Bible verse she had always clung to: *Trust in the LORD with all thine heart; and lean not unto thine own understanding. In all thy ways acknowledge him, and he shall direct thy paths* (Proverbs 3:5,6).

Ahanu had been awake for some time before he moved. His heart was a jumble of emotions as well. While he looked forward to the trip and the time alone with his two boys—Sucki had decided to go, much to Bly's disappointment—he dreaded leaving Siskia and all the little ones. Was he a fool for doing this? In the back of his mind, he knew part of this trip had to do with a pouch full of coins which lay beneath Spirit Rock. Were they still there? Could he get them? The more they blended into American culture, the more he realized just how much that money could help them. It certainly wasn't the driving factor, but it was a real desire and the guilt of how he had gotten them had slowly been dulled.

When he felt Siskia move to get up, he reached for her and held her close, dissolving all of Siskia's resolve not to shed tears. She clung to him as though her heart would break. Indeed, she wondered if it would.

"I promised God that I would be strong," she whispered, thankful that Joseph was sleeping soundly.

"I did too," Ahanu said softly, and Siskia felt a tear splash upon her cheek. It shocked her. Never, since the day of his conversion, had she seen her husband cry, and it both broke her heart and gave her resolve to be strong for him.

"I'll be alright. The grandchildren are already dividing up which days they will stay with *Nookomis*."

"That's because they have the best grandmother in the village," Ahanu quipped.

They lay still for a moment, just enjoying the special closeness which would not be theirs for many months.

"Is our love strong enough for this?"

Siskia's question surprised Ahanu. He stiffened. "Do you doubt it?" He could feel the smile forming on her lips and rolled over to kiss her. He needn't worry that the love relationship, which they had always enjoyed, would fade away as they aged. It was something that no one talked about with their elders, but at that moment, he knew it was as strong as ever.

*   *   *

Now that the goodbyes were over, and they were paddling up the Tuscarawas River, their excitement grew with every stroke. "We'll make great time since we don't have the women and children to slow us down," Joseph said excitedly as his oar dug into the water. Sucki looked over his shoulder at his father and smiled. They had given Joseph the front and allowed him to navigate. He had the body of a man but the heart of a child.

Joseph was right. They reached the place where they had put in their canoes by midday. It had been several winters since they had initially made the journey from Yellow Creek, but Ahanu had joined David and John on several of their missionary trips and knew the way well—at least as far as Yellow Creek. Beyond that point, it had been more winters than he cared to remember!

As would become their custom, the three men would scout out the villages before entering them. As they searched the village of Yellow Creek from their hiding place, they were amazed at what they saw. The Indian village was gone and in its place was a small town. Houses clustered together along the banks of the Ohio—not many, but when they had last seen it, there had been none!

Ahanu sat back on his haunches and thought as his boys watched him. He shook his head. "I wonder where our people have gone," he whispered. His face was etched with worry, but when he looked up into the anxious faces of his sons, he pushed the worry aside and smiled.

"We will find them," he said quietly. "If not, you two are about to get a lesson on living off the land. Our ways have become soft."

He saw the surprise on their faces and chuckled. "This trip is going to be memorable in more ways than I thought."

Sucki looked at Joseph as a smile grew on his face. He nodded. "We will learn well, father. You will be proud."

Ahanu had thought they would be able to use canoes on the rivers, but the canoes had gone the way of the Indians as well. The three travelers would have to walk the entire distance unless he could find some friendly Indians.

The old trails were clearly seen from years of foot travel. It was obvious they were still in use. As they neared Fort Pitt, the memories of their time in Logstown flooded his mind. David had told him to travel north of the Fort which would bring him closer to Indian villages, even some Moravian villages of believers which had been established before the war.

How thankful they were to finally find some of their people! That night, in the little village of Tionesta, they were treated well and slept well. The good people of that place filled their sacks with good food and told them which way to go. Ahanu's only worry was that it was a new way for him, but they had told him of the unrest along the Siskëwahane River. "Best to stay among our people and come to your place from the north," one of the older chiefs said. "Bald Eagle is stirring up the whole area with his raids."

Ahanu's face flushed as he remembered his time with the man.

"You know of him? Of course you would if you came from there. Then you understand my words."

As they made their way east, the mountains that Ahanu remembered from his childhood began to rise before them. Sucki and Joseph soaked in the sights with great admiration, never having lived in a mountainous area. At Sinnemahoning they were able to borrow canoes and flow with the Sinnemahoning Creek, a welcome change for the foot-weary travelers.

Joseph lay asleep in the back of the canoe as Ahanu and Sucki paddled on. The beauty of the area was breathtaking, and Ahanu drank it all in. He especially loved to watch Sucki's reaction to the majestic mountains and thick mountain laurel which was just coming into bloom.

"How could you leave all this behind?" Sucki whispered, partly not to awaken Joseph and partly not to disturb the nature around them. They had already passed several herds of elk grazing along the creek. They thundered away as the canoe approached their watering hole.

"It was not my choice," Ahanu answered quietly. "No one ever leaves their home without good reason. You will soon understand if you don't already that there are things more precious than land."

Sucki knew he was referring to his growing brood. He was right. As a young father, he knew already that he would do whatever he had to do to protect them.

As the waters of the Sinnemahoning drew near the Siskëwahane, the current was swift and the rapids rocked the boat. Sucki's eyes gleamed with mischief as he looked back at his father. Ahanu knew his intent and leaned to the right just as Sucki's paddle hit the water next to Joseph sending a shower of frigid droplets on the sleeping giant. The young man awoke with a start just as Ahanu and Sucki maneuvered the canoe onto the Siskëwahane River.

"You'll pay for that big brother," Joseph said as he wiped the water from his face, but he was soon taking in all the sights.

They had made the trip in one month and as they drew close to the Great Island, Ahanu's heart began to race. It was as picturesque as he had described it to his sons on their travels.

The island looked the same from a distance, but as they grew nearer, Ahanu saw no movement. Then he remembered Brother Zeiseberger's words. *Famine and small pox had struck the village.*

They docked their canoes in the same place where Ahanu and the others had launched from so many winters ago, but it was overgrown with water rushes. The sandy bottom was still there and the canoe slid through the shallow waters, parting the rushes, until it could go no further. Sucki jumped out and pulled the craft to land.

The path was crowded with weeds and the fields were and overgrown tangle of goldenrod and thistle. The boys followed their father as he led the way to where a thriving village had once stood. The remains of their longhouses were still there, but they had succumbed to the weight of the winter's snow and the summer's rain and wind.

Someone had been there recently, for they saw the remains of a fire in a circle of stones. Memories flooded Ahanu's mind as he searched the landscape: his first sight of the village as he entered with Savanukah and their other two friends; Siskia's secret gift of clothing; her father's desire for him to marry his daughter; their wedding; Sucki's birth.

He turned to the boys and explained that famine and small pox had overtaken those that had stayed behind when they had left. "If any survived, they must have moved on long ago."

His heart was heavy, and he saw the disappointment in his sons' faces. He smiled. "But I will show you how it was when we were here." He walked back to the edge of the clearing. "This is where I first saw your mother. She was as graceful as a deer as she hurried to meet your uncle Machk." He continued to talk as they walked, and they were able to laugh together and cry together. He showed them the burial mounds and told them about their grandfather and mother and their great faith in the One True God.

"But come. Let us see if French Margaret's Town is still here." He smiled as he took one last look at Great Island and entered the canoe.

As they floated down the Siskëwahane River to the western shore of the Legaui-hanne Creek, the area was eerily quiet. No hustle and bustle of trade, no canoes or campfires, only the sound of the gently rolling water as it lapped up against the shore.

Ahanu kept alert and watchful, not wanting to be surprised by an unseen enemy, red or white. As the mouth of the Leguai-hanne came into view, he steered the canoe over to the left side of the river and into the waters of the Leguaihanne. Sucki and he paddled hard against the current but were soon in calmer waters.

"Let's pull in over there," Ahanu said as he pointed to a small clearing to the left. They beached the canoe and got out of the canoe. Ahanu signaled for them to be quiet and pointed to the fresh footprints in the wet earth. With great stealth, they followed their father up the path and into the woods.

A single cabin stood among the giant pines and maples and sitting in front on a stool was an old man whittling wood. He whistled as he whittled and never looked up, but called to them in a clear voice, first in their language and then in English.

"I have no money. I am here alone. You are welcome, but if you mean harm, then keep on going up the trail."

Sucki looked at his father questioningly. Ahanu didn't know whether to trust him or not. With a silent prayer, he motioned the boys to follow cautiously and stepped out into the clearing.

The man had been leaning back against the logs, but set the four legs of his stool on the ground and looked up for the first time. He didn't seem surprised to see them. He showed no fear of friendship. "State your business," he said matter-of-factly.

Ahanu came nearer. "I am Ahanu and these are my sons. We come from Ohio Country."

"Name's Russell," the man offered. He cocked his head to one side. "What in the tarnation are you doing way over here?"

Ahanu smiled at the man's frankness. "I lived here long ago. My people were Susquehannocks, and I have come to show my sons their roots and visit my dead ancestors."

"Well I'll be. I ain't never thought I'd see the likes of a Susquehannock. They died out years ago, and what was left of 'em, those manic Paxton Boys done killed in cold blood. Real shame on my people, I'll tell you. The Lord Almighty will judge 'em."

Ahanu's face brightened. "Are you a believer?"

Russell's face scrunched up. "Well, I suppose you could say that. My dear mama, God rest her soul, brought me up on the Good Book. Haven't read it for years and ain't many folk around here to converse with. You call yourselves Christian?" he asked sincerely.

They all nodded. Ahanu looked around, remembering the day of his conversion. "I stood here and listened to a preacher named David Brainerd tell of Jesus. I became a believer that day," Ahanu finished in reverential awe.

"You don't say," the old man said excitedly. "Here in French Margaret's Town?"

Ahanu nodded.

"Well, I'll be. That was before my time, but I heard stories about that." He shook his head sadly. "They were better times when Injuns and white folk knew how to git along. Also before the small pox epidemic." He huffed. "That killed off most the Indians and then renegades from Bald Eagle's band have done run off most of the white folks. He's dead now, but his savagery lives on."

"But why do you stay?" asked Sucki. The old man fascinated him.

Russell chuckled. "I guess I'm part bear and part rattler. Then agin, maybe there's a little bobcat in me too.

Anyone in these parts knows me and leaves me alone. I ain't hurtin' no one, and I ain't grubbin' for the land. I'm just finishin' out my days here in this spot."

He stood and motioned to his door. "Why don't you come on in and have a bite?"

Ahanu looked at the sky. He knew they could make it to Spirit Rock, especially if they could keep canoeing. "Thank you for your kindness, but I would like to get to Spirit Rock before the sun sets."

"Spirit Rock? Ain't never heard of it."

Ahanu explained where it was, but the old man shook his head. "Ain't nobody livin' up thata way. You should have clear sailing. Stop on by on your way back through."

"We will," Ahanu promised.

Russell held out his hand, and Ahanu shook it, then Sucki, and finally Joseph. "What's your name, sonny?"

Joseph smiled and told him.

"Good name, lad. Perhaps you will grow up and save your people like Joseph did in the Bible."

Joseph looked at him in surprise. He had never thought of that, and the old man's words felt like a prophecy.

The trio waved as they headed back to their canoe and started upstream. The depth and smoothness of the water made paddling easy even against the current and Ahanu wondered why they had never traveled by canoe before. He recognized the large elm at the edge of the wide meadow and pushed the canoe in its direction. They didn't disembark, but Ahanu told of his first visit to the area and then of his conversion. The boys drank in every word before they pushed on.

The shadows of the trees were growing long by the time they reached the foot of the mountain where they would need to travel by foot. They stashed the canoe out of the water and hid it in the low-lying branches of a giant white pine.

Ahanu felt as though he were a young man once again. They were right at the spot where he had stopped and listened to Savanukah and the others' conversation. In fact, where the canoe now lay hidden was the exact spot where he had hid. He shared story after story with his sons as they made their way up the mountain. The path was nearly gone, but Ahanu knew the way.

He debated where to go first and chose Spirit Rock. If they hurried, they would be there just as the sun set. His heart raced as he realized it would have been exactly around this time when Sucki had been sacrificed on Spirit Rock. He did not keep track of the moon's phases like his ancestors had, but he knew it had been near the end of this month.

"Father, slow down," Sucki called as Ahanu pushed ahead. He laughed.

"Can't you keep up with an old man?" he taunted and the boys took the bait. They both rushed past him, seeing their destination in the distance.

The sun hung just above the horizon like a molten ball of fire just as the three Susquehannocks reached the rocks. They stood side by side panting for breath. The view was spectacular. Streaks of red, orange and pink fanned out from the sun like streams of liquid fire, drenching the valley before them in ethereal dusky hues.

Ahanu's throat clogged with emotion, and tears ran down his cheeks. He put an arm around each of his sons, thanking God for this magical moment.

They all stood and watched as the sun slipped away, slowly putting out its lights but not before spraying the entire sky once more with darker shades of amber and purple.

Without a word, Ahanu knelt and his sons followed suit, bowing their heads in prayer.

"Oh Father," Ahanu began but could go no further. He wept uncontrollably, overwhelmed with both his blessings and his loss.

"Heavenly Father," Sucki began. "Thank you for bringing us to this place. Thank you for keeping us safe and well and for giving us the strength to make this journey. But most of all, thank you for saving our souls. Thank you for the man, David Brainerd, whose words sparked Father's conviction of sin. Thank you for Mother's faith and strength of spirit when Father needed it most." He paused momentarily and was going to begin again when he heard his brother's quiet voice.

"Thank you, Father for sending Jesus to die for our sins. Thank you for Brothers David and John and their faithful witness. Thank you for our family. Keep them safe and bring us back together again."

They continued to bow in silence, not wanting to end the sacred moment.

"Great God of Truth, thank you. You took my broken heart and life and gave me beauty for ashes. Help our people to understand the truth of Your Word, and maybe find peace with the white man."

Again they knelt in silence until Ahanu uttered, "Amen."

He stood and pulled them both into his arms. "How proud I am to call you both, son," he said in a husky voice. "There is more to show you, but we will make camp here, and I will tell you my story."

*   *   *

Ahanu took them to the site of his village the next day. There was nothing there, and trees had grown up in the clearing. Several places there were lumps in the leaves and new summer growth where wigwams had once stood. They visited their ancestral burial grounds although there was nothing much to see.

"Your great-grandfather's sprit lives in you both. I have seen him in your eyes. Never forget you are a Susquehannock," he said fiercely. "They may take our land and our homes. They may even spill our blood, but they cannot take away who we are and where we came from."

That night, as they sat around the fire, Ahanu told them of his past: his childhood, his people's stories which his grandfather had told him, and his time with Bald Eagle.

"I am ashamed of my actions, and for that reason I cast the coins in the crack in Spirit Rock," he said as he jutted his chin in that direction. "Tomorrow, I want to see if we can find those coins," he said quietly.

Sucki looked at Joseph. After all that their father had said, they wondered why he would want them, but they kept silent.

Ahanu couldn't sleep that night. It was as if all the host of hell were tormenting his soul. Raweno came to him, laughing and taunting his soul. In his dream he was standing at the base of Spirit Rock. The coins were within his reach, but when he stretched out his hand to take them, they ran red with blood. Blood flowed all around him. He looked at his hands and they were covered with blood. In horror, he looked and saw the bodies of those he had killed lying on Spirit Rock as demons danced around them chanting, "Raweno!"

He sat up in a cold sweat, still feeling the darkness. He could not see them, but they were here, in this place of spiritual darkness—the place of pitiful sacrifices.

Silently, he scrambled to his feet and stumbled to the edge of the cliffs. He dropped to his knees and began to pray, never stopping until the visions and voices were gone. He shivered in the cold and looked out across the valley. A full moon was bathing the mountains in its light, casting shadows into every fold in the landscape.

Peace reigned in his heart, but he was exhausted. He would not seek the coins. Perhaps someone else would find them someday, but they were not meant for him.

*   *   *

Ahanu awoke to an empty lean-to and sat up quickly, too quickly. His head was foggy from last night's nightmare and lack of sleep. He looked around for the boys but they were gone.

He looked out through the woods and saw that Joseph was sitting on the rocks. He went to him but the lad was so deep in thought that he never heard his father's approach. As Ahanu came closer he realized that he was not thinking but praying.

He looked for Sucki, but he was nowhere in sight. Quietly, he sat down beside his son and took in the breathtaking view. The sun was to their backs and was just about to break over the trees behind them. Distant treetops were tinged in golden morning sunlight and a wisp of fog laced its way above the Leguai-hanne Creek, gracefully rising with the sun. Far below, in a wide meadow, a mother bear and two cubs meandered towards the creek.

When Ahanu came out of his reverie, he found Joseph's eyes upon him. He could not name the look in his eyes. Wonder? Questioning? Sadness? Perhaps it was a combination of all three. He put his hand upon Joseph's shoulder, much as he would have done to his equal. The gesture did not go unnoticed, and Joseph sat a bit taller. "What's on your mind, son?"

"I want to stay here, Father," Joseph said quietly.

Ahanu nodded. Joseph had no idea how much sadness the statement put in his father's heart. "Me too."

Joseph's face brightened. "Then why don't we bring Mother and the others back here?" he said excitedly.

Ahanu's face was full of pity. "We can't, my son. This land is not ours."

"But neither is Gnadenhutten."

It was true, but it had been purchased or given to the Moravians for the express purpose of building a mission. "But it does belong to someone."

"Why couldn't we buy this land? Or why should we even need to. It belonged to our ancestors," he said fiercely.

Ahanu shook his head. "It is not that simple."

The two were sitting in silence when Sucki returned. He was none too quiet and was whistling a tune, but when he saw their long faces, he stopped. "Why the long faces?" He was secretly excited to be on their way back to Ohio. The ache in his heart for his wife and children had nearly grown unbearable.

Joseph stood abruptly. "I want to stay," he said and ran off into the woods.

Sucki looked at his father questioningly as Ahanu rose to his feet. "He likes it here," was all he said.

It was a quiet hike back down the mountain. With their minds elsewhere nothing was said about the coins until they had reached the bottom. Suddenly, Joseph stopped and looked at Ahanu. "Your coins, Father. We forgot to get your coins."

Ahanu shook his head and kept walking. "Forget them, son."

It was about time for the afternoon meal when they pulled the canoe into the bulrushes at Russell's cabin. They didn't worry about being quiet this time and were in quiet conversation when Ahanu stopped abruptly, nearly causing Sucki to run into him.

Lying in the doorway of the cabin was the still body of the old man. Ahanu ran to him and reached for his hand. It was still warm. He gently rolled Russell over and placed his hand on the man's forehead. He was burning up with fever.

"Help me carry him inside," he ordered, and both boys came to their father's aid.

The inside of the cabin was dark, but in the corner was a bed. They gently laid him down and stood back to assess the situation. Looking around the cabin, they could tell that it was usually neat and clean, but in a basin were several dirty dishes and a pot of crusted stew sat at the edge of the potbelly stove in one corner.

Ahanu found a kettle and handed it to Joseph. "Get some clean water."

Joseph nodded and was out the door.

Ahanu had gone to a cupboard to look for some food or medicines. "Sucki, see if you can find some garlic growing nearby. You know where to look."

Sucki turned and hurried away just as Joseph reentered the cabin with fresh water.

Ahanu pointed to a cloth on a rack. "Take that and cool his forehead and arms with it. I'll make a fire for something hot to drink. He took the bucket from Joseph and poured some of the water in a cup and into the kettle. "See if you can get any of this into his mouth."

Joseph hurried to the task, placing the bucket on a nightstand and pulling a chair beside the bed. He began by dipping the cloth in the cool water and laying it on the man's forehead. In a matter of seconds, the cloth was warm, and he started again. After several times, he patted the man's face, neck and arms with cool water and then took the cup which Ahanu had placed beside the bucket and held it to the man's lips, which were cracked because of dryness.

He slid his free hand under the man's head, tilted it up and then put the cup to his lips. At first the water just drizzled down the man's neck, but on the third try, his mouth parted and the water entered his mouth. Involuntarily, he swallowed it and began to cough.

Joseph looked alarmed, but Ahanu encouraged him to keep trying after a moment. By the fifth sip, the man seemed to rouse and drank the water voraciously.

"Not too much, Joseph," Ahanu warned. "We do not know how long he has been without food or water."

Sucki came through the door carrying a bunch of garlic and grinning from ear to ear. He held up the bundle proudly.

"Good work, son, both of you," Ahanu said looking from one to the other.

At that moment, Russell's eyes fluttered open. At first he seemed alarmed but then he recognized their faces. "Boy, am I glad to see youins!" he croaked in a raspy voice.

"How long have you been ill?" Ahanu asked, taking the garlic from Sucki and deftly breaking it apart and cutting it into pieces. He dropped it into the water which had just started to simmer.

"Oh, just about as long as you were gone. I wasn't feeling too perky the day you showed up and went downhill fast. Don't know if I'd made it if you hadn't come along. Was powerful thirsty and was going to get water. That's the last thing I remember." He sniffed the air. "Whatcha cookin'?"

"Garlic for your fever," Ahanu said as he stirred the pot.

"Never heard of that, but I'm ready to try anything." All the talking had tired the man. "I'm as hungry as a bear. There's some salt pork in the smokehouse out back," he added and then closed his eyes. Before Ahanu could answer him, he was asleep again.

By that evening, they had cleaned up the cabin, washed some of the dirty bedding and cloths, and had a stew simmering on the stove. Sucki had found honey in one of the pots on a shelf and a bit of tea. Ahanu mixed some of each into his concoction, and Joseph helped Russell take some of it before he ate some of the stew.

Once Russell's stomach had some food in it, he was asleep once again, and the three men walked out into the front clearing.

Sucki was the first to speak. "What are we going to do? We can't leave him alone."

Ahanu could hear the frustration in his voice. "You are right. Unless someone comes along, we need to stay with him until he recovers."

"How old do you think he is?" Joseph asked.

Ahanu picked up a twig and started to break it into pieces. He tossed the tiny bits into the water as he thought. "Older than me. Maybe seventy winters."

Nothing more was said as they all were lost in their thoughts. "We will see how he is in the morning," Ahanu said.

Both sons nodded. That night, they sat along the water until it was time to turn in for the night. Ahanu made a bed on the floor of the cabin to keep watch over Russell. His fever spiked in the night, and Russell mumbled in his sleep for a while but after another sip of water, he settled down for the night.

In the morning, he seemed worse. The fever was ravaging his body, and he had no appetite. Day after day he lay in his bed, and the three Indians cared for him and fervently prayed for wisdom.

A week went by, and the old man held on. How he was still alive was a mystery to Ahanu. With hardly anything to eat and only sips of water and the tea mixture, they feared he would soon die.

"Whatever he has, it's going to kill him if he doesn't soon get better," Sucki said one day as he stared at the sickly form wasting away in the bed. He was frustrated. He wanted to go! He wanted to be home with his family!

Ahanu shook his head. "I know your frustration, son. It is past time for us to be on our way, but we can't just leave him." He thought for a moment. Suddenly, his face brightened. "I remember that there was another village further down river. I will see if there is anyone there to help."

The boys were hopeful as Ahanu left the cabin and paddled away.

Ahanu paddled swiftly, knowing that he couldn't miss the village. It had been quite large and was also at the mouth of another creek. But as he turned to paddle up the creek he searched both sides of the water. Just like Great

Island, he could see where the village once stood. He pulled up to the bank and secured the canoe.

With urgency in his steps he nearly ran up the path. *Surely, there must be someone!* But the place was also deserted. Broken down longhouses were scattered here and there, reminders of another time. His heart ached. What were they to do? He needed answers. He fell to his knees and implored his Father to lead them.

Sucki and Joseph knew as soon as they saw their father's face that it had been a futile trip. Ahanu shook his head and went into the cabin. "We need to pray, boys. I have no direction, but this man needs us, and he needs our God to heal him."

They all fell to their knees and poured out their hearts to God. Around and around the tiny circle they prayed, begging and pleading for God to heal Russell.

They had just finished praying the Lord's Prayer when Russell groaned. Ahanu jumped to his feet and went to him, taking the ever-present cup and putting it to Russell's parched lips. He felt his head and turned to the boys.

"He is cool. His fever is down. Boys! God has given us a miracle!"

"Well, that's the first time I've ever been called that," muttered Russell, and they all laughed.

*   *   *

Russell slowly gained his strength back but it was obvious that the man wouldn't be able to be left alone for weeks. They asked if there was anyone to help him, but he had no one. One evening after supper, Ahanu asked the boys to walk with him.

They headed into the woods and along an old trail. The trees towered above them, shutting out much of the late afternoon sun. It was cool here and so peaceful, even though their hearts were troubled.

"I'm not sure what to do," Ahanu confessed. "If we do not leave soon, our families will be worried, but I'm not sure that Russell will survive on his own."

"Let me stay," Joseph blurted out. Both men looked at the young man as though he had lost his mind.

"No," Ahanu said flatly.

"But we can't stay forever."

"You aren't staying by yourself."

"I wouldn't be by myself. Russell would be with me."

"Talk some sense into him, Sucki." But Sucki was silent.

"We've already talked. I'm leaving," he said quietly. "I cannot be away from my family any longer."

Ahanu stopped and looked at Sucki and then at Joseph. He could see that they were serious.

"Your mother will kill me," Ahanu said. "I cannot leave you here, Joseph. I would rather die," he said fiercely

"Go, Father, and when Russell is better, then I will come."

Ahanu scoffed.

"You were my age when you set out on your own and you had no direction... or the Lord," he added quietly. He looked into his father's eyes. They were full of anguish. "Father, I want to stay. I believe God wants me to stay."

"But..." Ahanu did not know what to say. "I will pray about this."

"We will pray with you," Sucki offered, but Ahanu cut him off.

"No. Go back to Russell."

They looked at each other and then at their Father. They had never seen him like this before. His eyes were deep pools of sadness, and his jaw twitched as he clenched his teeth. He turned abruptly and hurried away.

He walked quickly and then began to jog. Soon he was running as fast as he could. It felt so good. He stretched his legs as far as they would go, running like the wind.

Several times he caught woodland animals unawares and they bounded into the forest.

When he thought his heart would beat out of his chest, he began to slow down. He had followed the path along the river and turned to an outcropping of ledges near the water. Climbing to the top, he sat down and allowed his pulse to slow down. He looked up into the cloudless sky and watched as an eagle came soaring up the river, swooping down to catch his dinner. The strong majestic wings lifted the bird high into the air and into the woods on the opposite side of the river.

"Why, Lord? Why did You let this happen?" He pulled his knees up and wrapped his arms around them, resting his chin there, much as he had done as a young boy. Indeed, the run had made him feel young again—back to a simpler time.

He thought of Siskia. What would she do if he returned without Joseph? What would happen to him? The area seemed quiet. Ahanu had been surprised at Joseph's interest and desire to live off the land. He had proven himself capable. He would have Russell.

Ahanu had known for a few weeks now that Sucki was chomping at the bit to get back to his family and he didn't blame him. Being away from Siskia had been difficult enough, and he couldn't imagine being away so long from his children as well. He bowed and prayed for wisdom, but he already knew what the answer was. If Russell was in agreement and would care for Joseph, he would stay behind.

*   *   *

The following morning after breakfast, Ahanu told them of their plan to leave Joseph behind to care for Russell until he could care for himself.

Russell looked at Ahanu as though he didn't understand. He then looked at Sucki, and lastly at Joseph. He swallowed hard, and his eyes misted. He was not a praying man, but he had asked the good Lord for this very thing. He had grown fond of the young man. Many evenings the two of them would play checkers, something Joseph had never done. He had become an expert and had even beaten Russell a few times.

"I don't know what to say," he said in a raspy voice, full of emotion. "I would be honored to have your son stay here with me."

Ahanu tried not to show that his heart was breaking. He nodded quickly. "Then it is settled. The boy wants to stay." He looked at Joseph. Their eyes locked momentarily, and Joseph wondered if he could really do it. But Russell's voice interrupted his thoughts.

"I want you to know, that if he chooses to stay even when I'm stronger, all of this will be his. I have no one else to leave it to," he said in quiet conviction. "I even have a little money stashed away. I know I said I didn't, but no one would ever find it unless I showed 'em where it was."

They stood in awkward silence for a moment. Ahanu went to Joseph and put his hands upon his shoulders. He searched his face. "Are you sure, son?"

Joseph's eyes were filled with tears. He could only nod. Ahanu pulled him into a strong embrace and held him as long as he could and let him go.

He strode purposely to Russell and shook his hand. "If you change your mind and want to come to Ohio, you would be welcome."

Russell nodded. He didn't trust his voice but had to speak. "Thank you. You saved my life," he said hoarsely.

Ahanu nodded. He looked at Joseph one last time and then hurried from the cabin. Sucki nodded to Russell, came to Joseph and held him in a brotherly embrace and then hurried away.

It was a silent ride up the Siskëwahane River. Both men paddled in silence. Before they knew it, they were passing Great Island.

"We will keep on the Siskëwahane, but we will need to keep a sharp eye out for trouble," Ahanu said.

There was silence for a moment and then Sucki spoke. "I don't know if I could have done what you just did."

Ahanu could hear the admiration in his son's voice. "Your children are babies. When the time comes, you will have the strength, even when your heart is breaking."

Traveling by canoe was much faster, even though some spots were low. It was now early August, and Ahanu thought they could be back before harvest time. The further they got from Joseph the more his heart ached to get home to Siskia.

The trip brought back so many memories for Ahanu. He was thankful they passed by Bald Eagle's Nest without any trouble. Kittanning would be the next village where there could possibly be danger, but they wouldn't get there until the next day. That night, Ahanu thought it best if he filled Sucki in on their stay there.

He listened with rapt attention as Ahanu told of Pontiac and his love for Siskia. He had heard the village was quite a beehive of activity. Many Indian raids had been staged in Kittanning against the British. Would it be a safe place now that the British had lost?

That night before falling asleep, Ahanu decided it would be best to pass Kittanning and Fort Pitt in the cover of darkness. They could cover plenty of distance now that they were paddling with the current of the great Allegheny and Ohio Rivers. From there, it wouldn't take them long to get from Yellow Creek to home. Home—the word sounded as sweet a meadowlark's song!

Sucki liked the idea when Ahanu told them of his plans, and father and son made deep strokes into the water, pushing the canoe swiftly through the water. Their conversation was animated as they talked about getting home and all they would do.

Back and forth the Mahoning Creek meandered and at times Sucki felt that they were going in circles. Only stopping when necessary, they were on the Allegheny River just as darkness crept in about them. The cooler night air felt good against their damp skin. The river was much wider and deeper and the water moved swiftly through the tall overhanging trees.

As they approached Kittanning, the smell of wood smoke threaded its way through the air. Ahanu felt anxious. How glad he would be if they could just slip by the village.

As they drew near, they stayed far to the western shoreline and dipped their paddles noiselessly into the river. Ahanu could see the shoreline just ahead with several canoes lined up, just as they had been so many years ago. He thought once again about Pontiac and Captain Hill and the fact that both men were now dead. How good God had been to him! He took a moment to silently thank the Lord for all He had done for him and his family. His mind went to Siskia and then to Joseph.

Suddenly, there was a commotion on the opposite shore. They had been seen and even as he watched, several warriors were directing their canoes towards them.

"Say nothing," he hissed to Sucki.

As the warriors shouted to them, Ahanu held up both hands high. "We come in peace," he shouted. Sucki raised his hands as well.

"Come with us," one of the Indians shouted none too friendly. How different from when they had arrived the last time, but he knew that two men could be more of a threat than many canoes with families. They could be spies or scouts from a warring tribe.

Ahanu and Sucki paddled to the eastern shore between two of the other canoes. Before they could get out of the canoe, two of the warriors were pulling their canoe out of the water.

They were escorted to the fire ring where the flames cast dancing shadows all about them. Ahanu searched the faces of those around him. There were only men—the women and children were all in bed. A giant of a man stood opposite of him and Ahanu's heart dropped. It was Beedeedee, the man he had fought and beaten what seemed like a lifetime ago. He started to look away, but not before he saw that the man recognized him.

With a roar of rage, Beedeedee lunged toward Ahanu, but just like the last time, Ahanu's swift movements allowed him to slip away as the giant crashed to the ground.

The others laughed, but Beedeedee scrambled to his feet and was ready to lunge again when a stern voice stopped him. "Enough Beedeedee."

Ahanu turned to see who had spoken. He was a little younger than Ahanu, but by his stance and demeanor, he knew he was the chief. Then he realized that it was Blue Feather, one of the men that they had beaten.

Blue Feather smiled cruelly. "I see you remember me." He looked at Sucki. "And has your son grown to be as good a fighter as his father?"

"We come in peace. We only wish to pass through your village and return to our family," Ahanu said.

"You will fight first, but this time you will fight with us not against us."

Ahanu kept his gaze steady and confident. "Our God calls us to live in peace," he said quietly.

Blue Feather threw his head back and laughed. He sneered at Ahanu. "Ah yes. I remember your God. If He is so strong, then He will help you to help us win our fight."

Ahanu started to say something, but Blue Feather shot his hand into the air and stuck him across the face.

"Silence! You are our prisoners, and you will fight or die! Take them away," he commanded, and two of his men bound their hands behind them and pushed them toward two trees where they were pushed to the ground and bound to the trunk.

They searched them for any weapons or knives and left them, laughing and taunting them as they walked away.

Ahanu watched their movements, completely absorbed in his own thoughts until he heard Sucki huff. He looked over at his son who fought to keep tears of frustration from his eyes. Ahanu's heart ached. "I'm sorry, Son," he whispered.

Sucki looked surprised. "This is not your fault, Father."

"Yes it is. I should not have come this way, or I should have paid better attention to what was ahead of us in the water. We should have..."

"Father, stop. We are in God's hands."

That one solitary statement stopped Ahanu's litany of excuses. His look of frustration and anguish slowly dissipated in the light of this simple yet profound truth. He sighed and laid his head against the tree trunk. "You're right."

"He will see us through." Sucki looked across the clearing to the men that still gathered around the fire. He tried to hear their conversation but could only catch bits and pieces. He strained to hear more, then he turned abruptly to Ahanu.

"They are fighting with the British."

Ahanu looked puzzled. "But the war is over."

"Not here," Sucki said and listened once again. "They are waiting for British soldiers to arrive and then are heading southeast to Hannastown."

"So that's what Blue Feather meant when he said we would fight with them. They are attacking the colonists." He nearly added, *and killing innocent men, women, and children,* but he knew Sucki already knew this. News of renegade Indians wreaking havoc all over the Allegheny Valley had reached Gnadenhutten and was one of the reasons this trip had almost been postponed again. Past images flashed in his mind making him sick to his stomach. *I will not do it!* he wanted to shout.

"We need to pray, Father," Sucki said quietly. He saw the torment on his father's face. His uncle Machk and

Savanukah, his father-in-law had shared some of what they had done before their conversions. Machk had told him of his father's thirst for revenge, getting caught up in the moment of storytelling and saying more than he probably should have.

Ahanu looked into Sucki's sympathetic face and nodded. Before he could say a word, Sucki began.

"Oh Father, we need your help. Please give us wisdom. Help us to be strong and face whatever you have set before us. May these wicked men be destroyed, and may your precious name be glorified. Please give us wings as eagles. Help us to run and not be weary, to walk and not faint." He heard Ahanu's grunt of approval and continued. "May your angels keep watch over us in this dark place and watch over our families as well. And Father, may we see them soon. In Jesus' Name. Amen."

Sucki kept his head bowed. As hard as he tried, he could not keep back the tears. Ahanu longed to touch him but his ropes kept him bound and out of his reach. "Thank you, Sucki. You are a joy and a comfort to my father-heart. I am proud of the man you have become."

Sucki wiped his eyes on his sleeve and leaned his head against the tree. "How can you say that when I cry like a baby?"

Ahanu jutted his chin out. "Those tears show that you are strong in heart, stronger than any of these fools. You are brave too, but better to weep than to talk foolishly."

Oh, how Sucki loved his father! His wisdom had always been a beacon of light into his soul, showing the way to righteousness. And now, in their darkest hour, it blazed like the sun at midday, bringing comfort and strength to his fearful heart.

The next morning, a brave came to them and roughly untied their ropes. Ahanu stood and towered over the youth but then saw that he held a gun. "Go," the boy said gruffly and jerked his head in the direction of the nearest longhouse.

"I must relieve myself," Ahanu said.

"Not now. You go," he said more determinedly and poked Ahanu with the barrel of the gun.

Ahanu was tempted to take the thing from him and wrap it around his neck, but simply walked away from him instead. Sucki followed his brisk pace, and they heard the boy scrambling to keep up with them.

As they drew near, the doorflap flew open and Beedeedee stood there glaring at them. Ahanu ignored him and entered the longhouse. As his eyes adjusted, he saw Blue Feather and the other leaders at the far end of the structure and walked confidently to them.

He stopped before them and felt more than saw Sucki come up to stand beside him. Ahanu had told him that Savanukah had beaten Blue Feather with his bow, and the pride that he felt for his people made him stand a bit taller.

Blue Feather just stared for a moment. Even though the tournament had been over forty winters ago, it was still fresh in his mind. It had been the only challenge he had ever lost, and it tore at his pride like a briar of thorns. Now, here stood one of them—those Praying Indians. His eyes glimmered with excitement.

He wasted no time in laying out the plan before them. "We wait for the British and the cover of a new moon. Then we will attack the white man's village at Hannastown. You will fight for us."

Ahanu was only silent for a moment. Then, with quiet conviction in his voice, he answered. "We will not fight."

Beedeedee had been waiting for his answer and came forward pinning Sucki to his chest and laying his knife against his scalp. Sucki struggled against the giant, but it was no use.

Ahanu watched as the blade pressed again his son's skin and a trickle of blood ran down his forehead.

"Are you sure of your answer?" Blue Feather asked, his voice bursting forth with the pleasure of victory.

Ahanu looked at Sucki. He was so brave but Ahanu could see his fear. He looked back at Blue Feather and raised his chin. "We will fight."

Blue Feather smiled and nodded once to Beedeedee. By now, blood ran across Sucki's forehead and into his eyes but he did not wipe it away. He wanted to shout, "No!" but he would obey his father.

"Take them away!" Blue Feather commanded, and Beedeedee came up behind Ahanu grabbing his arms and nearly lifting him off the floor. Ahanu thought his arms would snap, and the pain was excruciating, but he would not give any of them the satisfaction of seeing his pain. Another warrior had hold of Sucki, and they were led from the longhouse and to another structure which was much smaller. Without ceremony, they threw them into the hut and stood as sentinels before the door.

Ahanu scrambled to Sucki and quickly took a cloth from his side pouch and wrapped it around the wound. He was sitting back on his haunches checking to make sure the bleeding was stanched when the flap was opened and a young woman entered. She had a bowl with food in it and a flask of water which she quickly sat down before them.

Ahanu watched her and studied her face. Her eyes were downcast and her hair was pulled over the right side of her face. He looked at her hands when she set down the food and noticed that they were scarred and grotesquely malformed. His mind was working hard to bring back to focus their time in Kittanning, and he suddenly remembered, but before he could say anything, she was gone.

"What is it, Father? Did you know her?" Sucki asked.

Ahanu nodded slowly. "Yes, I believe I do." He looked at the food and realized how hungry he was. "Let's pray and then I'll tell you her story."

They bowed in prayer, once again asking for strength and wisdom, and then shared the food and water. Ahanu took a slow sip of the water, not certain how long they would have to make it last, and handed it to Sucki. His actions did not go unnoticed, and Sucki did the same.

"Shortly after we arrived here, there had been an accident. A young girl had fallen into the fire and was badly burned. It was horrible." He stopped talking for a moment as he relived the time. "Her family didn't think she would live. Her father, a proud man, didn't think she should live," he added quietly. "But she did."

Sucki nodded in understanding. The Indian culture was not always kind to the deformed.

"She loved you and your mother and would follow Siskia around like a puppy. She's just a few winters older than you and she loved to try to carry you around, which, of course, you did not enjoy." They shared a smile—the first in a long time.

"What is her name?" Sucki asked.

Ahanu smiled sadly. "Yellow Bird. As a young girl, her hair was the color of the sun and as curly as lamb's wool."

Sucki looked surprised, and Ahanu went on. "Somewhere in her bloodline was the blood of white men, probably another reason her father did not favor her even before the accident." Ahanu shook his head sadly. "Her mother suffered for that. It wasn't long before the man took another wife, and Yellow Bird's mother became more of a slave than anything else."

"Who is the father? Did you know him?" Sucki asked. Ahanu could hear the anger in his voice. He took a moment to answer, not wanting to look up. Sucki waited.

Finally, Ahanu's gaze met his son's, and he spoke so quietly that Sucki could hardly make out the name.

"Blue Feather."

*   *   *

For the next few days a routine seemed to be put into place, and the prisoners were mostly ignored. Twice a day, food came, and they were allowed to relieve themselves under supervision, but other than that, they were left alone.

The brave who had first taken them to the chief's longhouse came every other day opposite of Yellow Bird. He was surly and fairly threw the food at them before picking up the empty containers.

The next time Yellow Bird came in, quietly Ahanu called her by name. She nearly dropped the dishes, looking up and into his eyes.

"I am Ahanu. This is Sucki. My wife is Siskia. We were here when you were young." He spoke rapidly, hoping she might say something, but she looked like a frightened rabbit and scampered away.

"Do you think she knew us?" Sucki asked.

"I don't know," Ahanu said. He had a plan, and Yellow Bird was a big part of it.

The next time she came, he spoke to her again. Terrified, she shook her head and put her finger to her lips, looking furtively over her shoulder.

"You know me?" Ahanu whispered.

A faint smile came to her lips as though it didn't know how to get there. She nodded and leaned close. Ahanu did so as well. "I will come tonight if I can," she said and was gone.

That night, the men waited but she did not come. The following night they waited again and had just about given up when the flap opened slowly and she crept in. They huddled in a tight circle and whispered into each other's ears. "The guards are sleeping. They could get into trouble, but no one would believe me if I told on them." She hurried on. "Do you know their plan?"

"To attack Hannatown?" Ahanu offered

She nodded and said, "But they also plan to use you to strengthen the warriors and new braves into action."

Sucki looked at her questioningly.

"They will torture you until you beg for mercy," she said sadly. "I've seen them do it before."

They sat in silence, the reality of their demise sinking in.

"Your mother and wife was good to me," Yellow Bird continued. "She told me about Jesus."

Ahanu knew this, but just nodded.

"Will you take Mother and me with you if you escape?"

Ahanu saw the fear and pleading in her eyes and reached for her deformed hand. At first, she pulled away, but he held firm. "You have my promise."

She smiled again, transforming her face into a beautiful sight even with the scars. "I have a plan," she said. Her chin was set, and she continued. "They will all get drunk the night before the raid. The British will bring more rum. When they have drunk it, they will come for you, but we will be gone." Her eyes were wide with excitement as she continued. "I will have a canoe ready downstream and Mother will be there for us. They will have you tied to the tree as they drink, but I will cut your cords. Stand ready and watch for the right time and then meet me in the woods behind this hut. I will show you the way."

Ahanu was astonished. She had it all planned out. He thought it through for any trouble spots. He only saw one. "But if they catch us, we will all die. Are you ready to die?"

The biggest smile yet came to her face, and her eyes danced with joy as she nodded. "Jesus is my Savior and best Friend. Without Him, I would have died long ago."

As though Yellow Bird had prophesied the future, the British came. They brought the rum and all day long, the Indians and British drank and celebrated. Ahanu and Sucki heard their raucous laughter and bits and pieces of conversation, and as the day wore on, they could hear more and more.

Suddenly, the flap flew open, and the two guards hauled them out into the open. They were put on display, just as Yellow Bird had predicted and drug to the two trees where they had been secured that dreadful night when they were first taken captive. It had been night before. Now, to Ahanu's disgust and horror, they saw the dark blots on the tree and ground where blood had dried.

The whole tribe looked on, their eyes bleary with liquor and the thirst for blood. Surprisingly, Blue Feather was sober. He cockily strode towards them to the hoots and howls of every warrior while the British watched with equal delight.

"Your time is at hand," he said as he drew close to Ahanu. His face was just inches away as he spoke. "You will soon be ready for the fight of your life."

Ahanu worked hard to keep his breathing steady and his eyes quiet of any revenge or anger. At that moment, he realized that his Lord was standing near him, just like David of old. *The battle is the Lord's.* Those words flashed into his mind, and he drew strength from them. He said nothing nor made any facial expression. He simply stood there like a statue.

Blue Feather's liquored breath made him want to vomit but still he stood firm. The chief was infuriated and stepped back to slap Ahanu across the face. The blow nearly toppled him, but he slowly stood erect once more.

Blue Feather spit in his face, but still he did not show any sign of weakness or aggression.

Sucki's jaws were clenched, and he wanted to scream a thousand insults, but he too stood still.

With one last look of disgust, Blue Feather lifted the bottle he held in his hand to his lips, took a long draft, and spit it in Sucki's face.

Sucki's look of astonishment made him roar with laughter and the wicked leader strutted away.

Neither prisoner spoke, but a few moments later they felt the bands around their hands relax and the rope around their waists and feet go limp. Yellow Bird carefully tied slipknots into the ropes so they would easily slip off with only a tug but still looked to be tied.

"You will know when the time is right," was all she said, and then she slipped unnoticed into the woods.

Once again it seemed as though they had been forgotten. A wild boar had been roasting in an open pit, and the smell of clams simmering in a pot wafted through the air. Soon they were feasting and becoming more insolent even to each other.

Father, give us wisdom. Show us your timing. Before Ahanu had finished the words, a fight broke out. Soon bedlam reigned, and he knew he had his sign from God. Quick as lightning they were free and running through the woods. Yellow Bird appeared out of nowhere and led them to the canoes. Her mother, Kimi, was already seated in the canoe.

Without a word, they jumped in, Ahanu in front, Kimi and Yellow Bird in the middle, and Sucki in back. Kimi had the paddles in hand and handed one to each man, and they were on their way. The canoe was just far enough downstream that they couldn't be seen, so they wasted no time masking any noise. The canoe shot through the water nearly causing the women to tumble backwards. Yellow Bird looked up in surprise and laughed softly. Free! For the first time in her life she was free.

By the time tempers had sizzled out and amends were made, the prisoners were long gone. More fighting broke out, and innocent bystanders were accused of letting them go. It seemed as though they had just vanished. Search parties were sent in every direction, but when word came to Blue Feather that his wife, Kimi, and daughter were missing and one canoe was also gone, they knew they would never catch them. He cursed and swore, but the British urged him to forget it. They were more concerned with tomorrow's work than a few missing Indians.

Words were few until the foursome knew they were out of harm's way. Even then talking was superficial. The men continued their energetic pace, and both were too winded for words anyway.

As they came near Fort Pitt, Ahanu slowed his pace and Sucki followed suit. Truth be told, he was ready for a break. He had gained a new appreciation for his father.

Ahanu turned around to face them. He looked at the women and smiled weakly. Slowly, his breathing became normal, and he could talk. "Thank you, Yellow Bird. We owe you our lives." The young woman blushed under such praise.

"I fear I was acting selfishly," she answered quietly.

"It is not selfish to fight for a just life and gain freedom in the same act," Ahanu assured her. He then looked at Kimi. She had once been a vibrant, youthful beauty, but now she looked to be older than the hills. Her eyes were watery pools imbedded into dark circles and her hair was limp and gray. He thought of Siskia's eternal beauty and thanked God that he had been able to spare her from a life such as Kimi's. He spoke her name softly. "Kimi, you will be welcome in our village."

Tears sprang to Kimi's eyes and ran down her cheeks. She could say nothing, but only nodded.

Ahanu looked back at Sucki. "I do not want to make the same mistake at Fort Pitt. It is in the hands of the Americans, but I don't want to take any chances."

"You know best, Father. I trust you completely."

Their eyes locked for a moment, and emotions ran high. Oh, how thankful they were to be alive! Ahanu nodded and then looked away, thinking through their situation.

"I think it would be best to pass under the darkness of the night since it is new moon once again." He looked at the shoreline and motioned to a clearing in the thick brush which ran along most of the river's edge. "Let's stop there," he said and in no time, they had pulled the canoe out of the water and out of sight.

Kimi took a satchel from the canoe, which neither Ahanu or Sucki had noticed, and followed the men into the woods. There were the remains of a campfire beside a log, and they all sat down, stretching their legs before them.

Kimi opened the sack and produced dried venison jerky for all of them and a few nuts and berries. They all bowed their heads, grateful once more for God's hand of protection and guidance.

The rest of their journey sped by. Fort Pitt was silent as they glided by near the opposite shore. They were nearly hidden by the overhanging trees. The next day they arrived at Yellow Creek and hid the canoe in the bushes and headed for Gnadahutten. The men were anxious to get there and wanted to push through the night, but they didn't want to wear out the women.

When Kimi sensed that they were stopping for the night because of them, she asked how far it was to their home.

"We will be there by midmorning if we get an early start," Ahanu had said.

"Then if we keep going, we can be there tonight?" Kimi asked.

Ahanu looked at her. "Yes, but..."

"But nothing. We are strong. Do not stop for us."

Ahanu looked questioningly at Sucki and then at Yellow Bird. They both nodded in agreement and the foursome set out for home. Their steps were light and the Lord blessed them with a clear night. Even without the aid of the moon, the path was easily visible.

Sucki's heart raced. He would be with his family tonight! He knew Ahanu felt the same way. It had been nearly twice as long as they had expected. Harvest time was nearly over. He felt chagrined at the thought of Bly and the boys doing all the work, but he would make it up to them.

How thankful they were that someone had left a canoe at the Tuscarawas River and Stillwater Creek. It was the last leg of a very long journey.

It wasn't long before both women were fast asleep. Ahanu smiled back at Sucki. He could see the whiteness of his broad smile even in the darkness of the night. An owl hooted along the creek, and the sound of an animal's feet padding softly away from the water could be heard.

They rowed in silence, anxious to turn the last bend and then they were there—the cabins and other buildings of Gnadenhutten could be seen in the distance. Their pace quickened once again, and they beached the canoe one last time.

Ahanu had a strange feeling as he helped the women out of the canoe. Sucki had run ahead, so ready to see his family. Suddenly, a cry of bitter agony broke the silence. Sucki came running, kicking in the doors of every cabin as he came.

"What is it?" Ahanu nearly shouted.

"They're gone! They're all gone!" He fell to his knees and cried.

"What do you mean?" Ahanu asked but he ran past Sucki and to his own cabin. Sucki was right—the cabin was empty. He ran everywhere, even into the church and the cooper's shop, but everything was gone. *Where could they be?* A thousand dreadful responses came to his mind but he refused to think on any of them. *We will find them, if it takes the rest of my life!*

Chapter Thirteen

Though They Slay Me

A thousand shall fall at thy side,
and ten thousand at thy right hand;
but it shall not come nigh thee.
Psalm 91:7

Exhausted from the long journey and overwrought emotions, the four all found a place to sleep away what was left of the evening. Ahanu had decided he and Sucki would canoe to Coshocton and see if Chief Newcomer had any answers. They'd be back by noon.

The next morning, the sound of footsteps woke Ahanu with a start. He lay still and listened. Silently, he went to the door and looked out. One lone man was foraging around the front of one of the cabins. He looked harmless, but Ahanu was taking no chances.

He slipped out of his cabin and circled around the buildings until he was behind the man. As swift as an arrow he was on top of the man. Ahanu flipped him over and saw fear in the white man's face.

"Please, don't kill me. I was just looking for food," the old man whimpered.

Ahanu checked him for weapons, and then released his hold. "Where is everyone?" he demanded.

The man's eyes were open wide with fear and surprised. "Gone. The British done drove them off to Sandusky just a few days ago."

Ahanu tried to process the information. "Why? Where's Reverend Zeisberger and Brother Heckewelder?"

"They's been arrested and hauled off to Fort Detroit for treason."

"Treason?" Sucki cried. Ahanu looked up to see his son heading to them. He stood up and offered the man his hand.

"Where is this Sandusky?" Ahanu asked.

"It's a far piece from here, 'bout two three days' journey up on Lake Erie."

Ahanu had heard of the place from Brother David. His burden for lost souls reached to every tribe, but he had had little success in that area.

"We must go," Sucki nearly shouted.

Ahanu nodded. "Go tell the women our plans." Sucki turned and was off like a shot. Ahanu's heart ached for him—so much uncertainty! He turned back to the man and tried to calm his own fears and anxieties. "What is your name and where are you from?"

The man's countenance relaxed a bit. "Name's Jed. I live on down the Tuscarawas a piece, me and my woman. We don't mean no harm. Wouldn't of know'd about your people except we heard the British troops marching on by. They're a noisy bunch. Don't care who hears 'em, but then there was a mighty big passel of 'em."

Ahanu shook his head. "Why would they do this? Our brothers never did anyone harm. My wife and family have been with Brother Zeisberger for almost twenty winters now. We believe in the one true God."

Jed smiled, showing several missing teeth. "I should have know'd. You can tell, you know. True Christian folks will treat you fair."

"I'm sorry for jumping you," Ahanu said, but the man was waving him off.

"Don't apologize. I hate to think of what I might have done if I saw someone snoopin' round my place, especially with my mind full of worry for my kin."

The two men talked a bit more. Jed knew the way to Sandusky and gave excellent directions. He said his goodbyes and wandered away, knowing that they'd be gone soon. He had enough sense not to rummage any further till they were gone.

*   *   *

Siskia sat alone in their makeshift structure. They were not welcome here, but with both missionaries arrested and their men gone, she, Bly, and the children had done their best. Togquos and Waneek had been so much comfort and help to all of them. *"Oh, Ahanu, where are you! Will you never return?"* Her mind was a constant battleground. She would think the worst and then run to her Savior for comfort. She needed to be strong for Bly and the children, especially the children. They seemed to ask every day when Father and Grandfather were coming back. She saw the anguish in Bly's face as she smiled and told them soon, but would it be? Would they ever come back? And what was happening to them? Winter was nearly upon them and the others were already stretched to the limit with food. If only they could have harvested their crops before they were ordered to leave.

The trip should have taken three days, but they made it in two. It was dark by the time they arrived at the main cluster of buildings. Most of the villagers were already in their homes for the night, but Ahanu knew there would be someone on lookout. He was right.

Seeming to appear out of nowhere, a young brave stood before them. Before he could do or say anything, Ahanu spoke. "We come in peace. We are from Gnadenhutten and are looking for our families."

The young man relaxed a bit but kept his weapon handy and in plain view. "They are over there," he said jerking his head to another circle of buildings.

Ahanu nodded his thanks and turned away. He was in no mood for confrontation or pleasantries. He needed to find his family.

As they approached the buildings, he was astonished to find that most of them were nothing more than rudely constructed huts, much like the one in which he and Sucki had been held prisoner.

Sucki rushed passed him. "Bly," he called as he drew near. In only a moment's time, one of the flaps flew open and a young woman was running his way. She threw herself into his arms weeping.

"You came," she cried. "We were so worried."

Before they could say another word, Siskia came running as well. When Ahanu saw her quick, graceful movements, his mind went back to the first time he had seen her. He had loved her then, but those emotions were as nothing compared to the deep devotion he had for her now. She too threw herself into his arms, the tears flowing freely. "Oh Ahanu!" It was all that she could say.

Others came from the remaining huts and one of them stirred the embers in the fire ring. In a matter of moments, they were all there rejoicing in their safe return, plying them for questions.

It was several moments before Siskia began to look around. Ahanu dreaded the moment. She looked at Ahanu, her eyes wild. "Where is Joseph?"

He took her hands and looked straight into her eyes. "He is safe, and he is happy."

She looked at him questioningly.

He told her and the others about their journey, quickly getting to the part about Russell. He shook his head. "We knew you would be worried, and we could barely stand to stay any longer, but he couldn't be left alone." He paused. "It was Joseph's suggestion that he stay."

"And you let him?" Siskia shrieked.

"We will talk about this later," Ahanu said kindly, but the tone in his voice left no room for contradiction. "Trust me," he whispered, his weary eyes pleading.

She stared into his eyes in agony. Her heart was breaking, but she nodded slightly and ducked her head—a sign of her submission.

Ahanu looked at the others. "What happened? Why are you here?"

Machk looked at Ahanu and then glanced at the two women who stood back beyond the circle.

Ahanu tossed his head impatient with himself. "I'm sorry." He stood and went to the two women. "This is Kimi and Yellow Bird." Siskia's head shot up. "Some of you who were at Kittanning with us may remember them... and Blue Feather." He looked at Savanukah who was nodding. "They are the reason we made it home alive."

Siskia suddenly rose to her feet and walked quickly to them. She looked first at Kimi and then Yellow Bird and pulled them both into an embrace. "Welcome. It isn't much but you are welcome to be here." Her eyes misted. "And thank you," she said huskily.

Bly came to them and joined the embrace. No words were necessary. They could see the gratitude in her eyes.

As the women joined the group, Machk began to explain what had happened. He shook his head. "Right after you left, we heard the Americans had destroyed Coshocton. It wasn't long until the British came and arrested David and John for treason. Then we were told we needed to move. They feared that we were aiding the Americans.

Ahanu huffed in frustration. "We cannot win in this war that is supposed to be ended. The British accuse us of helping the Americans, and the Americans burn our villages and arrest our missionaries who are innocent of any crimes!" He stood and paced. "Is there no end to this madness?"

"How did you know where to find us?" Machk asked, hoping to divert some of Ahanu's anger.

Ahanu stopped and looked around the circle. They were all watching him. He sighed and sat down beside Siskia. "We only arrived three days ago in the middle of the night. In the morning, an old man was foraging around the cabins and told us of your troubles and where you had been taken." His voice was so full of sadness, that it made Siskia feel ashamed of her outburst. She took his hand and squeezed it, but his mind was elsewhere.

"Will we be able to go back?"

Savanukah shook his head. "They brought us here to be close to the British Fort at Detroit."

"Plus, the Wyandots and Delawares in this village sympathize with the British," Degataga added in hushed tones.

"Don't they know we do not fight?" Ahanu asked.

Machk shook his head. "They will not listen, and their hearts are cold against the Gospel. That is the least of our concerns right now. We have so little food I am afraid it will not last through the winter."

"Disease! Famine! War! These are what the white man bring!" Ahanu hissed.

Machk was silent for a moment. He felt a great responsibility now that their spiritual leaders were gone. He and Chenoa had spent much time in prayer throughout the move and once they had arrived. "But they brought us the truth about the One True God," he said quietly.

Ahanu felt as though a knife had been driven into his heart. His head ached and his body was stiff from the excursion they had just endured. "We will talk in the morning," he said and rose to his feet. Siskia quickly followed suit and led him to their new home. Once inside, she held him and wept again. "Oh, Ahanu. I was afraid I'd never see you again."

He responded to her heart-cry and held her close. She felt so good in his arms. It had been too long since he had felt the calming effect of her presence. "I will never leave you again," he whispered fiercely into her hair and tightened his hold. Suddenly, he felt as though all strength had left him, and he fell to the pallet of furs, Siskia joining him. He sighed deeply. It felt so good to lie down. Siskia quickly pulled up the covers and started to kiss him, but he was already asleep. He was home! She could face anything now that he was here! She snuggled closer into the crook of his arm, smiling for the first time in a long time.

Ahanu slowly opened his eyes and looked a-round. Where was he? The surroundings were unfamiliar to him. Sunlight was creeping in under the doorway adding confusion to his already befuddled brain. He closed his eyes again and rolled over. The furs were soft and familiar. They smelled like Siskia. Thoughts of last night and the past few days came back to him, sparking his memory. He sniffed the air and smelled the delicious smell of fried food coming from close by.

Before he got up, he took a moment to talk to his Lord, something that had gone to the wayside over the past few weeks. He thanked the Lord for safety, for home and family, for strength and health. He prayed for wisdom and for their spiritual leaders and for Joseph and Siskia as well as the others. Feeling as though he was ready to face the day and a bit chagrined at the lateness of the hour, he slowly stood up and stretched, but his hands hit the roof. He was tempted to get angry and punch his fist right through the flimsy structure but chose to thank the Lord for a roof over his head instead!

Right after breakfast, the men and some of the women gathered around their makeshift council fire. More details were shared about the past few months. Ahanu had wanted to talk privately to Siskia concerning Joseph, but he knew she had been patient long enough. As he told of their time together, a longing for simpler days seemed to overshadow them. Memories of their long-ago homes and families came to mind making their present situation look ever more bleak.

"Will he come back when the old man is better?" asked Siskia.

"I do not know," offered Ahanu. He looked around at their surroundings. "Do we even want him to come back? Russell has offered to give him everything he owns. He hinted that he had money stashed away. Joseph could buy land there and make a home. There are no British there to drive him off, and the other settlers have also fled because of Indian raids."

Siskia looked alarmed. "Won't that put him in danger? They will think he was responsible."

Ahanu nodded. "That might happen, but Russell seems to have a good understanding of both Indians and settlers. I have confidence he will do right by Joseph, or I wouldn't have agreed to let him stay." He turned his attention to Machk. "I don't think these huts will make it through the winter."

"We've talked about that," said Machk. Having lived near the Great Lakes, he knew how harsh winter could be. "We planned to build longhouses now that we know we will be here indefinitely."

"What about the food?" Ahanu asked.

"Savanukah and Degataga have taken stock. If we can hunt for our meat, we may be able to make that which we harvested earlier last."

"Could we go back and harvest the rest?" Ahanu asked.

Machk shook his head warily. "I believe it would be too dangerous. I am just thankful you and Sucki were able to get through unharmed. God was with you."

"And can we get any food from the others?"

The men exchanged glances and shook their heads. One of the older men who was from the Delaware Turtle tribe commented. "We parted ways during the first war. We sided with the Americans, and they sided with the British.

They have not been friendly to us since, and our beliefs only add more fuel to their fire."

The circle was silent for a moment while everyone thought on his words. Then Machk spoke. "We need to take care of our own, but we do not want to stir their hearts against us. We will get a hunting party together today."

When the group split up, Machk came to Sucki and Ahanu. "You two should stay with your families. You've been away long enough."

Sucki's eyes brightened. "Thanks, Machk," he said and hurried off to find Bly.

"What if I took Siskia with me?" Ahanu offered. "She could be a great help and that would give us some time together and away from here."

Machk nodded. "Good idea. She really struggled when we left Gnadenhutten. Chenoa and I prayed for her and with her often."

Ahanu's face showed his deep gratefulness but then his countenance darkened. "I fear for Joseph in that way. He has no one."

Machk smiled sympathetically. "He does have Someone."

Ahanu understood. He shook his head. "I am so thankful to be back. My faith flickered in the wind of adversity."

"It is good to have you back, and Sucki."

Siskia was overjoyed to be going on the hunting trip. They gathered with the others but fell to the back of the group as they headed east and into the forest. No one seemed to mind or even notice. The time alone was exactly what both of them needed, and Ahanu was even able to fell a doe. The group had been very successful and came back into camp with enough meat to supply their needs. They had even planned to share with the Wyandot village, but when they saw the meat, they took what they wanted, leaving less than half of what the others had killed.

Over and over, the scenario was the same: God blessed the efforts of the Praying Indians only to have the Wyandots take it from them. It was a long winter. Thankfully, they had their longhouses erected before the first of the winter snows arrived, but little by little the food supply dwindled.

By March, their situation was dire. Many were sick, and others were weak from lack of food. A messenger was sent to Fort Detroit asking for permission to go to Gnadenhutten and gather what food they could from their fields. Permission was granted, and hope rekindled in many hearts.

The following morning, a force of nearly one hundred of their people headed south to Gnadenhutten to gather as much food as they could carry.

Sucki came to his father's longhouse and called to him, but it was his mother who came to greet him. Her face was etched with worry. "Your father is ill," she whispered.

Without hesitation, Sucki entered and went to the pallet which held his father's strong frame. He knelt and laid a hand on his forehead. It was burning hot.

Slowly, Ahanu opened his eyes and shook his head. "It is nothing." He tried to get up, but Sucki gently pushed him down.

"No, Father. You cannot go. You are too weak."

Siskia came and knelt beside him but said nothing.

Sucki looked into her worry-filled eyes. "Don't worry, Mother. We will soon have food, and he will get well." His heart ached for them and fear was pushing its way in. Without a word, Sucki began to pray. "Dear heavenly Father, we need Your help. Please take the sickness from my father's body, and please keep my family safe. May we soon rejoice and celebrate Your resurrection. Raise him up for Thy service, oh Father. Bring peace to our home." Sucki's voice cracked with emotion. He could say no more.

Ahanu's eyes were shut but he knew his son's struggle. "Father, hear our prayers. We pray in Jesus' name.

Amen." He reached for his son's hand and squeezed it. "Be safe, my son."

Sucki squeezed Ahanu's hand and then embraced his mother before rising to his feet. He took one last look at his parents and then hurried to the door.

*   *   *

Colonel David Williamson stared ahead as the trail wound its way along the Tuscarawas River. He rode with purpose as did the men that followed him. One hundred-sixty militiamen from Pennsylvania were on a mission to put an end to the brutal Indian raids that had haunted their homes and settlements for too long. They would end this madness once and for all if they had to kill every Indian in sight and burn every village—they would stop at nothing to bring peace to their land. Sure, Philadelphia felt the victory of Yorktown, but they didn't! The British still manned Fort Detroit and others, and the Indians were their blood-thirsty marauders.

As they neared the village, they heard voices. Raising his hand for silence, they stopped and dismounted, sending spotters ahead to survey the situation. They had been told that Gnadenhutten had been cleared out. Something was not right.

"There's about a hundred Indians working in the fields, Colonel," the scout reported. "They're unarmed, sir."

The colonel thought for a moment. "Good." He mounted his horse and motioned the men forward.

Machk looked up at the sound of horses approaching. They were nearly finished harvesting the corn. He looked past the rows and to the river as the never-ending string of troops came from the trail and made their way around the village. He stood and watched them approach, noticing that the others did so as well. They had nothing to hide. They were Christians who did not fight, but even as he thought the words, he wondered if these men knew it.

Williamson rode out from the circle of horses and approached Machk. "You are not to be here," he ordered.

Machk nodded. "We had been given permission to harvest our crops and take them to our village."

"Where is your village?" Williamson questioned.

"We are at Sandusky. We were ordered there by the British." Machk stood tall, keeping his eyes fixed on the man and trying to stay calm.

"It isn't safe for you here. We have been ordered to take you to Fort Pitt where you will be safe."

Machk hesitated. "Many of our people are waiting for us to return with food. They will starve," he said quietly.

"That is not our concern," Williamson declared. He looked at the buildings which once rang with the sound of voices singing praise to God and pointed to them. "Your men will go in there and the women there," he said as he pointed to another cabin, which had been Reverend Zeisberger's home. Machk looked at Chenoa. Her eyes were filled with fear but she squared her shoulders and led the way for the other women.

The doors were shut and bolted. Murmurs circled the room as anxious voices asked the difficult questions.

"What will happen to us?" one young boy asked Machk.

Machk knew he needed to be strong. He put his hand on the boy's shoulder. "Nothing that God does not allow." He looked over the boy's head to the others. It did not look good.

"Don't they know that we are Christians?" Savanukah hissed. His eyes were wild with fear and frustration.

"They would call themselves Christians, but I don't think they can believe that an Indian can follow Jesus and not fight."

"Then we must show them," a quiet voice from the far end of the building said. They all turned to look at

Abukcheech. He was now the oldest member of their clan. They had told him he didn't need to come, but he had insisted. His name had been changed to Caleb when Reverend Zeisberger read Caleb's story in the Bible. His words brought their minds and hearts back into focus. The enemy was just outside the door and their purpose seemed clear, but there was peace in their hearts.

"Caleb is right. We must be brave. Jesus will not fail us," Machk said, his voice gaining strength with every word. He began to sing one of their favorite hymns and continued to sing until the sun set.

Chenoa heard the singing over the weeping that was all around her. She had tried to encourage the women, but they would not listen. As she caught the phrase of the hymn, she began to softly sing along. One by one, the women became silent, and a holy hush fell upon them. Soon, they were lifting their voices in praise to their God as well.

Williamson had gathered his officers in a cabin at the far end of the village and was discussing their plan when a knock came to the door. He looked across at the sentinel beside the door in obvious annoyance and jerked his head with a quick nod.

A young man stood at the door, obviously nervous.

Williamson looked alarmed. "What is it, soldier?" he barked.

The soldier fingered the hat in his hands nervously. "It's the Indians, sir."

Williamson waited for more, but the man just stood there. "Well? What's the problem?"

"They're singing, sir. They're singing hymns, sir."

The officers looked from one to the other. They had been told that this village was a Moravian mission, but they didn't want to believe it. The discussion became heated. Many of the soldiers that rode with Williamson had witnessed firsthand the savagery of an Indian raid and had lost loved ones and property. They wanted revenge. Others argued that these Indians were different.

"They didn't have a mean look about them, and when we herded them into the buildings, they just walked right in—never even looked back."

"They killed my father!" one man shouted and the shout was echoed around the room.

"Silence!" Williamson shouted, and the arguing voices died down. He looked around the room. "We will decide their fate tomorrow," he said and marched out of the cabin.

He never looked back, but as he drew near his own cabin he stopped midstride. He could not understand the words, but he knew the hymn tune well. In fact, it was one of his favorites. Doubts and misgivings haunted his soul. He needed to lead, but without a doubt, he knew how the vote would fall in the morning. Heaven help them.

The Indians prayed throughout the night. Some would pray while others slept. As the first light dawned, they could hear the footsteps of the soldiers.

"Line up," Wilkinson shouted. He looked down the long line of grim faces. "Any who oppose the decimation of these Indians, step forward." Here and there a man took one step, but the vast majority held firm.

The colonel eyed the entire expanse. "If your conscience will not permit these actions, then you are released from your duty. Ride out immediately."

Not even twenty men slowly walked away, gathering their gear and mounting their horses. The rest were ready, itching to begin.

Wilkinson had ordered the men to gather any warriors that were in the group and bring them to the edge of the village.

The men's cabin door flew open, and a dozen soldiers entered, grabbing the young men and hauling them out the door. The others cried out to God for mercy.

Machk, Degataga, and Savanukah were among the twelve that were taken. Machk's mind ran in a thousand directions. His first thoughts were of Chenoa and then the children. He thought of his father and mother and that he would see them soon. Once again, his strong voice began to sing and the others soon joined him. They were going to die, but they did not fear death. Soon they would see Jesus.

"Oh Father, forgive them. Jesus help them," Savanukah cried as they looked down the barrels of twenty guns.

Williamson could not understand their words, except for one—Jesus. He pushed it out of his mind. "Fire!" Twenty guns exploded and twelve men fell to the ground. *Jesus! Jesus! Jesus!* echoed in his mind until he thought he'd go mad.

Chenoa cried with the others, but they had little time to weep. The door crashed open, and the room was flooded with crazed men with tomahawks, shouting and cursing, scalping and bludgeoning. "Jesus," she cried and all went black.

The same was happening in the other cabin. The blood flowed as tomahawks did the horrendous deeds of evil men. The wicked act was soon over. All were dead—all but two.

Sucki felt as though his head was on fire. He had been scalped, but not completely. He lay dazed for a moment and opened his eyes to look around. It nearly made him sick to his stomach, but the soldiers were gone. They were celebrating in their usual way. Closing his eyes for a moment, he came to his senses. Tearing the bloodied shirt of the one next to him, he wrapped his head and then tried to stand. A wave of nausea nearly toppled him. Steadying himself for a moment, he looked around the room. Right behind him was a window! Quickly, he pushed it open and crawled out and dashed into the woods behind the cabin.

As he worked his way to the women's cabin he was surprised to see a young boy come tumbling out of the window. He scrambled to his feet and ran to the woods. Sucki ran to him.

"Are there any others?" he asked frantically.

The boy was weeping, "Just my brother, but I don't think he's going to make it."

As they both looked on, both cabins burst into flames. The boy started to shout, but Sucki caught him and covered his mouth, holding him close and rocking him. They sat there watching as tears coursed down their faces. Sucki picked up the boy and carried him deeper into the forest. *Chenoa is gone! They're all gone!* He wanted to shout but held his peace.

*   *   *

Ahanu moaned. His mind was full of terror. Something was wrong, dreadfully wrong. For three days he had slept, only to awaken to feel water dribbling down his throat. His eyelids felt like rocks when he tried to open his eyes. Then this morning he saw Machk, Savanukah, and Degataga. They were singing and others were praying. It was such sweet music, and yet he also heard weeping and moaning.

Siskia looked up from her place beside the bed and crawled over to Ahanu. She felt his head. It was cool! Tears sprang to her eyes, and she whispered a prayer.

"Siskia," Ahanu whispered.

"Oh, Ahanu!" He lifted his hand to her wet cheek and then kissed it.

He tried to sit up but couldn't. He slowly shook his head. "I'm as weak as a kitten."

Siskia was now weeping. "But you are alive."

Ahanu looked at her. Something was wrong. He strained to sit up but couldn't. "What is it, Siskia?"

With his question, she wept even harder, lying down beside him. Her body shook uncontrollably. Ahanu rolled to face her and grabbed her arm. "Tell me," he demanded.

"They're gone," she wept. "All but Sucki and little Thomas are gone."

Ahanu rolled back and covered his face with his hands.

Siskia continued. "The soldiers killed everyone, accusing them of raiding the settlers."

"But Sucki is alive?"

Siskia only nodded. "He was scalped and left for dead but was able to escape. He lost a lot of blood, but he's going to be alright. But, Ahanu, the others..." She couldn't finish.

Ninety-six in all were dead. Sixty-two were adults and thirty-four were children. Ahanu remembered the argument that Sucki had with Bly and his oldest. They had wanted to do their part, but Sucki would not let them go, saying it was too dangerous. Indians from the Wyandot village and elsewhere continued to raid the settlers along the Ohio River. Their group never would have gone if the situation wasn't dire. Now, the village was nearly decimated.

When Sucki had recovered enough to speak, the small remnant gathered while Sucki told his story. He told of their bravery, how they knew they would die and yet they sang and encouraged each other in prayer and with scripture.

Several times his emotions overwhelmed him. "I will never forget their bravery and great witness to the soldiers. Some of the soldiers left. Most stayed, but I saw the look of confusion in their eyes as they heard us sing. One man threw down his tomahawk and wept. He thought that revenge would soothe his heart of its painful loss, but it didn't."

Ahanu thought back on his own thirst for revenge. He thought of Machk and Savanukah. *I should have been the one! I should have been the one!*

Three weeks later, Reverend Zeisberger and Heckewelder were released from Fort Detroit. They had heard about the massacre and hurried to those who were left at Sandusky. Their hearts ached for those who lost so much, comforting them with the Word. As their faith grew stronger, David prayed for the right time to tell them their plans. He called a council fire the next Sunday.

All eyes were on him as David looked to John for strength. He loved these people and hurt for their loss, but there was so much more work to be done. "John and I plan to move further west to spread the gospel to those who have not heard," he said quietly.

The people sat motionless. They were mourning. They were weary of moving. They were tired and hungry, searching for a peace that seemed to elude their grasp.

Ahanu spoke first. "I will go no further west. Our son is to the east, and if we go anywhere, it will be in that direction."

Siskia was surprised at his words. They had not discussed it, but she was inwardly filled with great joy. Perhaps they could go home again! But Ahanu was speaking.

"We traveled north on our journey to Great Island and visited a Moravian village in the wilds of Pennsylvania. If it is unsafe to go further, we will settle there."

An older man spoke up. He had been from Yellow Creek and had hurt his foot while felling trees. That injury had saved his life from going with the others back to Gnadenhutten. "I have heard that Cornplanter is on the move. He is negotiating for land for his people in that area and further north in New York. Perhaps we could go there."

For the first time in weeks a glimmer of hope flickered on their faces. Could they move east? Certainly, they would be rid of the British once and for all. Murmurs circled the group as they discussed the possibilities.

"It may be a good plan," John said. His heart ached for these wanderers. "At least the east holds more certainty than what we may find going west."

David nodded. "Well, if any of you decide you want to go with us, you are more than welcome. You have been brave in the face of this life's most trying circumstances. Your people have faced death with confidence. They shined bright in their darkest hour, and we may never know the eternal rewards which they have earned. We never know who our gospel light will illuminate. It may be the least likely of all we see."

Ahanu thought back to the day of his conversion. David Brainerd had no idea of the seed that had been sown in his life and the fruit that followed. He looked around the circle. So many were missing, but his family had been spared. Waneek and Togquos had been away scavenging for food when the party had left for Gnadenhutten. He shook his head. Truly, God's hand had been on them—all of them— even those who had died. They were with Jesus in heaven. How many of his people would be in heaven because of these missionaries? Slowly, he stood to his feet.

"Go with God. We thank our Father that He brought you to us. Our loss is great, but without your message of truth our loss would have been for all eternity." Heads nodded and murmurs of agreement could be heard all around the fire.

"We thank you for your courage to come to us—to leave your home and families to come to a strange land. Your faith has brought on much fruit, and may there be more in your next venture. We are not angry. We are just tired and sad—sad at your leaving and sad because of our loss. But we will not forget your great hearts and good teaching."

They had been together for so long, but now they would stand alone—without their chief and without their spiritual leaders. They would go with God as well, knowing the path may be difficult but not impossible.

That night, alone in their hut, Ahanu held Siskia close. She shivered, but it was not from the cold.

"Will we be safe?" she asked quietly. Losing so many of their friends had taken a toll on her courage. But Ahanu knew her strength was not found in her body or will but in her spirit.

He tightened his hold. "Yes," he said in quiet confidence. "I do not know what our God has planned for us, but whatever it is, this tragedy has shown me that His way is always best."

"Even for Machk, and Chenoa, and..." She couldn't finish. The thought of what they had faced, possibly watching their own children be murdered, was more than she could bear.

Ahanu was silent. He too had suffered many nightmares but always awakened to rest in the arms of Jesus. In some ways, he envied Machk. His whole family was now sitting at Jesus' feet. No more heartaches. No more upheavals. Finally, he spoke. "They are in a much better place, Siskia. They walk by sight while we continue to walk in faith. I do not know what God has planned for us, but every path that we take will eventually lead us to our true home... and to Jesus."

EPILOGUE

It was an end of a war and the end of an era. While many Indian tribes continued to make raids and fight the white man, Ahanu and what was left of their clan moved east to the Moravian Village near Tionesta, and later settled further south on Cornplanter's Tract. By 1803, Ohio became the seventeenth state to join the union. A homeland for the Indians called Ohio Country no longer existed. Settlers crossed over the Allegheny Mountains and poured into the land once promised to the Indians.

The only way for any Native Americans to survive was to acclimate into the white man's world. Cornplanter, a Seneca Chief originally from the Genesee River valley, understood this better than most. Son of a Dutch trader named John Abeel, Cornplanter noticed early on that his skin was a lighter shade of brown than his friends. His mother told him of his father whom he later saved during an Indian raid.

Cornplanter negotiated for Indian rights throughout his lifetime, even writing a letter to the newly elected president, George Washington. Eventually, he was granted a land tract along the Allegheny River which included the Indian village of Jenuchshadago.

It was to this haven of rest that the remnant of Gnadenhutten came for refuge and settled, finally finding a home. Cornplanter eventually became a Christian. Was he another convert who could trace his spiritual lineage back to David Brainerd? God only knows.

1955

George watched as the pyro technician put the last of the charges into place. He looked at the mountain's edge, soon to be a crumbled pile of rocks and debris, and smiled in satisfaction. He loved his job as foreman of Kane Construction. The company had won the bid for this section of the new highway, which meant he would be going home every night to his wife and kids.

Randy stepped back from the explosives and mentally reexamined each step of his work. Every detail was important in accomplishing a quality, controlled explosion.

"All set, Randy?" George asked. The excitement could be heard in his voice.

Randy smiled. "All set, sir." His boss's boyish delight always made him chuckle inwardly.

"Good." George turned on his heels and made the necessary warnings, shouting them into his bullhorn and finishing with the regulatory countdown. "...5, 4, 3, 2, 1!"

Within seconds, the ground shook and all watched as Randy's well-placed explosives liquefied solid rock. A giant dust cloud spread in every direction, billowing high into the air before it began to make its descent.

High above the explosion site stood Spirit Rock. The cliffs shuddered, but they rested on solid bedrock. The blast made little difference to the ancient altar... except for one.

Beneath the cliffs, a handful of coins tumbled from their ancestral resting place and trickled forth, down the hidden slope. Tarnished coppers and silver coins shook and slid to their new homes. Two gold coins, larger than the rest, led the way, still as shiny as the day they were minted.

As though guided by an Unseen Hand, the gold pieces came to rest near the opening of a hidden cleft. For the first time in over two hundred years, they reflected the rays of the late afternoon sun, sending forth their light like the beacon of a lighthouse. However, would their beckoning rays be sent forth to save life or to destroy it?

Fact or Fiction

One of the difficulties when writing historical fiction is that the reader doesn't know what is true and what is not. Below is a list of names and places. I hope it is helpful.

Name/Meaning

1. Spirit Rock — A real rock outcropping near Trout Run, PA but NOT called by that name.
2. Hassun/stone — *fiction*
3. Ahanu/He laughs — *fiction*
4. Shikellimy — *fact*—emissary for the Iroquois of Pennsylvania; settled in Sunbury
5. Togquos/twin — *fiction* (Ahanu also uses this name for his son)
6. Sucki/black — *fiction* (Ahanu also uses this name for his son)
7. Raweno — *fact*—creator god of the Iroquois
8. Anakausuen/worker — *fiction*
9. Taima/thunder — *fiction*
10. Chogan/black bird — *fiction*
11. David Brainerd — *fact*—all references to David Brainerd and his family are based on facts
12. Jonathan Edwards — *fact*
13. Westgate Inn — *fiction*
14. Siskia/bird — *fiction*
15. Pontiac — *fact*—a young Odawa war chief

who nearly turned the tide of the French and Indian in favor of the French. However, the possibility of him even falsely professing Christ and his involvement with Siskia are fiction.

16. Savanukah — *fiction*
17. Degataga — *fiction*
18. Kanatase — *fiction*
19. Terés — *fiction*
20. Chief Shawátis — *fiction*
21. Machk/bear — *fiction*
22. Great Island — *fact*—inhabited by Indians until the mid-1700s. A common meeting place for both Indians and early settlers. A large island in the Susquehanna River near present-day Lock Haven.
23. Siskëwahane or Susquehanna/mile wide, foot deep
24. Legaui-hanne or Lycoming/sandy stream
25. Chief Bald Eagle — *fact*—notorious enemy of early settlers who did send out war parties against the white men
26. Ralph Jamison — *fiction*
27. Moses Tunda Tatamy — *fact*
28. Otstuagy — *fact*—Indian village located at present-day Montoursville
29. French Margaret's Town — *fact*—Indian village at the mouth of the Lycoming Creek
30. Lawisahquick/middle Creek—Loyalsock Creek
31. French Margaret — *fact*—eldest daughter or niece

of the famous Madam Montour, an Indian interpreter who settled in Otstuagy after her husband's death. Her eldest son, Andrew Montour was also an interpreter and negotiator in Pennsylvania and Virginia and was a captain in the French and Indian War.

32. Punxsutawney/land of sand flies
33. Kittanning/on the main river
34. Turtle and Turkey clans *fact*—two branches of the Delaware Tribe
35. Captain Hill — *fact*—actual Indian leader
36. Logstown — *fact*—trading post for both Europeans (French first and later English) and Indians.
37. Half King — *fact*—also known as Chief Tanacharison, represented the Six Nations
38. Scarouady — *fact*—Oneida Chief who ruled with Half King
39. Conrad Weiser — *fact*—pioneer, interpreter and diplomat in the early 1700s especially for Pennsylvania
40. Tanacharison — Chief in Ohio Country
41. George Washington — *fact*—All his battles and travels mentioned in *Spirit Rock* are true; however, any encounters with fictional characters are fictitious.
42. Governor Dinwiddie — *fact*
43. Christopher Gist — *fact*
44. John McGuire — *fact*

45. Trader Frazier — *fact*
46. John Davison — *fact*
47. Chief Jeskakake — *fact*
48. Chief White Thunder — *fact*
49. John Washington — *fact*—known to the Indians as Caunotaucarius, which means Town Destroyer
50. General Braddock — *fact*
51. Colonel Thomas Gage — *fact*
52. Laurence Washington — *fact*
53. Daniel Boone — *fact*
54. Daniel Morgan — *fact*
55. Captain Beaujeu — *fact*
56. Alaquippa's Town — *fact*
57. Queen Aliquippa — *fact*
58. George Croghan — *fact*
59. Kanuksusy — *fact*
60. David Zeisberger — *fact*
61. John Heckewelder — *fact*
62. Yellow Creek — *fact*
63. Logan — *fact*
64. David Greathouse — *fact*
65. John Petty — *fact*
66. Sakari — *fact*
67. Colonel John Gibson — *fact*
68. Gnadenhutten — *fact*
69. Newcomer — *fact*
70. Russell — *fiction*
71. Hannatown — *fact*
72. Beedeedee — *fiction*
73. Blue Feather — *fiction*
74. Colonel D. Williamson — *fact*